Also by Patience Griffin

The Accidental Scot ✓
Some Like It Scottish
Meet Me in Scotland
To Scotland with Love ✓

The Trouble with Scotland

A Kilts and Quilts Novel

Patience Griffin

A SIGNET ECLIPSE BOOK

SIGNET ECLIPSE
Published by New American Library,
an imprint of Penguin Random House LLC
375 Hudson Street, New York, New York 10014

This book is an original publication of New American Library.

First Printing, April 2016

ISBN 978-0-451-47639-5

Printed in the United States of America
10   9   8   7   6   5   4   3   2   1

Penguin
Random
House

For Charla & Amber

PRONUNCIATION GUIDE

Aileen (AY-leen)
Ailsa (AIL-sa)
Bethia (BEA-thee-a)
Buchanan (byoo-KAN-uhn)
Cait (KATE)
Deydie (DI-dee)
Moira (MOY-ra)

DEFINITIONS

céilidh (KAY-lee)—a party/dance
fash—trouble
fat quarter—a portion of fabric measuring eighteen inches by half its width (typically twenty-two inches). In the U.K. a fat quarter is slightly larger, approximately 56cm wide x 50cm.
Gandiegow—squall
Irn-Bru (aɪərn'bru)—considered Scotland's national carbonated soft drink
ken—range of knowledge or understanding
manky—seedy
numpty—a stupid person
postie—postman
radge—crazy, mental
shite—derogatory term

Quilters of Gandiegow

Rule #4
Let the healing art of quilting take root.

Chapter One

A light Scottish summer breeze deposited a leaf on the hood of Ross Armstrong's red truck. He brushed it aside, dropped the rag he'd been using into a bucket, and stepped back, admiring his masterpiece—a newly restored 1956 Ford F-1. Ross hadn't done it all by himself, not by a longshot. His brothers, John and Ramsay, had helped, and Doc MacGregor had been invaluable, from rebuilding the engine to doing the new paint job. But Ross felt a sense of accomplishment anyway.

As if the wind had dropped something heavier than a leaf—perhaps an anchor—a thought hit him, crushing his good mood. *Now what am I going to do?*

For the last seven months he'd spent every spare second on the pickup, when he wasn't working on the family commercial fishing boat or helping out at NSV, the North Sea Valve Company. He'd filled his time, hoping to keep the women, *and men*, of Gandiegow from bugging him, trying to set him up with their daughters and granddaughters. Now that Pippa—his ex-long-intended—was married, the town thought he should be hitched, too.

Didn't everyone have enough to fuss over with Moira

and Father Andrew's upcoming wedding than to try to marry off Ross, too?

He had his own plans. Robert and Samuel were out of school for the summer, so they could take his place on the fishing boat while Ross did something else.

He just didn't know what.

He'd spent a lot of the time working on the truck thinking about a new career, how he might step out from the life everyone else had chosen for him from birth. His little brother Ramsay had made a change from being a fisherman to running his own business. Ross could do it, too. He'd been toying with the idea of hiring out his truck to haul goods, but it didn't seem quite right.

"There you are."

Ross groaned as he glanced back at Kit, the town matchmaker, barreling toward him. She might be his sister-in-law, but it didn't give her the right to meddle in his nonexistent love life. Sure as shite, she held her damned matchmaking notebook to her chest, and right beside her was Harry Dunn looking intently at him, too.

Ross tossed the bucket into the bed of the pickup, pulled his keys from his pocket, and hopped into the front. "Gotta run."

"Wait up," Harry hollered. "My niece is coming in today for the quilt retreat. She wants to meet ye."

Kit glared at Ross. "You'll never find another woman if you keep running away."

He turned the key and revved the engine. "Sorry, Harry. Sorry, Kit. Can't hear ye over the noise." He cranked the window up as fast as he could and pulled out.

"That was a close call," Ross said to the refurbished gray interior of the truck.

He wasn't being rude, only preserving what little sanity he had left. He'd done what the town had wanted. He'd waited years for Pippa to return so they could marry. She'd returned, all right, but instead of marrying him, she'd met and married her true love, Max. Max was a hell of a guy, and Ross wholeheartedly gave his blessing to their quick wedding. That should've been enough to satisfy Gandiegow. *But no.* The second Pippa was married, Kit started pestering Ross to take out the new schoolteacher, Kirsty. Against his better judgment, and to get Kit and everyone off his back, he'd gone to dinner a time or two with Kirsty. She was okay—nice-looking and everything—but his time would've been better spent chopping bait.

As he drove from the community parking lot and up the bluff, he caught a glimpse out of the rearview mirror of Kit with her hands on her hips. There'd be hell to pay for foiling her plans. He was going to have to talk to his brother Ramsay about setting his wife straight. Ross couldn't be tied down right now. This was his time to play the field. Hell, he wanted to wear it out!

Maybe he should drive to Lios or Fairge to do just that. But first he had to pick up some goat cheese at Spalding Farm for Dominic and Claire, Gandiegow's restaurateurs.

Farther up the road over the bluff, just past NSV, a coach bus came into view. Ross eased his truck to the side to let it pass. Harry's niece was most certainly on that bus headed for the quilt retreat. Just like before every Kilts and Quilts retreat, the gossip mill had been abuzz, but Ross had done his best to ignore it. He pulled back into the road and kept going.

He glanced back in his mirror at NSV, Pippa's father's factory. Ross worked there sometimes and had invested what cash he had, not regretting the decision. NSV would make money one day, but in the meantime, what was Ross going to do? A looming dread fell over him. *Have I wasted my life up until now?* His little brother Ramsay, for gawd's sake, changed his life. Ross had always worked on the family fishing boat. And that was fine, but shouldn't he want more? What did he own besides this truck and a few shares in NSV? He'd spent his thirty years doing the right thing, being an honorable man, and what had it gotten him?

As if a thick fog had lifted, everything became clear. He was done doing what everyone else wanted, done doing what was expected!

He glanced over at the quilted grocery bags beside him. *Except today.* He would run errands for the village. But later . . .

Later he would make a stand and take back his life.

At twenty-two, Sadie Middleton didn't like zombie movies, but as she stepped off the bus a mile out of Gandiegow, Scotland, she felt like the lead in her own dreadful film. *Sadie of the Dead.* Not some glamorous zombie either, but a plain zombie who wanted to vanish. The other women around her were excited, giddy about their first evening at the quilt retreat. Sadie felt only waylaid. Shell-shocked. Miserable. If she was still at home in North Carolina, she would be sitting on the porch with Gigi, her grandmother, drinking sweet tea and waiting for the July Fourth fireworks to begin.

Except they weren't in the US.

And Gigi was dead.

The gravel crunched under Sadie's feet as she made her way, along with the other quilters, to the North Sea Valve Company's factory door. Their bus had died and coasted into the parking lot, and they were to wait here until she and the others could be transported into the small town. She leaned against the building, unfolded the printed e-mail, and read it again:

Dear Sadie and Gigi,

Pack your bags! Your team has won the grand prize in the quilt block challenge. Congratulations! You are coming to Gandiegow! For complete information regarding your Kilts and Quilts Retreat and all-expense paid trip to Scotland, please e-mail us back.

Sincerely,
Cait Buchanan
Owner, Kilts and Quilts Retreat

Having read the note a hundred times, Sadie shoved it back in her pocket. It seemed a cruel joke from the universe—to receive this letter only hours after Gigi's funeral.

At hearing the news about the retreat, her brother, Oliver, had gone into hyperdrive, using his grief to propel him into action. While insisting Gigi would want Sadie to fulfill their dream of a quilt retreat abroad, Oliver had made all the arrangements for Scotland—packing her bags and having her out the door before Sadie knew what had happened. His bullying made the trip feel more like a kidnapping than a prize.

Sadie's grief had immobilized her, made her want to crawl under a quilt and never come out. She waffled between feeling despondent and angry. But the one constant was her guilt for the part she'd played in her grandmother's death.

Her quilted Mondo bag slipped from her shoulder . . . the bag that matched Gigi's that they'd made at their last quilt retreat together. Memories of that glorious weekend were stitched into Sadie, the moments long and meaningful. She pulled the bag up, held it close, and squeezed her eyes shut.

The last twenty-four hours were wearing on her. Sadie was exhausted, depleted. But she had to keep it hidden at all costs. She glanced over at her ever-helpful brother as he assisted the rest of the women off the bus. *Good*. He was being kept busy. She was sick to death of Oliver fussing over her and telling her what to do.

At that moment, two vans pulled up. A tall, nice-looking man got out of one and a very pregnant strawberry blonde got out of the other. As they spoke to the bus driver, the woman handed over her keys to him.

Oliver, who had only just finished unloading the last quilter from the bus, hurried to the couple who'd brought the vans. "Excuse me?"

"Yes," answered the man. From his accent, he clearly was from the States. Texas, perhaps.

Oliver pointed to Sadie. "My sister needs to be in the first group into town."

Embarrassment radiated from her toes to her scalp. *Dammit, Oliver.* Sadie ducked behind another woman as the two newcomers turned in her direction.

"Sure," the man said. "We can take her into Gandiegow first. I'm Max, by the way."

Oliver introduced himself, too, and unfortunately felt the need to explain further. "My sister is ill."

The couple's curious eyes transformed into compassion. The women around Sadie spun on her with pity as well, staring at her as if they hadn't just spent the last couple of hours on the bus with her in quasi-normal companionship. To them, Sadie had been another quilter, a fellow retreat goer. Now, she wasn't. She was to be flooded with sympathy. No longer included. On the outside because of her disease.

Oliver spoke to Sadie but pointed to the vans. "Get in. They'll get you to town." He'd said it as if Sadie's problem was with her ears and not her kidneys.

Without a word and anxious to hide her red face, Sadie walked to the van with a compliant exterior. On the inside, though, she was seething. She climbed in and took a seat in the back. A minute later, others were climbing in as well. No one sat next to her, leaving her alone to frown out the window at her overly responsible brother.

The couple climbed into the front of the van and began chatting with the other quilters. Sadie found out more about them and their connection to Gandiegow—Max and Pippa were engineers at the North Sea Valve Company and newlyweds. They kept up a steady conversation, asking the quilters about themselves, and explaining about the upcoming wedding between their Episcopal priest and a town favorite. Mercifully they left Sadie alone.

A few minutes later, when they reached Gandiegow's parking lot, a group of men and women were waiting for them.

"We're a closed community," Pippa explained. "No cars within the village. Everyone is here to help carry yere things to the quilting dorms." Sure enough, many of the women had wagons beside them, while the men had their muscles. "Deydie will want everyone at Quilting Central as soon as possible. She's the head quilter and town matriarch." Pippa made it sound as if they better do as Deydie bid or there might be trouble.

One by one, they disembarked from the van. When Sadie got out, a young woman in a plain plum-colored dress with a double-hearted silver brooch moved forward. Next to her was a young girl.

"I'm Moira," the woman said, "and this is my cousin Glenna. We'll help ye get settled into the quilting dorm."

Sadie followed them, immediately pleased with both of her handlers; Moira and Glenna seemed blessedly quiet and shy.

Even though it was early evening, the sun was still in the sky, due to how far north Gandiegow was. They walked through the minuscule town along a concrete path that served as a wall against the ocean with no railings for safety. Moira pointed to where Oliver was to stay, Duncan's Den, and then took Sadie next door to the other quilting dorm, Thistle Glen Lodge. It was nothing more than a bungalow set against the green bluffs of summer, which rose nearly straight up at the back of the town.

Glenna shot Sadie a shy glance, then turned to Moira. "Should I let Deydie know that she's made it?"

"Aye. We'll be along shortly," Moira said. The girl ran off between the buildings.

Moira led Sadie inside to the way-too-cheery interior and down the hall to a room with three beds. The decorations were plaid and floral—a little French country on the northeast coast of Scotland—and too optimistic and exuberant for Sadie.

Moira motioned for her to go in. "You can store yere clothes in the armoire. The kitchen is stocked with tea, coffee, and snacks. But all yere meals are provided either at Quilting Central or the restaurant. I can bring ye scones and tea in the morns, if ye like, though."

Sadie set her Mondo bag on one of the beds. Moira was nice, but Sadie wanted only to be left alone to crawl under the quilt and hibernate until life wasn't so crushing. And she was so very tired. People didn't understand that though she looked fine, she was often exhausted and feeling generally cruddy . . . her new norm. Patients with chronic kidney disease, CKD, usually weren't diagnosed until it was too late, already in stage four like herself, and in need of a kidney transplant.

She'd found out only last month. Gigi had promised to be with Sadie every step of the way. But Gigi was gone, leaving Sadie to deal with everything alone. Oliver couldn't; he had his own life, his cybersecurity consulting business. He didn't have time to sit with her while she had her blood drawn week after week. He couldn't put his life on hold while Sadie waited for the day to come when the doctors would move her to the active transplant list.

Sadie looked up, realizing she'd slipped into herself again, something she'd been doing a lot ever since her diagnosis.

Moira, though, seemed to understand and went to the doorway. "I'll give ye a few minutes to settle in. Then Deydie expects all the quilters at Quilting Central for introductions and the quilting stories." It was another warning that Sadie shouldn't dawdle.

She jumped at the sound of hard knocking at the front door.

Moira put her hand up, either to calm Sadie's frazzled nerves or to stop her from going for the door herself. "I'll see who it is."

Sadie dropped down beside her bag and smoothed her hand over the pinwheel quilt that covered the bed. A minute later she heard her brother's exasperating voice at the entrance. Heavy footsteps came down the hall. She thought seriously about crawling out the window to escape what was sure to be more nagging.

She didn't turn to greet him. "What do you want, Oliver?"

"I came to walk you to the retreat. We have to hurry though. One of my clients needs me to hop online and check for a bug."

If only Gandiegow didn't have high-speed Internet, then Oliver wouldn't have been hell-bent on coming to Scotland to keep an eye on me. But her brother's IT business was portable.

Moira saved Sadie. "Don't worry. I'll get her to Quilting Central safely."

He remained where he was. Sadie could feel his gaze boring into her back.

"Go on, Oliver. Your customer is waiting."

She still didn't hear him leave. Sadie rolled her eyes heavenward and heaved herself off the bed. She plastered on a fake smile before facing him. "I'm fine. Really."

"Okay. But if you need me, I'll be next door at Duncan's Den." The other quilting dorm, only a few steps from this one.

Sadie nodded.

Oliver held his phone up as if to show her he was only a call away.

"Come," Moira said. "It's time to meet Deydie and the other quilting ladies."

Oliver pinned one more worried glance on Sadie, then left. She grabbed her bag and a sweater.

Outside, Sadie trudged along, wishing to be anywhere but here.

Moira peeked over at her. "Gandiegow only has sixty-three houses."

"It's very quaint." For the first time, Sadie really looked around. The village arced like a smile facing the ocean, the little stone cottages an array of mismatched teeth, but seemed to fit together. The rounded green bluff loomed at the backs of the houses, a town blocked in, but cozy. Yes, the village was *quaint* with its oceanfront views from nearly every house. But sadness swept over Sadie once again. Gigi would've loved it here, as she'd often reminisced fondly about the small town in Montana along the Bitterroot River where she'd grown up.

Moira stopped in front of a building with a sign that read QUILTING CENTRAL. "This is it."

Without realizing that she should prepare herself, Sadie opened the door and stepped in. A tidal wave of anxiety hit her, the emotion so overwhelming, she wanted to flee.

The smell of starch.

White- and gray-headed women.

Fabric stacked and stashed everywhere.

All the things that reminded her of Gigi. If that wasn't enough to have Sadie bolting for the door, a crowd of women scuttled toward her. She backed up.

One tall, thin elderly woman clasped her arm, stilling her. "We're so glad ye're here. I'm Bethia."

A short battle-ax of a woman barreled through to get to Sadie, grabbing her other arm. "I'm Deydie. We've been waiting on ye."

Sadie was short of oxygen. She desperately wanted out.

Gray-haired twins, wearing matching plaid dresses of different colors, stepped in her path. The red plaid one spoke first.

"Sister and I were distraught when we lost our gran."

They knew. Sadie looked at the faces around the room. *They all knew.*

The green-plaided one bobbed her head up and down. "That was many years ago. We've all experienced loss." She gestured toward the crowd. "We understand what ye're going through."

The other whispered loudly to her sister. "But not about the kidney disease."

No! How could he! Sadie wasn't the all-out swearing type, but internally she formed a string of obscenities to sling at her brother that made her cringe.

"Back," Deydie said to the twins. "Give the lass room to breathe and to get her bearings. She's not well."

Well enough to scream!

A thirty-something woman, carrying a baby, made her way to Sadie. "I'm Emma. And this is Angus." She had a British accent, not a Scots like the others. She turned to Deydie. "I should take over, don't you think?"

Deydie nodded vigorously. "Right. Right. It should be ye." The old woman cleared the others away.

"Come sit down," Emma said. "The town can be a bit overbearing. But they mean well." She led Sadie to a sofa.

Deydie called everyone's attention to the front and began welcoming all the quilters.

Emma leaned over. "I'm a therapist. Most people when they're grieving should talk to someone. I wanted to let you know that I'm available if you need me."

A moment ago, Sadie thought the woman had her best interest at heart, but she was like the others, trying to suffocate her, trying to tell her how to deal with her grief. Sadie didn't deserve their attention. Her selfishness had killed her grandmother. She opened her mouth to set the well-meaning therapist straight, but the woman's baby fortuitously spewed down his mother's blouse.

"Excuse me." Emma stood with the little one. "We'll talk later."

Or not.

Emma's leaving should've given Sadie's senses a reprieve, but in some respects, all the women smothering her had been a distraction. The room, *this place*, was too much; she couldn't sit here with a huge group of women reminding her of her grandmother. And with Gigi newly buried. The guilt. The grief . . . everything. Sadie had to get out of here . . . escape.

She looked longingly toward the door, only ten feet

away. Everyone was listening to Deydie, finally not focused on her. Sadie stood nonchalantly and walked toward the exit, slowly and with purpose, as if she'd left her curling iron on back at the dorm.

Two more steps. She eased the door open so carefully that the bell above the door barely jingled.

She slipped out, gulping in the cool evening air as though it was water. But it wasn't enough. The town still felt claustrophobic. She'd do anything to get out of here.

The tide was up and the ocean was slapping itself against the walkway with increasing ferocity and passion. The sea was alive, the waves crashing, telling her to run.

And on the breeze, she heard the strangest thing . . . male voices singing. It was surreal. She followed the sound, heading back in the direction of the parking lot where the van had dropped them off. She stopped outside the first building in town, a pub called The Fisherman where the tune was coming from. The song pulled her up the steps and had her opening the door. As she crossed the threshold, the song came to an end.

The room was mostly filled with men, all sizes. The vast majority looked as if they could've done a magazine shoot for *Fishermen Now.* A few looked her way, but being plain, she didn't have to worry about anyone hitting on her or even approaching.

She put her head down, made her way to the bar, and sat at the far end on the only open stool. Next to her was a particularly large, rugged, all-muscle—and from what she could see of his profile—handsome man, undoubt-edly one of the fishermen, too. Another man, short and squat, stepped between them, partially blocking her view of Handsome.

Squat clamped a hand on Handsome's shoulder. "Ye'd like my niece, Ruth. She can cook and sew. She'd make ye a good wife. I promise, she will. At least meet her while she's here for the retreat."

The way Handsome was scowling over his drink, Sadie was certain he hadn't been one of the men singing moments ago. He looked as if he'd given up singing permanently.

The bartender waved to Sadie. "What can I get ye?"

"Water," she said automatically. Cola and alcohol were out-of-bounds. She would do everything she could to keep off the active transplant list for as long as possible.

Handsome glanced her way, and damn, he was good-looking. Not that a guy like him would notice someone like her. Sure enough, he went back to his drink without a word.

Squat was fidgeting, beginning to look desperate. "What do ye say? I told Ruth ye'd see her. Take her to dinner. Or maybe have a stroll to the top of the bluff." He chewed the inside of his cheek. "She won't mind the exercise."

Sadie felt sorry for Handsome. Couldn't Squat see that he didn't want to do it? The bartender set her glass in front of her and left to help a patron at the other end.

"Dammit, Harry," Handsome growled. "Ye're putting me in a hell of a spot."

Sadie made a snap decision. She reached for her glass and *accidentally* knocked it aside, spilling water all over Harry.

He jumped back. "What'd'ya do that for?"

She reached for the towel at the end of the bar and began blotting at the water on Harry's shirt. "So sorry. I guess I wasn't paying attention."

When Harry wasn't looking, she tilted her head at Handsome for him to make a run for it. This fisherman was no dummy. He was out the door before she could order Harry a drink to make up for the drenching she gave him.

Once Harry was settled and complaining to the barkeep about her clumsiness, Sadie decided to leave before she brought any more attention to herself. She headed for the door, no closer to finding a way out of Gandiegow.

Outside, she paused on the top step and spoke to the vast ocean in front of her. "I have to get out of here!" That's when she realized she wasn't alone.

Leaning against the edge of the building a few feet away stood Handsome. He walked toward her and stuck out his hand to help her down the last few steps. "I owe you, lass. Tell me where you want to go. I've got a truck."

Chapter Two

Ross couldn't believe the lass had not only saved him from Harry and his dreadful niece, but had read his mind, too. *I want out of here as well.* Her hand was warm in his and she held on tight. He glanced down at them linked together, and though it felt strange, it felt right, too. When he looked up, he saw his brothers, John and Ramsay, coming up the walkway that kept the sea at bay. Andrew MacBride, Gandiegow's Episcopal priest, was with them, too. Ross dropped Sadie's hand.

When John got close enough, he nodded in the lass's direction. "New friend?"

"Aye." Ross wasn't in the mood for explanations. Hell, he had none to give.

Andrew in his cleric collar looked at the two of them curiously, but said nothing. Ramsay wore a look of surprise that spoke volumes.

So what.

Aye, earlier Ross had skipped out when Kit, Ramsay's wife, had tried to set him up. And now here he was with a stranger . . . headed off to God-only-knows-where.

When Ramsay opened his mouth, John gently shoved him toward the steps.

"We better get inside before all the drink is gone," John said. "'Night, ye two."

"Good night," Ross said.

When his brothers were inside, he looked down at the lass again. "Were ye serious about getting out of town?"

"You have no idea," she said firmly.

He cocked an eyebrow at her. "And ye'd run off with a man ye don't know?"

She didn't hesitate, as if she already had his number. "I figured you for a nice guy from the get-go."

"How so?"

She shrugged. "If I hadn't rescued you, you would've agreed to go out with Harry-there's niece. And I'm not completely sure that you're off the hook yet. I expect you'll be strolling with Ruth to the top of the bluff before the quilting retreat is over."

She was probably right.

And she wasn't done. "I watched as you slipped from the pub. The townspeople seem to respect you by the way they were nodding in your direction as you left."

This lass saw too much.

She gave him a solemn stare. "Then the two who looked like you"—she pointed to where John and Ramsay had stood.

"My brothers," Ross interjected.

She nodded. "Your brothers saw us together. Witnesses, you see."

Ross shook his head. She may be right about him, but what if she'd been wrong? "Ye can't go around hopping into anyone's vehicle who offers."

She put her hands on her hips. "You don't know how badly I want out of here."

The lass was determined, he'd give her that. "Fair enough."

He really looked at her. She was shorter than him by at least a foot, with an innocent young face and brown bangs setting off her deep brown eyes. She had a birthmark above her mouth that reminded him of a heart. She seemed sweet, but her full-of-wisdom eyes contested her age, and at the same time they spoke of sadness and distress, too.

A wave of protectiveness came over him. "Do ye want to tell me what's going on?"

She shook her head *no*, as if that was her final answer. She glanced back at the rest of the town and then pointed to the parking lot. "Can we get going?"

"Aye. This way."

She walked beside him the forty-some steps it took to get there.

"Is that your truck? The red pickup?" She walked toward it with purpose.

It was the only truck in the lot.

She opened the passenger side. "I like it. It has character." She slid in and shut the door.

He did the same on the driver's side. "Where to?"

"Away."

He liked her resolve and how she knew what she wanted. He pulled out of the lot and up the bluff, leaving Gandiegow behind.

In contented silence, they drove for an hour, maybe a bit more. He should've asked for her name, but he didn't want to spoil the unspoken peace between them. From time to time, he would glance at her. The farther away from Gandiegow they went, the more relaxed she became. She mostly gazed out the front windshield, but if they passed something that caught her eye, she would look out her side window, too. She seemed to come awake, as if she'd been asleep for a long, long time.

When he pulled over the next rise, she grabbed his arm.

"This is it."

He slowed. "This is what?"

"Can we stop?" She pointed to an outcropping of rocks that overlooked the North Sea. "I need to sit right there."

"Sure." He pulled off the asphalt onto the grass.

She was out of the vehicle and shutting her door before he turned the ignition off. He got out, too, and watched her make her way through the tall grass to her spot.

She turned suddenly. "What's your name?"

She could've been part of a postcard. She wore a simple T-shirt dress and boat shoes. Her backdrop was the sea. A picture of purity.

"Ross," he answered hoarsely.

"Thank you, Ross." She turned back toward her destination.

He didn't move, watching her climb up and get settled. Maybe he should've asked her name back, but it felt perfectly natural to have things sit the way they were, part of the crazy magic since he'd met her. The next twenty minutes or so, he hung out at his truck. No one drove by on this Highland road, which was normal in these parts. As it grew later and the sun started to set, he made his way through the grass, too, to join her on the rocks.

As soon as he was settled, she gazed over at him.

"I like it here. I could stay in this spot forever."

"Aye. It suits ye."

They were quiet as the sun descended, but it was the strangest affair, as if they were at a symphony performance. Hushed. In awe. The air filled with tones of color. Ross had never experienced the sunset like this before. He looked over to see if the lass heard it—felt it—too. She was transfixed on the spot just off the horizon where the sun rested before falling into the edge of the ocean.

When it was over, she spoke very quietly as if they were in church. "I'm Sadie." She sighed with contentment. "Sadie Middleton."

The name jarred him out of the spell.

He hadn't listened to the gossip before the retreat goers had arrived, but invariably some had seeped in. And he sure as hell knew about *this one!* She was the one for which Deydie had said to take *extra care.* Her gran had recently died. And the lass was sick. Not a cold or anything minor, but truly sick. What a nightmare.

He hopped off the rock and glared up at her. "I'm taking ye back. Now!"

She cocked her head to the side as if she hadn't heard him correctly. Then she glared right back, or at least he thought it was a glare as the moon was rising.

She crossed her arms over her chest. "I'm not going anywhere."

"Ye're going back." Quick and decisively, he reached up and wrapped his hands around her waist. She gasped. Carefully, so as not to hurt her, he lifted her from the rock and set her on her feet. She weighed nothing. "Now, do I carry ye back to the truck, or will ye walk on yere own accord?"

Her stubbornness faded. He saw it by the slump of her shoulders.

She laid a hand on his arm. "I can't go back. Not yet." Her hand was cold.

"Lass, why didn't ye tell me ye were chilled?" He rubbed his hands over her arms. "Get to the pickup so I can turn the heat on."

"In a minute." She stilled one of his hands with hers. "First, hear me out."

He should have asked her straightaway who she was. He never should've let her sit on that damned rock so long. The town would crucify him if the American lass took ill. *Or became more ill.*

"I'll listen. But can you at least put yere sweater on? I'll get it from the truck."

She nodded. And as he walked away, the stubborn little thing scrambled back up on her perch.

He hurried. While he was at it, he also grabbed the quilt that Maggie, John's wife, had tucked behind the pickup's seat. You never knew when you might get stuck out on a Highland road. He took the items back to Sadie.

"Here." He handed her the sweater, then climbed up beside her, wrapping the quilt around her shoulders. "Now talk."

When she didn't immediately speak, he gazed down at her.

She was worrying her lower lip. "I could sit here for a year."

"Well, that isn't happening. Ye've got five minutes."

She ignored him, her eyes fixed on the horizon, captured by the massive full moon. "The ocean is vast and makes my worries seem small in comparison."

Now *that* he understood. "I'm a fisherman. Sometimes I think the Almighty made the sea for just that purpose."

She was quiet for a long moment. "I can't go back tonight. I need this time."

"Ye can't sit out here all night either."

She pulled the quilt tighter around her shoulders and he squelched the urge to wrap his arm around her to keep the quilt in place.

"I promise to go back tomorrow," she said in a small voice. "Just don't rush me. I know what I need, and it isn't a bunch of people."

A strange notion hit him. She didn't need a bunch of people, but she needed him?

"All right." The words came out before he knew what he was doing. He sighed. There would be hell to pay for this. "Let me call my brother John and tell him what's up. Then I'm going to take ye down the road. There's a B and B that might put us up for the night. And we'll go back early in the morn. Agreed?"

She nodded.

He allowed her to stay on her rock until the moon fully rose. When he went to get down, she didn't argue, but willingly slid down, too. As she walked beside him, she was quiet, subdued, but better than when she'd come into the pub hours ago in Gandiegow.

She kept the quilt around her shoulders as she climbed into his truck. It occurred to him that she was the first woman besides one of the old quilt ladies to actually ride in it with him.

After going a couple of miles down the road, he pulled

into the lane with the B and B sign, the one he'd seen many times when he'd driven to Inverness. Thankfully, the lights were still on.

He left the pickup running. "Stay here while I see if they have a vacancy."

As he walked to the front door, he pulled out his phone and called John.

There was no polite *hallo*. "Hold on," his brother whispered. The bed creaked, the door opened and closed, and then he was back on. "Why are you calling so late? Ye know I have to get up early for the boat. And so do you."

"I know. But I might be a few minutes late in the morning."

"If ye're not there, we'll leave without you. I have to set an example for Samuel and Robert." Maggie's teenage cousins.

"I'll try to make it, but do what ye have to do."

"Who was it that ye left with tonight?" John asked.

Ross reached the B and B's front door. A note had been pinned to it:

Ring bell, then go around to the back entrance.

"Nobody," Ross answered. "I've got to run." He hung up.

Within a few minutes, Ross had secured a room. *A room.* He walked back to his truck . . . Maybe his news would make Sadie want to return to Gandiegow tonight.

He opened her door.

A line between her eyebrows formed. "What's wrong? Didn't they have a place for us to stay?"

"Aye. They have a room."

"Good." She slipped from the vehicle.

But he blocked her from going farther, keeping one hand on the door and the other on the truck, and knelt to get closer to her eye level. "One, lass. They only have *one* room."

"Oh." She chewed her lip again, but this time it looked as if she was adding sums in her head. After a moment, she looked up at him. "Okay."

"There's another problem." *Gawd* help him for lying to the owner. "To secure the room I had to tell her I was with my new bride."

Sadie stepped back, bumping her legs against the truck frame. She stared up at him, incredulous. "No one is going to believe that." She waved a hand at him as if it was an awful joke. "Seriously. No one."

"They will. The missus was apologetic that there's only twin beds in the room."

"Thank God for small favors."

"I told her we'd make do."

Sadie's mouth fell open. Then she slammed it shut. She acted as if she might try again to say something, but then only shook her head.

"Come. Let's get you inside." He offered her his hand. "We've got to make her believe it. The missus was suspect at first, but I convinced her we're fiercely in love."

Sadie snorted. "It's going to take more than a little hand-holding to make it believable." But she laid her hand in his anyway.

They walked from the gravel driveway to the trellis at the edge of the garden. She stopped suddenly, tugging at him. "Wait." She let go and transferred a ring from her right hand to her left. "There. The illusion is complete. Thank goodness for Gigi's ring."

"Gigi?" he asked.

"My grandmother," she said quietly. "She gave it to me when I graduated in May." Sadie went still, as if the thought had flipped a switch that rooted her feet to the grass.

Gawd, he hoped she wouldn't start crying.

The missus of the B and B leaned out the back entrance. "Are ye coming in?"

Ross wrapped an arm around Sadie and continued walking, leaning down to speak in her ear. "I know I'm asking a lot, but can you pretend that ye're happy until we get to the room? As much as I love my truck, it would be damned uncomfortable to sleep in it tonight."

She nodded.

But the missus was watching them like a hawk. Ross kissed the top of Sadie's head. When they got nearer, he spoke to the woman, not believing for a second Sadie could hide her grief.

"Is she all right?"

Ross led the American lass inside. "We've had a long day. She's tired, is all. She'll be fine once I get her in bed."

Sadie stiffened.

The missus looked concerned. And then as if she was only now noticing, she glanced at their hands. *No luggage.* She glowered at its absence. "Just remember this isn't some manky hotel. This is my home."

"Yes, ma'am," Ross said, glad the woman had already taken his money.

"The room's upstairs." The missus stared at him hard for another moment.

Ross pulled Sadie to him tighter. "Come, luv." He ushered her to the stairs and up.

Once he had her inside the room and the door closed, he sighed with relief. The bedroom wasn't much, but it had the two requisite beds, simple patchwork quilts, and pillows. The only luxury as far as he could tell was the two fluffy robes hanging inside the opened armoire.

Sadie eased herself down on the closest bed. "Sorry."

"Ye've nothing to be sorry for. Do you want to use the loo first?"

"Yes." She rose gracefully and left the room.

He'd gotten himself into a tight spot. He wasn't sure how to handle the lass. Even worse, how was he going to handle Deydie and the rest of the quilters when they found out he'd taken her from the village and had her out all night?

He went to the window and stared out at the ocean until Sadie came back. He didn't say anything or look in her eyes as he walked from the room to take his turn in the loo. When he came back, she was wrapped in one of the robes, but he could see she was still fully clothed, the hem of her dress showing.

"I was cold," she explained.

He crossed the bedroom. "Lie down. Let's get these covers on you." He pulled the top quilt from his bed and spread it over her bed, too. He couldn't help himself—he tucked the covers around her like his mum used to do for him when he was a wee lad.

Sadie wasn't a wee bairn, but she needed his compassion so he gave it.

She gazed up at him with her deep brown eyes. "Thanks. For everything."

What could he say? It was his pleasure? Well, it had been . . . up until the point he'd learned who she was.

He turned off the lights, and the room went dark. The moon was high, though, and he had no trouble making it to his bed. He pulled back the remaining cover and lay down. How strange the day had turned out.

"Ross?" she said into the darkness.

"Yes?"

He watched as she wrestled with the quilts to face him, his tucking-in job wasted.

"Why aren't you married?"

"Where is that coming from?"

"I'm curious. I was right about you. You're a nice guy, and Harry's trying to set you up? There has to be a story behind it all."

They'd spent most of their time in silence today, but now she wanted to talk? He guessed he could say anything under the blanket of night . . . even the truth.

Ross sighed. "I was engaged once. Do ye have a beau back in the States?"

Sadie snorted again. "Not hardly. Tell me about your engagement. Unless, of course, it's too painful."

Ross could've produced his own snort, but he didn't. "Nay. Not painful at all. Her name is Pippa. She's a childhood friend. She runs the factory just outside of town. Our das set it up when we were kids."

"I met Pippa today, and her husband Max. They drove us into town after the bus broke down. You were engaged to her? An arranged marriage?"

"Something like that." He told her what had happened over Christmas, how his life had gone from *settled* to up-in-the-air. "Max came into town and stole Pippa's heart.

I'm happy for her. We were never more than friends."
And he'd made his mind up that if he was ever to marry,
it would have to start out with fireworks like it had with
Ramsay and Kit. *And Max and Pippa.* Love at first sight.
That way Ross would know for sure that what he was
doing was the right thing and not wasting his time. And
in this future relationship with his unidentified-as-yet
wife, they wouldn't be great friends at first . . . friendship
would come later. In this way—hell, in all ways—his mystery wife would have to be the opposite of Pippa. He
didn't even know what that would mean exactly, but
she would just have to be nothing like her. He finished
telling Sadie the rest, admitting one of his greatest flaws.
"But I was going to go through with it and marry her
anyway. I believed that doing what my father wanted me
to do—hell, what the whole town wanted—was more important than what I wanted. That it was the right thing."
And somehow, doing what everyone else thought was
right turned out to be wrong for Ross.

"I know what you mean. Gigi and Oliver wanted me
to become a dental hygienist, so I became one."

Ross could hear the frown in her words. He wanted
to ask her about it, but then she spoke.

"Have you ever lost anyone?" Her voice was quiet, but
her grief was palpable.

He thought about his da.

"A close friend?" she clarified.

The images of Duncan, his best mate, flashed through
his mind. "Aye." It had been one of the hardest things
he'd ever gone through, to watch his friend fight leukemia
and lose. "What about you?"

"Gigi was my closest friend."

"I lost my closest friend, too." Ross found himself opening up about Duncan. He hadn't talked about it with anyone, because everyone he knew had lived it along with him. Even though it tore at him to share with Sadie what had happened, it felt right at the same time. Then he went back a little farther and told her how the loss of his da hadn't been any easier. It had been sudden, no time to prepare, and no time to say *I love you* once more.

Sadie's bed creaked. He saw her rise and pad toward him. "Scoot over. I'm cold."

He could've argued that he was a big man in a small bed. But who was he to turn away a woman who needed him? He opened his arms and she slipped in. She didn't feel cold, but warm, and smelled of the outdoors, the ocean, and sunshine. He pulled the covers around them.

Sadie spoke into his chest. "I know what you mean about not getting to say *I love you* one more time. My parents went out for the evening and never came home. They were hit by a tractor trailer. I was six." She shivered.

He rubbed his chin over her hair. "Aw, lass, I'm sorry." He'd been lucky at least to have his father until he was grown.

"What about your mother?" she asked.

"She's in Glasgow. She moved in with her sister to care for her. Aunt Glynnis isn't well."

Sadie was quiet for a long moment. She was probably thinking about how she wasn't well either. Her silence gave him time to dwell on how bizarre this was. He was holding this sweet woman with no intentions of putting the moves on her. Not because he didn't find her intriguing, and not because she didn't fit up against him perfectly. He just wasn't the sort of man to take advantage of a woman in distress. She was completely safe with him. She was nice, and even adorable in a quirky kind of way, but not his type. He yawned. In the middle of it, he had a fleeting thought . . . *This lass is the opposite of Pippa.*

Sadie couldn't believe she'd been so bold. But she had to do it. She wasn't cold when she'd crawled into Ross's bed. He was the one who needed to be held. He was hurting and needed a hug, something a man like him would never admit. She had not done it for herself, no matter how good it felt to be in his arms. His yawn made her yawn, too.

She closed her eyes and snuggled in deeper. "Ross?"

"Hmm?" The hum of him relaxed her even more.

She sighed contentedly. "I know I promised to return to Gandiegow." She yawned again. "But can I have one more day to sit on the rock by the ocean before we go back?" She breathed him in and fell asleep.

Sadie woke, relaxed, well rested, and still snuggled against the Scotsman's chest. For a moment, she could imagine having this pretend life—whole, healthy, and sleeping in the arms of a kind man. But her current reality wasn't real.

His breathing was even and she was afraid if she moved, she'd wake him. But the restroom called. She slipped from his arms and stood. He rolled over, an arm and leg hanging over the side of the bed in the process. He was even more handsome in his sleep, if that was possible. She quietly left and went down the hall.

When she returned, Ross laid his phone on the bed and bent over to tie his army boots. "Get yere shoes on. We'll go downstairs, grab our breakfast, and leave."

Her heart dropped—they were leaving? Going back to Gandiegow? Now? Going back to being smothered? Rebellion had her planting her hands on her hips, making it feel as if she was speaking up for herself for what seemed like the first time. "I'm not leaving."

He stopped and glanced up. "Oh?"

As quickly as it came, her steam ran out and she dropped her arms.

He went back to tying his boots. "So ye've changed yere mind. Ye don't want to sit on yere rock?"

Her heart soared. "You're really going to let me have my day?"

He grinned at her and stood. "Part of the day. I texted my brother that we'll be back by supper."

She squeezed her hands together. "Thank you."

"I smell bacon. Can you play the satisfied bride for the missus below?"

Heat poured into Sadie's face. She still couldn't believe the woman had bought that they were a couple, even for a second, even a little bit. Ross—incredibly handsome and incredibly nice—could date anyone he liked. Sadie didn't belittle herself over her appearance; she liked who she was, had accepted she would never be beautiful. She was a realist. She peeked over at her fake husband. *Handsome* didn't come close to describing him. He was more, much more. He was nearly *perfect*.

She ducked her head. "Yes. I can pretend we're together." *But how could he?*

"Good, because I'm hungry."

They sat at the owner's table and ate their breakfast with the woman of the house looking on. Ross played it up to a tee and Sadie could see he had a mischievous

THE TROUBLE WITH SCOTLAND 33

streak. Whenever the missus checked in on them, Ross would pour it on thick, either kissing Sadie's fingertips or making love to her with his eyes.

Sadie, though she enjoyed every second, couldn't help but blush all the way through her porridge and bacon.

Oliver Middleton rubbed sleep from his face and walked into the small kitchen of Duncan's Den. On the counter, he found fresh scones, sausages under foil, and hot tea—very thoughtful. He rushed through his meal. He'd been online late last night with his client and never made it to the quilting retreat to see how Sadie was doing.

He was worried about her; she'd been dealt a shit-load lately. Last month her terrible diagnosis and this month, Gigi's death. Pain cut through him about his grandmother, about Sadie, about everything, but he squelched it. Taking care of his sister, making sure she was okay, was his number one priority. He'd promised Gigi. He hated that his grandmother had made him vow to keep it a secret from Sadie. He could tell her the truth now, but it wouldn't make any difference. It wouldn't bring Gigi back. But if Sadie had known beforehand, she might've been prepared for their grandmother's death.

Quickly, he dressed, finding the weather cooler here in July than in North Carolina. He went next door first, but no one answered when he knocked. He walked down the walkway, passing the General Store and the school. On the other side, he found the building marked Quilting Central and went inside. The place was crowded with quilters. He looked around, but didn't see Sadie. Two older women noticed him and hurried over.

"You must be Oliver, Sadie's brother," said the taller of the two. "I'm Bethia and this is Deydie."

The shorter, stockier one nodded at him. "Ye don't look a thing like yere sister."

Yes, he was blond, and Sadie had brown hair. He glanced around impatiently. "Speaking of my sister, I don't see her. How is she this morning?"

Bethia shot Deydie a worried glance.

Panic flooded him; alarm bells went off in his head.

Deydie crossed her arms over her chest. "Go ahead and tell him."

"Come with me, lad." Bethia pointed to the sofa.

"No." Oliver stood his ground. "Where's my sister?"

Bethia laid a hand on his arm. "We're not sure."

Oliver's throat closed and fire sparked behind his eyes. "What do you mean *we're not sure*? Where is she?"

Deydie stepped directly in front of him and cranked her head back, staring him down. "She ran off. At least that's what Coll told his wife, Amy." She pointed to a younger woman across the room. "Amy let us know this morning."

"We've been in this town less than twenty-four hours and you've lost my sister!" Oliver didn't wait to hear more. He wanted answers and he wanted them now. He marched over to the black-haired woman who at least knew something. She bent over to pick up a baby from a playpen before he reached her.

She gave Oliver a big smile, but it faded quickly. She must've known he was pissed. She handed the kid off to someone else, saying something in Gaelic as she did.

When he reached her, he didn't feel the need to introduce himself. "Where's my sister?"

"Hold up there," a male voice said from the doorway. Another man followed.

By the looks of them, the two were brothers, although one was redheaded and the other dark-haired. They approached Oliver.

"I'm John and this is my brother Ramsay."

The rest of the room went quiet, listening in. Oliver didn't give a rat's ass who overheard. "Where is my sister?"

John put his hand on Oliver's arm. "Why don't we go outside and talk?"

Oliver shrugged him off. "No. You'll answer my question. Now."

"Yere sister's in no danger. She's with my brother Ross. They're fine."

"What do you mean? Why is she with your brother? How do you know he has her?" Fear and anger swept through Oliver. "Where are they?"

"They left together from the pub," John said. "Last night."

"What?" Why was Oliver only hearing of this now! "Your brother kept her out all night?" Had he kidnapped her? No. That seemed too far-fetched. But didn't these people realize that he was responsible for his baby sister? "Your brother better not have touched her."

"The lass looked willing," Ramsay provided.

Oliver wanted to punch him.

Deydie glowered at Ramsay, but then stepped in front of Oliver as she'd done before. This time, her eyes held just the right amount of compassion, reminding him of Gigi. Tough, but with a good heart.

"Ye're not to worry, lad." She patted his arm. "If she's

with Ross, she's in good hands. No harm'll come to her."
She thumbed at the other two brothers. "I'd trust Ross
over the two of them." She was a woman who didn't
mince words. As gruff as she was, something about her
forthrightness eased the panic that Oliver felt.

Bethia took his arm. "Let's get ye one of Claire's
scones."

Deydie latched on to his other arm. "It'll help."

He'd already had a scone, but the two of them calmed
him. He let himself be led away.

As Sadie sat on her rock and soaked in the ocean, she
thought on how the day couldn't have gone better. They'd
picnicked with a hunk of cheese and a loaf of bread
they'd bought from the grocer in a nearby village. Ross
was a wonderful companion—not suffocating her or giving her any special consideration. He treated her as if
she was normal. And he didn't talk her to death.

She watched as storm clouds formed on the horizon,
and her mood grew dark with the sky.

She glanced over at Ross sitting next to her. "We're
going to have to leave soon, aren't we?"

"Aye." He motioned to the increasingly angry sky.
"We can't sit here with that on top of us."

Sadie wished she'd taken that auto mechanics class in
high school so she'd know how to disable the pickup. "I
don't want to go."

"Sorry, lass. We'll have to head back and face them."
His stoic demeanor spoke volumes.

"Oh."

He said he'd be in trouble with the people of Gandiegow, but she hadn't let herself worry over it. But now she felt terrible putting him in the middle. "Then let's get it over with."

He jumped off the rock before she could move. With his hands gently around her waist, he helped her down. He was kind, attentive, and she appreciated everything he'd done.

Before leaving, he pulled out his phone. "I'm going to let my brother know that we're on our way."

Sadie should call Oliver, but she wanted to hang on to her illusion of independence for as long as possible. Maybe she shouldn't have purposely shut off her phone, but she had to put the world on mute to achieve the quiet she needed.

The drive to Gandiegow was filled with comfortable silence and she soaked in every last second, knowing this would be the last of the peace. An hour later, as they were driving down the bluff to the idyllic village, Sadie steeled herself for the barrage ahead.

Ross parked the truck and turned to her before getting out. "Ye're going to be all right, lass."

The words themselves were reassuring, and she wanted to believe him, but too much had gone wrong to think things could ever be right again. She rallied a smile for him, opened her door, and let her feet hit the asphalt. Her adventure was over. A deep sadness filled her.

Ross got out and came to her side of the truck. Before she lost her nerve, she grabbed his arm, tugging, until he bent down so she could kiss his cheek. The stubble tickled and pricked her lips. "I'll never forget what you did for me." Never.

He stared into her eyes as if registering her for the first time, and he seemed shocked by what he found there. "Lass—"

"Sadie!"

She swung around to find Oliver barreling toward her. She'd never seen him this upset.

"Where the hell have you been!"

Chapter Three

Oliver's face was rage red from his neck up to his hairline. Sadie's view was blocked when Ross stepped in between them.

"Out of the way," her brother growled. "I need to speak with my sister."

"Not until ye've settled down," Ross said firmly.

She put her hand on her protector's back. "It's okay." Ross's back was rigid, strong.

"Are ye sure, lass?" As if Oliver might hurt her.

She stepped around him, brushing the Scot's arm. "I'm sure."

Oliver jabbed a finger at Ross. "He better not have laid a hand on you."

Sadie's cheeks went instantly hot. Ross hadn't done what Oliver was suggesting, but she had slept wonderfully, wrapped in the Scot's arms. She couldn't look up at his handsome face to see if he was remembering, too.

She took a deep breath and squared off with her brother. "Oliver, I'm a grown woman." She wanted to stomp her foot, but it wouldn't help her cause.

"Why didn't you have your phone on?"

"Sorry. I needed a break."

"Very mature, Sadie," Oliver said, slicing her with his words.

Even worse, Ross glanced at her as if he might agree with her brother.

"I didn't mean for you to worry."

"But I did." Oliver ran a hand through his hair. "I'm responsible for you."

She glanced heavenward. He was giving her the same old story. She'd be wasting her breath to tell him that she could take care of herself.

Oliver captured her arm and pulled. "Come. They're all waiting for you at Quilting Central."

She tugged back. "No. I can't handle it right now. Maybe later." *Or never.*

"But this is why you came," Oliver complained.

"No. I came because you packed my clothes and put me on a plane. If you remember, I was the one who wanted to stay home, in bed, under the covers."

This whole time, Ross remained quiet. She looked up at him now to gauge what he was feeling.

He stepped forward, her human roadblock once again. "I'll make sure she gets to the quilting dorm."

Oliver moved closer, ready to argue.

Sadie stepped between them again. "I'll be fine, Ollie." She hadn't used her pet name for him in years. "I want to lie down for a while."

It wasn't his nickname that did the trick. Oliver gazed at her, concerned.

"I'm tired. It's nothing more than that. Promise." She and Ross had stayed up very late talking, but she wasn't going to share that with her overprotective brother. "I'll see you later. Okay?" But suddenly she was worried about him. "What are you going to do? Work?"

"Deydie, you met her, right? She wants me to help with the computers at Quilting Central. Something about quilting software needing an update. I'm heading there now. Come with me."

A real yawn produced itself at exactly the right moment. "I can't. I'm bushed."

"But we will talk. Tonight." His bossy brother tone was back.

"Fine."

Ross reached into the truck and grabbed her purse, holding it out for her. He nodded to Oliver as he passed. Sadie had a weird moment of feeling sad that these two would never get along. But why should she care? She and Oliver were here for only the week. Thinking about the hovering quilters and Quilting Central, a week felt too long. She glanced up at Ross's kind face . . . and at the same time, a week wasn't nearly long enough.

Oliver stomped off.

Sadie touched Ross's arm. "I need something to eat before I head to the dorm." Her meds were due. "Does the pub have sandwiches?"

"Aye. But instead, I'll introduce you to Dominic's pasta at Gandiegow's restaurant."

"Thanks. Sounds great."

As they made their way from the parking lot, she decided to set Ross straight. "You know, my brother would never hurt me. He's just overprotective."

"And he has a temper," Ross added.

"Yes, he does." She wanted to tell Ross not to worry, but that rang too much of a relationship, which they weren't in. They'd had their Bonnie and Clyde moment—without the crime—and now they would go their separate ways. Well, after a meal anyway.

At the restaurant, people stared at her, or maybe it was Ross. He was nice to look at. Or more likely they were wondering why he would be with her.

From behind the counter, a strawberry blonde with a baby on her hip hollered to them. "Take a seat and I'll be right there."

"Thanks, Claire."

He chose a table and held out a chair for Sadie. It was crazy, but his attentiveness made it feel like a date . . . which it wasn't.

As soon as they were settled, Claire hustled over with their menus. The door to the establishment opened and Emma, the therapist, came in with what had to be her family—a tall man who was holding baby Angus. As soon as Emma saw Sadie, determination gathered in her gaze.

Sadie wasn't up to a lecture about death and healing and *it-takes-time*. She groaned. Unfortunately, she did it out loud.

"What?" both Ross and Claire said at the same time.

Emma made a beeline for them. Claire must've mistaken Emma's real target, because she held out her baby girl for Emma to take. "I'm glad ye're here. Can the Wee Bit sit with you while ye're eating? She's teething and wants constant attention."

Emma hugged the girl and kissed her head. "Certainly, Nessa can sit with us. She's always welcome."

"I'll grab a teething ring from the freezer for ye."

As soon as Claire left, Emma zeroed in on Sadie. "May my husband and I join you?"

What could Sadie say? *Sure, as long as you don't hound me about talking about my grief.*

Ross transferred himself to the chair next to Sadie. "Sit here. There's plenty of room."

Emma nodded toward her companion. "Sadie, this is my husband, Gabriel. He's the town's doctor."

Sadie nodded. "Oliver mentioned that a physician was in town." And that he could deliver her hormone shot tomorrow. "It's nice to meet you."

Gabriel gave her a warm smile. "It's nice to meet you, too." He handed off his boy to Ross. "I'll get the high chairs and be right back."

Emma settled in across from Sadie. "This is lovely—a dinner date."

Lovely? Sadie inwardly cringed. Being cornered at dinner wasn't her idea of a good time. *Ross the Roadblock* would undoubtedly not see Emma for the threat that she was and would be no help to Sadie this time.

But Emma surprised her. "I hear you went on an adventure. That's wonderful. You look refreshed."

Baby Nessa drooled a smile in Sadie's direction while Angus in Ross's arms grabbed at her sleeve.

Gabriel returned with the high chairs and positioned them on either side of himself, which left Emma's sleeve-grabbing baby next to Sadie. Now he was going for the single-pearl necklace Gigi had given her for her twenty-second birthday.

Sadie loved kids, and truth be told, they loved her. She'd been a very popular babysitter through high school and even college. The counselor at the nephrologist's office said motherhood wouldn't be off the table because of Sadie's kidney transplant. With extra care and monitoring, she could have children like anyone else. But she'd seen *Steel Magnolias* and what had happened to Shelby when she'd had a baby. Granted, Shelby had the complication of diabetes against her, but Sadie couldn't help but compare.

Fear and doubt had settled into nearly every thought since her CKD diagnosis last month, weighing her old life against her new reality.

Ross touched her arm.

She faced him. "Yes?"

"Doc MacGregor asked you a question," Ross said kindly. "Ye looked a million miles away."

"Sorry." These moments of zoning out kept intruding and she was embarrassed to appear so unfocused. She was still adjusting to her new life, another side effect of finding out her future was no longer what she thought it would be.

"How is the Highland air treating ye, lass?" Gabriel repeated.

He'd cleverly masked his question of how she was feeling, but there was no need since Oliver had blabbed about her illness to everyone.

"I'm feeling well." *Even on little sleep,* which she didn't add. "When is a good time to stop by your office and get my shot?"

Gabriel gave her another warm smile, understanding that he could speak freely. "Do ye think ye can steal away from the retreat at midmorning? I know Deydie can be pretty possessive of her quilters' time."

"It won't be a problem." Because Sadie had no intention of returning to Quilting Central.

Ross eyed her as if he knew exactly what she was thinking.

Sadie diverted her attention to the children. "Nessa and Angus are cute names."

"Family names." Gabriel reached for his wife's hand. "We named our boy after my grandfather."

The boy reached out, grabbed Sadie's finger, and shoved it in his mouth.

Emma smoothed down the baby girl's ginger wisps of hair. "And little Nessa is named after Claire's mother."

Sadie couldn't help but long for the children she would or wouldn't have. At one time, she'd dreamed of naming a baby girl after Gigi, her feisty grandmother. *Her dead feisty grandmother.* Sadie studied the menu, hoping Emma wouldn't see the grief that poured from her like water from the tap.

Thankfully, the rest of the meal was uneventful, except for Nessa dropping her teething ring on the floor and Angus throwing chunks of cheese at Gabriel. The babies were a great distraction from any more talk of Quilting Central, grief counseling, and any number of topics that could make Sadie feel miserable. There was a lot of talk about the upcoming wedding between Moira and Father Andrew. Sadie learned the sad tale of how Moira's young cousin Glenna had come to live with her because her parents had died in a car accident recently. Sadie felt for Glenna as few others could.

When they were done, Doc and Ross argued over the check, but Claire announced their dinner paid for by way of them babysitting during the evening rush. Claire retrieved Nessa, snuggled the child to her shoulder, and left to see her husband, Dominic, in the kitchen.

Gabriel turned to Sadie, who was playing with Angus. "Speaking of babysitting . . . Sadie, how would ye like to barter? You and baby Angus seem to be getting along famously."

Sadie liked Gabriel. He didn't seem to think her crippled because of her CKD.

Emma intervened. "Don't put our guest in that position."

Sadie ignored her. "What are you thinking, Doc?" Ross had called him that during dinner. "One shot for an evening out?"

Gabriel smiled at her, and Sadie couldn't help but think all the Scottish men in this town were a bunch of charmers. Then he turned to his wife, blasting her with such a large dose of smolder that Sadie was surprised when Emma didn't catch on fire. "I'm in need of an evening alone with my wife. I'd love to take her to Fairge to the cinema or for a drive in the country."

Emma and Gabriel shared a meaningful glance as if there was a cottage tucked away in the hills waiting for them. Emma blushed then . . . as if she didn't have the privilege of going home with the gorgeous doctor every night. "That's a grand idea. You don't mind, do you, Sadie?"

"Not at all." As long as she wasn't to watch Angus at Quilting Central, she would be fine.

Angus started fussing loudly. Gabriel eased him out of the high chair and bounced him. "I think someone wants a different kind of dinner now, Mama."

Emma stood as well. "Yes. We better get home. Thank

you for letting us join you. And thank you for agreeing to watch our son."

The boy began to wail.

"Ross?" Gabe grabbed the diaper bag. "Give Sadie my cell number. And Sadie, give me a call to make sure I'm in the surgery when ye're ready to pop over for yere hypodermic."

"Good night," Emma said and they left.

Sadie was alone with Ross, except for the other patrons of the restaurant. "Dinner was great."

"Are ye ready to head to the quilting dorm? Or do you want to sit here for a while longer?"

She thought about Oliver finding her at the restaurant and not resting at the dorm as promised. "We better go."

She laid her cloth napkin on the table and stood, knowing her special day had come to an end. She thanked Claire for the lovely meal.

Sadie and Ross strolled out into the cool summer air. For the first time, she realized how she'd hijacked Ross's time. "I bet you're ready to be rid of me and return to your normal life. I didn't mean to impose upon you for so long." They'd spent the last twenty-four hours together.

Ross's eyebrows furrowed. "I've really enjoyed it." But he seemed perplexed by his own words.

She didn't tell him that she enjoyed it, too, but instead concentrated on the waves swooshing against the concrete walkway. Once again they fell into companionable silence as they trod along. When they reached their destination, Thistle Glen Lodge, Ross didn't leave her at the end of the walk, but went all the way with her onto the porch. When he laid a hand on the doorknob, he didn't immediately turn it. She faced him, not sure what to say—

how to say good-bye. She opened her mouth, but caught a movement from behind him.

"There ye are!" Deydie hollered. "Come on, lassie. Ye need to get to Quilting Central and git to work on yere quilt. We knew ye were back in town and we've been waiting the evening session on ye."

Ross looked at Sadie as if he was checking a barometer. "She's tired." How well he'd gotten to know her. "She needs to lie down." He turned the knob then and held the door open for her.

Deydie glowered at him. "Ye better not be lying down with her, Ross Armstrong."

He raised one eyebrow at Deydie, looking ready to give her a fierce comeback. But then he seemed to think better of it.

Deydie put her hands on her hips. "And who gave ye permission to take one of my quilters from town anyway?"

Sadie felt forgotten because Deydie's ire was all on Ross, *her champion.* Maybe she should've slipped inside, but she couldn't leave him to this old Scottish badger. "I'm to blame. It was my idea to get out of town."

Deydie shook her head. "He never should've done it. Get on inside, lass, if ye're tired. I'll have a word with Ross. Alone."

Sadie looked up at him, not for permission, but to make sure he was going to be okay.

"Good night, lass," he said resignedly.

Sadie wanted to thank him again properly for the time on the rock, and all he'd done for her—maybe dare to kiss his cheek again—but not with Deydie as an annoyed audience. Anyway, she hadn't formulated yet what would be a proper thank-you for him being a gentleman. She felt as if she'd made a friend and an ally here in Scotland.

"Good night, Ross." She slipped inside.

As soon as the door was closed, she heard Deydie light into him, her words clearly sailing through the two opened windows at the front of the quilting dorm.

"That girl is not for the likes of you. Ye need a lass who's not sickly. Promise me ye won't be courting her."

Deydie's words hit Sadie like a slap and she gasped before she could get her hand to her mouth. She ran down the hall to her bedroom and shut herself inside. She would not cry. She'd known from the first that Ross was out of her league; that's not where the injury lay. But it had never occurred to her that her CKD would be used against her like this. Her disease had quietly slipped into her life and wreaked havoc with everything and taken away so much. Now the possibility of love fell out of reach, too, another dream shattered because of her worthless kidneys.

Maybe she should've waited by the windows to hear Ross's response to Deydie. But the truth was, Sadie couldn't bear to hear him agree with the old woman. She dropped on the bed, and drew the quilt over her, before the first tear slid down her cheek. *So much for not crying.*

She thought about North Carolina, about going home. The only things that waited for her there were an empty house and her job of endless mouths with teeth to clean. Dental hygiene was extremely important. She knew that. It just wasn't her passion.

She hated every moment in the dentist's office, scraping tartar and handing out goody bags with toothbrushes and dental floss. But right now, it looked preferable to another second here in Gandiegow.

Ross's gaze snapped to the open window when Sadie gasped, and then he turned his glare on Deydie. Of course, he had no interest in the American lass, but at least he had compassion. He'd been taught to respect his elders, but he was raging mad at the town's matriarch now.

"Did ye hear that? You've hurt the lass. And she's had enough pain, don't ye think?"

Deydie was a tough nut—bullheaded and single-minded. She glared right back. "I spoke nothing but the truth. She's not right for ye. Ye're a strapping lad. Ye need a woman who can be yere match in every way."

He could almost hear her say *like Pippa*, but she stopped short of uttering it. For a moment, she seemed to be chewing on her own words, maybe even reconsidering.

While he had the advantage, he said what was on his mind, and to hell with the consequences. "Don't take this the wrong way, but the only person who is allowed to counsel me on who I *court* . . . is myself." He was done doing what Gandiegow told him to do. And didn't the townsfolk realize he couldn't be tied down now? He'd never gotten to sow his wild oats, not really, and play the field like a normal bloke. No. He'd always been attached to Pippa. Sort of. He needed to get away from Deydie, and his own thoughts. "If ye'll excuse me, I'm going to check on Sadie and make sure she's okay."

Deydie harrumphed, but she didn't stop him from opening the door and going inside.

"Lass?" Ross called out.

"Go away." The voice was muffled.

He headed to the bedroom and knocked on the door. "Can I come in?"

"No."

He cracked the door to the darkened room. A ray of light from the hall shone on Sadie as she lay on the twin bed with her face to the wall.

"Are you all right?"

"Grand. Or whatever you Scots say." The lass had a sarcastic streak, but could he blame her?

He padded across the room. "Scoot over."

When she didn't budge, he nudged her with his knee. "I need more room than that. Remember? I'm a big man and this is a small bed. Now, scooch." When she still didn't move, he slipped his arms underneath her, picked her up, then settled himself on the bed, ignoring her sharp intake of air. She was half-sprawled across his chest.

"Deydie was way off base." Though he held her close, he wasn't interested in Sadie, beyond being her friend, but he didn't want her hurt either. "She never should've said what she said. I'm sorry for it."

Sadie kept her face turned away from him. "Didn't I say that I'm fine? It doesn't matter."

"But it matters to me," he confessed. He wasn't going to examine why. He liked holding her in his arms. He liked her being near.

Maybe he could make a career of protecting the lass.

A brilliant idea came to him. "I need yere help, Sadie Middleton." One where she could focus on something else besides all the tragedies that had befallen her.

She did look up at him then. "What? Me? Help you?"

"Aye." He brushed back a piece of her hair so he could see her face better. "I want ye to do me a favor."

"I'm more sleep-deprived than I thought. What could you possibly want from me?"

Ross settled her back to his chest, ready to give voice to the words he hadn't spoken to anyone. "I've been trying to figure out what I want to do for the rest of my life."

She nodded. "Me, too."

"So there's another thing we have in common, besides needing to run away every now and then." The thought contented him somehow. "But what I noticed about you is that when you needed yere time away to sit on yere own, you took it."

"Oliver would say I was being selfish. And Deydie thinks that plain, little sickly me is out to snare you." She did her little snort thing that was unladylike, and at the same time, adorable.

"It took conviction to do what you had to do—sit on yere rock and the hell with the rest of the world—and I admire ye for it."

"Admire me?"

"Aye. I've always done what others wanted of me." Working on the fishing boat and going along with marrying Pippa.

Sadie patted his chest. "I'm no poster child for independence. I became a dental hygienist because Gigi and Oliver decided it would be best. I hate sticking my hands in strangers' mouths." She shivered.

And Ross had been engaged to a woman he didn't love because everyone else thought it was best.

"What is it that ye want to do?" he asked. "That is, if there was no other consideration in the world."

She guffawed pessimistically. "My biggest fantasy? To read twenty-four hours a day."

He chuckled. "Lass, ye can't make a living reading."

"I know. But I thought if I could become a librarian, then maybe that would satisfy me." She put her hand up as if he was going to contradict her. "I know librarians don't sit around reading all day, but at least they get to talk about and think about books for a living. And they get to help people find wonderful books to read. Being a librarian would be the best job in the world." Her voice hitched.

Now that he had taken her mind off Deydie, he didn't mean to get her upset in a different direction. "Will ye help me?" He didn't know if he was asking for her to help him find what he wanted, or to help him not bend to the will of Gandiegow.

"I'll help. But on one condition."

"Anything."

"You have to get Deydie and the others off my back. I'm not going to return to Quilting Central, no matter what. Can you do that for me?"

He kissed the top of her head in answer. He trusted that Sadie knew what was right for herself, and if she thought Quilting Central was going to hamper her in any way, then he was going to run interference for her. *For now.*

He stared at the far wall, bracing himself. Once Deydie figured out what was going on, she was sure to tear into him again.

"It's going to be okay," he said to both of them.

Ross heard a noise at the front of the house. Had someone just come in? Footsteps stalked down the hall.

It wouldn't do either of them any good to get caught in bed together. Sadie seemed to hear it, too, as she stilled and her head cocked to the side to listen. He kissed her head again—not sure why he did it—and slipped from the twin bed.

"Sadie?" It was her damned brother, Oliver. "Are you asleep?"

Ross stood there frozen, hoping he wouldn't see him.

"What the hell is going on here?"

"Aw, hell."

Oliver flipped on the switch and stomped into the room. "Is this what you meant when you said you would get my baby sister back to the dorm safely?"

Ross glared at her brother. "She's hardly a baby." At least he hadn't caught him in her bed. But it did look incriminating. "It's not what you think."

"My ass." Oliver glared at Sadie. "Have you been crying? What did he do to you?" The chap looked ready to take a swing at Ross.

Before Sadie could say anything, the front door slammed again with more footsteps down the hall.

"Lass?" It was Deydie, dammit. "I came to make sure that ye're . . ." The old woman peered around Oliver.

Sadie scrambled out of bed, muttering, "Grand Central Station." She swiped the hair from her face.

Deydie forced her way past Oliver. "Why've ye been crying?" She glared up at Ross as if he'd brought on Sadie's tears.

He held his hands up. "Don't blame me. Ye're the one with the barbed tongue."

Deydie didn't get a chance to rip him apart because Oliver turned to the town's matriarch. "Is this how things

are run around here? Anyone can get in my sister's bedroom whenever they want?"

"Now wait a minute," Ross interjected.

Sadie shaded to the color of a deep-sea redfish.

Ross was in a strange position and not sure what to do
next. He could tell Oliver what Deydie had said and how
he was only checking on the lass, but he had no real explanation why he was in her bedroom with the lights out.

Deydie glowered at Ross and jabbed a finger at the
bedroom door. "Ye better get home."

This time, he didn't mind doing what Deydie told him
to do, but he hesitated anyway. He faced Sadie.

"Are ye going to be all right?" In other words, did she
want him to hang around and sort things out for her?

With still-watery eyes she gazed up at him. "I'll be
fine." She spun on her brother. "Nothing happened. Ross
is a *gentleman* with a capital *G*. You ought to apologize
for accusing him of something he didn't do." Her eyes fell
on Deydie, but she seemed to bite back whatever retort
she wanted to deliver in that direction.

Ross's feet wouldn't move, not until he did something
more for Sadie. "Deydie, our little quilter here is a guest
in our town. Don't you think we should treat her like
one?"

Oliver's gaze went from face to face. "What's that
supposed to mean?"

"Aye." Deydie patted Oliver's arm in a more grand-
motherly way than Ross had ever seen her treat her own
granddaughter, Cait. "Everything is okay here, lad. Let
me have a few minutes alone with yere sister."

He was surprised when Oliver nodded his head in
agreement.

Ross wanted to reach out to Sadie and squeeze her shoulder, or something, because he hated leaving her alone with Deydie. But at least the old quilter seemed to want to make things right. He just hoped she wouldn't do it in a way that would cause more harm, as Deydie had a tendency to do.

"'Night, lass," Ross said instead. He felt sure this was the end of whatever friendship he'd started with her, no matter the promises they'd made to help each other. Deydie would get the lass back to Quilting Central and Sadie would have no need of him. Sadness hit him hard as if he'd been blindsided by a wave. But he should've seen it coming.

Chapter Four

Sadie crossed the room and pulled her robe from the armoire while Deydie waited with her hands in her skirt pockets, as uneasy as Lucifer at church. Suddenly Sadie was bone tired. She never should've zapped her reserves the way that she had.

Deydie stood before her, still a force to be reckoned with but now with a hint of compassion in her eyes. "Ye see, lass, I've been busy with this wedding. I never meant to—"

Sadie put her hand up. "Don't worry about it." The old woman had only been speaking the truth. "Let's just forget it ever happened. I'm going to bed."

The double crease between Deydie's eyebrows relaxed. "Ye do look peaked. I'm going to make ye a cup of chamomile before I go." She hustled to the door, but stopped. "I'll let ye out of the quilting session tonight, but I'll expect ye at Quilting Central first thing in the morn."

Don't hold your breath. But Sadie kept the thought to herself.

Deydie scrutinized Sadie in silence, then finally exited without a word.

Sadie flipped on the small lamp beside her bed, already missing Ross's presence. She'd grown quite accustomed to him, but she'd have to sleep alone tonight. She shut the door, pulled off her dress, and donned her purple plaid pajamas. She was too weary to go in search of the kitchen and the promised tea. She flipped off the light, climbed into bed, and fell fast asleep.

Her rest was fitful as her mind whirled with storms, and the strong arms that were there to save her were just out of reach.

By morning time, she had a plan to get out of the Kilts and Quilts retreat. If Deydie was going to use Sadie's kidney disease against her, then she was going to use it right back—*in her favor*. She would feign sickness to get out of spending time with the ladies who reminded her too much of Gigi. She hadn't pretended to be ill since she was in grade school, holding the thermometer under the hot water faucet, right after her parents had died. But she was playing sick today, using the time to stay in bed to read.

Through the wall, female voices and laughter seeped in as the dorm came alive with movement and excitement. Sadie worried one of the women might take it upon themselves to rouse her, but when no one did, she realized Deydie had told them to let her rest for a while.

The front door opened and closed several times and then the dorm became quiet. Sadie rose, padded into the kitchen, and helped herself to one of the boxed scones and coffee in the carafe. After filling up, she went back to her room, propped herself in bed, and pulled out her novel to fuel her soul. Just as she settled the book in her lap, she heard a noise. Or at least she thought she did. But when she heard no more, she went back to reading. Two seconds later, she realized she was being stared at . . . by Moira.

"Sorry," the woman said. "I stopped to check in on you. I was quiet in case you were sleeping." Moira's brow slightly rose when her eyes landed on the novel.

Sadie scooted farther under the covers. "I'm not feeling well . . . I thought I should rest." She hated not being completely aboveboard with this nice woman, but sometimes a girl had to look out for number one.

Moira gave her a shy smile as if she understood.

Sadie shrugged, grinning back.

"I'll make ye a cup of tea," Moira said.

"You don't have to. I had some coffee a little while ago."

"I'll fix ye a cup of green tea just the same." Moira gestured toward the novel. "You have to keep up yere strength." Before Sadie could respond, she left.

Sadie went back to reading and became so engrossed in the story, she almost missed Moira slipping into the room and setting the steaming teacup beside her.

"Thank you."

With a smile, Moira nodded and departed.

Sadie was immediately back in the story—a romance set in medieval Scotland with a gorgeous alpha male and the strong woman who tamed him.

The front door opened and closed again. *What was it with Gandiegow? Could she not get a moment alone?* This time the footfalls down the hall weren't Moira's. Sadie jammed her bookmark in place and shoved the novel under the covers as Bethia appeared in the doorway.

"Are ye well, lass?"

Slowly Sadie cracked open her eyes as if just waking.

"Moira said ye're a bit under the weather." Bethia chewed her lip as if two seams didn't meet up properly. "Is there anything I can get for ye? I'm a healer, a certified herbalist. Moira said she'd made ye some tea, but if there's anything I can do, I'd like to help."

Sadie sat up a little, trying to assure the woman with a smile. "I only need to rest today." She would have to come up with another excuse to get out of quilting with the gray-headed ladies tomorrow.

Bethia still looked concerned. "Should I get Doc MacGregor?"

"Heavens, no. It's only jet lag." Though Sadie had weathered the worst of it with Ross by her side. "I'll lie down for a while and then I'll be fine."

Bethia fussed with her covers, felt the teacup to make sure it was still warm, and pulled the blinds shut. Sadie would have to open them after she left. With a few more assurances that she would be fine, Bethia finally departed, leaving her alone.

Sadie breathed a sigh of relief as all went quiet again. As she pulled her book from its hiding place, the front door slammed—*hard*—and familiar heavy footsteps marched down the hallway.

She groaned, no need to even look up to see who it was this time. "Hi, Oliver."

He frowned at her, the opposite of Bethia's concerned

ministrations. "Why are you in bed instead of at Quilting Central?"

Bethia must've gone straight to Oliver and ratted her out. Maybe the elderly woman wasn't so sweet after all.

Sadie had seen this side of Oliver often since her diagnosis—angry—and at first it'd taken her off guard and had hurt deeply. She had spent a lot of time worrying what she had done to upset her brother. She touched the novel under the covers. Gigi was the one who told her to look in her books for the answer. *Men are basic,* Gigi had said, *with only a few emotions. They can get angry waiting on a red light, angry over being hungry, or angry over heaven only knows what.* Between Gigi's advice and her favorite novels, Sadie had figured out that Oliver was missing the gene that would allow him to exhibit his true feelings: *fear.*

"It's no big deal. I'm taking it easy today," Sadie said.

With his eyebrows pinched together, he ran a hand through his blond hair, making his perfect cut stand on end. "The trip was too hard on you. Maybe we shouldn't have come."

Now there's an idea. But it was best to keep it to herself.

The front door opened again, her ears picking up the slight squeak of the hinges and the whoosh of the door sweep on the hardwood floor. *Oh, good grief. Will I be holding audience all day?*

"Lass?" Deydie hollered. "I've come to talk to ye."

Oliver seemed relieved to hear the old woman's voice. Sadie wasn't.

Deydie materialized in the doorway with her hands

on her hips. She scrutinized Sadie for a few seconds. "As I suspected, ye're only playing at being sick."

Sadie smoothed down the quilt. "I'm resting."

"I'm not a numpty. Ye look better this morning than ye did last night. And I expect ye were fine then, well enough to come quilt, too."

Sadie didn't say a word, her gaze going from one accusing face to another. She felt taxed for real now. She scooted down and yanked the quilt up. "Shut the door on your way out."

Deydie harrumphed.

Yes, they were brave words, considering the daggers her brother and Deydie were shooting at her.

Oliver pulled himself up straight. "I'll be back to check on you."

A promise or a threat? The two finally left, closing Sadie's bedroom door behind them.

She stared at the far wall for a long time.

A rap sounded on her bedroom door.

"Please, leave me in peace," she said to the hard oak.

"Lass? It's me—Ross."

Relief washed through her. "Come in."

He cracked the door open only a little and peered inside. "Are they all gone?"

"Yes." She smiled at him, understanding that constantly crossing Deydie could lead to dire consequences. "What are you doing here? Aren't you supposed to be fishing?"

"Aye. I've already been out and back from the morning run. We'll go out later this afternoon."

"What's that in your hands?" Sadie asked.

"Oh, aye, the reason for the visit." He held up a shirt

with a tear in it. "I need a favor." His eyes sparkled with mischief as if they were back in the breakfast room at the B and B and he was pulling the wool over the owner's eyes.

"What kind of favor?" Surely he didn't want her to play his bride again.

He shook his head. "At great peril to myself, I snuck a sewing machine out of Quilting Central when I saw Deydie heading toward yere dorm."

"Why would you do that?"

"I set it up at our cottage—ye know, the one I share with my brother and his family."

"That doesn't explain *why*."

"Oh. I need ye to repair this tear." He had such a forlorn expression on his face that it was comical. "It's my favorite shirt. And you owe me."

"Owe you?"

"For all the trouble ye got me into with Deydie and the quilting gaggle before." He seemed embarrassed. "I mean, quilting ladies. They think I coerced ye into running out on them. I'm happy to take the fall"—he lifted up his torn garment for emphasis—"if ye'll fix my shirt."

From where she sat, the shirt's demise looked suspicious—more calculated than accidental. "I don't believe for a second that that shirt is your favorite. It looks brand-new, with the folding creases still in it." Why had he ripped his shirt on purpose?

Pulling a dramatic face of mock hurt and disbelief, he glanced at the garment as if she couldn't possibly be seeing the same shirt that he did. "'Tis my favorite." He held up his right hand. "Promise."

She noticed his other hand was behind his back.

"Then how did you tear it? With your pocketknife?"

"I caught it on a nail. On the boat," he added as an obvious afterthought. "Will ye get out of bed and come to the cottage? I want to show ye where I live before I have to go back out on the water."

"But why didn't you bring the sewing machine to me so I could work on your shirt here?"

Confusion crossed his face, the first bit of honesty she'd seen from him since he'd come into her bedroom. "I dunno."

She smiled, shaking her head at him. "Okay. I'll fix your shirt. But I'll be a while. I need to shower first." After her running-away adventure and her crying jag last night, she needed to wash away some of the grit of life.

"I'll wait in the living room. Don't be long."

"I know what you're doing," she said pointedly.

"What?" he asked, all innocence.

But she couldn't work up any real indignation over it. He wanted her up and moving around, and he was willing to slice a hole in a brand-new shirt to get her to do it.

She swung her legs over the side of the bed. "Go on. I'll be out soon. *So I can fix your shirt.*"

He laughed. "Bring yere book along with ye. Ye'll have a few minutes to read while I dig out those dunga-rees I need hemmed."

She glanced down, and sure enough, the corner of her book peeked out from under the covers. What could she say? She'd been found out. She waved at him as if her hand was a paintbrush. "There's no way you need your pants hemmed." If anything, he would have to have them let out, as tall as he was.

"Ye get ready. I'll be waiting in the other room." He sauntered out, chuckling deeply to himself.

Sadie sighed, thinking how Ross had come to know her so well, and at the same time, she knew she would have to watch herself with him. He was getting to her. Her life was in enough upheaval as it was without her becoming a victim of a broken heart, too. Around Ross, she felt herself slipping into a kind of gooey mess, part butterflies, part hormonal, and part wishful thinking. A girl like her had no business getting dreamy-eyed over a man like Ross. She wasn't Jane Eyre, where everything worked out in the end with Mr. Rochester. She was plain Sadie Middleton, and had enough to worry about without troubling herself with a crush over a kind, gentle Scotsman.

Ross strolled from her bedroom, feeling as if he'd bested the prize fish. In his gut, he knew Sadie should get back to sewing as soon as possible . . . even though he had promised to get her out of Quilting Central. *Back on the damned horse and all.* If he had to, he'd face off with the quilters of Gandiegow to keep his end of the bargain with Sadie.

And for some reason, he didn't mind the thought of her and her sewing machine being at his house. Though how he'd come up with the plan seemed more like fate than brains on his part.

As if it was meant to be, he'd run into Father Andrew, who asked Ross to deliver a message to Moira, his fiancée. Then, when Ross stopped at Quilting Central to see Moira, she told him about Sadie lying in bed. Moira had pointed out the sewing machine assigned to Sadie, and then turned away, perhaps even blocking everyone's view as he'd unplugged the cord and walked off with it. As if Moira had given him the suggestion telepathically with her soft voice and incline of her head. The town might think Moira was quiet, but she had a cunning streak in her that was sure to keep her future husband on his toes.

Waiting, Ross paced the floor of Thistle Glen Lodge, grabbing a periodical from the stack on the coffee table as he passed by . . . a quilting publication. A fishing magazine would've been preferable, but the quilt on the front looked like the one his mother had made for his confirmation. His mum had called the pattern a Mariner's Compass.

How he missed his mother. She'd been in Glasgow with Aunt Glynnis for two years now. He would go see both of them soon, and maybe take his nephew Dand along. John and Maggie could use the time alone, except they wouldn't exactly be alone. Baby Irene was seven months old and had yet to sleep through the night. She was a handful, but the cutest little bug he'd ever seen, and she loved to cuddle with her Uncle Ross.

His thoughts turned to Sadie and he glanced down the hallway as she came out of the restroom all trussed up in a long robe. His pulse kicked up. A normal, natural reaction, he told himself. Everyone thought they'd been irresponsible, sneaking out of town the way that they had, but they were two unattached adults, and he'd gotten her back to Gandiegow safely, hadn't he?

Funny, spending time with the lass was the most interesting thing he'd done in a long while. Even more interesting than working on his truck.

A minute later, she appeared from the bedroom in a

purple sundress, the color of foxglove in full bloom, making her brown eyes stand out like a lone thistle in the glen. Remembering to breathe, he sucked in a lungful of air.

He felt damned uncomfortable. As if he was wearing a vise instead of a loose polo shirt. "Are ye always this slow getting ready?" He tried for teasing, but his voice was a mite strained.

She gave him a sideways glance. "You didn't have to wait that long. Besides, I hurried."

"Well," he groused congenially, "I would hate to be waiting on ye when ye were taking yere time."

She snatched the torn shirt from the back of the couch. Hell, good thing she remembered it because he'd forgotten all about it. He prayed John wouldn't notice that his new shirt had gone missing, and that Ross had taken the fillet knife to it.

He walked with Sadie through town, the pathways empty this time of day, for which he was grateful. Not that he was embarrassed to be seen with the lass . . . quite the opposite. He just didn't want to explain why he wasn't taking her to Quilting Central as expected. Her eyes darted everywhere, taking in his village.

"I can't imagine living here," she said on a sigh. "The North Sea out your front door. Do you know how relaxed I'd be if I had all this?" She gestured to the ocean, the cottages, and the bluffs.

"I'm pleased ye like it." It was an odd thing for him to say, but he meant it. He pointed to his family's white cottage, not the last cottage in town but nearly. "This is it." He sauntered up the walk with Sadie trailing behind. He opened the door for her, trying to see his home through her eyes. The big, open living room, their everyday things scattered about—fishing magazines, Dand's box of Legos, a pile of clean cloth diapers neatly stacked on the counter near the washer.

When John got married, they'd all worked together to update and expand the cottage. Da had built a new bedroom for John and Maggie and an extra bedroom that was now Dand's. After his mother moved to Glasgow, Ross had moved out of the bedroom he and John had shared growing up and taken his parents' old space. It had been strange at first, but now the room was all his own. Ramsay's old bedroom was now a nursery for Irene.

"This is lovely," Sadie said to him. "It's so welcoming."

"Maggie runs a tight ship. We all help out." Ross transferred his wellies to the boot mat, their proper spot.

Sadie gestured at the sewing machine. "For me?"

He nodded. "Ye can use thread and whatever ye need from Maggie's sewing things." He went to the wooden cabinet near the hallway, lifted it by the handle, and brought it over to Sadie. "This was Maggie's gran's. Open it here." He raised the lid on one side. "The shelves pull out at both ends." Completely opened, it looked like stairs on each side, bursting at the seams with sewing stuff— scissors, thread, buttons, patches, and ribbons.

Sadie's brow furrowed. "Are you sure she won't mind?"

The door to Maggie's bedroom opened and out she walked. Ross cringed; he hadn't known his sister-in-law was home. He was fairly certain Maggie wouldn't take it well that Sadie was here, that she'd see the American lass as a threat. The moment he was no longer engaged to Pippa, Maggie had been suggesting rather strongly that he marry one of her sisters.

She came farther into the room, her eyes darting to

Sadie, the sewing machine, then to Ross holding her gran's sewing cabinet in his hand as if he was holding little bug's baby carrier.

Maggie raised an eyebrow. "This is new, Ross. Are ye needing thread to whip yereself up something from me sewing basket, or were ye showing off yere muscles for our guest?"

He glanced down to see his taut bicep. He raised and lowered the cabinet as if getting in a few reps like the lads on the telly. He set the cabinet down.

"Little bug sleeping then?" he asked.

"Aye. I heard ye come in earlier." Maggie eyed the sewing machine in front of Sadie again. "I didn't realize Quilting Central was moving here. Does Deydie know?"

Ross caught the downturn of Sadie's features.

"The lass has promised to mend a few things for me."

Before he could wave her off, Sadie held up John's ruined shirt. "I'll do my best, but it's not ripped on the seam."

Maggie's face turned leathery with anger as if the reality of what he had done was hard to chew. Surprisingly, though, she held her tongue, gluing on a hard smile instead. "Ye're welcome to the dining table but, Ross, ye'll have to clear it away for the supper. Ye can set it on the treadle machine over there when she's finished."

Sadie eased into the chair in front of the machine, keeping her eyes on Maggie. "Will the noise bother the baby?"

Maggie snatched the clean diapers from the counter. "Nay. We're a loud household. Less so, though, since Ramsay moved into his cottage with his bride, Kit." She nodded to the cabinet. "Help yereself to what ye need. Ross, can I have a word? Outside by the burning barrel?"

Aw hell. Maggie had held it together for Sadie's sake, but she looked ready to cut him like the knife that had sliced through John's new shirt.

Ross set the sewing cabinet next to Sadie, giving her a wink to shoo away the concerned expression clouding her face. "I'll be back in a flash."

He followed Maggie, who was still clutching the clean diapers to her chest. When she closed the door behind them, she pounced.

"Have ye gone radge?" she hissed. "Are ye not thinking straight? The lass should be at Quilting Central where she belongs. If I let her stay here today, we'll both be in it with Deydie."

He held his ground, though it was pretty shaky. Deydie could make his life miserable if he didn't return Sadie to the bosom of Quilting Central. "She's staying. 'Tis my house, too." And to hell with convention, and Deydie, and what the rest of the town thought.

Maggie eyed him with suspicion. "What's going on here? Do ye fancy her?"

He said nothing while she glared holes into him. He owed her no explanation.

Dand came running toward the cottage.

"Mum! Did ye hear? Mattie and Cait will be home soon!"

Maggie kept her glower on Ross. "I heard. Now go inside and clean up. Ye can have a biscuit after ye do. Ye're expected over at yere aunties'."

Dand wiped the hair from his eyes. "Can Mattie spend the night as soon as he's back?"

"We'll see how ye're doing with your chores then."

"Aw, Mum."

Ross thought he better warn his nephew. "My friend Sadie is sewing at the dining room table."

"And be quiet when ye go in," Maggie warned. "Your baby sister's sleeping."

The boy ran for the door and slammed it on his way in.

Maggie sighed heavily. She seemed to listen for a baby's scream, and when it didn't come, she spun back on Ross. "Did the lass tell ye that she's sick? That she needs a kidney transplant? Do ye not know that she's not for Gandiegow? We have the doc, but no hospital to care for the likes of her."

He put his hand up. "Stop. I don't fancy her. I only wanted to . . ." He broke off. *Make her happy?* He couldn't say that. He didn't care if Sadie was happy or not. He didn't fancy anyone right now. He wanted to date lots of women . . . make up for missed opportunities. Maggie had it all wrong. "Quilting Central is too painful for the lass. It reminds her of her dead gran. Have a heart. Keep Deydie and the others from pressuring her into returning to Quilting Central."

Maggie seemed to consider his words and he couldn't help but drive the point home.

"Remember what it was like when ye lost yere own gran." The rest of them would never forget what Maggie had gone through. "It took ye a year to thread a needle again. Ye said it yereself that yere gran was the one who taught *you* to sew. I think it shows great promise that the lass is willing to sit in front of her sewing machine, don't you?"

Maggie looked out to the sea for a long moment. "All right then. She can stay."

The crashing of the waves was a welcome sound compared to her lecture, and for several moments there were no words between them. But then Maggie had to go and ruin it. "Ye'll have to tell Deydie what ye're about."

"Aw, hell." He was done talking and trod back to the cottage to check on Sadie.

When he got inside, she wasn't sitting behind her sewing machine. He glanced around to the sofa and saw Dand cuddled up to her with a book stretched across their laps.

Sadie went on reading what seemed like a most unconventional rhyming book, putting on various voices and seeming to have the time of her life while Dand giggled and guffawed.

Ross interrupted. "What are ye reading?"

Dand held up the book. *"Dinosaur Poo!"*

Sadie shrugged. "I gave him a choice between *Dinosaur Poo!* and *Princess Penelope*."

Dand tugged on her arm. "Come on. Keep reading."

At that moment, Maggie came through the door and stopped suddenly. Sadie glanced up for a second, but kept reading. Dand didn't notice that his mum was standing nearby, gobsmacked. When the book was done, he jumped up, grabbed another from the shelf, and then settled himself back up against Sadie.

Maggie came to stand next to Ross. "How did she do it?" she whispered. "Dand doesn't like books."

It was true; Dand couldn't read a word. They'd tried everything to coax him into wanting to read. Almost everyone in town had given him a book and taken a shot at persuading him to try. But the kid hadn't given a whit about books and could barely sit still. He cared only about roughhousing and playing outside. To see him now sitting on the sofa listening to a story was quite a surprise.

Ross shrugged. "What can I say? The lass has a way about her."

"I believe it's a miracle," Maggie said. "For both ye and Dand."

"Why me?" Ross asked.

"Because the lass just handed you the perfect excuse to give to Deydie for why she needs to stay here to sew."

With a click of the mouse, Oliver sent the first computer on the back table of Quilting Central to sleep. Only four more to go. He scanned the flurry of the room, realizing why no one had taken the time to update the computers—too busy quilting. Rotary cutters sliced through fabric, steam wafted from irons as quilters pressed away, and rows of women zipped through seams like bankers counting bills, their movements practiced, automatic, precise.

Gigi would've loved it here.

With his eyes slightly blurring, he moved to the next computer, removing his glasses and cleaning the lenses with the hem of his oxford shirt. His glasses weren't completely to blame. But there was no time to think about Gigi; he had to stay focused on helping Sadie. He had just settled into the chair and started to do a security scan when Deydie plopped down a stack of software boxes next to him.

"I've changed my mind, lad." She gave him a frightening grin. "My granddaughter Caitie and I talked about it, and decided we better go with the top-of-the-line embroidery software, too. Something more to offer the quilters."

He stared at the pile of work in front of him. The only way he'd been able to do what he'd done so far was because his US clients weren't awake yet. Oliver glanced at his watch. Well, they'd be up soon.

"I'll see what I can do," he said.

Determination shot from Deydie's eyes. "Ye'll do better than that. I promised the retreat goers that I'd show them how to use the embroidery software and the machines so they could design their own tags before they leave."

Oliver smiled, shocking both himself and perhaps her. She couldn't know how much her bossiness was helping him—keeping him so busy doing her bidding that he didn't miss Gigi so much. "Okay. I'll work on it as I can. I do have a full-time job with my current clients."

Deydie patted the pocket of her skirt as if her checkbook was lodged there. "I told ye to keep a tab and I'll be happy to pay ye when ye go." But she had a funny gleam in her eye as if she was cooking up some sort of plan.

"I'm only here the week," he reminded her, something he'd said many times since she'd assigned him his duties. He liked it here, but he was beginning to understand that maybe Gandiegow might not be so good for Sadie. Maybe he shouldn't have strong-armed his little sister into coming. If he made things worse for her, he'd never forgive himself.

"Aye. The week," Deydie said. "Right."

Just then the door to Quilting Central opened and a

gorgeous woman with long brown hair glided in. Oliver was . . . mesmerized.

Deydie nudged him, smiling like a wrinkly Cheshire cat. "That's Kirsty, the new schoolteacher. I told her ye were here. She wants to talk to ye about new computers for the school."

Oliver tore his gaze away from the very attractive schoolteacher and back to the not-so-attractive Deydie. "I won't be here long enough for new computers to be ordered and set up."

As Kirsty's gaze landed on him, she smiled and skated his way.

The foundation under his feet shifted. His black-and-white vision turned to Technicolor. His jumbled thoughts turned to poetry. And the room turned brighter. *Kirsty.* Her name rang in his head like a bell, calling him home. Deydie eyed him closely. She must've seen it in him before the thought could fully form in his head. But quite suddenly, he wasn't in such a rush to get back to the US after all.

Chapter Five

Ross left Sadie at the cottage so she could work on his shirt. He'd better face Deydie before she figured out where he'd stashed the American lass without asking permission from the quilting gaggle. He sighed deeply. This wasn't going to be pleasant, but he marched on to Quilting Central anyway.

The moment he walked through the door, Deydie caught sight of him. Glowering, she plowed forward in his direction. The old she-badger had a sixth sense when it came to trouble.

"What is it, Ross?" She said his name as if she'd downed a dram of spoiled goat's milk.

"We need to talk about Sadie."

At her name, her brother's head popped from behind a computer. Deydie put her hand up, motioning to Oliver as if to say *I have this*.

Ross cringed; an audience wouldn't help his cause. "May we speak in private?" he added quietly, *and politely*. Anything to get on her good side.

How he'd gotten himself wrapped up in this mess, he didn't know. He'd become Sadie's champion of sorts, which had left the damned town getting the wrong impression. He could see it on their faces. But he was in it deep already, so he waded in farther. "Outside?" *Where no one else can listen in.*

Deydie glared at him a second longer, but followed him, grabbing the watering can on the way. Once they were on the other side of the door, she handed it off to him. "Make yereself useful."

He took the can, filled it, and began watering the baskets of flowering geraniums, giving himself a moment to collect his thoughts.

Or to bolster himself up.

"Go on." Deydie acted as if she wasn't going to like what he had to say. She tapped his watering can. "I've got things to do, Ross. Ye're wasting my time. I have quilt retreats back to back, plus Moira and Father Andrew's wedding coming up. Spit it out. But don't be tellin' me that ye're keen on Sadie."

Ross blanched. "I'm not keen on anyone."

The old woman huffed like she didn't believe him.

This was ridiculous. He wasn't looking for a relationship. Couldn't anyone understand that? But he wasn't in the mood to discuss his love life right now. He expelled a pent-up breath. "Sadie isn't coming back to Quilting Central."

Deydie's glower grew, her face flushing red.

He stopped her before she burst. "She *can't* come back to Quilting Central. Not yet, anyway." The lass might never be able to join others in quilting again, but he would do his best to help her.

"Explain yereself, or get out of my way. I have work to do." Deydie moved toward the door.

Ross blocked her path. He had planned to tell her how Sadie was reading to Dand, but right now, it was more important for Deydie to know the truth. "Can't ye see that being at Quilting Central is hard for the lass? It reminds her too much of her dead gran—you, Bethia, all the quilters. The fabric, the smell of the place, I suspect, are all hard on her, too." Now it was time to come clean. "Ye may not like what I did, but at least I got her out of bed today."

Deydie glared at him as if he'd done it by ravishing the lass first.

He put his hand up to stop her rabbit-trail-thoughts, and to bring an end to her glare. "As we speak, Sadie is actually sewing, which I think is a remarkable improvement over hiding in her room, don't you?"

"Where is she?" Deydie barked.

"At my cottage."

Deydie cocked her head to the side as if she hadn't heard correctly. "She's where?"

"I set her machine on our dining room table and gave her a shirt to work on." There would be hell to pay when Maggie told John what Ross had done to his new shirt. "She's there now."

Deydie stepped forward and stared him down, even though he was more than a foot taller than she. "Who gave ye the right to take a sewing machine from Quilting Central?"

He wanted to say *the Almighty*, but Deydie would take her broom to him for blaspheming. "It was the only way to help her."

"Help her what?"

"Help her ease back into life without her gran."

As if each syllable was a raindrop and Deydie's single-mindedness was parched earth, his words seemed to finally seep in. Her fierce scowl slowly faded. "All right." But then her brows pulled together in realization and determination fell into place on her face like pegs in a hole. "If she won't come to Quilting Central, then we'll come to her."

"No!" That's not what he wanted at all. He opened his mouth to protest further.

But Deydie was the one who put a hand up this time. "Hold on to yere boxer shorts. We'll not bombard her all at once, but she needs to get used to us. We'll take turns visiting her. Maybe bring her a project or two to work on."

But Ross knew Deydie, and working Sadie to death didn't seem right, especially since the lass wished for some peace and quiet. And more time to read.

But Deydie was as set on her plan as the concrete of the pier. "Aye." She was nodding to herself. "Kirsty was looking for extra hands to make the back-of-the-chair bookholders."

"What?"

Deydie pushed past him. "I'll get it set up. Then we'll pay a visit to the lass at your house. First, though, I need to speak with Kirsty."

"No." But Deydie was already back inside. Maybe he should've started off by telling Deydie how Sadie had gotten Dand interested in reading books. But that ship had sailed. And here he was left holding the watering can and feeling as if he hadn't helped Sadie at all. He had only made things worse.

*   *   *

Sadie sat alone at Ross's dining table. Maggie was down the hall in her room, caring for baby Irene. Dand was off to spend time with Maggie's sisters. She smiled, thinking of the fit Dand had thrown when it came time for him to leave. He wanted to stay cuddled up next to Sadie while she read to him, and only the promise of more books later had calmed him enough to go willingly to his aunts'.

She sighed. Maggie was pleased that Dand wanted to read, but Sadie could tell that she wasn't pleased that she and Ross were spending time together.

Sadie had been nothing but trouble since she'd arrived in Gandiegow. She'd monopolized Ross's every second—she snorted—*since picking him up at the bar*. Here Oliver had thought Ross had kidnapped Sadie that first night. The truth was that she was taking up all of Ross's free time and she felt kind of bad about it . . . except that she'd enjoyed every minute.

She hadn't heard the conversation between him and his sister-in-law, but it was a safe bet that Maggie felt the same way about her that Deydie did. Couldn't these people see that Sadie agreed with them all—she wasn't good enough for Ross. Seriously, she was no love match for a man like him. Ross's other sister-in-law, the matchmaker, should put the town at ease. She was a professional. Surely Kit could see how ridiculous Maggie and Deydie were being. The idea of Ross with her . . . Sadie snorted again.

She repaired his mutilated shirt the best she could. When she was done, she turned off the machine and held his favorite shirt up. Unfortunately, it would never look brand-new again. She shrugged to the empty dining room and set the sewing machine on the treadle as Maggie had told Ross to do. She grabbed her book and headed for the door.

But before she reached for the knob, there was a quiet rap on the other side. Should she answer it? Sadie glanced at the closed door of Maggie's bedroom. The rap sounded again, harder this time. Not hesitating any longer, she opened the door to find a petite dark-haired woman standing on the threshold with Oliver, who was holding a wicker basket filled with denim material, scissors, and thread. *How strange.*

She wasn't the only one who was feeling strange if the look on her brother's face was any indication.

As his eyes fell on her, then scanned the interior of the cottage, he said, "I came with Kirsty to make sure you were all right."

Yeah, sure. Sadie knew the truth. He was making certain there wasn't an orgy going on. "Don't worry," she said. "Everything's on the up-and-up."

Oliver glanced around again. "Where's lover boy?"

Sadie rolled her eyes but answered her brother anyway. "Out on the family fishing boat with his brother John." She put her hands on her hips. "And he's not my lover boy."

"Sure," Oliver muttered, still lurking in the doorway.

Kirsty waited patiently, seeming to take their sibling bickering in stride, but Sadie was embarrassed. Having her brother treat her like an inept teenager was wearing thin.

Kirsty gave Sadie a warm smile. "May we come in?"

"Sorry." Sadie stood back, but felt a little weird about letting people into a house that wasn't her own.

Kirsty motioned to Oliver. "Put my things over on the table."

Sadie was surprised that this *Kirsty* had Oliver's number. Her brother, usually as alpha and indignant as they come, didn't seem to mind doing as she bid.

Kirsty touched Sadie's arm gently. "I'm Gandiegow's schoolteacher." She glanced around until she saw the sewing machine that Sadie had been using. "Deydie said ye could help with a project for the school children."

"She did?"

"Aye." Kirsty held out a sewn piece of cloth that looked like a one-sided saddlebag. "I thought to cut down on the clutter at the schoolhouse. We have cubbies, but wouldn't it be nice if the children's chairs held a book or two?" She slipped the contraption over the back of a dining chair and dropped Sadie's book inside the pocket. "See?"

"Clever."

"Will you help?" Kirsty asked with a warm tone.

Oliver stared at the schoolteacher as if he were wishing upon a star. Sadie had never seen him like this. Oliver had a crush. A big one.

When Kirsty turned away, apparently to scope out the work area, Sadie took the opportunity to wave a hand in front of her brother's face.

The trick worked, breaking the spell. Oliver glowered at Sadie with the disgust of the proverbial older brother. He must have it bad for the teacher, though, because before Kirsty wheeled back around, a smile had returned to his face.

Kirsty pulled a pattern out and spread it on the table. She explained how, if they worked together, it wouldn't take long to get the chair pockets done.

"So?" Kirsty finished. "Will ye help?"

"Of course, she will," Oliver answered for her.

Just then, Maggie's bedroom door opened, and she came in with baby Irene, whose dark red curls were going this way and that. She sucked her thumb, taking them all in with her deep blue eyes.

"We've more company," mother said to the baby.

"Maggie, this is my brother, Oliver." *The bully.*

Now Sadie caught the longing glance Kirsty cast at Oliver. But at least the schoolteacher was more discreet than Oliver's tripping-over-himself infatuation. *Good Lord.* When had they had time to fall head-over-heels-in-crush?

For a brief second, Sadie wondered if she'd be able to get her brother out of this town and back home. But it would be fine. Oliver was more career-focused than anyone she'd ever met. He would never leave his clients in the US for a woman, even if she was as sweet as Kirsty seemed to be. Oliver was more levelheaded than that.

The cottage door opened and two women she hadn't met came in with baskets. Moira and little Glenna trailed behind.

"We've brought sandwiches," the taller one said.

The younger of the two newcomers made a silly face at Irene, and the baby smiled around her thumb.

Maggie handed the little one off to the woman, who had to be close to Sadie in age. "These are my sisters—Rowena and Sinnie."

The women said hello, but Sadie could tell the younger one, Sinnie, wasn't nearly as outgoing as Rowena.

Rowena lifted her head in acknowledgment.

Within a minute, Deydie and Bethia turned up, too.

The room was beginning to feel tighter than the Spanx Gigi had bought last Christmas. Sadie looked to Maggie to see if she minded the growing number of people overrunning her house. Maggie didn't. Neither did baby Irene. The cherub was chortling loudly at the faces her aunt Sinnie made at her.

Deydie and Bethia took up spots at the table, opening up their notebooks. As Deydie pulled a pencil from behind her ear, Amy along with the matronly twins arrived. Now, every open space was filled.

This is all too much. Sadie started to rise, hoping to slip out.

But Deydie caught her arm. "Stay. Ye've work to do," she said glancing around. "Moira? Get over here. We need to go over this list."

But Sadie had a question. "Who's at Quilting Central supervising the retreat?"

"Claire and Dominic are feeding our guests their lunch," Bethia said. "We only have a short while."

Maggie and Rowena were handing out drinks and sandwiches, while Moira took Amy's spot, looking self-conscious.

Deydie examined her page. "Did ye double-check yere wedding date against the waxing and waning of the moon?"

"Nay." Moira bit her lip, looking dismayed.

Bethia flipped to a page in her notebook. "No worries. I took care of it. The date's fine. It's during the waxing."

"Good. 'Tis bad luck to wed during the waning." Deydie made a check mark on her list. "Now, Moira, we need to talk about the wedding cake. This is where ye and Andrew are to splurge."

Maggie spoke up as she handed off another glass. "She's asked me to make the brandy-flavored fruitcake. I've been gathering the supplies. Rowena and Sinnie will help."

Deydie grabbed a sandwich, frowning. "Fruitcake is traditional, I'll grant ye, but I—I mean, most of us like chocolate. What do ye say if we change it to the town's favorite?"

Maggie set a glass down in front of Deydie. "If *Moira* wants it, I can make one layer chocolate and one fruitcake."

Moira nodded. "That would be fine."

Deydie ran a finger down her page, but kept talking. "Because we're doing our version of the Penny Wedding, the rest of us will bring the food and drink."

The one named Ailsa spoke up. Sadie had dubbed her half of the *plaid twins*, as she and her sister had on matching plaid dresses again. Ailsa's was green. "We're all happy to pitch in. It's the least we can do for the good Father watching after his sheep."

Aileen laughed, the twin who was red-plaided. "And finally getting around to making Moira his bride."

A cheer went up around the room.

"Quiet down." Deydie went back to her list. "Moira, how is the 'wedding sark' coming? Will ye have Andrew's shirt done in time?"

Moira shifted in her chair. "I've only the buttons left to do."

"And Glenna's dress?"

Moira smiled over at her young cousin who was eating her sandwich. "'Tis done."

Bethia leaned over and touched the brooch that Moira

wore every day. "It's a lovely luckenbooth that Andrew gave ye."

"It was his mother's," she said quietly.

Bethia sat back, giving the bride a compassionate nod as if she was Moira's grandmother. "When ye and Andrew have yere first bairn, ye'll have to pin this to the babe's first quilt for good luck."

Deydie cleared her throat. "I think we best get through the wedding before we discuss the bairns."

Moira's face turned a darker shade of red than her plum outfit.

Deydie tapped her pencil. "The last thing we need to discuss is the wedding dress. Ailsa? Aileen? How's it coming?" Before they could answer, Deydie turned to Sadie and explained, "Moira wants to wear her mama's wedding dress. Of course, it's Andrew's responsibility to pay for his bride's dress, so he's paying for the alterations."

Amy leaned over and spoke to Sadie. "Pixie died a while back."

"Sister and I have it nearly done. Moira, we'll be ready for ye to try it on come next week."

"Good. Good." Deydie wrapped her sandwich in a napkin and stood, as if calling the meeting to an end. The crowd began moving toward the door. "Wait a minute. About the rest of ye and what ye're going to wear to the wedding."

Sadie thought this was a strange statement.

"Wear yere best dress, any color ye want, except green or black."

Black seemed obvious because of its link to funerals.

"Why not green?" Sadie braved.

Deydie nodded as if she approved of her speaking up and asking questions. "Because green is the color of the fairies. Bad luck to wear green to a wedding."

The ladies nodded as if this was common knowledge. Sadie would've liked to have seen this wedding, but she wasn't going to be here that long.

"We better get back to our quilters," Bethia said, rushing for the door.

Deydie had one more thing to impart before leaving. "I need a few of ye to stay behind and help Sadie here with the chair pockets."

"We'll stay," Rowena said. "Sinnie and I want to help cut them out."

Sinnie nodded as well.

Oliver tapped Sadie's arm as he headed for the door. "I'll talk to you later."

Sadie figured it would be a while, as he mostly had his eyes set on Kirsty.

Maggie wove through the few remaining people as they went for the door. "I'll get the extra scissors." When she reached the treadle machine, she pulled open the top drawer and produced two pairs of Wiss scissors. "Here they are."

Scissors like Gigi's.

The sight of those slightly tarnished steel scissors made something in Sadie's chest constrict painfully. Tears filled her eyes. She willed them away, blinking furiously at the oar propped against the far wall.

Maggie eased beside her, speaking quietly. "Can ye grab Irene a quilt from the nursery in the first bedroom?" She pointed to the hallway. "It's that way. Take yere time."

Sadie left her uneaten sandwich and hurried away, hoping the few who remained hadn't seen. She slipped into the bedroom with a crib set up in the corner. She grabbed a tissue from the dresser top and quietly shut the door, taking a minute to pull her erratic emotions together. She wiped the first tear away and blew her nose.

She missed Gigi so much. Would these gut-wrenching moments ever end?

But the truth of it settled into her—*the guilt*—the fact that Sadie couldn't go back and undo what she'd done. Her heart, her brain, her whole being screamed with *if onlys*. If only she hadn't longed for more than plaque-filled mouths to fill her time. If only the graduate school application hadn't been due that day. But the biggest *if only* would have been the easiest to change . . . if only she had picked up the fabric at the quilt shop like Gigi had asked, then her beloved grandmother wouldn't be dead.

Out at sea, Ross stood at the bow as he and John made their way back to Gandiegow. Ross's best ideas came to him while he was on the water with nothing between him, the wind, and his Maker. He glanced at the wooden cross hanging on the mast, knowing the Almighty had a hand in everything when it came to fishing. The weather belonged to Him, the catch, and whatever good ideas a fisherman had on the ocean. Today was no different.

A helluva plan was forming as the town came into sight and Ross glanced heavenward with a nod of thanks. It would work. When they reached the dock, he stepped off and moored the *Indwaller*, the family fishing boat.

The moment the boat was secure, he waved to John. "I'm off."

John nodded and went back to his logbooks inside the wheelhouse.

Ross had been around the quilters of Gandiegow for his whole life, and knew that when they were stitching they were either gabbing about the townsfolk, or were comparing notes about the books that they were reading. A quilting book club as it were. Cait and Graham kept a pretty extensive library at the mansion up on the hill, and Deydie and the rest of the women had read most of the novels there. Maybe it was time to bring the books a little closer to the center of town, to provide better access for the villagers and retreat goers alike without the hike up the bluff.

A library at Quilting Central.

And the perfect person to take on the project was back at his cottage, fixing a tear in his shirt . . . well, *John's shirt.* But before Ross could do anything, he'd have to run it past Deydie, not a prospect he was looking forward to.

First he headed home to check on Sadie. It had been hours since he'd left her alone with his sister-in-law. At the cottage door, he heard female voices within. When he stepped inside, he found the house scattered with women. But none of them were Sadie. Maggie stood in the kitchen pouring tea into mugs and Emma and Claire were passing around boxes of scones.

"What's going on here?" He took the cup Maggie offered. "Where's Sadie?"

Emma handed him a plate with two blueberry scones. "She had to go to the surgery."

Panic washed through him. "Is she all right?" He didn't mean to raise his voice.

Emma lifted an eyebrow as if to question what he was about, but she answered him calmly. "Gabriel is giving her a hypodermic."

All eyes were on him, the packed room quiet.

He revised his question, directing it at Maggie. "What I meant was, after I left, was everything okay here at the cottage?"

Maggie's eyebrows pinched together. "Yes and no."

She explained what had happened with Sadie and the scissors. "It was thoughtless of me," she said, finishing. "I should've anticipated it. Every gran in the world has owned a pair of Wiss scissors."

"Nay." Ross took a quick sip of his tea. "I think it's good for her." If only her kidneys could be fixed with the shedding of a few tears.

Emma wrapped her arm around Maggie's shoulders. "Ross is correct. Sadie has to travel through her grief. There are no shortcuts to the other side. Things that remind her of her grandmother will make her weep now, but someday, those same things will make her smile. You'll see."

Maggie nodded as if remembering how it had been for her.

The women went back to chatting among themselves. Ross gulped down the rest of his tea and took his scones to his room. He changed quickly and within a few minutes was headed to Quilting Central, wondering if he would see Sadie on his way. He didn't.

Inside the building, Bethia was showing the transfixed

retreat goers how to construct a particular block. Ross glanced around the room, found the perfect corner for the library, and headed for it.

Mentally, he sized up the area. Shelves could angle into the corner, making a V. He imagined a small desk and a chair with Sadie manning the catalog. But there probably wouldn't be enough books to make that necessary.

"What are ye doing?" Deydie said, making him jump.

"You can be stealthy when ye want to be," he said.

She eyed him closely. "What's on yere mind?"

"Have you ever thought of putting a library in this corner?" he said quietly so as not to interfere with the instruction going on.

Deydie pointed to the far wall where quilting books lined several shelves. "We have a library."

"I mean novels. It could be another feature for the Kilts and Quilts retreat. The quilters could grab a novel to cozy up with at night."

Deydie's face squished up as if she was mulling over the idea. After a moment, she stepped closer. "And what's *yere* interest in this supposed library?"

He could've given her a line about how every Gandie-gowan was affected by the Kilts and Quilts retreat, but he told the truth instead. "I thought we might entice Sadie back to Quilting Central by asking her to set up a library here."

Deydie harrumphed. "*We* nothing. I'll talk to the lass." She eyed him suspiciously "Ye say that ye don't, yet ye sure act like ye have some feelings for the lass."

"I'm only being a good Samaritan." But the words rang hollow so he tried teasing—one of his younger brother

Ramsay's tactics—to get the old woman off his scent. "I want to go to heaven one day. Best to begin doing some good deeds now, don't ye think?"

The old witch just stared at him as if she could read his true motives. *Whatever they were.*

Ross threw his hands up in frustration. "The library is just an idea." *Not a marriage proposal.*

Deydie nodded. "Aye. It's a good idea. I'm just surprised it came from ye, is all." She waddled away, but stopped after a few feet, cranking her head over her shoulder. "I'll take care of it from here. Do ye ken?"

"Aye." He'd stay out of it.

He took a deep breath. *If only he could.*

When Sadie returned to Ross's house, this time with little Angus in her arms, she saw that thankfully the quilters were nearly cleared from the premises.

Emma put down her English paper piecing and stretched out her arms for her child. "So someone decided to wake up?" The boy squealed as she took him. She held him on her lap while undoing the clasp of her nursing bra. She settled him to her breast, modestly adjusting the folds of her blouse. "Thank you for bringing him over, Sadie. Maggie and I had so much planning to do for the céilidh after Moira's wedding."

"What's a kay-lee?" Sadie asked, feeling a bit stupid.

"A céilidh is a dance and celebration. We were meant to have one at the summer solstice, but the weather prevented it." Emma winked at her. "Scots drinking during bad weather is not a wise idea."

"The waves were splashing over the walkway at the

solstice," Maggie added from the kitchen where she was fussing with the roaster. "Everyone had to stay indoors and batten down the shutters."

The heavy-duty shutters with locks on the outside of the windows were hard to miss.

Just as Sadie sat down at her machine and picked up the next chair pocket to work on, there was a brief rap at the door, and Deydie and Bethia came bustling in.

"We're just taking a break from Quilting Central," Deydie announced.

But Sadie didn't believe her. And no more than five seconds later, Deydie spun on her directly. "I'm needing yere help, lass. I hear ye know books, like novels and such."

"Did Oliver tell you that?" *Of course Oliver told her. What hasn't he blabbed?*

"Quilting Central needs a library. I've decided that ye're going to make us one." As an afterthought, Deydie added, "Quilters are avid readers. Did ye know that?"

Sadie was living proof. Besides reading, she loved to listen to audiobooks while she was behind her machine. She chose more fabric and stitched the next seam, mulling over what Deydie had said.

"I thought if ye weren't up to quilting with us that the least ye could do was to help me with the library."

Why couldn't this woman leave Sadie alone? What about all the chair pockets she'd been assigned?

Bethia moved closer, examining Sadie's stitches, and said in a much gentler voice, "It wouldn't take much of yere time. Do ye mind very much?"

Sadie finished the seam, lifted the presser foot, and

shut off her machine. "What are we talking about specifically? Do you want me to make a list of books I think your quilters would like?"

Irene started fussing, and to Sadie's surprise, Deydie reached for her and took her in her arms. As the baby cuddled against her massive bosom, the expression on the old woman's face turned soft, maternal. She maneuvered the baby to her shoulder like an expert, patting her back gently.

"I'll need ye to look at the space in Quilting Central. I'll put Ross to making yere shelves for the books, or finding ye some. Fix up the corner however ye like."

"Why me? I'm no expert."

"From what I hear, ye're more of an expert than most of us."

Oliver again.

This was really getting ridiculous. "But I'm only here for the week."

Deydie lifted her eyebrow as if to say *We'll see*. "Then ye better get started. It would mean a great deal to us, lassie." She tilted her head toward the baby and said, "We all help one another here."

Bethia clasped her hands in front of her while she waited for the answer, making Sadie wonder if she was praying or holding her breath.

"All right." Just this once, she could go to Quilting Central. It should take only a few minutes at most and then she could get back to making the chair pockets for the school.

Deydie handed Irene back to Maggie. "Come on then." Her softness faded as gruffness returned. "The day is wasting away." Maybe they should take the baby with them to make Deydie more pleasant.

Sadie followed the women back to Quilting Central, the sun bathing her with warmth and at the same time, the breeze off the ocean cooling her. At the doorway, she took a deep breath, preparing herself for the onslaught of emotions that had hit her the first time she'd walked into the building.

When she opened the door, she peered in cautiously, and sure enough, she wanted to run. But Gigi's words about keeping promises pushed Sadie inside. Everyone looked up, but then looked away, like it wasn't polite to stare at a train wreck. Only Oliver, at the back by the computers, nodded in her direction.

Bethia took her arm. "We were thinking the library would look nice over here. See how the light comes in the window?"

Yes. They could even place a couple of comfy chairs or a small love seat under the sill.

"Get over there to get a closer look." Deydie's bossy tone was back, full force.

As Sadie walked over, the first wave of panic subsided. This time at Quilting Central didn't feel as overwhelming as before. The first time, the quilters had all rushed her, making her feel crushed and suffocated. But now the women kept to their seats as if they'd been stitched to them.

Only the plaid twins came forward. "We haven't been properly introduced," the one in green said. "I'm Ailsa and this is Aileen, my sister."

Her red plaid twin bobbed her head. "Bethia and Deydie said we're to help ye with the library. Whatever ye need."

"Aye," said Ailsa. "Are ye staying for next week's retreat as well?"

"Oh, no. I have to get back," Sadie said. But what did she have to get back to? The dental office had told her to take all the time she needed—the office manager knew that Sadie was less than thrilled with her job of cleaning teeth.

Deydie hustled over, as if to say *Time's up.* "The lass has to get back to work here. And so do ye two. How is Moira's wedding dress coming along?"

Ailsa opened her mouth to answer, but Deydie cut her off.

"Never mind. I'll come and see for meself." Deydie walked away with them, and Sadie saw her nod at another gray-haired woman.

That gray-haired woman snagged another on her way over to Sadie. They introduced themselves as Freda and Maxie.

"Freda is working on three quilts. One for her new husband, the McDonnell, and then matching quilts for their soon-to-be grandbabies," Maxie explained.

Freda had to be in her fifties, but she was blushing like a young bride, thoroughly in love. The two of them spoke with her for only a moment and then they too went back to their seats. Maxie nodded at the next set of women who stood.

As if Sadie was captain of some strange ark, two by two, the quilters came over to chat with her. And it was no coincidence. The more Sadie thought about it, the more certain she was that Oliver was behind this, too.

Deydie returned with a pad of paper. "Ye'll need this. For yere figuring."

Sadie had had enough of this charade. She hated Oliver's interfering, but she gave him points for cleverness. Luring her to Quilting Central by way of a library was brilliant. And truth be told, Sadie was anxious to get started—research what books to load on the shelves. Maybe she could borrow Oliver's laptop and search online.

Before anyone else could descend on Sadie, she grabbed the notebook and headed out the door. Outside, on the ocean breeze, she caught the scent of garlic in the wind and headed for the restaurant, hungry because she'd missed lunch.

When she opened the door, she expected to see Claire taking orders, but instead Emma was there waiting on tables. Claire was nowhere in sight.

Emma waved to Sadie. "I'll be right with you."

Wasn't she just back at the cottage?

While Sadie took a seat, she thought *What a funny town.* The village had a therapist who doubled as a waitress. While Sadie had been getting her shot from Doc MacGregor, a man had stopped by to ask the doc to give his boat engine a tune-up. And then there was Deydie, who seemed to think it was her job to organize everyone else's life, including Sadie's. As if she could ever help Sadie get over losing Gigi.

Claire came through the front door, calling, "I'm back." She grabbed an apron from the hook behind the counter. "Who's up next?"

Emma gave her a brilliant smile. "Me. I'm starved." She turned toward Sadie. "Join me for a snack?"

"Okay."

Emma slipped her apron over her head and chose a table by the window. "The view is great from here."

Before Sadie could answer, two more customers came in—a woman and a boy of around eight. When he saw Emma, his face lit up and he ran to her.

"Mattie! You're back!" She caught him, the two of them hugging. He let go and she ruffled his hair. "Oh, my goodness, you have grown. What have they been feeding you in New Zealand?"

The boy didn't answer, but Emma went on as if he had. "Well, it's about time you came to see me. I heard through the grapevine you had returned."

"We just arrived home," the woman said in a Scots-American accent. "We stopped by the surgery and Gabe told us where to find you."

Sadie recognized this woman. Thirty-something, cute. Yes, she'd seen her in *People* magazine in the story about Graham Buchanan, the BBC movie star from Gandiegow. She was his wife and she'd written his biography. Sadie had checked the book out from the library.

She stuck out her hand to Sadie. "I'm Cait. Deydie's my gran. She told me all about you."

I'm sure she did.

Cait laughed. "By the look on yere face, I see you've had a run-in or two with the ole bird. She's a good woman. Ye'll get used to her ways. In the meantime, don't hold my family ties against me."

Cait had a genuine smile and Sadie liked her instantly. "I won't."

At that, Cait's face clouded with empathy. "The quilt block that you and yere gran made was beautiful. Deydie sent me the pictures of the finalists. Hands down, yours was the best entry. I was so sorry to hear of yere gran's passing." She said it with such compassion that Sadie was put at ease.

Cait nudged Mattie. "You wanted to find Emma. Go on now and ask her."

That's when it registered that the boy hadn't made a sound—not when he'd run to Emma, and not when he'd hugged her.

Mattie faced Emma, serious, seeming to work up the words from deep inside. "I need to make an appointment." Sadie feared he had a severe stutter, but his voice was only quiet, hesitant. He seemed to struggle with every word.

Emma gave him an open smile that said *well done* even if her words didn't. "Do you want to wait until you get settled in, or would you like to start later today?"

Mattie looked up at his mother—correction, *his adoptive mother*, according to Graham's biography.

Cait shrugged. "You decide."

Mattie faced Emma again. "Today."

"How about you come by the doctor's quarters at three when Angus is down for a nap?"

Mattie nodded.

"Do you want to join us?" Emma glanced at Sadie for belated permission.

Cait shook her head. "Nay. We're headed to Quilting Central. I want to say hello to all the ladies. Graham has a two-month break and I want to take advantage of every second of being home."

Emma seemed to deflate a little. "Then you will head back to New Zealand with him?"

Cait's eyebrows pinched together. "I'm not sure. We've missed Gandiegow." She tipped her head in Mattie's direction. "We'll make our decision before school starts. Right, Mattie?"

The door to the restaurant burst open and Dand stumbled in. "Ye're home! Want to go to Spalding Farm with me and my da?"

"Well, hello to ye, too, Dand." Cait turned to Sadie. "This is John and Maggie's boy."

"We met earlier today."

Dand grinned up at Sadie. "She taught me how to read."

Cait and Emma both looked skeptical, and Sadie smiled at the boy's exuberance. "Yes. Dand and I read a stack of picture books together."

"It was loads of fun," Dand said to Mattie, giggling. "We read about dinosaur poop."

Mattie crinkled up his face, but he was grinning, too.

Dand turned and tugged on Sadie's hand. "Ye can read to Mattie, too."

Sadie smiled. "Maybe."

Dand turned on Cait. "Can Mattie come with us? We won't be gone long."

Cait touched her boy's arm. "Go on, Mattie. I'll run by Maggie's and pick you up afterward. Ye two stay out of trouble."

But the boys weren't listening as they dashed out the door.

Cait's smile faded, her eyes still on the empty doorway. "He's slid backward. In the last month or so."

Emma wrapped her arm around Cait's shoulders. "Don't worry. It's normal. We'll get it sorted."

Cait seemed to remember Sadie standing there. "Mattie has been struggling with mutism. He witnessed a terrible boat accident out by the rocks. All of the fishermen on board drowned."

"No." Sadie's heart went out to Mattie. "I'm so sorry."

"He's made a lot of progress," Emma said encouragingly. "He's come a long way."

"Aye," Cait agreed. "I'm torn. I want to be with my husband, but Mattie needs you, and Deydie, and Gandiegow."

Emma squeezed her again. "No decisions have to be made today."

Cait hugged Emma, bid them both good-bye, and then she was gone.

They had a pleasant meal of mini chef salads and buttery garlic bread, and then Emma hurried home to care for Angus.

Sadie stayed at the table near the front picture window and sketched a layout for Quilting Central's library. She also made a list of genres—quilting fiction, mysteries, mainstream novels, the history of crafting, and romance—books she thought would appeal to the retreat goers. Then she settled herself to gaze at the ocean. She would never tire of a view of the water.

Not a moment later, she caught sight of a man sauntering in her direction—his size, shape, and gait so familiar that her pulse even recognized him, racing more than it should. As he got closer, Ross saw her through the window, too, and waved.

Grinning, he walked into the restaurant. "Can I join you? I'm starving."

"I've eaten. But sit so I can show you what I've been

working on." She thrust the opened notebook toward him. "Oliver found a way to get me back to Quilting Central. Oh, but I'm sure you've already heard. Deydie said you were making the shelves for the library."

"This was Oliver's idea?"

"It has to be. He's a master manipulator. I've seen him operate my whole life."

The door to the restaurant opened.

"Speak of the devil," Sadie muttered, then plastered on a smile.

Her brother saw her, took in Ross, and then made a beeline for them. Sadie expected him to lambaste Ross, but he chose a different tack. "Deydie said you're putting together a library for her."

"Like you didn't know."

Oliver looked confused, then pulled his wallet from his back pocket, slipped out a credit card, and held it out to her. "I thought you would need this to buy some books online for it. My contribution."

Wasn't that just like her brother? Just when she wanted to stay mad at him, he had to go all generous and noble on her.

Sadie took the card, but before she could say anything, Ross piped up.

"Not online. Just now, Sadie was asking me to take her to Glasgow so she could shop for books. Tomorrow. Waterstones, right?"

This was news to her.

Now Oliver looked uncomfortable. "You're not going anywhere alone with this guy. We know nothing about him."

Ross's back straightened at this attack on his character but he didn't take the bait. "My nephew Dand is going along."

"How old is your nephew?"

"Dand? Six. No, seven last month. We'll be staying the night with my mother and my aunt Glynnis. Maybe two nights, depending on how many things need to be fixed around the house in Glasgow." Ross pulled Sadie's notebook over and ripped out a sheet, scribbling on it. "Here's my mum's phone number and the address of where we'll be. Call if ye like." He handed the paper off to Oliver.

Sadie huffed. Didn't they both know that she could manage her own life? But in truth she was probably more excited than irritated. Although Ross was being as highhanded as Oliver, she relished the idea of getting out of town again for a while.

To Oliver's credit, he looked a little embarrassed when he took the paper from Ross and shoved it in his front pocket, crumpling it. "Maybe I will check up."

But then he renewed his jerk-brother status. "Keep your hands off my sister anyway."

Like Ross would dream of doing otherwise.

Without another word, Oliver stomped over to the counter and placed a to-go order with Claire.

Sadie waited until she was sure Oliver wasn't listening and cocked an eyebrow at Ross. "Am I really going to Glasgow? Or were you just messing with my brother?"

"Aye. I promised to help get ye out of the retreat, didn't I?" His eyes twinkled with laughter. "But I'll need to let my mother know as soon as possible that we're coming."

"And Dand? Is he really going with us?"

"He's out of school. My mum would love to see him."

"But you haven't talked to Maggie about it yet?"

"It'll be fine."

"I guess I'll go then."

And an idea started to form. Ross was helping her stay away from Quilting Central, and she had promised to help him back. It just wasn't going to be the assistance he expected.

Sadie smiled at her plan, knowing it had nothing to do with a new career, but instead his peace of mind. While they were in Glasgow, she would find Ross a woman.

Chapter Six

After he ate, Sadie strolled beside Ross as they made their way back to his house. Inside, all was quiet. There was a delicious aroma of a roast in the oven, and the cottage felt warm and cozy. Or maybe it was being near Ross that made her feel this way.

Sadie went to her place at the dining room table, ready to get back to work on the chair pockets. Ross stepped to the refrigerator and pulled a note from a clip.

He held it up to Sadie. "Maggie's at the store."

So they were alone; the time was now then.

"Ross?"

But as he turned to her expectantly, the front door flew open and in clattered Dand and Mattie.

"Then I pulled out my slingshot and shot him," Dand was saying. As he motioned to his friend over his shoulder, he stumbled on the hall rug. "I'll show ye the feather I knocked off."

Dand's bedroom door had barely slammed behind them when one of Ross's brothers appeared. His eyes took in the scene.

The brother cocked an eyebrow. "I'm not interrupting, am I?"

For a moment, Sadie thought Ross looked embarrassed, but certainly she was imagining it.

Ross nodded to his brother. "This is Sadie Middleton. Sadie . . . John, my older brother."

"It's nice to actually meet you." John gave Ross a pointed look.

Sadie knew what it was about. He was referring to the night she and Ross ran off together.

John's gaze fell on the fabric spread out on the table. He was nice to not mention the mess she'd made of his house.

The door opened yet again, and Maggie stepped inside with Irene cradled to her chest in a baby carrier, the little one hanging on to Maggie's long black braid.

"Wife." John eased the cloth grocery bag from her shoulder and kissed her on the lips. He walked into the kitchen and deposited the bag on the counter.

Maggie undid the strap of the carrier. "Can someone hold Irene while I finish the cooking?" She let the strap fall, and without a glance in the men's direction, she put Irene in Sadie's arms. "Thanks."

Ross's gaze snapped to Sadie. "What about me?"

Sadie shifted the child out of his reach and bounced her. "I have her. She's mine."

The warmth and weight of a baby was wonderful. "Go do some guy stuff."

Ross moped away, plopped on the couch, and put his feet up. "Done."

"What's this I hear about ye going to Glasgow tomorrow, Ross?" Maggie said from the kitchen.

Ross cursed under his breath before cranking his head over his shoulder to his sister-in-law. "I want to see Mum. I thought I'd take Dand with me if that's okay with you two."

Sadie watched Maggie's face. She seemed to be waiting patiently for the rest.

Silence loomed. Ross dropped his feet to the floor and turned to Maggie. "If it's not okay, I can go without him."

Still Maggie remained quiet.

"Oh, for heaven's sake," Sadie said. Didn't Ross have a clue? She walked past the stubborn Scot, kicked his shoe, then spoke to Maggie. "Ross is taking me also, so I can buy books for Quilting Central's library."

John looked to Maggie. "Quilting Central has a library?"

But Sadie was the one who responded. "Ross is going to build shelves, and I'm going to stock them. Or do the best I can before I have to leave on Saturday." Time was passing quickly.

The tension was thick. Sadie knew it was because she and Ross were spending too much time together. She'd heard the whispers that Maggie wanted one of her sisters for Ross. Sadie wished she could explain that she wasn't after him. The idea was laughable, really. She only wanted to help him find someone new. But she hadn't even told him her plan yet.

John broke the silence. "Brodie Wallace is back in town."

Sadie looked at Ross questioningly.

Ross sat back down. "Brodie's a friend of ours whose grandfather has been sick on and off for a while now. I suppose he's come home to help old Abraham."

John sat on the other end of the sofa. "Aye, I've noticed his cough is worse of late."

There was a ruckus at the front door as it swung open and Ross's brother Ramsay came in with his wife, the matchmaker. "*Gawd*, woman, ye have balls."

They both laughed, but when Kit saw Ross, she narrowed her eyes at him. "You and I need to talk. You know, don't you, that you're going to have to meet with Harry's niece. He promised her." She held her hand up. "I know *you* didn't promise, but still. You don't want to hurt her feelings, now, do you?"

Ross's eyes flitted heavenward. "Not now, Kit. I beg you."

"After dinner then," she said with finality, "we'll talk."

Sadie gave Ross a pitying look, feeling better about the plan she was working on for Glasgow. If he started dating, surely the people of the village would leave him alone then.

"Are you staying for dinner, Sadie?" Kit asked.

"Aye," Maggie said. "Stay."

"Thank you. I'd love to." It would beat going back to Quilting Central and eating with the quilters. For some reason, she didn't mind the hubbub at Ross's cottage.

Sadie continued to work on the chair pockets, but as dinnertime drew near, she cleared them away. Cait dropped in briefly to retrieve Mattie, and John and Ross set the table. The entire house reverberated with jibes, laughter, and love.

Dinner was a predictably loud affair, as the brothers kidded one another and a gurgling Irene was passed from person to person, even Dand taking his turn with his little sister.

For a moment, Sadie wished Oliver was here to experience the fun. She, Gigi, and Oliver had had wonderful family dinners—far quieter than this, but just as full of love.

But not anymore.

When no one could eat another bite, Kit announced that she and Ross would be doing the dishes.

"Sadie, ye have to help, too," Ross said.

"Of course." She would be his buffer and moral support against his matchmaking sister-in-law and her onslaught of eligible bachelorettes.

Kit took her place at the sink to wash, but before she could open her mouth, Ross was talking.

"Sadie, I've been meaning to ask ye, what's it like in North Carolina?" He winked at her. "Are the summers the same as here?"

She knew what he was doing. "The weather is hot this time of year. We spend a lot of time on the beach or indoors where there's air-conditioning." She went on a bit longer about the beauty of North Carolina, then turned to Kit. "I hear from everyone that you're a matchmaker. How did you get involved in such an interesting career?"

Kit began explaining how she'd progressed from matching her wealthy friends to starting *The Real Men of Alaska*, and finally finding her way to Scotland and expanding her business here.

And while Sadie had Kit, she decided to pump her for useful information. "So how do you go about deciding who is best for whom? Let's take Ross, for instance."

"Let's not," Ross interjected. "It's not polite to discuss my love life with an out-of-town guest."

Kit tossed her dish towel at Ross's head. "You need

my help, brother-in-law, or you'll end up a lonely old fisherman."

"Nay. I'll have all of ye to nag me to my dying day."

"How exactly would you go about picking out a woman for Ross?" Sadie might've said too much because Kit looked at her sideways and Ross swung around to look at her, too. "I mean choosing the right mate for a man. Or a woman, for that matter."

Now Maggie was looking at her strangely. "Are ye asking for yereself?"

"Heavens, no." Sadie glanced at the clock on the wall and watched the hand tick while she tried to come up with a way to dig herself out. "It's late. I'm just so tired. I better get back to the quilting dorm."

Ross pointed at the door. "I'll walk you. To make sure ye don't get into any trouble."

That only made things worse. Now Ramsay and John were looking at her, too.

Ross grabbed the novel she'd been reading that morning off the treadle machine. "Ye don't want to forget this."

Outside, Ross jumped right in, or maybe down her throat. "What was that all about?"

She had wanted to tell him her plan earlier, when she'd thought he was in the right frame of mind. Now . . . not so much. "I have an idea of how to help you. A way to get Gandiegow off your back."

His raised hackles relaxed. "All right. I'm listening."

"When we're in Glasgow, we should go out," Sadie said.

He frowned at her.

"Oh, I didn't mean you and me. But we should go to a pub or something."

He still looked bemused.

She put her hands on her hips. "So we can find you a woman."

"We?"

But he seemed relieved that she wasn't the woman in question, and her heart gave a sad little sigh. Logically she knew Ross wasn't for her, but apparently subconsciously, a fantasy life she didn't know existed had taken over wanting things it couldn't have, not in a million years.

"And what would this woman be like?" He was all in now.

"I don't know yet. But you'll let me be your wing-man—I mean, your wing-woman—at the pub?"

He seemed to be thinking about it. "And what about ye? What about finding you a man?" He stopped for a second, considering. "Unless ye already have one at home you failed to mention."

Sadie snorted. "No. Not hardly. I already told you that."

"Why not?"

She blushed—not only for the crazy thoughts that she'd been having about Ross, but for the truth. "It's embarrassing."

"What's embarrassing?" He stood there, waiting patiently. "Tell me."

"Dating has always seemed a lot of trouble, as far as I'm concerned. I've always been more interested in books than men." There. She'd said it. She finally glanced in Ross's direction, and she found him grinning.

"What?" she said. "You think it's funny that I'm pretty

clueless?" *Not completely clueless*, but he didn't need to know about the experiences she'd had.

"That's not it at all," he said. "Go on. Tell me more."

"I guess I just don't know how to be all that feminine. I don't know a thing about clothes or fashion, though Gigi did her best to teach me; it just didn't take."

Ross scanned her from head to toe as if she had assets worth looking it. He didn't seem repulsed by what he saw . . . quite possibly the opposite. But she had to be mistaken.

He touched her arm and got them moving again. He was silent for a long moment as they cut through the path to the back of the bluff. She waited for him to say something about his assessment, like, *Oh, I think you look great.* But who was she kidding?

Finally he spoke. "Maybe I can help."

"Help what?"

"We're here."

Sure enough, they were back at Thistle Glen Lodge. The lights were out, so clearly the rest of the dorm occupants weren't back yet from Quilting Central. Sadie could read her book in peace and not have to speak with another human being tonight.

Ross walked her to the door, opened it, and flipped on the foyer light. The chandelier put him in half shadows.

"Do you want to come in for a drink?" she heard herself asking, as if having an out-of-body experience. *Am I out of my freaking mind?*

Talk about embarrassed. Her face heated up. She wanted to crawl into a hole and hide forever. Why had she done that? She sounded as if she was propositioning him. Everyone knew *drink* was code for *sex.* "Sorry." Her cheeks felt as though they'd been torched. If only she was in half shadows.

To her surprise, he didn't seem to be put off by the idea. He studied her face intently, as if he were actually considering it.

If only I were more interesting to look at.

"I can't stay," he finally said. He gave no more explanation than that, just turned and walked away at a clip without so much as a good-bye.

She stood in the doorway, disgusted with herself. *Stupid, stupid, stupid!* She knew exactly who she was, accepted it, and was completely comfortable in her ballet flats, yet now she felt like doing something crazy. Run after him. Throw her arms around him and hang on. Soak him up.

Because when she was around Ross, she felt as if she was *more*.

More Sadie than she'd ever been on her own.

Stupid. Stupid. Stupid! Ross took long, determined strides away from the quilting dorm and toward the pub. Everything in him wanted to turn back, drop anchor beside Sadie at Thistle Glen Lodge, have that drink she offered, and see where things would lead. But she wasn't part of his plan. She was here for only a short period of time. She was his friend. And for some reason, which he couldn't figure out, she was derailing him. But he would keep his hormones under wraps and his bearings true. He'd missed out on years of freedom and was determined to claim it now.

He should head home to bed, but the Inquisition waited for him at the cottage.

It was times like this that he missed Duncan the most. He could really use a shot of whisky and a chat in front of the fire with him. But Duncan was gone, and life had moved on. The only problem was that Ross hadn't.

He entered the pub and sat at the far end of the bar, where he'd first met Sadie, and where he'd taken it upon himself to spirit her away from the town for their twenty-four hours of freedom. What he wouldn't give to be away from Gandiegow now.

But the two of them, plus Dand, would be going away together tomorrow. They should've discussed their travel plans, instead of how she wanted to find him a woman.

But at that moment, with the light falling on her, she'd looked just like an angel. An angel! *Gads!*

Coll appeared in front of him. "What will ye have?"

"A dram." Just a little something to take the edge off. But before Coll could put a glass on the counter and fill it, Ross changed his mind. "Give me an Irn-Bru to go instead." He wouldn't sit here and drink alone. He'd take his soft drink and have a visit with Duncan . . . at the cemetery.

Can in hand, Ross headed up to the top of the bluff. He loved all the seasons in Gandiegow, but the summer weather made it an easier hike to the top to visit his old friend. And his father. And countless others who had died. Right after Duncan's death Ross had made the trip several times a week, bringing a bottle of something stronger than what he had now to share with his friend, at least in spirit.

He must've been caught up in his thoughts, because it wasn't until he'd nearly reached Duncan's grave that he noticed another person in the cemetery.

Brodie Wallace, paying his respects in front of his cousin Joe's tombstone. Brodie and Joe had always been close, but an odd pair—Joe outgoing as they come, Brodie quiet as the bluff. When Brodie hadn't come back for Joe's funeral, the whole town had gossiped about it, judging Brodie harshly for making Abraham bury his grandson alone, even though Joe's widow was with him at the graveside. But Ross always thought Brodie must've had his reasons. Good men always did, and didn't need to broadcast an explanation to anyone.

Ross glanced at Joe's tombstone. Poor bastard. Too young to die. He'd been in a horrific car accident in America. Ross was glad Brodie was back to take over Abraham's fishing business.

Brodie looked up and nodded as he came up beside him. "Ross."

"Brodie." It didn't feel right to leave straightaway, so Ross added, "I just heard ye were back."

"Aye. For a while, it seems."

"Abraham can use a hand. He wouldn't take help from the rest of us."

"Aye. Stubborn."

The wind picked up. They stood there a while longer, neither of them talking.

Finally, Brodie stepped away. "'Night."

Ross nodded and moved on to Duncan's tombstone, sipping his soda.

The evening was calm, but there was a storm brewing inside of Ross. What was he going to do about Sadie? Since she'd arrived in town, she'd turned things upside down for him. He was no longer thinking about his future and what he wanted to do, but was occupied with taking care of her. What did that say about him? And why in the hell had he let himself become so involved with a woman from the States?

He closed his eyes and took a deep breath. Answers came to him along the breeze, lifting his spirits. He had promised to help Sadie stay away from Quilting Central, and in his own way, he'd kept that promise, plus had also begun to help her by easing her back into Quilting Central's bosom with the library. But Sadie's offer to help him find a woman should be reciprocated in kind. He had no delusions of finding her a man while she was here in Scotland, but he could at least prepare her for when she got home. *But do I really want to ready her to be with another man?* He ignored that question. Yes, with a little coaching and practice, he felt Sadie could be the perfect catch.

And being a fisherman, he wondered who would reel her in. All the men he knew flashed through his mind, not one of them right for Sadie. It would take a special kind of man to appreciate her for who she was, to see past her kidney disease. And her meddling brother, Oliver. Aye, Ross would put his mind to it, feeling sure if he did, he could find the right man for Sadie Middleton.

Sadie woke early, still thoroughly embarrassed about last night. She hated that she'd put Ross in such an awkward position. She wondered now if he would even take her to Glasgow with him. Well, if he did show up, she would make sure not to do that to him again. He was her friend and she couldn't ask for more.

She wrapped her robe around herself and readied for the day while the rest of the dorm slept on.

Packing for the trip into Glasgow, she felt strangely nervous about meeting Ross's mother, but didn't know why. Maybe she was only excited because, she, Ross, and Dand were off on an adventure, as Emma had called it.

As Sadie wheeled her bag into the living room, Ross and his energetic nephew arrived.

"Are ye ready, lass?" Ross smiled at her, no trace of the awkwardness that she'd feared.

And because she had no control over her own reactions, her stomach squeezed in delight at the sight of him. She tried not to grin back. "Yes."

Dand ran up and grabbed her bag. "First Mate said I should be a gentleman and get yere bag for ye." He grinned and she saw that he was missing a bottom front tooth. He smiled even bigger when he saw her realization. "The Skipper knocked it out last night when he got me in a half nelson. Mum said that tooth should've come out a long time ago and that Uncle Ramsay saved us a trip to the dentist in Inverness." He pulled back his lip so she could see the gaping hole. "Ye should've seen all the bluid."

Sadie laughed. "Yes, you certainly have quite a hole there." She'd never met a cuter kid. "Why do you call your Uncle Ramsay 'Skipper'?"

Dand spoke over his shoulder as he wheeled her bag out the door. "Because he runs his own boat. He can't be Captain because Da is the only captain."

"And you're First Mate?" she asked.

"Aye." Ross smiled, but there was something behind it. "It's a long story. I'll tell ye on the way to Glasgow."

But as soon as they were settled in the truck, Dand began a loud, animated story about the horses he'd seen at Spalding Farm that lasted for the next hour as they drove through the beautiful wilderness of the Highlands.

Suddenly, the truck became silent. Dand's warm body leaned up against her.

Ross nodded. "He talked himself out."

Sadie glanced down at the child between them and smiled.

Instead of Ross telling the story of Ramsay and his boat, he quietly told her some of the ideas he'd been entertaining as a second career, like using his truck for a hauling business.

"But nothing feels right," he said. "There has to be something out there for me to do."

"You'll know when it comes along. It'll feel perfect," she assured him.

A contented silence settled over them. The gentle hum of the engine, the sun shining through the window, the child sleeping next to her, and Ross confident at the wheel . . . all had a hypnotic effect on her. Sadie relaxed as though into a warm bath. She closed her eyes for only a moment and woke when Ross shut off the truck outside a cute whitewashed stone cottage with two dormer windows peeking out on the second floor.

Her driver glanced over at her, nudging Dand at the same time. "Hey, sleepyheads, we're here. Are ye ready to see yere gran and auntie?"

Dand started to clamber over Sadie to get out but Ross put a hand on the boy, stilling him. "Remember now, Aunt Glynnis isn't well. We'll not be loud in the house. Understand?"

"Ah, Uncle Ross. Mum and Da already said for me to behave."

"Quiet and behaving are two different things." Ross looked as if he didn't believe the boy could do either. "I need both from ye, Dand. Or else yere mum won't let me take you on yere own again."

Nice threat.

Sadie opened her door and Dand scrambled out past her. She started to slip from the truck, her stomach a mess of nerves, when Ross grabbed her hand. "And you, lass, ye better remember to keep it down in the house. Ye're such a hell-raiser."

She was grateful for his teasing and smiled back.

Ross grabbed their bags from the bed of the truck. By the time they made it to the door, Ross's mother was outside hugging Dand.

"Who is this grown man? What have ye done with my wee grandson?"

"Ah, Nan, ye saw me last month."

She hugged him again. "But ye've grown." She tugged at Dand's bag. "Did ye stick baby Irene in your knapsack so I can see her, too?"

Dand giggled, shaking his head no. "But I packed a load of books for me and Sadie to read!"

Ross's mother looked past Dand and smiled at her son; then her gaze fell on Sadie. Her eyes lit up and she pulled Sadie in for a hug as well. "Welcome, Sadie. Ross told me about ye. We're happy ye're here. I'm Grace." She let go.

Sadie was shocked at being hugged so warmly. "Nice to meet you."

There was such a kindheartedness in Grace that Sadie couldn't help but like her instantly. She was tall, as Sadie would expect of the mother of the strapping Armstrong brothers. At first Sadie thought Grace and Ross shared the same nose, but there were differences. Grace's nose was hawk-like in an elegant way. Her motherly manner immediately put Sadie at ease, making her feel more comfortable than she had back in Gandiegow.

Grace held the door wide for her, but she didn't let Ross in so readily, instead pulling him in for a long hug. "I've missed ye. Verra much."

"Ah, Mum," Ross said, sounding much like Dand. "I haven't been here two seconds and ye're already laying on the guilt."

Sadie didn't think it was guilt at all.

Grace squeezed him harder. "It's been near half a year since I've seen ye. Since I was back for Pippa's wedding."

Maybe Ross does know his mother.

"I'm a busy man." He said nothing about Pippa or the wedding. "But I'm here now. Can ye let it go?"

"Come in then. Glynnis is resting." Grace turned to Sadie. "That's my sister."

"They're twins," Dand added. But then he stopped short. "They don't look alike anymore."

"Because ye're great-auntie has been sick," Grace supplied, smiling gently at Dand. "I'll get the kettle on. Ye made great time, aye?"

Ross stopped his mother with a hand to her arm. "If it's all the same to you, Mum, Sadie and I are going to pass. She wants to get straight to the shopping."

Grace shrugged, taking the news well. "Settle in and

then get going. Dand and I are going to have a bite to eat. Will ye have something before ye go?"

Ross looked to Sadie as if she'd said something. "Nay. Sadie wanted to check out the pub."

Grace laughed. "I can see she's a demanding lass."

And Sadie had barely said hello.

Ross put his hand to her back. "I'll show you to yere room first."

As he guided her to the stairs, his hand unnerved her, heated her up and made her tingle. She stepped away, but tripped on the hall rug. He caught her around the waist and pulled her back into his chest, making everything worse.

"Whoa. Are ye all right?" His breath was on her neck.

She sagged, afraid she might faint . . . dead away. *Then he could scoop me into his arms and carry me upstairs like a Scottish Rhett Butler to my Scarlett O'Hara.*

Good lands! Her imagination was on overdrive. Sadie should check herself into the Only-in-Your-Dreams Ward.

She moved away from him. Quickly. "I'm fine." She held on to the banister, concentrating as she climbed the stairs rapidly, making sure to firmly plant one foot in front of the other.

But when she reached the top, she realized she didn't know which room was hers. The bungalow was small, but there were four doors to choose from.

Ross took the stairs at a normal pace, making her feel even more self-conscious. She was a rational person. Why, then, did she feel so shaken up by the touch of Ross's breath on her neck? She shivered.

When he joined her at the top, he pointed. "In there."

She turned the handle and spoke over her shoulder quietly. "Thanks." She started to escape into the room, alone, but Ross blocked the door with his hand.

He put a finger to his lips. "Shhh. Let me in for a minute." He didn't wait for her consent, but stepped in and shut the door behind him. "I want to talk to you about what we're going to do this afternoon."

She froze like a rabbit. Except she wasn't scared of him. She was terrified of where her logical brain had landed and of the images popping up.

"What's wrong?" He gazed at her for a long moment, like he had done last night. But this time, he wasn't running away.

She should answer him, but she couldn't tell him the truth. She hated to admit it even to herself. She was seriously attracted to him, which was utterly ridiculous. Nothing could come of it beyond sitting up late at night, mooning over him, like she'd done last night. What had she been thinking when she'd agreed to come to Glasgow with him in the first place?

The bedroom was small and he took up most of it with his all-male presence. She had to answer him, but what could she say?

He cleared his throat and looked away, staring past her shoulder. "I'll give ye a minute." He might as well have said what was really on his mind . . . *I'll give ye a minute to pull yereself together.*

She would need more than a minute. She'd need a lifetime.

He spun around and left the room.

She exhaled.

Then collapsed on the small bed, her wound-tight nerves unraveling like thread from a spool.

Ross was no dummy. She'd gone completely mental, and he knew it. Was this just another one of the stages of grief . . . *falling for a Highlander*?

Well, she better take the next few minutes to get a grip, because they were headed out to shop for books. She glanced in the small mirror on the wall. She was still plain Sadie, but she took a moment to primp her short brown hair anyway. And for fun, she applied some berry-colored lipstick.

Bravely, she opened the door and went in search of Ross. Downstairs, tucked at the back of the house, she found him in the kitchen, leaning against the counter. Dand and Grace were at the dinette table, the three of them chatting quietly.

Grace looked up. "There ye are." She gave Sadie a brilliant smile. "Ye know, ye're the first lass Ross has brought home for me to meet."

Like she was Ross's girlfriend! Sadie tripped again, this time on thin air.

Chapter Seven

In a flash, Ross caught Sadie, pulling her to him. Chest . . .
to . . . chest. *Oh, God!*

Grace jumped to her feet, too. "Are ye all right?"

Sadie wanted to disappear. "I'm okay. Just clumsy."
She gazed up into Ross's eyes.

He looked concerned. Sadie hoped he wouldn't question her about her stumbling.

If he did, what could she say? *Midday drunkenness?
Uneven floor? Localized earthquake?* The truth was she
had a serious hormonal imbalance when it came to a
certain excessively gorgeous fisherman. Finally she settled on the perfect explanation, one he couldn't refute.
She would lie and tell him it was her kidney disease. Sure,
it was dishonest to use her illness as a scapegoat, but at
least it would prove good for something.

He didn't ask, fortunately, and she pushed away, trying to act as if she wasn't falling-in-crush with him, and
stood unassisted.

Grace seemed amused. "Let me get you some tea."

Sadie put her hand up, not looking her in the eye. "No,

no. Ross is right. We should get to the store and pick out those books."

"Aye." Ross ruffled Dand's hair. "Remember what I told you. If ye aren't the perfect sailor while I'm gone, ye'll be walking the plank when we get home. Ye hear?"

Dand saluted with a biscuit in his hand. "I'll be good, First Mate. Promise." Crumbs flew everywhere.

Sadie said a quick good-bye, slipped from the kitchen, and headed toward the front door. She'd have to apologize to Ross for being such an addlebrained klutz.

He was right behind her. Sadie raced for the truck and hopped inside before he could hold the door open for her. She was comfortable around Ross, but she wasn't comfortable with her crazy feelings. He slid into the other side.

She laid a hand on his arm to get his attention, but glanced away when he turned in her direction. She bit her lip. "Sorry." She waited a moment before daring to look at him.

He shook his head, seeming confused. "For what?"

Hadn't he noticed that she had embarrassed him in front of his mom? "For, um . . . for, um . . ."

Ross grinned at her. "We'll stop and get ye a strong ale. That'll fix yere stammer." His gaze dropped to her hand still on his arm.

She scooted back to her side of the vehicle, taking her hand with her, and faced forward. "Yeah. Right. A strong ale should do it."

Ross surprised her a few minutes later by pulling into a train station. "It's only a twenty-minute ride into Glasgow." He patted the steering wheel. "We'd take that long looking for a place to park the truck."

He bought their tickets as she waited. She couldn't remember ever being on a real train. The train at the zoo when she was five didn't count. When they boarded, Ross pointed out a place for them to sit together. She looked out the window as the train pulled away from the station, ignored his warm body next to hers, and concentrated on the scenery until they arrived in the center of Glasgow. Ross took her hand and helped her step down from the train. He needed to stop touching her and taking care of her every need.

He took her straight to the pub as promised, and filled her with delicious food, not teasing her when she passed on the ale because it wasn't good for her kidneys.

"So what's the plan?" she said after finishing her last bite. "Which bookstore are we going to first?" She was excited to check out the bookstores in Scotland.

"We have to make a detour first."

"What kind of detour? I promised Deydie a library for Quilting Central, and Oliver's credit card is ready for some action."

"Did ye notice the shop next to the pub?"

She shook her head.

"It's a little dress shop."

"Why would you want to go to a dress shop?" Did he want to buy something nice for his mother?

"Ye mentioned you knew nothing about clothes. I thought we could do a little exploring to help ye figure out what you like."

She stared at him, dumbfounded.

He shrugged. "We don't have to, if ye don't want. I kind of like yere brown dress."

She glanced down at her old standby. It was comfortable. It was modest. It was old. "I guess I could take a look."

"That's the spirit." He put his hand out to help her up. "Come on."

This is the last time, she told herself as she took his hand. But she vowed to find the right moment to talk to him about being such a gentleman. Did he know that when he touched her, it was too much? *Way. Too. Much.*

The shop next door turned out to be perfect. The dresses were classically cut with a touch of whimsy. She gravitated to a rack of dresses and began flipping through the hangers. Finally she pulled out a red one and held it to her chest, checking the length while Ross stood back and watched.

Because the sales clerk was busy, Sadie turned to Ross. "What do you think of this one?" She stepped in front of the full-length mirror.

He came closer, standing behind her, but not too close. "The real question is whether *ye* like it or not."

"I like the cap sleeves. And it isn't too short."

"Do ye like it enough to try it on?"

She did.

He took the red dress from her. "I'll keep this while you find some more."

She picked out four dresses, giving them to him one at a time. Ross pointed at another rack.

"Take the green one there. It'll look nice with your eyes."

But the green one was fun and flirty, not nearly as conservative as the ones she'd picked out. She started to tell him it wasn't her style, but he'd been so good to her that she couldn't say no.

Sadie pulled the green one from the rack and went to the sales clerk for a changing room.

"Follow me." The woman guided her through an archway. On the other side was a half-circle couch, facing the curtains to two dressing areas.

The sales clerk hung Sadie's things in one of the rooms. "Ye get started with these while I bring yere boyfriend back to help ye decide."

"He's not . . ." Sadie tried, but the woman was already gone. Sadie pulled the curtain and stared in the full-length mirror, getting a good look at herself. If she was honest about her brown dress, she should've stopped wearing it two years ago. Maybe three. And burned it. She pulled it over her shoulders and laid it on the lone chair.

The green dress, the one Ross had suggested, called to her first. She took it from the hanger and slipped it on.

She jumped when Ross spoke from the other side of the curtain.

"When ye're ready, let me take a gander."

She peeked out. Ross was leaning back on the dainty sofa with his hands behind his head, a man at leisure with his legs sprawled. She pulled the curtain shut. This was stupid. He shouldn't be here.

"Why don't you go back to the pub?" she suggested. "I'll meet up with you in a little while."

"Why don't ye stop stalling and get out here?" He laughed as if he was thinking of a joke. "Or do I need to come in after ye?"

"He wouldn't dare," she said to the little dressing room.

"Don't challenge me, luv. I never back down."

Sadie about melted all over the green dress. He'd called her *luv*. Not for the first time, and she shouldn't think anything of it. He'd called no less than three women *luv* since she'd arrived in Gandiegow. Granted, they were all old enough to be his mother or grandmother.

"I'm coming." She whipped back the curtain and stepped into the waiting area.

He leaned forward with his elbows on his thighs, taking her in from head to toe. He seemed to be schooling his reaction. "Do you like it?"

"I don't know."

He unfolded himself from the sofa and came to her. He laid his hands on her shoulders and spun her toward the full-length mirror. "Take a look and decide."

He still had his hands resting on her, and it was hard to concentrate on anything except where he touched. She shrugged away, moving closer to the mirror.

What she saw first was how the green dress made her brown eyes stand out. Then she noticed the angle at which the dress hung, flaring at just the right spot, making her look as if she had hips. Which was surprising, considering her boyish figure. The fabric was light, fairylike, and she felt . . . she felt . . . she felt *pretty*. She gasped.

Ross moved closer, a smile spreading over his face. "Now you see it, too."

She wanted to hear what he saw, but was too self-conscious to ask, so she nodded instead.

"I think that one's a keeper. Now, go try on a dress that ye picked out."

The red one had looked interesting on the mannequin, but on Sadie, it looked like a Red Cross tent. She didn't even have to show that one to Ross though he complained that he wanted to see it, too.

As she tried on each dress, her style became clearer—what she liked, what looked good. In the end, she approached the checkout counter with two dresses, a pair of slacks that gave her a shapely butt, and a white sweater that would go with everything. Ross took the green dress from her.

"What are you doing?" She grabbed for it. "I want that."

He held it out of her reach. "I picked it. I'm paying for it."

"It won't fit you."

"Verra funny." He stopped and stared at her, as serious as a storm forecast. "Let me do this." He paused for a second. "With no argument."

"Fine," she grumbled. But why would he want to spend his hard-earned money on her?

By the time they were back outside, it was four o'clock.

"Will we have time to get the books and be back at your mother's for dinner?"

"Nay."

"I'm sorry." She lifted the one small sack that he'd allowed her to carry. "I shouldn't have taken so much time in there."

"Are ye really in that big of a hurry to get back to Gandiegow?"

She thought about it for a moment. "Well, no. But we are expected." Oliver was probably tallying every second she was gone.

"My mum will want the extra time anyway."

"To spend with Dand?"

"No. *To interrogate you*." He nudged her. "How about a stroll before heading back to the train station?"

"Sure." She shifted her sack.

He put out his hand. "Here. I'll take it."

"No. I'm fine. But tomorrow, I promise to let you carry as many of the books as you can handle."

They walked around the city and he shared the sights with her, having an irresistible way of telling a story that kept her completely enthralled. Too soon, they were headed back to the train. But once they took their seats, she realized she was spent, worn out in a good way. She closed her eyes and tried to prop herself against the window. The train jolted forward, making her hit her head.

"Come now." A giant arm sank around the back of her shoulders and pulled her close. "Lie yere head here. I won't tell a soul."

With her eyes still closed, she smiled and leaned into Ross's warm, strong body. He relaxed her, but she was too aware of him to actually doze. Before she knew it he was squeezing her shoulder.

"We're here."

"Thanks," she mumbled, scooting away from him. She thought about her plan, how she was going to help him find a woman. It didn't sit well with her, but she would, no matter how wrong it felt. "Are you looking forward to tonight? Do you think your mother will mind that you're going out again?"

"I'm sure she'll grouse a little. It's her way. But she'll be fine with Dand to keep her company."

"Is that why you wanted to bring him along?"

"One of the reasons." He didn't elaborate.

When they got back to the house, Grace and Dand

were sitting in the parlor with Glynnis, who was lying on the couch with pillows propped under her legs.

"Rossy," Glynnis said a little weakly. "Come here and give yere favorite auntie a *scwunch*."

Ross grinned and walked toward her. "First of all, ye're my only aunt. And secondly, I'm too old to be called *Rossy*." He leaned down and gave her a tender hug and a kiss on the cheek.

"Ye'll never be too old to be my Rossy, and don't you forget it."

He took her hand. "I think ye're right, Auntie." He motioned to Sadie. "This is my friend, Sadie. She's from the States."

"Oh, I've heard," Glynnis said, a sly grin on her face.

"Mum, have ye been gossiping?"

Grace raised an eyebrow as if he dared to lecture her.

"Do ye have something to hide, Rossy?" Glynnis laughed hoarsely. "It wasn't Grace who told. Dand had quite a bit to say about Sadie."

She and Ross turned to the boy.

Dand continued folding a piece of newspaper into a hat, not looking up at them. "I just said that Aunt Sadie was yere new girlfriend now that Pippa married Max."

"What?" Ross and Sadie said together. Except Ross's *what* was a boom, and Sadie's was a squeak.

"We're just friends," Ross declared.

"Friends," Sadie said quietly, though she felt a little hurt by how adamant Ross was.

Dand turned to them. "But ye two ran off together. I thought when two people run off together that they're getting married."

Sadie wanted to be anywhere but here.

With a frown etched on his face, Ross sat on the recliner and motioned to Dand. "Come here, lad." He patted his knee.

Dand ambled over and crawled into Ross's lap. The women were captivated.

Ross stared the boy in the eye. "Ye can't jump to conclusions without knowing all the facts."

"What are the facts?" Dand asked sensibly.

Yes, Sadie wanted to know them, too.

"The fact is that Sadie and I are friends, *grand friends.* The Almighty must've wanted me to meet Sadie and for us to get along so famously, because we've become good friends awfully fast. But just because we took a little trip doesn't mean that we're getting married."

"But when Gus and Donna slipped out of town, Father Andrew had to marry them when they came back. Her da made sure of it."

Ross looked heavenward, his sigh wrought with exasperation. "That was different. Gus and Donna were . . ." He was apparently at a loss for the right words. "Sadie and I are . . ." He seemed stuck for a moment here, too. "We're only friends, Dand. Nothing more."

Well, he'd certainly made that clear!

But Ross wasn't done with the boy. "There'll be no more gossiping, okay? A man just doesn't do it."

Dand slipped off his lap and slammed his hands on his hips. "Aw, Uncle Ross, I don't gossip."

"Yup, ye did, just like ye belonged at Quilting Central."

The boy turned red and stomped his foot. "Did not."

"Ye watch what you say in the future. Do you understand?"

Dand's indignation drained and he hung his head. "Aye."

Ross ruffled his head. "No harm done."

But Sadie felt otherwise. "I'm going to take my things up." *And regroup.* Ross was a nice guy, and he'd just made it clear to everyone that she needed to find some Roundup and douse the crazy weeded fantasy that had taken root in her head.

"You rest if ye need," Grace said, leading Sadie to believe that Deydie, or Ross, had told her about her CKD. Or had Dand filled everyone in on that, too? "Dinner will be in thirty minutes."

"Thanks." Sadie hurried from the room.

Upstairs, she focused on hanging up her clothes in the tiny closet and not replaying the earnestness of Ross's face while he was talking to his nephew.

There was a knock on the door. "Sadie. Let me in."

"I'm lying down," she lied as she hung up her new slacks.

The door opened and Ross came in, closing it behind him. "Lying down?"

She didn't need to explain herself to him. She hung the green dress. "What do you want?"

"We need to talk about tonight."

"Yes. I'm going to find you a woman." Though it would kill her. "I'm looking forward to it."

"I need ye to do something for me."

"What?"

"Put the green dress on and I'll show you."

The magic of the green dress was gone, complete history. She couldn't feel pretty in it now, even if she wanted to.

"Humor me," he said.

She didn't budge. She wasn't dressing up for him. Her drab brown dress was fine.

"If ye won't do it for me, then do it for Mum. She'll expect you to be dressed nicely for dinner. It's what they do here in Glasgow. I'll step out." He walked to the door and opened it. "But I'll only give you a minute. That's sixty seconds. One, two, three . . ." He gave her a look that said if she didn't do as he bid, he'd change her clothes for her. And not in a sexy way.

Ross left. Begrudgingly, she pulled the green dress from the hanger and donned it within the allotted minute.

She thought he would just walk back in because apparently here in Scotland they didn't believe in privacy.

But he surprised her when he quietly tapped. "Ye ready?"

She pulled the door open. "Happy?"

"Not yet." He stepped in. "Stop looking at me like I'm the enemy. I'm here to help."

"Help with what?"

He cleared his throat and shifted from foot to foot. "I figured while I was finding someone to date, that you could practice picking up blokes."

"What?" A million thoughts tumbled through her brain. "Why?"

He shoved his hands in his pockets and glanced back at the door. "You were the one who said ye didn't have much experience."

Good. At least he had the decency to be embarrassed.

"What are you suggesting, then?"

"I thought I could give ye a few pointers so you could

chat up a man or two at the pub. Give ye some practice." He frowned, but went on. "So when ye go back home, you would be more comfortable with it."

But she knew what he really meant. That if she was to get a man, she'd have to learn to use her womanly wiles . . . because she had no physical assets to work with. She was hurt and angry, but in the end, she couldn't argue with his logic.

"What do you propose? I learn to throw myself at men?"

He glared at her. "*Gawd*, no! But ye could put out a little bait and then lure them in."

"*Put out?*"

"That's not what I mean. Come here," he rumbled.

She stayed where she was. "Why?"

"I want to show ye how to walk." He reached out and took her hand. "Come." He pulled her to him.

She brushed up against his chest, but stepped away quickly. "I'm fine the way I am."

"I agree," he said. "But I'm not the one ye're trying to catch. Besides, all of us could use a little help now and then. Ye're going to help me tonight, right? So I'm going to help ye now."

"Fine. Then show me how this seductive walk should look." She reached for her purse. "Wait. Let me get my phone so I can videotape this for your brothers."

"Funny. All I'm asking for ye to do is to sway yere hips a little as you sashay across the floor."

"Show me." She dropped her purse.

Ross awkwardly strutted across the room. It was hilarious to see him try to be feminine.

"Now it's yere turn."

She shook her head.

He took a step toward her.

"Fine." She marched across the small room instead of demonstrating the sexy walk he wanted.

"No." He came up behind her, placing his hands on her hips. "Like this." He moved them side to side.

She went hot and at the same time became covered in honest-to-God chills. Warmth spread low in her abdomen. It was hard to catch her breath.

But she did. "Stop that. I can do it."

"Then go on."

She glanced over her shoulder to glare at him, but finally did as he said, swaying her hips as if she was walking a runway. "Are you happy?"

He looked perplexed. "I guess it's okay."

"Now can we go down to dinner?"

"It's not ready yet." He stepped away from her, looking irritated. "Go stand over there."

She needed space from him, too, so she perched herself by the window.

He scanned her from top to bottom, and didn't look pleased with what he found. She wanted to yell at him that he was the one who'd picked out the dress!

"You know how to flirt?" he said roughly.

"Of course, I know how to flirt." The truth was that she never felt like doing it though. The men she met didn't seem worth the effort.

"Well, do you know other stuff?" he said painfully.

She turned away and put her hand up. Oh, God, if he was asking about her sex life, it was none of his business.

"Not that," he said. "I mean, do ye know that ye're supposed to ignore men and act aloof?"

She planted her hand on her hip—*where he was touching her only moments ago*—and abruptly dropped it to her side. "Is that the kind of thing you like? You're only interested in a woman if she's playing games?"

"Nay," he said heatedly. "Other blokes go for it. I like a woman who is honest, straightforward, true." But that declaration seemed only to put him more on edge, because he sounded almost angry.

She couldn't figure him out. He was all over the place.

"I'll probably have to teach ye how to kiss, too." He looked troubled by the prospect, maybe even uncomfortable mentioning it.

"Get out, Ross."

He took her arm, but it was as if just touching her made the anger fade, and in its place was warmth. "I'm concerned." He cleared his throat. "That if ye get the chance to kiss a bloke tonight—or back home—that, um, that ye, um, might not know what to do."

"What?" But she was distracted because he was rubbing her arm with his large hand, as if she might be cold.

He paused for two more caresses. "I don't want ye to be uncomfortable, Sadie."

God, she loved it when he said her name. It hit her deep. His voice was as rich as chocolate mousse.

But did he think that she'd never been kissed? "I've kissed people," she said defensively.

"Yere gran doesn't count," he said.

Was he serious? Sure, she might be plain, but she did have some experience.

He dropped his hand, looking superior—the older, wiser one.

Either he thinks I haven't kissed a man, or that I'm no good at it. Suddenly, she had a wicked idea. *If he's willing to go there, then I'll let him show me how it's done.*

"Fine," she said. "What do you propose?"

He stepped closer. "I could give ye a kissing lesson, if ye'll let me."

Chapter Eight

"**D**o your worst." Sadie leaned in, closed her eyes, and waited for the Highlander. But the kiss didn't come. She opened her eyes.

He hadn't budged. He *tsked* with that superior gloat still plastered on his face. "That's not how it's done." He gave her a patient look, as if she would be lost if it weren't for him.

She mimicked his deep brogue. "What do ye mean, *That's not how it's done?*"

He raised a chiding brow at her. "If ye really want to knock a man for a loop, eye contact is yere best bet."

"Kiss with my eyes open?" She'd never kissed anyone that way. And in the movies, they certainly didn't stare at each other during lip-locks either.

"Nay. But look the fellow in the eye before the kiss. Take his measure. Make sure he's worthy of the kiss. And if he is, then ye can deliver a message to him."

"What kind of message?"

He shrugged good-naturedly. "Tell him with yere eyes why ye're going to do it. Are ye making a promise to be his and his only? Or are ye taking pity on the poor bastard that no one else will kiss him? Or are ye bored, with nothing else to do? There are a thousand things one can say with the eyes."

"Oh?"

"Kissing is all about *intent*."

And Ross's intent was simply to teach her *how to do it right*.

"Okay," she said like a good student. "I'm ready to try again."

He stepped forward.

She gazed into his blue eyes. They were beautiful, soulful, and yes, wise. But they held a hint of playful mischief. His eyes . . . caused her insides to go crazy. Uncomfortable with anticipation.

Then he discombobulated her further by cupping her face tenderly as she fell under his spell.

And holy crap, he was right. She could see so much. Though the things she read in his eyes, she couldn't believe, not even for a millisecond. She saw promise written there. She could see this moment, she could see tomorrow, she could see the rest of her life. It was deep, rich, and everlasting. It all hung in the balance, now and forever, locked in their gaze.

She knew Ross was wielding his charm, and she shouldn't fall for it. But she caved as easily as a cream puff, wanting his lips on her so badly that it hurt.

"Uncle," she whispered as she leaned in, keeping her eyes open. His pupils dilated as if he was surprised by her bravery. At the last second, when their lips met, his eyes, her eyes, drifted shut.

She kissed him. Tenderly at first, hesitantly . . . acting as if she didn't know exactly what she was doing. But she did. She was a good kisser. She just wouldn't pull everything from her arsenal at once, because she wanted to *teach him* a lesson.

Okay, that wasn't necessarily it either. She'd wanted to kiss him from the first moment she saw him sitting at the bar. She shifted a little, nibbling at the corner of his mouth, which seemed to drive him half crazy. His right hand left her cheek; he wrapped his arm around her waist and pulled her in tight, his left hand still cupping her face. She rubbed circles into his shirtfront as she kissed him full-on. He opened his mouth to say something, but she took the opportunity to deepen the kiss. He growled approvingly, as if her tongue in his mouth was the biggest turn-on he'd ever had, and he squeezed her tighter.

And he kissed her just as deeply back . . . *damn him*. Her focus evaporated and the kiss took on a life of its own. No longer could she think clearly. She was in the moment with him. Savoring it. Savoring him. She clutched at his shirt, pulling him closer.

She was just settling in for the long haul when he broke it off, breathing heavily.

Their faces were only inches apart. She brought her eyes up to meet his. "Well? How did I do?" Her voice sounded strange, as if it belonged to someone else, perhaps a sexy movie star.

His eyes narrowed as if he was trying to figure her out. But then he seemed to change tactics and a hint of new mischief began to grow in his gaze. He tilted his head as if mulling over her question. Finally, he spoke. "It was a good start . . ."

"But?" she asked.

"I think ye're going to need more practice."

He didn't wait to hear what she had to say. He dove in and captured her lips. He must've forgotten he was supposed to stare deeply into her eyes. Or maybe his lips were impatient. Either way, this time he was showing her what it was like when he was in complete control. She whimpered with the utter joy of it, winding her arms around his neck, pulling him down to her. She could've died a happy woman at that moment, knowing what it was truly like to be kissed with passion.

Rap, rap, rap. It took a second to seep in, but they both jumped apart at the same moment a young voice filtered through the hardwood door.

"Uncle Ross? Aunt Sadie? Nan says it's time to come down to tea." He pounded again. "What's going on in there?"

Ross ran the back of his hand over his mouth as if wiping Sadie's kiss away. He opened the door. "Shhh, Dand."

"It's okay," the boy said. "Aunt Glynnis is downstairs." He stopped talking and stared at Sadie. "Are ye all right?"

She caught sight of herself in the small square mirror on the wall. She was as red as her dress was green. Her eyes were bright, expectant. And her lips swollen. She caught her tingling bottom lip in her teeth. But then noticed Ross was staring at her mouth, so she stopped. "I'm fine, Dand." She didn't look back at Ross, but followed Dand out the door.

So that was that. She'd kissed the great, big, gorgeous Scot. She'd had her fun. She'd played with fire. But now she felt burned. There was always a price to pay. And in this case, it was reality—Ross wiping her kiss away as if it was an unwanted drip of gravy. She couldn't help but replay it over and over as she walked downstairs to dinner.

She hadn't seen the future in his eyes. It was only a mirage. And she wasn't some sex goddess tempting the beautiful Highlander. She was plain, old Sadie Middleton.

But plain, old Sadie Middleton had been kissed. Thoroughly. Completely. And was now changed because of it.

Ross stood alone in Sadie's room and ran a hand through his hair. He needed a minute to calm down. The lass had taken him off guard, completely knocked him for a loop, and nearly brought him to his knees. Either he was one hell of a teacher or Sadie was a fast learner.

He smiled. Or she'd pulled one over on him.

"First Mate!" Dand shouted from the bottom of the steps. "Nan says, 'Now!'"

Ross glanced about the empty room. Sadie's brown dress lay crumpled on the bed. He picked it up. "I should make her put this flour sack back on before I take her out tonight."

But they weren't going on a date! He was finally free of being promised to Pippa. Attached to no one. This was his time to cast his line in new waters, enjoy his freedom. He wouldn't do it forever, maybe for the next five or six years, and then he would settle down and have a family.

He exhaled. But Sadie's kiss seemed to have peppered holes in his plan. He wanted to bring her back up here and kiss her again. To see if it had really been, well, *all that*.

Instead, he screwed his head on straight and trudged down the stairs to dinner. All through the meal, Sadie wouldn't look in his direction. His mother, though, was doing enough looking for the both of them. She wouldn't stop gazing from him to Sadie, then back to him again. For once, Ross was thrilled that Dand wouldn't hush because he kept the conversation rolling.

As Dand and dinner wound down, Ross shifted toward his mother. "Is it my turn to do the dishes?"

Mum gave him a knowing smile. "Nay. Dand and I have the kitchen."

"Aw, Nan," Dand complained.

His mother ignored the kid. "Ye and Sadie better get along on yere date."

The lass who had been quiet all through dinner came to life. "We're not going on a date!" She looked scandalized.

What, wasn't he good enough for her? But he came to his senses and backed her up. "Not a date, Mum. Sadie wants to do a little research."

"Research? Really?" His mother wasn't buying it.

"She's wanting to experience the nightlife here in Scotland."

Dand popped up and ran for the shelf where the board games were stashed. "Then ye can stay here with us, First Mate. Aunt Sadie can do her research all on her own."

The boy had a lot to learn. "Sorry, Dand. A good Scottish man protects the womenfolk. You remember that." He turned to his mother. "We'll clear the dishes first. Come on, rat. Ye'll help."

Sadie picked up two serving dishes. His nephew grabbed

several plates. The three of them went through to the kitchen. She put her things down and hurried back to the dining room, leaving the two of them alone.

Dand clanked his plates on the counter and turned to him. "Are ye sure ye don't love Aunt Sadie?"

"What?" What had gotten into this kid? "Why would ye say that?"

Dand scratched his head like John did when he was pondering a tough puzzle. "Ye two are acting funny. Aunt Kit says that's a sign that two people might be a good match."

Gawd. Dand had become a strange sponge, soaking up all the wrong things. "Go get more dishes." Ross would have to speak with both Maggie and Kit about what they said around the boy.

Ross remained in the kitchen and started the tap, soaking the dishes for his mother.

The wise thing to do this evening was to *not* go out with Sadie. But he quickly nixed the idea of staying in. The way his mother was looking at him, she'd have him and Sadie engaged before the kitchen was cleaned. Mum was completely off base. Glynnis and Dand, too.

Sadie returned with the last of the dishes.

"Are ye ready to get out of here?" he said.

She nodded.

He dried his hands. "I'll tell Mum and Aunt Glynnis that we're going. Ye might want to run up and grab your new sweater."

She nodded her head, still not making eye contact. Was this how the rest of his stay in Glasgow was going to be?

After only a mild interrogation from Glynnis and

Mum, he met Sadie at the front door, and grabbed the extra key from the hook. He looked down at her shoes. "Are those comfortable?"

She stuck out one slender foot, accentuating the delicate line of her legs, and the flats she wore. "Will I be dancing?"

He was glad she was back to speaking to him. And for a brief second, he wondered what it would be like to hold her in his arms and move to the music. He started to answer, *maybe*, but decided better of it. "We're walking to the pub."

She nodded, glancing away, apparently back to the silent treatment.

He held the door open and pointed as she sailed through at a fast clip. "It's this way."

The evening was cooling off, kind of like how things had cooled between him and Sadie. They were going to have to clear the air. They couldn't spend the whole evening not speaking to each other.

"Hold up." He lengthened his stride to catch her. When he did, he gently pulled her to a stop.

She looked down at his hand and he dropped it.

"We need to talk about what happened in the bedroom." But his words sounded too intimate. "Hell. That came out all wrong."

The look she shot him made him even more uncomfortable. He was like a bug she'd pinned to a board. Her gaze was cutting. But the longer she looked at him, the more her indignation turned to hurt, the place between her eyebrows cinching together.

"You may want to talk about it, but I don't." She took off walking again.

Well, hell, that went smoothly. He watched as her hips swung side to side. What made him think he could improve upon her walk? And that shade of green in her dress brought out the color of her eyes. Though he couldn't see her eyes because she was halfway down the street by now.

He hollered to her. "I was just going to say that there couldn't be a repeat."

She slowed for a second.

He half jogged to catch up to her. "I said, we can't do that again. Did ye hear me?"

Sweet Sadie turned into the head stinger in a riled hornet's nest. She was red in the face, her eyes glistening with anger, and if she'd been a man, he would've been preparing himself to block the punch that was getting ready to coldcock him.

"I heard you," she ground out. "Can you stop talking so we can get to the pub and find you a woman?"

Her words, though not a fist, had the same effect as a punch to the face.

"Perfect." He was feeling a little riled, too, and he wasn't exactly sure why.

They finished the rest of the walk in heated silence. The pub was loud with voices and the one-man band who was playing his guitar and singing. Sadie seemed not to notice the musician or the crowd. She appeared to be on a mission, her eyes scanning the room the moment she stepped indoors.

She nodded in the direction of the bar where a tall strawberry blonde sat, nursing an ale among the noise. "What about that one?" she said in a raised voice.

He bent down to hear her, and rolled his eyes when

he figured out what she'd said. "Can we at least get a drink before the hunt begins? I'm thirsty. What about you?"

But the lass was a little like Deydie; when she latched on to an idea, she wouldn't give it up. "That one won't be alone for long. You should grab the opportunity. Before someone else does."

Ross gave the woman a second glance. She was very attractive, but he wasn't interested. Not his type. "She reminds me too much of Pippa."

Sadie gave an exaggerated sigh, tugged on his arm, and then went on tiptoe to speak in his ear. "Well, give me your list of requirements so I'll know what to look for."

But it wasn't her words that made his brain pause. Was she blowing on his neck to drive him crazy? Nay. But to have her so close . . . He shook his head to brush off the sensation. He focused on answering her. "Requirements? It's easy. You saw Pippa. I want the opposite of her." And that disturbing thought hit him again. *Sadie is the opposite of Pippa, every last inch of her.*

"I'll work on it. But you have to go over and practice on her, while I round up a few women." She pushed him in that direction.

He wasn't used to being pushed around, or told what to do. He didn't budge.

She stuck out her hip, propping a hand there. "Why are you being so obstinate?"

"I can scout out my own *birds*. And while I do, ye go practice yere dating skills with those blokes over there." Ross scrutinized them. They looked out of their element, perhaps American themselves, the three of them. Maybe on holiday from university. No harm in her speaking with them. "Give me a little space to work my magic," he said, trying to lighten the tone between them. He and Sadie were friends, and he needed to start acting like it.

She looked at the men skeptically, probably taking their measure like he had. She gave a little shrug. "We'll meet back up in thirty minutes."

"An hour." He needed a break from her. Perhaps a cold shower and a double whisky, too. He had to eradicate the memory of Sadie kissing him so he could get on to cavorting.

Sadie turned and walked away. And just like that . . . he felt a twinge of loneliness in the crowded pub.

Gawd!

He walked to the bar and ordered that whisky. With drink in hand, he noticed a group of women standing by the bandstand. They weren't watching the musicians, but skimming the room, on the lookout for someone to catch. He'd help them out. He sauntered over, ready to work that magic he'd been bragging about.

But before he said hello, he glanced around to see how Sadie was making out with the Americans. Only she wasn't with them. Ross quickly scanned the room. She was with two large, redheaded twins—Scots, by their kilts. One of them left her for a moment, went to the bar, and brought her back a drink. Ross hoped she hadn't opted for alcohol, for her kidneys' sake.

She took a sip. And as if she knew she was being stared at, she shifted her eyes until they fell on his. Like she was fine and dandy, she lifted her glass to him and raised her eyebrows in some cocky salute.

Ross was cemented to the spot. He heard the women behind him, being loud and obnoxious. Sadie wasn't loud and obnoxious. But she was occupied. Determined, he turned back to the group of women.

He found out they were up from London, city lasses, having a holiday in the *wilds* of Scotland. To him, Glasgow was about as rowdy as Mum's tame house cat. The women wasted no time, pulling him onto the dance floor. Ross took the opportunity to move about so he could catch glimpses of Sadie. She seemed to be holding her own with the two Scots. The women around him were unabashedly vying for his attention, shaking their assets at him like racing flags. But their attempts affected him as much as one of the elderly quilting ladies shaking a hanky in his face. He was bored shitless.

The song changed and the alpha of the females wiggled into his arms for a slow dance. The way she clung to him, he had no choice but to accept her invitation. He was miserable. He looked around for Sadie once more.

This time, though, things were different. He could no longer see her face, her suitors' bodies partially blocking his view. But he could tell that they'd backed her into a corner. And he could see one of the bastards running his hand up and down her arm. Ross came to a complete stop on the dance floor. The redheaded Scots were laughing it up. At the end of the joke, the other one wrapped his tree-stump arm around Sadie and pulled her into his side. Ross caught a glimpse of her face. And he saw red. She was biting her lip, clearly uncomfortable.

"Oy." The bossy woman swatted at Ross's chest. "Why'd you stop dancing?"

He grabbed her arms and set her away from him. "Sorry, lass." He nodded in the direction of Sadie. "Looks like *my cousin's* in a bit of trouble."

He didn't wait to hear her response, but marched over to fix whatever mess his *cousin* had gotten herself into.

But by the time he crossed the floor, Sadie had wiggled out of Beefy's grasp and seemed to be lecturing them. She wore a stern librarian's frown, as if they'd spoken too loud in her book sanctuary. But those two weren't deterred.

"Come on, hen," Beefy cooed, trying to get her back in the corner. "Ellar was only joking aboot ye putting yere hands on our dangling bits."

Ross had heard enough. He grabbed Beefy by the arm, spun him around, and punched him in the nose. Da always said *go for the nose if ye're serious about taking a man down*. It worked. But Ellar retaliated with a left hook to Ross's eye. And then a punch to the gut. Apparently, the twins had more relatives in attendance, because a group of men put down their drinks and rushed toward him.

Ross didn't wait to see if they wanted to discuss the weather. He grabbed Sadie's hand and ran. Outside, he yanked the rubbish bin in front of the door and turned into the alleyway. Five seconds later, the bin crashed and he knew they were coming. He pushed Sadie into one of the many doorways and crushed himself up against her, keeping them both out of sight.

He looked down at her. Her eyes were big, staring back at him. But then she changed, her shock fast turning into indignation. When her mouth opened with the lecture that was sure to come, he didn't hesitate but captured her tongue-lashing with his lips. He kissed her into silence.

It worked. He could tell she was stunned once again. He heard voices in the road outside, but their efforts seemed fruitless. They couldn't see them in their cubby-hole unless they knew where to look, and the bums must've been too lazy, or inebriated, to come into the alleyway and search. The voices began to fade.

Ross kept kissing Sadie, even when he knew the men had given up the hunt. This was much more fun than the pub anyway. When he realized he was growing hard, and pushing into Sadie more for desire's sake than for keeping them hidden, he pulled away. "Sorry. I had no choice."

"I know." She was breathing hard, but frowning. "*There can't be a repeat.* Or so you said." She ducked under his arm, freeing herself. "Does this alleyway lead out? Or do you have a clue?"

The passage curved and he was certain they'd find an outlet at the end. "Aye, it leads out."

She took off, putting space between them, acting as if she knew exactly where she was going. The lass had a habit of running away. And she was intent on getting away from him, which made him even more resolute in pursuing her.

Hmm. Maybe he'd been wrong about *what Sadie did or didn't know about men*. He ran a hand through his hair. He'd wasted his time trying to teach her how to land a bloke. She seemed to know instinctually all on her own. At least where it pertained to him.

Ross chased after her, determined not to put up with the silent treatment again. When he caught up, he pulled her to a stop. "What were you thinking?"

She stared at him with feigned innocence.

"Don't pretend ye don't know what I'm speaking about. Those two back there."

She raised an eyebrow. "I was practicing, as *you* suggested. You should've stayed in Taylor Swift's arms on your side of the pub. I was handling things just fine my own."

"Aye. Fine. Ye were almost forced into handling Ellar's dangling bits." He shivered.

"Quit exaggerating. Didn't you notice that I had worked my way out of it until you turned all Incredible Hulk on me? I'm a big girl. I can take care of myself."

"As I told Dand, it's a man's job to take care of *his* woman." Ross paused. "I meant to say, to take care of *a* woman." His words had bent on him and jabbed him in the gut, a little higher than where Ellar had punched him. "It's what we do. *I do*." He felt agonized. "We're friends, Sadie." He was almost pleading, and he didn't know for what.

Her frustration boiled over and she gave him an impatient eye roll. She shook her head as she looked him up and down, as if she didn't like what she saw. "Unbelievable."

"Let's get you home."

Unfortunately, it was relatively early. Late enough that Dand would be in bed, but not his mother. Ross was thirty years old, but it made no difference to his mum. She would scold him for fighting, and odds were, her tirade would escalate, because he'd been fighting in a public place, *ta boot*. He may be a grown man, but the closer he got to Aunt Glynnis's house, the more his feet dragged.

At the door, he pulled Sadie to a stop. "I'm sorry."

She got a satisfied smile on her face, accepting victory.

"Not for protecting you," he clarified. "But for man-handling ye the way I did."

She looked at him vacantly.

"In the alley."

"Oh." She touched a finger to her lips.

For a second, he relived what they'd done in the al-leyway while he had her pinned to the door. But he needed to be absolutely clear. He wasn't sorry about the kiss. Not in the least. It had been the best part of the evening, rivaling the satisfaction of smashing in Beefy's nose. "No. I'm sorry for crushing ye in the doorway. I shouldn't have been so rough." He never wanted to be rough with her. She might be feisty, but he knew she was breakable. "Are we okay then? Ye're done being angry with me?"

Lightning flashed. Then thunder rumbled.

She gave him her *Sadie smile*—genuine, full of sun-shine.

"We're fine." Her smile dissipated. "But I feel bad. The whole point was to find you someone new. A woman to get Gandiegow off your back. We'll just have to try harder tomorrow night. Okay?"

But Sadie was a nice lass. And the thought of taking her back to the pub and having the likes of Ellar and Beefy pawing her made Ross's blood turn to fire.

No, he would return her to Gandiegow; at least he could trust the men there.

But can I? He thought about everyone he knew. No one seemed right for Sadie. The right man had to be like her: *true, genuine.* And the thought of her going back to the States and dating there didn't seem right either.

He came to a decision. He would talk to Sadie about joining a nunnery. She'd like it there . . . plenty of time to read.

Ross opened the door and they stepped inside.

Mum emerged from the parlor. "Ye're back early."

He watched as his puffy eye registered with his mother. He put his hand up. "Mum—"

But one measly hand wouldn't stop her. Neither would a fleet of battleships. "Ross Alistair Armstrong, ye've been fighting."

He was a man. He was a Scot. At one time she'd understood that boys fought, but now without Da, she seemed to have forgotten that basic fact.

His mum looked outraged, ready for a fight herself. "Did ye take Sadie to the dirty pub? Ye should've taken her someplace nice. And to fight . . . Ross, what were ye thinking?"

Sadie slipped in front of him, touching his mother's arm lightly. "No, Grace. It's all my fault."

He laid a hand on Sadie's shoulder. "It's okay, lass."

She ignored him, keeping her attention on his mother. "It's not what you think. It was me. An accident. I—I elbowed your son in the face."

His mum was no dummy. She looked from the height of Sadie's elbow up to his eye. "Were ye hanging from a ladder when ye did it?"

Sadie laughed nervously, glancing up at Ross.

How is the lass going to get out of this one? Anxious to see, he stood by silently, waiting.

His mother pinned her with a stare. He'd seen this look before when he'd tried to dig himself out of a hole.

Sadie clutched her hands in front of her. "It's like this. Um, I dropped my purse. I didn't even know that I'd dropped it." She nodded her head as if she liked the story that she was spinning. "Ross was a gentleman and bent over to get it. I wasn't watching what I was doing and whacked him in the face when he came up."

Mum returned her attention to him with her lie-detector eyes.

Gawd. He'd have to back up the lass. He hid his swollen knuckles behind his back. "Aye. That's exactly how it happened." As long as Mum didn't see his bruised abdomen, he and Sadie might be in the clear.

But his mother surprised him. A flash of understanding registered across her face, and something puckish played in her eyes.

She wasn't buying one bit of their story, but she wasn't calling them on it either. *Why?*

Mum pointed to the stairs. "Well, Sadie, since ye injured him, ye'll have to tend to the cut above his eye. The first aid kit is in the linen closet."

Ross spun her in the direction of the steps, wanting to get away from his mother's all-knowing gaze. But he made it only a few feet before his mum spoke one last time.

"Sadie, run in the kitchen first, luv. Ross'll need a bag of peas from the freezer for his sore knuckles."

He paused, but then leaned down and spoke to Sadie. "Do as Mum says. I'll retrieve the first aid kit and meet ye upstairs." He turned back to his mother. "'Night."

"Night, Rossy," his mother said. And that was exactly what he felt like, a mischievous lad.

He went upstairs to the loo, found the first aid kit, and

took it back to his room. He could take care of this himself.

A second later, there was a knock at the door. He answered it. Sadie stood there with the bag of peas. "Thanks." He took it from her and started to shut the door.

She blocked it, stepped in, and closed the door behind her. "Put the peas on your hand, while I work on your face."

"I've got it."

"Your mother said I needed to tend to you. I don't think it would be wise to get on the wrong side of her. Do you?"

He agreed. But also, Sadie seemed so determined, he felt as if he really didn't have a choice.

He glanced around, but already knew the only place to sit in the small room was the bed.

As he sat on the comforter, his thoughts drifted toward what beds could be used for, and how good it had felt to have Sadie crushed up against him. But this Nurse Nightingale had only one thing on her mind: seeing to his wounds.

She edged up to him and brushed his hair back from his forehead. He wanted to wrap his arms around her and pull her in close. Maybe nuzzle her perky little breasts through her green dress. They weren't much, but they were perfect on her . . . and enough for him. She leaned closer to get a better look at the cut, and he felt himself overheat.

He told his brain to switch subjects. "Ye didn't have to cover for me with my mum."

"I know." Sadie grabbed an alcohol pad and ripped it open.

"Why did ye do it?"

She wiped at his wound and he winced.

"Sorry. I have to clean the area. Who knows the last time Ellar washed his hands?"

Ross winced again, thinking about Ellar and his dangling bits. He snatched up the first aid kit. "If there's a bottle of alcohol in here, I want ye to pour it in the cut for a good long minute."

She laughed and the sound reminded him of chimes rustling in the wind. She opened another alcohol pad, ran her hand through his hair again, and then scrubbed the cut harder. "To answer your question: I helped you with your mother because you helped me with the twins. We're even."

"I didn't know we were keeping score."

She was leaning over him and he couldn't help himself. He looked down her dress, confirming what he suspected. No bra, only perfect little breasts. He cleared his throat, stared at the chest of drawers across the room, glad the first aid kit was in his lap.

She put her other hand on his shoulder—to either balance herself or to drive him wild—not having a clue what thoughts were rolling and tumbling through his mind. How easy it would be to pull her new dress over her head. He could gaze at her bare body for a couple of hours. And perhaps kiss her perfect breasts for a couple more.

He put his hands on her waist, intent on pushing her away, but suddenly he was in a tug-of-war with himself. *Push her away or crush her to me.*

"Out," he growled, his saner side winning. He shoved her gently, putting breathing space between them.

Standing a foot away, she looked hurt, her eyes asking *why*.

He didn't know.

Why did she have this effect on him? Why had she come to Scotland? Why did he have a damned whisky at the pub? The alcohol had to be the reason for what he was feeling.

"Go! Go read. Go to bed." He didn't care what she did as long as she was gone from him. "I'll see you in the morn."

She looked really upset now, more hurt than if he'd poured alcohol into one of her open wounds. She spun around and stumbled from the room.

"Aw, hell," he said to his aunt Glynnis's wallpaper. Sadie didn't deserve to be treated like that. She was his friend.

He sat there for a long moment as the idea that had been spinning around in his head from nearly the first made him reach for his phone. He needed to do something to make up for his bad behavior . . . because apparently Sadie was *keeping score*.

Ross called Doc MacGregor.

To find out what he would need to do.

And tomorrow, when they arrived back in Gandiegow, Ross was going to hop aboard the family fishing boat, and stay out to sea until either the lass was headed back to America, or until he was needed further.

Doc picked up on the first ring, gave him the information, and promised to set it up. Afterward, Ross was left alone with his thoughts. Sadie's hurt expression gnawed at him.

"Dammit." He couldn't let her think it was something *she did*. Well, it had been something she did. Standing close to him. Looking at him as if he was the admiral of the fleet, making him hard when he shouldn't be.

He needed to clear things up with her—even if he wasn't entirely sure what to say. He certainly couldn't tell her the truth. He left his room and lightly tapped on her door. "Sadie, lass? Are ye decent?"

"Yes," she said quietly on the other side.

"May I enter?"

"That depends."

He ran a hand through his hair and leaned closer to the closed door. "I've come to apologize."

"Then come on in."

He did and stopped short. She was adorable, stretched out on the bed wearing purple plaid pajamas, holding a book in her lap. "What are ye doing?"

"Reading."

He cleared his throat, trying not to laugh. "Really?"

"Yes, really. What's so funny?"

"I dunno," he deadpanned. "Maybe because ye're reading yere book upside down."

Chapter Nine

Sadie flipped her book right side up, making sure to act as if she always read upside down. Besides, what did he expect? She hadn't been able to concentrate since he'd jumped down her throat. She'd barely gotten her book open before he'd walked in. She'd wanted to read, but then she'd lain there thinking about why he was angry. She'd tried to be gentle, but he'd told her to clean his wound well.

She gazed up at him. He was so lovely to look upon, just like Captain Wentworth, the seafaring man in her book. But Ross was real. She had to admit that she'd liked running her fingers through his hair. She should feel bad for taking advantage of him, because she'd run her hand through his hair a second time, because really, when would she ever get a chance like that again? She'd gotten to kiss him repeatedly . . . *three times total!* But who was counting?

This was no time to bask in the revelations of his kiss, though she'd known by looking at him, Ross would be amazing at it. She should just be grateful for all the glorious blessings she'd had today, instead of pondering Ross's sudden mood change.

She pulled the covers up and gazed into his eyes. He was just standing there. Why wasn't he getting on with it? "You wanted to apologize?" she reminded him.

"Aye." He didn't seem to know where to start.

She helped him out. "You growled at me. Remember?" Suddenly it occurred to her that at the time, he really seemed angrier with himself than with her.

He cleared his throat, acting uncomfortable. "Oh, aye, the growling. It's to be expected."

"Why's that?"

"I have a condition." His contrite manner faded away as his eyes filled with merriment.

She'd play along. "What kind of condition?"

"Can't say it aloud. But I'll give ye a hint. It's going to be a full moon in a bit. I couldn't help myself."

"I thought the moon had to be out for that particular condition to take hold?"

He shifted. "Not when ye have it extra bad like me." His confession seemed real. He wasn't playing anymore.

"Oh?"

"I'm sorry, lass." His brogue was thick with emotion.

Unfortunately, her crush on the Highlander grew a bit stronger, and her denial of it weaker.

"Will ye forgive me?"

She looked away, speaking to the quilt that lay over the rocking chair. "Sure. You did it well."

"The apology?" He moved closer.

She cranked her head back to watch him as he came near. "Yes, the apology."

"Scoot over."

He didn't wait for her to move, instead insinuated himself on top of the quilt beside her. "I need to rest for a moment. All this talking has worn me out."

She scooted, but only an inch or two.

Staring straight ahead, he nudged her shoulder as if they were a couple of pals. "I really wasn't angry with ye."

"I know."

He jerked toward her abruptly, staring at her, seeming a little panicked and worried. "How did ye know?"

"Easy," she said. "I didn't do anything wrong." At least she hoped she hadn't. "I just figured it was some leftover testosterone from the fight at the pub. You didn't know what to do with it, so you slung it at me."

He nodded. "Aye. Right. Testosterone." He leaned his shoulder against hers and left it there. "And ye didn't deserve for me to bark at you."

"Growl," she corrected.

"Growl." He rested his head back against the wall and closed his eyes.

For a long moment they were wrapped up in their own silence. She was so comfortable with this man. She could soak him up like warm sunshine or wrap him around her like a quilt. Either way, she wanted him near.

I'd like to kiss him again, the unrealistic part of her whispered. This time she wanted to do it for no other reason than because it felt so good to have his lips on hers.

But he had something else on his mind. "Read to me, lass."

She looked down at the novel in her hands, *Persuasion*. "I'm sure you won't like it."

"It'll be grand. Start right where ye left off." He paused for a second and chuckled, his eyes still shut. "Now that yere book is right side up."

Her cheeks burned, but he couldn't see them. She opened her book and found the place . . . where Captain Wentworth was ready to confess his love for Anne Elliot in a letter. For a moment, Sadie started to go to a different spot in the novel, but it wouldn't hurt Ross Armstrong to hear how it was supposed to be done. She had a feeling he knew perfectly well how to woo a woman, but he probably had no idea how to seal the deal. And this was something that a devoted Highlander like him would have to learn. After all, the two of them would be heading out again tomorrow night, hopefully to a different pub, so they could find him a woman. His shoulder was warm against hers, but she felt sad. And Sadie was certain that one day soon, Ross Armstrong would make someone a happy lass indeed. Not her, of course.

The thought unsettled her.

"Go on," he rumbled.

Maybe she shouldn't educate him on how to do it right. "How about I find a nice fishing magazine to read to you?"

She started to rise, but he stilled her with his hand.

Sadie sighed, maybe a little too dramatically. "It's the climax of the book. We should start at the beginning."

"Nay. Read to me where ye're at."

She looked down at the page, but knew the passage by heart. "This is a letter written by Captain Wentworth. He's ignored, or tried to ignore his ex-fiancée for most of the book."

"All right."

She cleared her throat and started. *"I can listen no longer in silence. I must speak to you by such means as are within my reach."* She stopped reading. "I love the old way of speaking. Don't you think it sounds rich?"

Ross chuckled. "I think ye're hedging."

She glanced at the page again. Well, he asked for it. She got on with it, the words that burned through her, that gave her a longing that would never be satisfied. *"You pierce my soul. I am half agony, half hope. Tell me that I'm not too late, that such precious feelings are gone forever. I offer myself to you—"*

Ross put his hand over the book, halting the words.

She looked up at him. He seemed to be working hard not to have a repeat of his werewolf moment from earlier.

"Enough," he said calmly. He scooted from the bed.

She wanted to follow him. But she pinned him with accusation instead. "You were the one who wanted me to read."

"Aye. But ye need yere rest." He looked at her with kind eyes, but she could see the fire behind them. Or more likely, she was imagining fire and passion. Jane Austen had a way of evoking wishful thinking . . . and poor eyesight.

She chewed her lip, wanting more from him. But he'd already given her more than a plain girl like her should ever expect.

He walked to her door.

"Good night, Ross." She was shocked by how husky her voice sounded.

"Good night, Sadie." He pulled the door open, but stopped and spun on her. "Tomorrow, when we're at the bookstore . . . we should do some shopping for you. Ye need new books."

"I have plenty. And my e-reader is full."

He pointed to the book on the bed. "Ye need something besides that." He acted as though *Persuasion* should be banned.

"What kind of books do you suggest?"

He scratched his head in a show of thinking hard. "How about a murder mystery? Or science fiction? Or a book on how to hang curtain rods?"

"Romance not your thing?" she said boldly.

"Aye," he admitted, "for a single man like myself. I'm not interested in happily ever after." He didn't let her say more. He walked out and shut the door behind him as if he meant it.

Well, that was perfectly clear. And Sadie better get her head out of the clouds. Wishing for things that could never be was crazy thinking. She was a practical girl. Except when it came to the books that carried her away.

And maybe when she looked into Ross's blue eyes.

She picked up the novel, but couldn't stomach any more of Anne Elliot and Captain Wentworth's happy resolution. Perhaps it was time to give up on Jane Austen altogether and move on to more realistic books. Jane Austen made the real world unbearable, because who truly found their Mr. Darcy, Colonel Brandon, or Edmund in the end?

She laid *Persuasion* on the nightstand, turned out the light, and sank under the quilt. But when she closed her eyes, she could feel Ross pushed up against her in the alleyway. She could feel his lips on her. And as if she was writing her own fairy tale, she gave way to her fantasy of what it would be like to be Ross's woman. To make love to him. She knew it would be wonderful. And she envied the woman he would find at the pub tomorrow night. She envied his future wife, too. And though she had squelched these feelings in childhood, she looked up at heaven.

"Why couldn't you have made me pretty?" she whispered. She sighed heavily and threw off her covers as the next thought hit her. She knew God did things for a reason, but it just felt a little as though He was picking on her. It was bad enough that she'd never be able to win the heart of a man like Ross, but then to stick her with bum kidneys felt like overkill.

She'd been down this path many times since her diagnosis; it never was productive. She closed her eyes and thought about the view of the ocean from her rock. How it made her feel as if anything was possible, and how tomorrow was a good time to put her feet back on the ground.

Sadie slept hard. She woke to sunlight coming through the curtains, washing over her face. She glanced at her phone . . . ten o'clock! She couldn't believe she'd stayed in bed so long. She grabbed her toiletry bag and headed for the bathroom.

On the way, she saw Ross's door was closed, too. Was he still asleep? She heard Dand downstairs, talking fast.

Sadie went in the bathroom, cleaned up for the day, and donned her other new dress. She grabbed her pill bag and headed for the steps. Before leaving North Carolina, Oliver had made sure everything was sorted and in her bag. She was grateful now that he'd taken care of that detail. She'd been too distraught over Gigi to remember.

Downstairs, she found Grace and Dand at the kitchen table, playing cards.

Grace glanced up and smiled. "Good morn, Sadie. Sit. I'll get yere breakfast."

Sadie put her hands up, making her pill bag rattle like a maraca. "No. I can take care of it myself."

Grace went to the stove. "I know ye can." She grabbed a plate and filled it from a covered cast iron skillet. "Ye're going to love this breakfast casserole. It's my daughter-in-law Kit's recipe."

Kit was one of the people trying to set Ross up. But Sadie didn't say that to Grace.

Dand popped up and pulled out a chair. "Will ye read to me today, Aunt Sadie?"

"Give the lass a minute to get her bearings," Grace said.

Sadie smiled down at the boy as he beamed up at her. "I will do my best to make time." She ruffled his hair. "Okay?"

He guided her over to the chair, but she still didn't sit. She couldn't stand it anymore. She had to know. "Ross sleeping in this morning?"

Grace laughed. "Heavens, no. He was up early. When I got out of bed, I found him visiting with Glynnis in her room."

Sadie glanced around.

Grace was too observant. "He's running an errand."

Sadie's eyebrows rose as she waited for more information.

"He didn't say where he was going. Only that he'd be back." Grace pulled down a mug. "Will tea work?"

She hesitated. "Yes. Tea's fine." Sadie had the sneaking suspicion that someone had filled Grace in on her CKD. Ross didn't seem the type to divulge her medical history to anyone. But it was clear that he and his mother were very close . . .

Dand brought the sugar bowl over and plopped it on the table in front of Sadie's chair, only spilling a little. "Nan doesn't let me have more than a spoonful, but ye can have as much as ye like in yere tea."

Sadie shook her head. "No. I'll take mine plain. I have to watch my sugar intake."

Grace paused halfway to the table with Sadie's plate still in her hand. "Oh. There's no sugar in the breakfast casserole, but I should've asked first if it would be all right."

Sadie sagged a little. "So Ross did tell you? That I have chronic kidney disease?"

Grace stopped short. "No. But ye just did." She gave her a kind smile. "Sit and tell me what that is."

Sadie dropped into her chair. She didn't like talking about it, but her doctors said it was important to communicate with everyone she knew, to educate them. Kidney disease didn't get the attention, or funding, that it deserved.

"Chronic kidney disease or CKD means my kidneys are gradually losing their functionality." She told her the rest, about how she would eventually need a kidney transplant, about what she was doing to take care of herself, but not how alone she felt. Or her worry over who was going to take care of her when she did need to have the surgery. She did share with her a little about Oliver and how he'd brought her to Scotland.

Sadie was prepared to clam up as soon as she saw the pitying look, the one everyone gave her when they found out about her kidney disease. But Ross's mother surprised her.

"'Tis a shame, but we all have our burdens to bear," she said matter-of-factly. "Glynnis has had MS for years. And things haven't been easy for me since my husband died. But we persevere, as will you; I'm certain of that. Love and community get us through."

What happens, though, when you don't have either?

But Sadie felt a little better. Grace had put things into perspective.

Sadie laid a hand on her arm. Ross's dad was gone, and it never occurred to her what Grace might be going through, how she must miss him. "I'm so very sorry for your loss. I can't imagine."

Grace smiled at her stoically. "There's only one constant in this world: *change*. And there's no shortage of sorrow. But we get through, one day at a time."

Tired of the conversation, Dand ran off to play in the backyard. Sadie hoped they would move on to much lighter subjects, but Grace was a prospector, tunneling in, searching for the mother lode.

"So what is it that ye do, Sadie Middleton? Besides read to my grandson and act as traveling companion for my favorite middle son?" She laughed at her own joke.

Sadie sighed, not wanting to even say the words. "I'm a dental hygienist."

"But?" Grace prompted.

"It's not my calling," she admitted.

"I see." Grace was astute and understood so much with few words. "And the brother ye told me about?"

"Oliver," Sadie said.

"Aye, Oliver. How does he feel about ye being a dental hygienist?"

Sadie laughed derisively. "He *loves* the idea." Since he and Gigi had been the ones to cook it up while sitting at the kitchen table. *While Sadie sat by silently.* She was only now understanding how important it was that she stand up to her family and be truthful. Gigi would still be alive if she had.

Grace gazed at her patiently, as if she knew Sadie was working things out.

She felt such a kinship to Ross's mother, who was so warm and easy to talk to. She found herself telling her all about Oliver's overprotectiveness, and how suffocating his hovering was. Grace nodded empathetically, as if she'd seen this kind of thing before.

Finally, Grace leaned forward and said, "So tell me this, must ye be a dental hygienist to make a living? Or do you have the freedom to change professions?"

Sadie had thought this through before; she could get a job at the university while she worked on her library science degree. Gigi and Oliver were her only obstacles. And now Gigi was gone.

"I'm still working that out," Sadie finally answered.

"This has been a good chat." Grace stood. "Come. Let's corral Dand and take a walk. That's enough grilling for now, don't ye think?"

Sadie smiled. She really, really *liked* Grace. Ross was lucky to have such a woman as this for his mother.

Grace opened the back door. "Dand, let's take a walk, luv."

The three of them put on light jackets and made their way down the street. Sadie and Grace stopped and admired the gardens while Dand collected rocks and jumped in mud puddles.

When they returned to the house, Ross was there.

Sadie wondered where Ross had been, but she didn't ask.

Apparently, he had no such compunction. "Where have ye been?" He looked at his watch. "We've a lot to do today."

Grace shot her son a stern warning with her green eyes. "We were taking a walk and smelling the roses, getting to know each other. She's lovely, Ross."

He nodded toward her as if she was no more than a statue. "Aye. But Deydie called me on my mobile and needs us to pick up some fabric for Father Andrew and Moira's wedding reception. Something about tablecloths." He made the task sound distasteful.

"I see," Grace said. "Then ye better not dawdle. Who is marrying them anyway?"

"Doc MacGregor's da. He'll be coming up from Edinburgh to do it."

Grace turned to Sadie. "Ye best grab yere purse and get on with it. When Deydie calls, we all jump to attention . . . even here in Glasgow."

Sadie did as she was told and was in the truck before Ross or Grace had to tell her twice.

But at the bookstore, Ross patiently let her browse. Sadie had drawn up a preliminary list, but she found that once she was surrounded by books, she lost all track of time. Ross gave her room and space to wander the aisles. Every once in a while, he would appear and switch out her full basket for an empty one. The third time he ambled up beside her and retrieved her full basket, he asked, "How are you doing, lass? Can we break for some food?"

"Yes, we're done here," she said. She followed his glance down at her basket. "Oh, these romantic novels aren't for Quilting Central; they're for *your* edification."

"Verra funny, lass."

After the books were bought and stored in the large plastic containers in the back of the truck, they walked to a small café for lunch, then hurried on to the fabric shop. But when they arrived, the clerk was clearly agitated.

"But I told the woman on the phone that we were out of that particular lace."

That sounded like Deydie.

"Sadie, ye'll just have to choose. Deydie said if they didn't have it, then you should pick out something else."

"Why me?"

He raised his eyebrows. "Do I look like I know about such things? Now if we were talking about fishing line and bait, I'd be yere man. But I know Moira. She'll be fine with anything ye choose."

"Do you have Moira's number so I can check with her?"

He frowned. "I wouldn't give it to ye even if I did. I'm sure the town fussing over her is stressing her out enough as it is. Ye met her. She wouldn't want the attention. I think that's why Deydie left it up to you."

Sadie was still hesitant. "Let me call Deydie, then."

Ross laid a hand on her arm and—suddenly she was

suffused with warmth. Oh, she knew she was reading more into his touch than was really there, but she relished it, like the first bite of a fresh-from-the-oven apple pie. *With ice cream on top.* She even closed her eyes and soaked in the feeling.

"Are ye okay?" Ross asked. "Have we overtaxed ye?"

Yes. He'd overtaxed her senses.

She opened her eyes, embarrassed. "I'm good."

He was right. She was making too much of everything. These were little decisions.

"Just think of what you would want for yere own wedding."

"I would hate a big wedding," she admitted. "All the flowers and fuss." She'd want nothing more than her vows and the man she loved standing beside her, claiming her for all time. *Yeah, I've read too many romance novels.*

"If I were to get married, I'd probably elope." Although suddenly an outdoor wedding sounded nice. An image came into her head—of her rock by the ocean, where she'd spent her first evening in Scotland with Ross by her side.

But wishful thinking would get her nowhere. She was never going to marry.

Putting her mind firmly to the task, she chose a simple white cotton fabric for the tablecloths and an old-fashioned lace for the overlays.

As Ross loaded it all in the truck, she asked, "Are you looking forward to tonight?"

He cocked his head to the side, clearly confused.

"Did you forget? We're going out again. This time we really are going to find you a woman."

He shook his head. "I want to head back to Gandie-gow tonight." He helped her into the truck and then started it up.

"Are you afraid we'll run into another set of twins and you'll get into another fight?"

He glanced over at her seriously. "Aye."

"Ross, your mother said it was the 'dirty pub'." She laughed. "Surely not all the pubs in Glasgow are like that."

He gave her a pointed look. "It's not the pubs I'm worried about."

She held up her hand. "I solemnly promise to stay away from the likes of the twins."

"That's not it either." Ross took her hand and lowered it. "I think it's best to get you back."

She had the feeling he wanted to be rid of her. Well, they'd spent a lot of time together since she'd arrived in Scotland, and he was probably sick of her company.

She had to save face. "Yes. I think we better head back too, if I'm to get the library at least marginally set up before I go home to North Carolina."

"Ye're leaving tonight?" Grace asked, studying these two closely.

Ross opened his mouth, but she had more to say.

"That's a long trip to make this late. I'll worry."

Ross looked abashed at her guilt trip. "I—"

"It's me," Sadie said. Grace had the lass's number; she could tell she was going to save Ross once again. "I'm the one who wants to get back. After all the books I bought today, I'm afraid I won't have time to make any headway on getting things set up before I fly home."

Grace changed tack, because she'd just had an idea.

"I understand. Aye. Ye have to get back tonight. Just promise me that ye'll be safe. And if ye get tired, Ross, that you'll stop and rest."

Ross kissed her on the cheek. "I promise, Mum."

Grace sighed heavily. At least Sadie looked happy while reading to Dand before dinner. But something had happened with these two—Ross and Sadie—while they'd been out. She had a feeling it had to do with that crazy and misguided arranged marriage her husband had dreamt up long ago. She was worried about her son, not because he was heartbroken, but because he'd been burned by being tied down to everyone else's dream for him. Grace's hope of seeing her middle son happy was fading.

After they ate, Ross took up his plate and said, "I'll help with the dishes and then we need to get on the road."

Sadie had barely touched her food, but she stood, too.

These two were quite the pair. Even though they were clearly at odds, they seemed to back each other up at every turn.

Grace laid her napkin on the table. "Don't worry about the dishes. Dand and I will take care of cleaning up."

"Aw, Nan, I—" Dand complained.

Ross raised an eyebrow, silencing him.

Immediately, Dand shifted gears. "I know, Uncle Ross. I'll be good for Nan and Aunt Glynnis."

Ross nodded to the lad and then turned to the American lass. "Sadie, can you be ready in five minutes?"

"Yes."

Ross instructed Dand what to clear next. Everyone left the dining room except for Grace.

Living here in Glasgow, she'd had no say when Ramsay decided upon his wife. Of course, she adored Kit—Ramsay couldn't have chosen better—and Grace loved her immensely. But it would've been nice to have been involved, even in some small way. It was hard being away from her bairns, though they were grown men now. Maybe she could do something to help Ross. She'd had her one true love, and she wanted that for him, too.

Sadie reappeared with her quilted bag over her shoulder.

Grace rose and pulled her in for a hug. "I'm so glad ye came to visit." What she really wanted to say was that she liked her a lot, that Ross liked her, too, and that she would fit well into the Armstrong family.

Sadie hugged her back. "It was lovely to meet you, too. I had a wonderful time. Thank you for everything."

Dand came running into the room and slammed into them. "Ye were going to leave without saying good-bye?"

"Ye'll get to see her," Grace said. "When I take ye back. Remember, we have to be there for Moira's wedding." She'd met the priest a couple of times and was happy Moira had found the perfect man for her.

Dand dropped his arms. "But Sadie will be gone by then."

Ross walked into the room with his bag, a pillow, and a quilt.

Grace turned to him. "Is that true?"

"Aye." Ross shifted the load in his arms and took Sadie's bag from her. "When did ye say yere flight was?"

"Saturday."

Grace thought she would have more time, that Sadie

would still be in Gandiegow when she went to Moira's wedding. *This isn't good. Not good at all.*

"Can't ye stay longer?" Dand whined.

Sadie shook her head *no*, but then brightened as she smiled down at him. "I almost forgot." She pulled a book from her bag. "I got you something special when I was out today."

Dand took it, but he looked as if he'd rather have Sadie than the book. "Who's going to read to me?"

Grace put her arm about her grandson. "I will."

"We're all going to survive, squirt. Promise." Ross's tone sounded resolute, which wasn't really a comfort. "We've gotta go, Mum."

"I know." Grace pulled him in for a hug. "I love ye, Ross."

"Me, too." He kissed her cheek and let her go. "Is it okay that I borrowed a pillow and a quilt?"

"Ye know it is." He'd probably taken it for the lass in case she got cold and tired. Ross could be a thoughtful man, if thickheaded.

Grace and Dand watched from the doorway as Ross led Sadie to her side of the truck. When she was buckled in, he stowed their things in the back, and got in the driver's side. A minute later, the two of them were gone.

"Nan, can't we do anything to make Aunt Sadie stay?"

Maybe. "Run into the parlor and get a board game set up for us. I have a call to make first."

Dand looked up at her. "To who?"

"Never mind that. Go on now. And see if Aunt Glynnis needs a fresh cup of water. I'll be there in a minute."

Ross was fighting his feelings, and Grace understood

why. For so long, he'd been attached to Pippa, and now he was free. But love had a way of showing up unexpectedly and knocking on your door at the most inopportune times. It had been that way for her and Alistair. She'd been all set to move, a job lined up in London, her dream of living in a big city about to come true. But then Alistair, whom she'd known all her life, had pulled his boat into the dock, and asked her to go for a ride. The rest was history. What a blessing. She was glad she'd answered the door when love knocked. Otherwise, her life wouldn't have been as rich and full.

Grace waited until Dand shut the door before lifting the receiver from the old rotary phone hanging on the wall.

She resolved to have no misgivings about what she was going to do. When she was younger, she resented the meddling old women of Gandiegow for doing what they did best—*meddle*. Grace reassured her nagging conscience that her motives were pure. She was getting involved out of love. She chuckled to herself. If questioned, all the busybodies of Gandiegow would say they did it out of love, too. Thirty-five years ago, she would've never foreseen becoming one of them . . . and aligning herself with the head busybody, Deydie!

But Grace liked Sadie. More important, Ross liked her, too. Without Grace's help, he would be pigheaded and screw it up, and all because Alistair, her beloved husband, and Lachlan, Pippa's father, had insisted that the two children marry one day.

Intervening was the only way to save her son from missing the wonderful life that awaited him. She would be his saving grace.

Deydie picked up. "Hallo."

"It's me, Grace. I'm calling for a favor." She knew she would have to tread lightly with Deydie, as well as her son. "It's about Sadie."

"Did they get the material for the tablecloths?"

"Aye. They're on their way home."

"How is the lass feeling? Did she tell ye she's sick?" Deydie said it as if Sadie's illness was a curse.

But Grace knew better. "Aye. She told me about her illness. She's feeling fine."

Deydie cleared her throat.

Grace knew what that meant. Deydie was ready to let loose with some gossip.

"Did she also tell ye that I found Ross in her bedroom?"

"Nay." Grace didn't know how she felt about that. What mother wanted to know the comings and goings of her grown son's bedmates?

Deydie continued. "But I put a stop to it straightaway. Ross doesn't need a sickly lass. I promise to watch them close. We'll make sure to keep them apart."

Now what was Grace supposed to say? She couldn't come out and tell Deydie the reason for her call if the old woman couldn't see the truth . . . that Sadie might be Ross's one true love. But what could Grace say to Deydie now to make her keep Sadie in town?

"How's her brother?" Grace offered, to buy herself some time.

"Now that one is hearty and hale. And handy. I wouldn't mind having him around permanently. He would make quite the addition to the community."

Now there was an idea! "From what I learned from

Sadie, I expect the best way to keep Oliver in Gandie-gow is to have the lass stay as well. She said he's terribly protective of her."

"Aye. Ye're right. He's a good lad. But what could I do to make the lass want to stay?"

Well, asking Sadie to clean Gandiegow's teeth wasn't the way to go. "How about having her teach at the quilt retreat? Do you have one going on next week?"

"I do, but I don't think the lass will do it willingly. She isn't fond of Quilting Central."

"Hmm." Grace thought fast. "How about if ye tell the lass that one of the teachers had to cancel and ye have no one at all to take her place?"

"But the town is filled with capable stand-ins," Deydie complained.

Grace smiled into the phone. "You know that. And I know that. But Sadie doesn't."

Deydie cackled. "Och, Grace, ye may have lived in Glasgow these past two years, but ye're still a Gandiegow woman at heart."

Grace had to admit it was true. But she would have to be careful with Ross. She couldn't push Sadie on him like Pippa had been forced on him all those years. Grace had only bought her son some time.

Chapter Ten

Ross didn't look at Sadie as he wound the truck through Glasgow. He didn't say anything either. He wasn't happy driving home so late, but he knew it was best. He wanted her out of the city to keep her safe from the Glaswegian men. But he needed to keep her safe from him as well. Hell, he needed to protect himself, too. Her kisses were addicting. The second he arrived home, he was going to put a hundred nautical miles between him and the American lass.

Without letting his eyes leave the road, he adjusted the pillow and quilt between them. "This is for you, in case ye get tired. It's a long way back to Gandiegow." His voice sounded strained.

She didn't say anything.

He glanced over at her. "Are you okay?"

She shrugged.

"Talk to me, Sadie."

"I'm fine."

"Ye're not. Now tell me."

She looked out her window. "But it's stupid."

"What's stupid?"

"I'm going to miss Dand." She paused for a second. "And I really liked your mother."

He'd been warned his whole life about women and their crazy emotions. But this rogue wave that she'd tossed at him seemed real, especially the way she chewed her lip. He kind of felt honored that she would tell him the truth. "Are ye buckled up well?"

She gazed over at him. "Yes. Why?"

"I want ye safe and secure. Lay yere head on the pillow and get some rest." He couldn't do anything about her missing Dand—*and his mother*—but he could heed Doc MacGregor's advice about how to help her: Make sure Sadie doesn't get overly tired.

She didn't move. She just sat there, staring at him.

He patted the pillow. "Come on, lass."

Finally, she did as he asked and laid her head down.

He wanted to comfort her, perhaps caress her arm, but he couldn't. "Are ye warm enough?"

"I'm okay." She had her sweater on so he guessed that she was.

They were finally out of the city and he pointed the truck north, relieved to be on the road home.

He honestly couldn't understand how anyone could live in a city like Glasgow, landlocked as it was. Sure, it had the River Clyde, but it wasn't the same as having the North Sea as his playground. Ross loved seeing his mom, but he missed the ocean. He missed fishing. He was certain that's what was wrong with him. That as soon as he got home and back on the boat, he would feel more like himself. He glanced down at Sadie lying beside him. Aye, his strange feelings really had nothing to do with her at all.

The pillow was a good call. She looked to be sound asleep.

"Sadie?" he said quietly.

She didn't stir.

Poor thing. He laid his arm across her and held on to her . . . in case he had to make a sudden stop or something.

But there was no traffic on the road this late. He used the time to think on his future, about what he was going to do next with his life—new job, new career—but he kept glancing at Sadie and found no real answers. As he drove farther into the Highlands, he felt better and not so worried about his next step.

It was one o'clock in the morn when they came down the steep road leading into Gandiegow. He got out, grabbed the bags from the back, and opened Sadie's side of the truck. She was stirring, but he didn't see any need for her to fully wake. He scooped her into his arms.

"I can walk," she said quietly, almost as if she didn't want to bother the town.

"Nay. I've got ye. Ye're only dreaming anyway." She weighed little more than Dand. It occurred to Ross how fragile she felt. He held her closer. "Sleep now."

She cuddled into him, and he smiled.

At Thistle Glen Lodge, without jostling his load, he maneuvered around to open the door. Soft lights had been left on in the hallway and the kitchen. He walked her to the loo and gave her a little squeeze. "Pit stop." He pulled off her shoes before setting her on her feet.

When Sadie slipped inside, he quietly set her bag down and unzipped it carefully. Her purple plaid pajamas were on top. He pulled them out and tapped at the door.

She cracked it open and looked out.

"Yere night things."

"Thanks." She took them. "Good night, Ross." She stared at him a second longer and then closed the door.

But he didn't budge. The job wasn't done. He was a man who saw things through to the end. He waited for her to come out and enjoyed the shocked surprise on her face.

"I said good night," she whispered.

"Aye." He took the clothes she held in her arms. "Just making sure ye get to bed all right."

"I'm a big girl."

"You? Ye're the size of a mite." And not a girl, but a woman. A woman with a delightful bit of fire in her eyes.

"I never asked you to be my manservant."

"Take advantage of me while ye can."

They both stared at each other under the light in the hallway. He hadn't meant it in a sexual way, but her eyes dilated, and the air between them sparked.

"I didn't mean—"

She put her hand up, cutting him off. "I know."

She stepped in front of him, and when she passed, he stretched out his hand and let the fabric of her pajamas brush his fingertips.

Silently, he followed her into the bedroom, but he didn't have to worry about being too quiet; the snoring in the next room could've woken his mum in Glasgow.

Ross leaned down and spoke in Sadie's ear. "Will ye be able to sleep with this noise?"

She shivered, but surely not because he was standing so close. More likely, she was chilly.

She turned and whispered back. "I have earplugs."

He stilled; her breath on him felt like a butterfly's caress. While he was immobilized, she climbed into bed.

He regained his senses and pulled the quilt up, tucking her in. Everything in him wanted to lean down and kiss her, taste her sweet lips again. But he couldn't. He just couldn't! He'd confused them both enough already. He was way overdue for some distance from this lass. He needed to get out of here.

He turned to leave, but her hand slipped into his. And then she tugged.

It was the bravest thing Sadie had ever done, getting his attention. But she needed to thank Ross for being so kind to her, so gentle, so good. She needed to thank him for taking her to Glasgow to buy books, and for letting her meet his mother. She needed to thank him for being such a good friend to her.

And all the while, she was pretty certain she was lying to herself about all of it.

She pulled him down, his hands landing on either side of her. She was just going to make it a quick thank you kiss. A peck on the cheek.

What she intended, though, was not what she did.

She clutched his shirtfront, stared into his face—registering only his hooded eyes in the moonlit room—and then pulled him to her lips. She was hungry for his kiss, maybe even a little desperate. She angled her mouth over his and kissed him with all she had. He didn't pull away, but adjusted his position, as he sat down beside her. He wrapped her in his arms and kissed her back. He seemed a little desperate, too.

They were a couple of starved creatures, feasting on

each other's mouths. But something changed. He rested his hand on her cheek, and the kiss turned tender. And it was as if the tenderness was the thing that killed it.

He pulled away. "I have to go." His face was so very close to hers.

"I know," she whispered. "It was only a dream."

He let go of her and she scooted under the quilts. She closed her eyes so she didn't have to see him leave.

Quietly, he pulled the door closed behind him.

Yes. It had been a dream. All the time she'd spent with Ross had been just that.

Sleep should've been elusive, but she needed to only pretend that she was back in his truck with his arm tucked protectively around her, and she fell into a deep sleep.

In the morning, Sadie woke before the rest of the quilters. She could've lain there all day, reliving the kiss in this very bed, but instead, she tucked the memory away, knowing she would pull it out often when she was alone in Gigi's house back in North Carolina. She crawled out of bed. She had a lot to accomplish today . . . because tomorrow, she was going home.

It didn't take long to get ready. She liked that she was super low maintenance, which would serve her well when she had her transplant. She had only to shower, comb out her wet hair, and dress. She didn't bother with makeup or curling irons. She was who she was, and that was okay with her.

When she arrived at Quilting Central, she was relieved no one was there . . . *yet.* She went to her corner, prepared to get as much done as quickly as possible before they descended upon her. She knew it would be hard to be around the gray-haired ladies, but Sadie steeled herself for what had to be done. As she scooted furniture to the side to make room for the book nook, she began to envision how the library space should flow. She was so caught up in her own thoughts that when the bell above the door jingled, she jumped.

"It's just me," Ross said in his soothing baritone.

"I thought you would be out with your brother fishing this morning," she said.

He lifted his arms, showing the first two bags of books that she'd bought in Glasgow. "I thought ye might want these first."

The air between them was an awkward mess, and it was all her fault. She shouldn't have kissed him last night. But at the same time, she was glad she had. It was her way of saying good-bye.

"Sadie, I—"

Deydie hustled through the door. "Why are ye two here so early?" she barked.

Ross set the bags next to Sadie and headed for the door. "I'm not really here. I'm just dropping these off, then I'm catching a ride out with Brodie to meet up with John."

Deydie snatched up her broom and blocked him. "Ye're not going anywhere, laddie."

Ross raised an eyebrow as if her broom was nothing more than a twig.

Deydie's broom stayed firm. "Ye promised to make the shelves for the library. And that's what ye're going to do. Today. And if it's help ye need, then get Max or Abraham to assist ye."

He glanced at Sadie, and then looked at Deydie as if

help wasn't the problem. "I already set it up with Brodie. He's waiting for me on his boat. And I've texted John that I'd meet up with him at the fishing grounds."

Deydie jabbed her broom as if holding off a ferocious lion. "Then ye can undo it."

He snarled a little.

Deydie then turned on Sadie. "Why are ye here early, missy? Shouldn't ye be in bed, resting? Ye look like shite."

Ross whipped around in Deydie's direction. "Now, see here—"

Sadie stepped around him. "I needed an early start if I'm to get the library set up before I leave."

Deydie put her broom down and leaned on it. "Ye're not going anywhere either."

Sadie tilted her head to the side, because the old woman had gone batty. "That's what I just said. I'm going to stay here today and work on your library."

As Deydie shook her head, her jowls jiggled. "Nay. Not today. I mean to say, ye're not going anywhere tomorrow." She set her broom against the wall and came to her. "It's all squared away. The next retreat is starting soon." She looked off in the distance, seeming to talk to herself. "And why we thought we could handle another retreat *and* Moira's wedding is beyond me."

"What do you mean, it's all squared away?" Sadie said, trying to get Deydie to make sense.

"We're short a quilt teacher, so ye're going to do it."

Sadie wobbled a little. "What?"

Ross reached for her, but she saw the moment he stopped himself. Instead, he took a step away.

"Ye have plenty of people in this town to teach quilting," he said.

Although the words seemed to be in her defense, Sadie's heart sank. She felt certain he just wanted her gone.

Deydie was shaking her head dramatically. "Nay. The wedding, Ross. Everyone is busy. And Oliver said the lass would be happy to do it."

Oliver again! Well, she wasn't being pushed around by him anymore. "I'm sorry, but my airline ticket is for tomorrow."

"It's all taken care of. Kilts and Quilts made yere reservation in the first place, so I changed it. Ye're here for another week." Deydie held up her hand as if Sadie could actually form any words in protest.

Her throat was too dry.

Deydie pointed to the calendar on the wall. "Before ye say any more, I know the retreat is only for three days, but ye have to stay a wee bit longer. We need all the hands we can get."

"I'm not a quilt teacher," Sadie said quietly. She never planned on quilting again, in fact. She loved it, but couldn't do it. That was her penance for causing her grandmother's death.

Deydie dug in the pocket of her dress and pulled out a folded sheet of paper, which she opened and thrust at Sadie. "Moira designed this using yere quilt block that won the challenge. It's for the retreat goers."

Sure enough, the quilt block that she and Gigi had imagined, and made, was in the center of the quilt, the medallion. Surrounding it was a combination of Rail

Fence blocks set in threes with a Nine Patch block set in between.

"Ye'll teach them how to make yere quilt block. These quilters have enough skill to finish the rest of the blocks and put them together when they get back home." Deydie seemed proud of herself for coming up with this plan.

Sadie straightened to her full sixty-four inches, feeling like a giant for once, next to Deydie. "But I have to get back." She had to leave. She looked over at the number one reason why—Ross. If she stayed, she'd probably get her heart broken. She'd developed a one-sided crush. It was best to get out of town with her heart and dignity intact.

Deydie dug another piece of paper out and handed it over. "And here's the quilt ye're going to make for yereself."

"What?" she protested. "*I'm* not going to make any quilt." But then Sadie looked down at the design, staring at it for a long moment. Once again her quilt block was in the center, but this time, the blocks surrounding the medallion represented a Sampler.

"Oliver mentioned yere gran loved Sampler quilts. With the winning block that the two of ye made, it would make a fine memory quilt." Deydie set a hand on her shoulder as if to steady her for the rest. "This is going to be a beautiful, special quilt. Oliver contacted one of your gran's quilting friends, and she went over to yere house and put together some of yere gran's favorite fabrics. The box is on its way. It should be here tomorrow."

What? No! Gigi's favorite fabrics are going to haunt me here?

"I have to leave. I have to get back home," Sadie repeated more forcibly.

Deydie cackled at her. "That's not what Oliver says. He says ye're free to stay in Gandiegow as long as we need ye."

Oliver could go to blazes! He'd only said that because he was hot for Kirsty, and he wouldn't let Sadie out of his sight for one second.

"And we need ye!" Deydie pounded her on the back, but stopped suddenly. "I didn't hurt ye, did I?"

Sadie looked around desperately for someone to help get her out of this. But the only other person there was Ross. He didn't look happy about her staying, either, if his scowl was any indication.

Sadie had to admit that it hurt to know he didn't want her there. *I thought we were friends.* Not typical friends, perhaps, but friends with kissing benefits.

"I suggest ye hurry up there, lassie. Ye have instructions to write up for the teaching of yere block. Do what ye can do with yere books, and while Ross is building the shelves, ye can camp out over there and make yere lesson plans."

A part of Sadie had to laugh. She'd been steamrollered most of her life, but Deydie was in a league of her own when it came to bossiness.

Now Deydie turned on Ross. "Why are ye just standing there? Ye've got to get to work on these shelves."

Ross shoved his hands in his pockets. "I'll finish unloading the truck first. Where do you want the fabrics?"

"Bring them here. We'll get the tablecloths sewn and then ye can drop them off at the restaurant. It's going to be a hell of a reception."

The door to Quilting Central opened.

"There's the groom now," Deydie said. "Father, come over here. I want to speak to ye about the wedding."

Father Andrew backed away a little, looking ready to make a run for it. "I—I just stopped in to pick up a basket for Mrs. Bruce. She asked if I could bring it by, as her youngest has a cold." He stayed glued to his spot as if coming in farther would be against his religion.

Deydie waddled away to retrieve the basket from the table.

Ross met him at the door and muttered under his breath. "Get out while ye can, Andrew. That woman is on a roll."

"I heard that, Ross," Deydie hollered from clear across the room. "I think the good Father should help ye today with the shelves. If not, I'm sure he could help with the decorations for the wedding reception."

Andrew looked at Sadie and her bags of books. "Let me drop this off first, and then I'll come back and help with the shelves."

"Good decision," Ross said.

Andrew took the basket from Deydie and slipped out the door.

Ross glanced one more time at Sadie before he left, too.

She thought she would breathe easier now that he was gone. Until she looked at Deydie.

The old woman was glaring at her. "Put yere bait away, lassie. Ye won't catch that one. For yere sake, I hope ye don't have yere heart set on Ross." Sadie heard the unspoken words. *He's too good for the likes of ye . . . with yere plain face and second-rate kidneys.*

"I don't have my heart set on anyone," Sadie protested haughtily. "I need him to get my shelves finished, is all."

"Then ye better mind how ye look at him. He's not going to be the captain of yere vessel."

Enough with the fishing analogies, already.

"I have work to do." Sadie turned back to her books.

But two seconds later, when the door opened again, she swung around in stupid anticipation . . . and was let down.

Oliver came through with a couple of boxes in his arms. "For you," he announced to Sadie.

"Me? What is it?"

"Actually, it's for Quilting Central's library. I got a deal on a laptop and a bar code scanner in Inverness."

Did she seriously need a bar code scanner for this small library? Couldn't they just do it the old-fashioned way? But Oliver looked so pleased with himself.

"I already cleaned up the computer and loaded the software for the scanner. I'll show you how to use the wand and input the books."

"Thanks, Oliver," she said. "You've gone to a lot of trouble."

He turned pink around his ears. "It wasn't a big deal."

Maybe, though, he was feeling guilty for signing her up for things he didn't have the right to.

"So Deydie tells me that *you've* volunteered to be an instructor for the next quilt retreat."

Oliver's ears went from pink to red. "Funny, sis." He set the boxes on the sofa.

"What gave you the right to volunteer me? And who made you my keeper?"

"God," he shot back.

"Cut it out, Oliver. I mean it."

Before he could answer, the door jingled again. Sadie was certain this time it would be Ross, but Kirsty blew through the door, literally. She had to pull the door closed behind her.

"The wind's really picked up," she sang out.

Oliver gazed at the schoolteacher as if she was a sleek new CPU. "What's going on?"

She held up the scanner wand with the attached cord. "Ye left this at my flat." Then she noticed Deydie, and blushed. That's when Sadie realized that Kirsty's lips looked swollen and well kissed. And she was positively beaming at Oliver as she handed over the wand.

Sadie rolled her eyes at her brother. Yes, there was the reason she was stuck in Gandiegow: Oliver's hormones.

To Sadie's, and apparently Kirsty's, surprise, Deydie nodded her head approvingly. "Come here, lass, and get yereself a cup of tea. Ye look thirsty." She latched on to Kirsty's arm and dragged her away, whispering conspiratorially.

"What do you think?" Oliver asked her.

"That you should prepare yourself for a shotgun wedding?"

Oliver was the one to roll his eyes this time. "Not that. Do you think the equipment will work for the library?"

Sadie thought it was overkill, but what good would it do to say so? "It's perfect."

Once again the door opened. She was being ridiculous . . . waiting stupidly for Ross to reappear. She was cranking her head around so often that where her neck was she should've installed a hinge instead. This time, it was Father Andrew returning, wearing a pair of faded jeans and a T-shirt. He could've been one of the local fishermen.

"Hold the door," a familiar voice said. Ross came in with a tool bag in one hand and a couple of boards in the other. "Abraham had these lying around. Can ye get the other end, Andrew? I'm about to drop them." The wind blew the door toward Ross and the boards slipped from his hands, hitting the floor with a clatter.

Deydie came charging at him. "Be careful. If ye scratch the hardwood, I'll fillet ye, Ross Armstrong!"

Andrew scrambled to help pick them up. Together the two of them carried the boards over to where Sadie stood, and she moved back to give them room.

Oliver glared at Ross as if to warn him not to even look at Sadie.

Now the women of Gandiegow began to pour into the building, and Sadie did her best to ignore those who reminded her most of Gigi. Not all of them, after all, were up in years and gray-haired.

Moira appeared with a tray and set it on the coffee table. "Some refreshments?" she said, with a smile for her beau.

Andrew came to stand by Moira and kissed her cheek, love shining in his eyes.

"How are the wedding plans going?" Ross asked.

Andrew rolled his eyes. "Don't ask. The quilting ladies have taken it to new artistic heights."

"But I like Gandiegow's traditions," Moira said quietly, glancing at Deydie.

"What kind of traditions?" Sadie asked.

"Well, some of them are pretty common, I guess. But we have some . . . superstitions, I suppose," Moira said.

"Tell me." With her glass in hand, Sadie sat down on the sofa, where Moira and Andrew joined her.

"Little things. Like good omens. One of Mama's favorite stories was that Papa surprised her with a sighting of a gray horse."

Andrew and Ross both nodded their heads as though they understood.

"What's special about a gray horse?" Sadie asked.

Moira smiled at her fondly. "It's considered good luck for the bride to see a gray horse on her way to the kirk. So Papa left nothing to chance. Apparently, it took him a trip two shires over to find a gray horse, and then several hard-earned pounds to get the horse transported to Gandiegow for Mama to see." The bride glanced up, as if imagining the horse walking down the steep road leading into the village. "In Mama's mind, that was true love."

Moira glanced over at her betrothed and smiled at him, but with a hint of tears in her eyes. Her parents were gone; Sadie could relate. But now Moira was beginning her new life with her true love.

Andrew took her hand and squeezed it, and as if that didn't seem enough, he kissed it, too.

Deydie hurried over. "I need ye two over there to look at swatches. It's yere day we're planning here. Everything has to be done right."

Andrew rose, offering his hand to Moira. "Duty calls."

"Thanks for the refreshments," Sadie said.

"Ye're welcome."

Sadie watched as they strolled away, arm in arm. She refused to glance at Ross to see if he was as affected by the love that poured from them, too.

Oliver waved a hand in front of Sadie's face, making her jump.

"When did you come back over here?" She looked about the room, but Kirsty was gone.

Oliver began fiddling with the computer cables. "Kirsty had to run back to the school to get paper for Bethia. Something about the wedding shower. I'll pull a table over here and get you set up."

"Thanks. That would be great."

Ross began pounding with his hammer. Andrew returned and joined in the construction.

Oliver quickly set her up. But as he was showing her how to get started, Kirsty walked back into the building. One nod from her and Oliver deserted Sadie, heading for the door and following the schoolteacher out as if tethered to her.

Well, Sadie couldn't judge. She was overly focused on a certain Scot too. In fact, she couldn't help but drink in every word that was being said between him and Father Andrew as they worked on the shelves a few feet over.

"I don't envy ye." Ross glanced to where the women were chattering away about the wedding.

Andrew shrugged. "I want to marry Moira, no matter what it takes." He nodded in the direction of Deydie and her followers. "My advice to you is when ye go to get married, don't let them talk ye into a big wedding. Run off and elope."

"Don't worry. I'm not going to marry for a long, long time." Ross locked eyes with Sadie, as if he was making his point loud and clear.

He was doing that a lot lately. And she didn't understand why.

She was feeling a good sulk coming on. If only she could go home today, she wouldn't be subjected to feeling like this. In the next second, she was braving a glance to see if Ross was still looking in her direction. He wasn't, but Emma was. She broke away from the group across the room and made a beeline for Sadie.

Crap. Sadie needed to watch her emotions. By the determined line of Emma's mouth, she had therapy on her mind.

Sadie put her head back down, pretending to be engrossed in scanning and entering the books into the computer. She liked Emma, but she wasn't in the mood to have her mental state dissected.

"It's time," Emma said. "I've left you alone long enough."

Sadie didn't reply. She only reached for the next book.

Emma sat, laying a hand on her arm. "I can see Deydie has put you to work. I'm sorry. If you don't want to babysit, I fully understand."

Sadie's head shot up. "Babysit?"

"Yes. I've been putting off buying a dress for the wedding." Emma glanced back over at the crowd of women. "I had hoped those last few baby pounds would melt away first." She patted her hips good-naturedly. "I've decided to embrace them instead. Gabriel says he likes that I have meat on my bones—*more to hang on to.*" She laughed again. "His words, not mine."

Sadie thought Emma was beautiful. Perfect.

"When would you like me to watch Angus?"

Emma squished up her face as if she hated to ask. "Today? This afternoon? If that works for you. I could put Angus down for his nap and then Gabriel and I could sneak out."

"Yes. This afternoon would be fine."

"One o'clock?"

Sadie barely got her "yes" out before Deydie started hollering.

"Emma, if ye're done jabbering, can ye run up to the big house and get my other notebook?"

Emma smiled at Deydie. "Of course. No problem."

"Big house?" Sadie asked.

"Graham Buchanan's home."

"Oh. That's right." She knew the star lived in town, but had forgotten to ask which cottage was his, Cait's, and Mattie's. She was just starting to realize that maybe she'd been a little self-absorbed lately.

"Would you like to come with me?" Emma said.

"To Graham Buchanan's house?" Sadie automatically turned to Deydie. The old woman would probably bite her head off for leaving before the job was done. But Quilting Central was filling up and getting louder by the second. "Sure," Sadie said. Besides, when else would she have a chance to peek inside a bona fide movie star's house? She closed the lid to the laptop, glancing around.

"Leave it there. It'll be fine. No one will bother it."

Sadie stood and followed Emma out, all the while proud of herself for not checking to see if Ross was watching her go.

Deydie didn't miss the look on Ross's face as he watched Sadie leave. "Damn."

"What's wrong?" Bethia asked.

"It's Ross. That lad is acting as if he might be smitten with the American lass." Deydie shoved her hands in her dress pockets. "I specifically told him to stay away from her."

Bethia got that look on her face, the one she wore when a lecture was on its way. Deydie had seen that look her whole life from her best friend and she was damned tired of it.

Bethia slipped her arm in hers and pulled her away from the others. "Maybe we should leave Ross alone and let him make up his own mind this time. Wasn't trying to marry him off to Pippa interference enough?"

Aye. They'd gotten in a little over their heads then. "But this is different. The lass isn't well. Life in Gandiegow is no summer picnic. It takes a special kind of woman to survive here on the northeast coast of Scotland."

Bethia nodded her head. "But we're not going to interfere this time."

Deydie glowered at her before turning back to Ross. She was definitely going to have to do something. First, she'd make sure Sadie was kept busy around the clock, and she would have to tell Kit to step up her efforts to find Ross a *suitable* mate. Deydie glanced around at all of her quilt ladies. They were a force to be reckoned with when they all put their minds to it. Perhaps if Ross wouldn't listen to reason, Deydie would just have to enlist the whole quilting circle.

Chapter Eleven

As Sadie strolled along the walkway with Emma, she gazed out at the ocean. Later today, she would sit on one of the little benches outside of Quilting Central and work on what Deydie called her "lesson plan." How had she got wrangled into teaching a quilting class?

Emma nodded toward the Armstrongs' cottage. "Maggie mentioned that you've been reading to Dand."

"It's a pleasure. He's so energetic and inquisitive."

"Maggie said it's made a huge difference. Did she tell you that before you started reading to Dand he wasn't interested in books at all? You've turned things around for him."

Sadie smiled. "Really?" She'd actually made a difference with a few picture books? "Well, I've enjoyed every second. He loves stories."

She remembered vividly when the reading bug took hold of her. Her parents used to read to her before bed, making it her favorite time of day. After the evening they went out and didn't return, Oliver took over the responsibility of reading to her, as if he'd been handed the baton. He was only ten, but he never missed a night—

until, of course, she was old enough to want to keep her reading selections to herself. Her hard feelings toward him lessened a fraction. Because he bullied her so often, she tended to forget what a good brother he could be, too.

Emma pointed to the path behind Deydie's cottage. "This leads up to the big house." She continued on with the previous thread. "You have earned points with Maggie. And the rest of the town, I suspect."

The steep path led to what looked like a new castle built next to a ruin. When Cait answered their knock, a cute little sheltie ran out.

"Dingus! Come back here," Cait shouted, laughing. The dog circled the yard and ran back in the house.

As Cait showed them around, Sadie kept a lookout for Graham, hoping for a glimpse of the famous actor.

Cait touched her arm. "My husband's away on a publicity junket."

Sadie's cheeks burned.

Emma laughed. "You might be jumping to conclusions, Cait. Maybe Sadie was looking for Mattie."

"Sorry," Sadie said. "I was just curious."

Cait smiled. "Graham will be back for the wedding. You can meet him then."

Sadie's hopes fell. She would be gone before Moira and Andrew's nuptials.

Emma stopped short and stared at Sadie. "I just had a brilliant idea. Cait, did Maggie tell you about Sadie reading to Dand?"

Cait laughed. "Are you kidding? She can't stop talking about it. She's so grateful."

Emma touched Sadie and Cait, as if linking them. "What if Sadie gets the boys together a few days a week and reads to both of them?"

"Why together?" Sadie asked.

"I'll explain," the therapist said. "I've been trying to come up with new ways to help Mattie feel more comfortable speaking."

But didn't they understand that she was going home soon? Not tomorrow, apparently. But in the very near future. "What do I need to do?"

"You could start a reading club for Dand and Mattie. Begin by reading *to* them. Then suggest that each one of you take a page to read aloud. Eventually, have the boys take turns. I want Mattie to get used to hearing his own voice again. It might be easier if he was reading and telling a story."

Cait clasped their hands, completing the circle. "Emma, ye're brilliant. This sounds wonderful. You don't mind, do you, Sadie? It would be such a blessing to have yere help."

"Of course, I'll do it." She sighed. "But I'm not here for that long."

"Whatever time you can give us will be appreciated." Cait hugged them.

Emma laughed. "This has been a productive outing. I better grab the notebook for Deydie. I have to get home and relieve Gabriel from baby duty."

"Sadie, would you like to stay for a cup of tea?"

"I'd love to but I'm sure Deydie is wondering why I abandoned my post. Did you hear about the library at Quilting Central?"

"Aye. What a grand idea. Ross did well thinking it up. Who knew that he cared about the Kilts and Quilts retreat so much?"

"Ross?"

"Yes." But then Cait faltered. "Oh, um, maybe it was someone else who came up with the idea. Yes. It had to be someone else."

Always the therapist, Emma looked concerned. "What's wrong, Sadie?"

"I'm fine," she answered. Why would Ross pretend the library was Oliver's idea? "Thanks again for the invitation. I better get back, though."

"Yes. I have to run as well."

She and Emma left, and hurried back down the bluff.

A few minutes to one, Sadie made her way to the doctor's quarters, bypassing the doctor's office downstairs and heading up the steps as instructed. She knocked quietly on the door to the flat for Angus's sake, and Gabriel opened it.

"Thanks for doing this, Sadie." He showed her around, pointing out Angus's room, the kitchen, and the pantry in case she became hungry. He pulled a list from a magnet on the refrigerator and handed it to her. "Emma has written out a schedule. We're heading into Inverness to look for her dress and then out to dinner. I hope it's okay with you that we'll be gone that long. I tried to get Emma to agree to an overnight in the big city, but she won't be separated just yet from her bairn."

"Mothers always know best," Sadie said. If she were going to be here longer, she would've gladly offered to watch Angus overnight as soon as Emma was ready.

She'd done it many a time as a babysitter. It was fun to play house in someone else's home.

Emma rushed into the room. "I'm ready. Did you give her the list?"

"She's all set," Gabriel assured her. "She has my mobile number. Everything will be fine."

"Right." Emma picked up her purse. "Call if you need anything. No matter how small."

"Angus and I will have a great time."

After a few more worried looks, Emma left with her husband.

After Sadie checked Angus to make sure he was asleep, she settled herself on the sofa with her notebook and the hand-drawn picture of the quilt she was supposed to teach. But as soon as she began to write the first instruction, she heard the downstairs door open and close. Her first thought was that Emma and Doc had forgotten something. But she heard only one pair of footsteps on the stairs. Then there was a light rap at the door.

She jumped up to answer it. Ross stood on the other side of the threshold.

"Can I come in?" he said quietly.

"It depends," she said.

He looked startled. "Depends on what?"

"Whether or not you'll tell me the truth."

He hesitated for a moment, then nodded.

She stood back and let him in.

"May I sit?"

She grabbed her notebook from the sofa, the only seating in the small living area. He sat down, seeming to take up most of the space in the room. She sat on the opposite corner, as far from him as possible.

Ross pinned her with his blue eyes. "Out with it, lass. The way ye're frowning, ye're looking more like Deydie every second. What's on yere mind?"

"Why did you say Quilting Central's library was Oliver's idea when it really was yours?"

The question took him off guard; she could see the surprise on his face. But he recovered in Ross style— quick, intelligent.

He shrugged. "I never said it was yere brother's idea. If I did anything it was to *not* correct you when ye said it was."

Is that what happened? He was confusing her.

"Why are you here?" she asked.

That question seemed to stump him, too. "I thought ye could use some company?"

"Are you sure? Because you don't seem convinced."

He paused for a long second, then sighed. "The truth?"

"It's what we agreed upon, remember?"

He shook his head. "Can I hide out here for a while, lass?"

"Why?"

"Harry's niece."

"Oh. Is she gunning for you?"

"Aye. Both barrels. And it seems the quilting ladies are egging her on, too. Will ye let me seek sanctuary?"

"What are you going to do after I'm done babysitting? The retreat isn't over until tomorrow."

Ross glanced about as if sizing up the place. "Maybe Doc and Emma would let me share a room with Angus."

Sadie laughed in spite of herself. "If I let you stay, what do I get in return?"

His eyes dropped to her lips. Or at least she imagined they did. But she couldn't trust her crazy eyes when it came to him.

"I know," she said. "You can have dirty diaper duty."

He didn't even balk. "Seems fair."

"Is Harry's niece all that bad?" Sadie wondered if the niece was as plain as she was, or maybe she had some abnormality.

"Nay. She's actually very attractive."

Envy pricked her.

He began listing her attributes. "She's a tall lass with golden locks. Her voice sounds like an angel. And she has a body that rivals that of Scarlett Johansson."

Sadie hadn't met Harry's niece, but she despised her. At the same time, Sadie had promised to help Ross with his love life. "If she's so dazzling, you should go out with her."

He shook his head. "She's not for me. Not my type."

"What is your type, then?" If she was going to help pick someone out, she needed to hear it straight from the fisherman's mouth.

"A lass who's looking for a good time and doesn't want to settle down." He glanced away. "Plus, a man needs to feel like he's the one doing the pursuing. She chased me down the walkway earlier and I had to hop on Brodie's boat to make an escape."

Sadie rolled her eyes. "Why can't women do the chasing every once in a while?"

"Because a man has to be the man."

"That kind of thinking went out of style the same time your truck was built."

He shrugged. "Then call me old-fashioned. I'm clear about what I want, and *don't* want. And I don't like desperate women."

Sadie was feeling uncomfortable. Underneath it all, she might be feeling a little desperate. *Desperate to kiss Ross again.* She wondered if he would kiss her while he was here. That thought had hung at the back of her mind since the moment she opened the door to him. She sighed, exasperated with herself. How did they ever get on this subject anyway?

He turned back to her. "What are we going to do with our time?"

She gazed at his mouth, wondering if he had any idea how she'd like to spend the next several hours in a clinch with him. Instead, she picked up her notebook and held it to her chest. "I don't know what you're going to do, but I have a lesson plan to create for teaching my quilt block." *Mine and Gigi's.* She squeezed the notebook tighter.

For her own good, she redirected the conversation. "And you're not completely off the hook for the whole library at Quilting Central debacle."

"Debacle?"

"You know what I mean. You had no right to manipulate me."

He laid a hand over his heart, as sincere as if pledging allegiance. "I only meant to help. I'm sorry I wasn't clearer about my part in it." He paused, then dropped his hand, turning serious. "I promise to never do anything to hurt you, *Sadie-lass*."

Her heart melted. "Okay. You're forgiven. Now stop looking at me like that."

"Have ye eaten?" he asked. "I missed lunch, hiding."

"I'm not hungry." Her stomach was a mass of unsettledness. Too many butterflies and no room for food.

He pulled out his phone.

"What are you doing?" she said.

"Placing an order at Pastas and Pastries."

"What about Harry's niece? You're going to chance running into her for the sake of some chicken Marsala and breadsticks?"

"Delivery."

But that gave Sadie something else to worry about. "Aren't you concerned about being seen here? News travels fast in a small town."

"Not if you trust the delivery man to keep his mouth shut."

Aye. Ross trusted his brother Ramsay, but he also wanted to drive home a point. He could choose who he wanted to spend time with, and he didn't need Ramsay's wife Kit to do the choosing for him.

Ross had tried to talk to Ramsay about his wife, but his brother only laughed . . . *like I have any control over what the lass does.* That may be true, but Ross felt pretty sure that if Kit brought up matchmaking Ross, Ramsay would let her know that he'd seen him alone with Sadie a *second time*. Seeing was believing.

Ross knew he was using Sadie to call off the dogs—the busybodies of Gandiegow. Should he come clean with her? Especially after promising to give her the truth? But he'd also promised to never hurt her. In most cases it was better to ask for forgiveness than permission. *But Sadie isn't most cases.*

He put his phone back in his pocket before dialing.

"I thought you were going to order food," she said.

"In a minute." He patted the seat beside him. "Come sit closer. I need to ask ye something."

She perched on the edge of the sofa. "So serious. What's up?"

"I really am famished," he started, "but there's also more to it." He confessed how he hoped if Ramsay saw them together again that it would help keep Kit at bay.

She shrugged. "If you're asking whether it's okay that you use me, I did say I wanted to help."

He reached out a hand to her, wanting to pull her in for a hug. But he stopped himself just in time. "Ye've got a good heart, Sadie Middleton. Ye're a good friend."

"Yes. A good friend." She rose and chose a place by the hearth, staring into the empty grate.

"Can I help with yere lesson planning?"

"No. I'm fine." But she looked uncomfortable standing by the fireplace.

"Sit down." He scooted as far over on the sofa as he could. "Ye better use this quiet time to get some work done before the little master wakes up."

She glanced toward the hallway. "I'll work at the kitchen table in the other room."

"Good idea." He stood and took out his phone for a second time. "I'll have Ramsay pick us up some food." He made the call and joined her in the kitchen. While she scribbled in her notebook with her head down, he put the kettle on and pulled down two mugs.

He liked to watch her work—the way she bit her lip while she thought. She drew a series of pictures, placing lines of text underneath. She was concentrating so hard that when Ramsay knocked on the door, Sadie jumped.

Ross laid a hand on her shoulder. "I'll get it."

He was expecting only Ramsay, but Kit was at the door as well.

"May we come in?" she said.

Ross wondered what would happen if he said *no*. He'd wanted to prove a point to his brother in a roundabout way; he hadn't wanted to come face-to-face with his matchmaking sister-in-law though.

"Sure." He took the sack of food from Ramsay and stepped back. "Sadie's in the kitchen."

"Oh?" Kit said. *Like Ramsay didn't run straight to her and tell.*

Ross shut the door and went back in the kitchen.

Sadie popped up from her chair as if she'd been caught in the act.

"It's okay, lass." Ross went to stand beside her.

Ramsay sauntered over to the cabinet and pulled out a stack of plates. "We thought we'd join ye."

More like chaperones, if Ross was reading Kit accurately. "So you're telling me that you two missed lunch, too?"

Kit and Ramsay shared an intimate grin. Ross rolled his eyes. Sadie blushed.

"I hope it's okay that we stay," Kit said. "We wouldn't want to interrupt."

Sadie moved her notebook to the counter. "I was working on the lesson plan for the quilt retreat."

Kit nodded. "I heard you were staying over." She glanced at Ross for good measure.

Was that Kit's way of finding out if Ross was staying over, too, as in *sleeping over*? Or was he just being paranoid?

Ramsay clamped a hand on his shoulder. "Relax," he muttered, as if he was the older brother instead of the baby of the family.

Ramsay went to his wife and ran a hand down her back. "Take it easy on him, sprite."

She seemed to consider his words and then beamed up at him. "All right. For you." She turned back to Sadie. "May I see what you've written up so far?"

Sadie handed off the notebook.

Kit's eyes ran down the page. "It looks good. Do you have someone lined up to do a test block from your directions?"

"I hadn't thought that far ahead."

"I'm happy to be your guinea pig. We could do it at Quilting Central tomorrow, if you like."

Sadie glanced at Ross, slightly panicked.

Kit's head swung from one to the other, registering every emotion as if she was a bar code scanner.

He stepped in. "Sadie's not completely comfortable at Quilting Central. How about ye do it at the cottage? I set up a sewing machine there, if you don't mind using it."

Kit nodded. "That would work."

Ramsay set a foil pan on the table. "How about we eat?"

The four of them said grace and dug in. As the meal went on, Ross relaxed, because Kit seemed to have gotten what she came for. He didn't know if she meant to double her efforts to find him a mate after this evening, or if she was going to leave off altogether.

Sadie, though, still seemed on edge. As soon as she took her final bite, wee Angus let out a cry. "Excuse me." She laid her napkin on the table and left.

Ramsay stood. "I believe that's our cue, brother."

"Where are ye going? What about the dishes?" Ross said.

Ramsay chuckled. "Ye'll have to take care of them. Kit and I have to run. We're off to an appointment."

Kit frowned up at him. "What are you talking about? What kind of appointment?"

Ramsay wrapped an arm around her shoulders. "My peace and quiet time."

"Oh, brother," Kit said.

Ramsay nodded. "She's a pretty determined woman, my wife. She insists on yielding to my every need in the evenings. She knows if I don't get enough attention from her that I become cranky."

Sadie walked in with Angus cradled in her arms at the same time that Kit reached up and patted Ramsay's cheek.

"You're so full of yourself," Kit said. "But I love you anyway. Take me home."

"Aye." Ramsay winked at Sadie. "Ye take care." And he guided his wife from the kitchen.

Ross was left alone with Sadie and the boy.

"What can I do to help?" he said. "Nappy change?"

"I'll get this one." She nodded to the plates on the table. "The kitchen is all yours." She walked away to the other room singing softly to the lad.

Ross had the kitchen tidied in no time. He found Sadie and Angus sitting on the floor with wooden blocks between them. He lay down beside them and propped himself up on one elbow, offering a rattle to Angus to chew on.

"So what about you, Sadie? How many children do you want to have?"

When she didn't immediately answer, he glanced up. She had her head bent down over the babe's.

Aw, hell. He'd stepped in it. "I wasn't thinking, lass."

"It's okay."

He sat, moving closer and wrapping his arm around her. "It's not okay."

"I can have children," she said quietly. "I love kids. But there are risks."

"If it's any consolation, I keep forgetting about . . . yere condition. I just don't see you as sick. Not in the least."

She looked up at him with a grateful smile. "That's probably the nicest thing anyone has said to me since I arrived in Scotland."

He squeezed her shoulder. And because he wanted to do more, like kiss her again, he dropped his hand and scooted away.

For the next few hours, they focused on Angus. Sadie gave him a bottle, then Ross burped him. When the lad messed his britches, Sadie filled the baby's bath while Ross cleaned him up enough to play in the water. The two of them made a good team. He knew it. He could tell she knew it, too.

At nine thirty, Sadie rocked Angus to sleep and stowed him in his crib. As soon as she walked out from the bedroom, Ross grabbed her hand and pulled her in for a kiss. He hadn't planned it, but being near her, working together, well, it had all been too much. More than he could handle anyway. Her surprise turned quickly to passion, and she wrapped her arms around him, kissing him back. Just as he was thinking they should move this to the sofa instead of the hallway, the door to the flat opened.

They jumped apart.

"We're home," Emma whispered.

Sadie balanced herself against the wall.

Emma came into the hall and stopped short when she saw Ross.

Doc came up behind her, took in the scene, and grinned. "Was the lad so much of a handful that ye needed backup?"

Sadie shook her head. "Your boy's an angel."

Ross crossed into the living room. "I took refuge here. Ye know how *they* can be."

"The quilting ladies?" Gabe laughed. "I heard about Harry's niece wanting a turn with ye."

"Sadie was nice enough to let me hide out."

Sadie walked into the living room and picked up her notebook from the floor. "Anytime you need me, I'll be happy to babysit. I'm here for an extra week."

Gabe winked at Emma. "We will definitely make use of ye while we can."

Emma latched on to Sadie. "Take a second and come see my new dress."

The two of them left and went down the hall.

"Well?" Gabe said.

"Well, what?" Ross answered back. There was nothing to tell.

Gabe nodded to where the women had been. "You and the American lass?"

"Nothing's going on. I'm tired of telling everyone that."

"I see." Gabe raised an eyebrow. "Perhaps you should make an appointment with me and have yere eyesight checked. I believe ye aren't seeing things for how they really are."

"Not likely."

Gabe chuckled. "If things change and you need someone to talk to about it, my door is always open."

"Ye're beginning to sound like yere wife the therapist." And Ross really needed to make this next part clear. "Sadie and I are friends. That's as far as it goes."

Gabe's eyes shifted as if they weren't alone.

Ross spun around and found Sadie standing there, frowning. He didn't like it when she frowned. Especially when it was directed at him.

"We better get going," Ross said.

Gabe nodded at the lass. "Have Ross walk ye back to the quilting dorm."

She frowned at Gabe as if to ask *why*, but she didn't go so far as to say it. Instead she gave a noncommittal good night to both Emma and Gabe, then left without looking at Ross. He had to hurry after her.

Once outside, he pulled her to a stop, wanting to fix what he'd done. "I know I'm sounding like a broken record."

"About what?"

"Don't give me that. You're as tired of hearing me say it as I am of repeating it."

She raised an eyebrow. She was going to force him to say it out loud.

"Everyone thinks we're together, and I keep setting them straight."

She looked him square in the eyes. "Of course. It's preposterous they would think such a thing."

He was surprised that she was so firm in her declaration.

"Why is it preposterous?" Ross asked, surprised at how defensive he sounded.

She started walking, speaking over her shoulder. "Because you're not my type."

He stood there kind of shocked.

If I'm not her type, then who is?

But there was a more pressing question, lingering at the back of his mind. *Something having to do with them kissing each other.* Had all the others who'd kissed her been knocked from their moorings like he had been?

Ross realized she was almost to the corner of the restaurant and the main walkway. He hustled to her, again, ready to find out. He caught up to her in between the buildings.

"Hold up." He gently pulled her to a stop.

The lass spun around and faced him with fire in her eyes. She was so alive. So enticing.

He was one tug away from having her in his arms, and kissing that mouth of hers he liked so *verra much*. "I'm not yere type?"

"Not in the least," she said with no hesitation, glaring at him, daring him with her eyes.

He accepted her challenge and dipped his head, pulling her to him, kissing her with all he had. *Trying to change her mind.* Instead of pushing him away, she clung to him as if she was caught in his net as much as he was in hers.

At that moment, the door slammed to the restaurant. As Ross pulled away, Deydie stepped perfectly in their line of sight. The old woman took in the scene and glowered. Whatever crazy urge that Ross had about taking things further with Sadie halted, stumbled, and fell dead in its tracks.

"Ross, ye and that girl git out of the shadows," Deydie growled.

Sadie stared up at him fuming mad.

He shrugged. What did Sadie expect? She's the one who dared him. Besides, he didn't make her kiss him back.

He stepped away and moved into the light.

Deydie pointed at Sadie. "And ye . . . git on back to the quilting dorm. It's time for ye to go to bed. Alone!"

Sadie stomped off without a backward glance.

"Good night, lass," he hollered after her.

Deydie put her hands on her hips. "I know what the problem is. What do they call it when ye're moonin' over a new lass after a broken engagement?" She glared at him a moment. "Aye, a *rebound*, that's it. Normally, I'd tell ye to have yere fun, but Sadie's a good lass. Not one for ye to rebound with. Have yere rebound with someone else."

Ross exhaled. "I thought ye didn't like her."

"Och, lad. I believe her to be a sweet girl."

"She is a good person," Ross agreed.

Deydie shook her finger at him, something she'd done a lot lately since Sadie came to town. "I tell ye, ye need a strong, healthy woman." She bobbed her head up and down. "Like Harry's niece."

Could she and everyone else give it a rest!

"I've got to go." He sidestepped around her.

"Mark my words, Ross," Deydie growled. "Sadie may be sweet, but for ye, she'll be nothing but trouble."

Ross didn't respond. Oh, he wanted to. He had a lot to say on the matter. Sadie wasn't trouble. She was fun. Thoughtful. Kind. And the problem that he had—if he was actually going to admit to having one—was that he wanted the lass. Maybe Deydie had the right of it and when it came down to it, his feelings for Sadie were nothing more than some kind of delayed rebound reflex. If that was the case, there was only one way to fix it.

Chapter Twelve

You're not my type tumbled around in Sadie's head as she rolled over in bed and stared at the wall. She was glad no one was around when she got back to the dorm, because she couldn't talk to another living soul tonight.

Of course, Deydie was right. Ross had given Sadie attention only because she was a rebound for him. A convenience. And a novelty. Not a Gandiegow lass. In reality, Sadie was no one at all. She needed to remember that for the rest of her stay in Scotland.

She rolled to her back and stared up at the ceiling, feeling the crushing weight of it on her chest. If only Gigi was here. Her grandmother would've known the perfect thing to say to turn all of Sadie's worries into insignificant grains of sand. But Gigi was gone, and Sadie was all alone to deal with her miserable life on her own.

And she wanted nothing more than for Ross to sneak into her room, climb into the twin bed with her, and hold her until the wave of grief passed.

Morning came too soon. As she lay there for a long moment listening to the snoring in the room next to hers, she had an epiphany. She was responsible for her own happiness, and that meant getting out of Scotland with *most* of her heart intact.

She rolled out of bed, deciding that today she would do only things that made her happy. First, she chose the green dress that she loved so much. And she didn't give a hoot whether Ross thought she looked nice in it or not. She took her things to the bathroom and got ready. And because it pleased her to do so, she blow-dried her short, bobbed hair, used the curling iron under the sink to put a curl at the ends, and applied a little lipstick.

"I'm plain, but I'm not all bad," she thought, tapping the little heart-shaped birthmark at the corner of her mouth.

In the kitchen, she grabbed an oatcake from the container on the counter and hurried off to Quilting Central. When she walked inside, she was startled to see that the library shelves were completed. She glanced around to see if little elves were scampering away. But the room was empty, save for her stacks of books.

She frowned, wondering what it meant. Why would Ross have worked on them last night? And if not Ross, then who?

She scanned in three books, but felt restless. She rose from the couch and went to the kitchen area, filled a mug with water, and placed it in the microwave for a cup of tea. She took it back to her place by the computer and forced herself to stay focused on the task at hand.

As soon as all the books were inputted, she began arranging them on the shelves. With a burst of wind, the door blew open and Sadie spun around to see if it was Ross. But it was only Deydie.

She looked startled to see Sadie there so early. "What

are ye doing here?" she asked brusquely as she laid a stack of cut fabric on the first table.

"I was putting the library together."

But Deydie had other things on her mind than books. "Ye need to get yere arse over to the kirk. The service is going to start any second."

"Kirk?" Sadie said automatically. But then she remembered . . . *the church*. "I think I'll just stay here, if that's okay."

"Nay, 'tis Sunday. We pay our respects to the Lord on Sunday, come hell or high water. Now, git off that couch and hurry over there."

When Sadie didn't immediately jump to her feet, Deydie made a move as if she was going to come over and yank her up.

Didn't Deydie understand that Sadie was feeling out of sorts with God these days? Hadn't He dropped more than her fair share of grief on her plate recently?

Deydie slammed her hands on her hips. "Have faith and trust all will be well."

The old woman had read her mind.

Sadie rose and walked toward the door.

Deydie nodded at her as she passed. "Ye look very pretty today."

That's a stretch. But Sadie didn't feel like getting into an all-out war.

The two hurried down the walkway as Deydie shoveled out orders. "Ye'll sit with me and my quilting ladies."

Sadie knew better than to ask what the older woman knew about the completed shelves at Quilting Central. Maybe she'd run into Ross after church and ask him.

But as they made their way down the aisle, Sadie scanned the room and didn't see him. Was he running late, too?

The service started with Andrew and the choir. Several times during the processional, Deydie leaned over and tapped Sadie's hymnal to bring her eyes back to the page instead of the room. As the service wore on, Ross still didn't appear. His family all sat in one pew together, but they didn't seem to be concerned about his absence; not a single one cranked his head back toward the narthex to catch a glimpse of him.

When it was over, Sadie made her way into the hall, looking for the answer to the whereabouts of her shelf-builder. When John headed for the door with baby Irene in his arms, she bravely cut him off.

"Hi. Good morning," Sadie said, feeling unsure. "I was looking for Ross. I wanted to thank him for finishing up the library shelves." She looked from side to side. "Do you know where he is?"

John gave her a kind smile. "Sorry, lass. Ross is gone. He's helping out on the *Betsy Lane*, a lobster boat. He won't be back until right before the wedding."

Ten days. *After I'm gone.* And he hadn't even said good-bye.

"T-thanks," she muttered.

Irene put her arms out to Sadie. Automatically, she took her and bounced her gently.

John watched her closely. "Are ye all right, lass? Do I need to get Doc? Or yere brother?"

Sadie plastered on a smile. "I'm happy Ross is trying something different. He was looking for something new."

"I know," John said.

And she suspected John might feel a little betrayed as well.

Irene stuck a thumb in her mouth and lay against Sadie's chest, contented.

Maggie materialized beside her. "Ye have a way with the babe. Do ye want me to take her off yere hands?"

"No." It felt good to be comforted by the baby in her arms. "She's settled in."

Maggie gave her a pitying look. "Why don't ye come to noon meal at our house?"

Sadie was going to decline, but Kit came up from behind and laid a hand on her back.

"She can't come, Maggie. She's going to lunch with us. Then I'm going to work on her quilt block; test it out."

Yes. The retreat started tomorrow and Sadie still needed to finish planning her lessons. But she felt a little empty inside. Knowing for sure she wouldn't see Ross again would take some getting used to.

Sadie glanced down and saw that Irene had drifted quietly off to sleep. As she handed the baby over to Maggie, Dand ran up and hugged her middle.

"Did ye ask her, Mum? Is Sadie going to come over and read to me this afternoon?"

"I—"

Sadie squatted down to Dand's level. "What do you think about you, Mattie, and me starting a book club? I thought the three of us could read together."

"That sounds great!" Dand turned and hollered across the narthex. "Mattie! Hey, Mattie!"

The other boy turned and waved.

Even though his parents were shushing him, Dand

hollered again. "Come here, Mattie! Sadie's going to read to us!"

Mattie brightened and rushed over.

Kit laughed. "Sadie, I believe the boys have changed your plans. I'll come over later. Right now, you have a date."

"Sounds good."

Dand looked up at his mother eagerly. "Sadie's going to read to Mattie and me."

Maggie smiled back. "I heard. But ye're going to have to let her eat first. Also, Mattie has to ask his mama's permission to come to the house."

The boys ran off to find Cait.

Then they all walked to the Armstrongs' cottage as Dand listed every book he wanted them to read. The little boys were helping keep her mind off of Ross's absence. *Well, mostly.*

Once inside Maggie shooed Sadie from the kitchen. "Go on now. I'll let ye know when it's time."

Sadie settled herself on the sofa between Dand and Mattie and began with Dand's favorite books. After two, she turned to Mattie. "Do you have a favorite that you would like for me to read?"

Mattie slipped off the couch and pulled out a book, handing it over to Sadie. He climbed back up and sat close as she read about the dragon in the cave. She couldn't help but compare the silent dragon to the boy next to her.

There was a pleasant buzz of activity in the cottage as Maggie pulled food from the oven and the refrigerator while John set the table. Sadie figured they had time for one more book before it was time to eat.

She chose an easy read from the pile. "I have an idea."

She waited for both of the boys to look her way. "Wouldn't it be fun if we took turns reading?"

Dand smiled from ear to ear. "Only if you help me with the hard words."

Mattie nodded solemnly.

Sadie started off with the first page. When she was done, she turned to Mattie. "Do you want to go next or do you want Dand to?" No surprise, he deferred to Dand with a nod. Dand read his page excitedly, struggling with several of the words. For a second, she waited to see if Mattie would come to his rescue. When he didn't, Sadie provided the help that was needed. Then she turned the page and said casually to Mattie, "Your turn."

Mattie leaned over and quietly read the eight words on the page, never looking up once.

"Wow," Dand said. "Ye read really good, Mattie."

Mattie gave him a crooked smile.

When the book was done, Maggie announced that it was time for lunch.

"Go wash up, lads." Maggie turned to Sadie when the children left the room. "What ye're doing is a fine thing . . . for both Dand and Mattie."

Sadie smiled. "I've always loved to read." She glanced down the hall to where the boys were. "I just never knew how good it felt to read to others. Until now."

John pointed out where she should sit. "If that's the case, I bet Mr. Menzies wouldn't mind ye dropping by to read to him. His eyes are bad, and he's been shut up in his house for the last couple of years. He always appreciates a visit."

"Sure. If you let me know what kind of books he likes, I'd be happy to."

John named several well-known thrillers. Probably books Ross would prefer to Sadie's Jane Austen collection any day.

The boys came running back in, prayers were said, and the food passed around. Once again, Sadie wished her brother could be here for the family dinner. But by the way he was making eyes at Kirsty during church, she imagined the two of them were enjoying a more intimate setting for their meal.

After eating, Sadie was pulled away by a text from Kit. *Change of plans. Emma is going to meet you at Quilting Central.*

"Go on," Maggie said. "John will clean up the kitchen while I nurse Irene."

But Sadie wasn't happy about Kit's text. What happened to her testing the quilt block at the cottage?

Sadie didn't think she could possibly sew at Quilting Central. She would just have to convince Emma to come back here. She walked to the door, but Maggie hurried toward her.

"Ye almost forgot this." She hefted the portable sewing machine from the treadle and handed it over.

Sadie's stomach churned the whole way to Quilting Central. It was one thing to set up the library; it was quite another to quilt, with all the memories it would dredge up.

But as it turned out, the place was empty. Either the quilters spent their Sunday afternoons at home or they hadn't arrived yet. Sadie was thankful to have the place to herself, if even for the moment. But then her stupid eyes landed on the completed shelves and the deep hurt of abandonment settled into her bones.

She positioned her machine on a table close to the door, in case a quick getaway was necessary, and noticed a cardboard box with her name written at the top. She pulled it closer. A lump formed in her throat. For a second she worried she would sob.

The restroom door opened and Emma appeared. "Oh, hello. The postie asked me to drop that box off here." She stopped suddenly, her cheerfulness turning to concern, and then she rushed to Sadie. "What is it? Tell me what's wrong."

Sadie scooted the box toward Emma. "Gigi's favorite fabric."

"Oh, sweeting." She ushered her to the sofa in the new little library.

All the losses were jumbling together. First Ross this morning, and now another reminder that Gigi was gone.

"I miss my grandmother," Sadie blurted.

Emma took her hand and squeezed. "Of course you do." She was quiet, letting Sadie sort through her thoughts.

"I want to talk to her. There are things I need to tell her." Sadie and Gigi didn't always see eye to eye when it came to men. But Gigi was the only one who could help make sense of the mess she'd gotten herself into with Ross. Gigi had a way of tackling problems from a different angle—ways Sadie never saw on her own. "There're also things I want to share with her. Good things." She looked around the room filled with fabric, projects, and love. "Gigi would be beyond excited to be here."

Emma nodded understandingly.

A sob erupted from Sadie, along with the words she never planned to utter. "But I killed her!"

Emma's look of alarm lasted only a split second. She took both of Sadie's hands and squeezed. "You are in a safe place. But first, let me lock the door." She jumped up and set the dead bolt.

The second she returned to her place on the sofa, Emma's eyes backed up her words. Sadie felt safe and confessed everything.

"I went against Gigi's wishes. She didn't want me to be a librarian. She said I'd never get a man if I buried myself in stacks of books. She was worried about me being alone in the world." Sadie motioned to herself. "She never made a big deal about it, but I knew she was referring to how plain I am."

Emma shook her head. "You're not plain, Sadie Middleton. You're you. The most perfect version of yourself."

Sadie nodded to assure Emma. "I know therapists have to say stuff like that, but you don't need to protect my ego. I'm okay with being plain. I'm a realist."

"I'm a realist, too. And your friend. And as your friend, I'm going to give it to you straight. Do you understand?"

Sadie braced herself, but she figured Emma wouldn't tell her anything new.

Emma gazed into her eyes with earnestness. "Anyone who meets you automatically loves you." She squeezed her hands again for emphasis. "Ask anyone in Gandiegow."

That statement delivered a hell of a wallop to Sadie's chest. On its heels came another.

But Ross doesn't love me. No man had ever loved her. And that was okay. Somehow, though, she knew she was responsible for running Ross out of town. She'd do anything to take back whatever she'd said or done that pushed him away. Had it been because she'd lied to him and said he wasn't her type?

Emma touched her arm as if to reassure. "Deydie and some of the others seem a bit harsh at first, but it's no reflection on you. It's their way of protecting their corner of Scotland."

Emma had misread Sadie's consternation. And Sadie couldn't bare her soul and talk about her crush on Ross. She could hardly admit it to herself.

"Now that we have that settled"—Emma glanced at the door as if it was a watch and their time was nearly up— "tell me why you believe you killed your grandmother."

Because Emma had woven such a deep layer of trust and confidence around them, Sadie felt safe to tell her what had happened. "The second I started my first dental hygienist job, I knew I couldn't do it. Not long term. Not even short term. I went behind Gigi's back and looked into going to graduate school for library science. But I didn't get around to applying right away because, well, I was spending a lot of time at the doctor's office, trying to figure out what was wrong with me. And when the diagnosis came, everything was up in the air, and I wasn't sure I could handle the graduate program. At the last second, I decided to go for it. The application was due at five p.m., and Gigi called at four and asked me to run by the quilt shop and pick up the fabric she'd been waiting for; her hair appointment was running late. I told her I couldn't do it. I didn't tell her why, and Gigi was upset with me. I figured I would wait and tell her after I was accepted into the program."

"So what happened?" Emma asked quietly.

"Gigi made it to the quilt shop as they were closing.

She was out of breath and holding her chest. The quilt shop owner said she collapsed just as she made it to the counter."

"Oliver told us she'd had a heart attack," Emma said gently.

"The paramedics said she was gone when they arrived." A tear slipped down Sadie's cheek. "If only I had gone to the shop when she asked me. I was sending in my application at the same moment Gigi died. My selfishness killed her."

Emma slipped her arm around Sadie. "No. You didn't kill your grandmother." She squeezed her shoulder. "But maybe taking the blame has been easier than facing the fact that you have to go on without her."

"What?" Sadie pulled away, feeling angry and confused.

"I didn't know your grandmother, but I'm certain if she was here right now, she would agree with me." Unwavering, Emma stared steadily into Sadie's eyes. "She would be proud that you were making decisions for your own life, moving in the direction that you felt was best for your future. Who doesn't want that for her child?"

"But Gigi wasn't my mother."

"True. But I understand from Oliver that she raised you both. She was your grandmother, but in a lot of respects, she played the role of mother, too. She would only want what's best for you. And as mothers, we tend to think that we know what's best . . . like I do for Angus. But if all goes well, one day I'll put myself out of a job, and he'll be able to start making decisions for himself." She paused for a second. "Just like you did."

The realization started to sink in. Sadie knew Gigi.

She might've been a little upset with her at first, but she had a way of accepting things, even faster than Sadie herself. Gigi was forever saying, *Nothing is more constant in life than change.*

Emma gave her an understanding smile. "I promise that when you're ready to go through your grief that you will give up blaming yourself. But in the meantime, I feel like I have to say it again . . . Gigi's death is not your fault."

Loud banging sounded at the door. Then Deydie squished her face up against the glass.

"Should I let her in?" Emma asked.

"If you know what's good for both of us."

Emma got to her feet. Sadie stood, too, and hugged her new friend.

Deydie pounded harder. Her muffled, "Unlock this door," filtered inside.

Sadie laughed, feeling lighter than she had in days. "I'm going to wash my face."

She took her time in the restroom. When she walked out, she felt self-conscious, but neither Deydie nor the other women who had shown up descended on her. Sadie was grateful. She was also grateful that one of them had moved Gigi's fabric box to another table, farther away. Sadie would have to face that box eventually, but now wasn't the time.

Sadie and Emma got down to work, setting up the machine as Emma explained how Kit had gotten detained by a call from a client. Sadie wondered if maybe it was fate.

She and Emma worked through the quilt lesson step-by-step. Kit's suggestion to test the pattern was a good one; they found several places to make the instructions clearer and were able to fix a measuring error.

Finally, Emma stood and stretched. "I should make my way home and care for my men." She hugged Sadie.

"Thank you for everything." Sadie was referring to more than the quilt block test.

Emma gave her a genuine smile. "You will do a brilliant job of teaching the quilters this week."

Out of the corner of her eye, Sadie noticed Deydie hanging posters along one wall. "What's that all about?"

Emma pretended not to notice. "I do have to go. Good luck."

That sinking feeling came over Sadie. She could've just left, but something told her she'd better speak with Deydie first.

She walked across the room and saw that on each poster was a famous quilting instructor from the US. Sadie had seen many of them on TV or had bought a book they had written about a certain aspect of the craft.

"What's all this?" Sadie motioned to the six posters lined up.

"Och, I guess I forgot to tell ye." Deydie nodded respectfully to the wall, as if the women themselves were in the room. "These are the students that ye'll be teaching next week."

Ross went below deck to his cabin to get his rain gear. On his bunk lay the blank piece of paper on which he'd tried to make a list of future careers that would fit him. His mind, though, couldn't focus on anything but Sadie. Then or now.

He snatched up his gear to go back outside. It would

serve him right to catch his death of cold. He was such a louse. A coward. Of course he'd left for Sadie's sake; she deserved more than to be his rebound fling. But she also deserved a man who wouldn't run out on her and not say good-bye. It was just that he didn't think he could do it. He would've taken one look at her sweet, beautiful face and been unable to leave.

That was one thing that bugged him about Sadie—she was always calling herself plain. When he'd first met her, he'd thought her pleasant-looking, but not necessarily a beauty. But he must've not been looking closely. If Sadie was plain, then so was the first flower in spring. Or the sunset over the ocean. Or a rainbow after a storm. And when he'd first seen her at the pub, he'd thought she was too young for him. But now she seemed perfect.

He hadn't left Gandiegow because he didn't want Sadie to be his rebound; he'd left because she was so much more than that. But he needed to pull his head out of the clouds. He wasn't ready to settle down, yet he couldn't treat Sadie like a fling, either. Being so attached to the lass would mean trouble for the both of them.

He tossed his pillow against the wall. "Why couldn't she have shown up five years from now?"

Ross pulled his rain jacket from his duffel and slipped it on. The job on the *Betsy Lane*'s crew had come along at just the right time. It put distance between him and Sadie, and that's what he needed to get his head screwed on straight. And they were scheduled for an offload right before the wedding, which was perfect. He would make it in time for Moira and Andrew's big day . . . and Sadie would be gone.

Chapter Thirteen

Sadie glanced at the six famous quilters talking among themselves near the back of Quilting Central. She leaned against one of the longarm quilting machines for support. She hadn't slept a wink last night. She was such a nervous wreck that she didn't have the wherewithal to worry over Ross . . . not too much anyway. She took a steadying breath. "Tell me again why these quilters are here."

Deydie cackled. "Ye're whiter than the muslin on that Four Crowns quilt I just took off the quilting machine for Kirsty. I think she means to give it to yere brother."

"The famous quilters?" Sadie reminded her. "Why?"

"They wanted their own retreat here in Scotland, and Caitie set them up." The old woman patted her back, more gently than she'd ever done before. "I told them ye were new to teaching, so don't be nervous. Besides, ye only have to teach two hours in the mornings. Three days of that ain't going to kill anyone."

It might. Sadie looked down at her hands. They were shaking.

"What makes you think I can teach them anything?"

And why didn't I go home when I had the chance?
Maybe if Sadie closed her eyes, she'd disappear like Ross
had. It would serve Deydie right for putting Sadie on the
tracks and sending the quilting train to barrel over her.

Life in Gandiegow, as far as she was concerned, was
a complete disaster.

Except she enjoyed reading to Dand and Mattie. Getting to know Moira, Emma, and Kit. And setting up the
library. But she certainly didn't enjoy how miserable she
felt about Ross being gone.

Oliver and Kirsty came through the door.

Sadie rolled her eyes. "Great. An audience."

"He's here to fix Caitie's computer."

"And judge me," Sadie added.

"Nay. He's here for moral support." Bethia handed
over a steaming mug of tea. "Take a sip and then we'll
get started."

None of this made sense. Sadie looked to heaven and
shook her head, not sure what the Big Guy was thinking
on this one. She headed up on the stage.

Bethia guided the six women to the front table. Sadie
expected them to look judgmental and critique her every
move, but instead they only welcomed her with warm
smiles. She should've known. Quilters were the best people in the world as far as she was concerned—more giving
than any other group.

But when Sadie opened her mouth to introduce herself, nothing intelligible came out. "Well, um . . . ah—"

"Get on with it, lass," Deydie hollered. "These ladies
don't understand gibberish."

Sadie reddened. "Sorry. I'm Sadie Middleton."

"She and her gran won the quilt block challenge," Deydie said.

They nodded at her kindly, and Sadie suddenly felt brave. She stepped off the stage and stood in front of the tables, holding her head high as if she was the equal of these mega quilting stars. She held up her winning quilt block. "My grandmother, Gigi, and I designed this quilt block because we've always loved thistles." She described how they'd worked on the block together and sent it in, hoping and praying to win the challenge. Then she had to tell the rest: how they'd won, but that Gigi had sadly passed away before finding out.

"Come sit with us." Dorothy Webb Parker patted the seat beside her. "Deydie told us about your grandmother. We're so sorry for your loss."

Each one of them gave Sadie her condolences. And this time, she wasn't angry with Deydie for sharing the news about Gigi. Because sharing the loss felt as though she was being lifted up by the community, instead of the grief weighing her down.

Dorothy examined the winning quilt block. "How did you approach the appliqué?"

Sadie answered her, and then the next question. Two hours flew by, and she found that she liked teaching, because while she was teaching, she also learned a lot. She learned she could get up and speak in front of others and be heard. And she learned that she liked helping people. Although these women knew so much more about quilting than she ever would, they hadn't known Gigi's secret to appliquéing.

When her time was up, Sadie gathered her bag with

three thrillers to take to Mr. Menzies's house. After reading to him, she had an appointment with Mattie and Dand.

Deydie stopped her at the door. "I'll expect ye back here this evening."

"Why?" Surely the old quilter didn't have another class lined up for her.

"Since ye missed yere retreat last week—with all the gallivanting ye did with Ross—ye're going to have to do some sewing. And it's time for ye to deal with yere box." Deydie pointed to the parcel that now sat on a small table next to Deydie's desk. "I'll be right there with ye when ye go through it."

But Sadie had faced enough challenges for one day and was going to put her foot down. "I don't want to—"

"Yere gran would want ye to get back on the horse. Let me hold the reins and help boost you up. It'll just be a few of us here. Think of us as yere quilting family." Deydie cocked her head and grinned. "Besides, ye're going to do it whether ye want to or not. Ye might as well pretend that ye have a say in it and agree now while ye have a chance."

Sadie sighed heavily. "Fine."

Deydie handed her a plastic container. "Moira has been cutting background fabric for ye this last week."

Sadie felt a squeeze in her heart. "With all she has to do to get ready for the wedding?"

"Aye. We want ye to get past yere grief."

She turned her head away, and saw Oliver watching her. The worry lines that had appeared between his brows ever since her diagnosis seemed to have faded. From this distance, he didn't look like the overbearing brother that she knew; he seemed more concerned and sympathetic. Or perhaps it was her perspective that had changed.

"I'll get past my grief," Sadie said, reassuring Deydie. Or possibly reassuring herself. She walked over to Moira, lifting the container up. "Thank you so much. Can I take you to lunch to repay you?"

"Nay." Moira smiled shyly. "But we can go to lunch to have a nice chat."

"Perfect."

Sadie left her background fabric in one of the cubbies and walked with Moira to the restaurant. After lunch, she read to Mr. Menzies, who was a delight because of his enthusiasm. Then she had to rush back across town to make her date with the two boys.

Though she was busy every minute, whenever she walked from one end of town to the other, her gaze would wander out to the sea, hoping to catch a glimpse of Ross. But his leaving was a clear message . . . Sadie needed to let go of an impossible dream.

At seven o'clock, she arrived back at Quilting Central. As Deydie promised, there was only a small crew of quilters there: Bethia, Moira, and Cait. The retreat goers were apparently whooping it up at the pub under Kit's supervision. Yes, having fewer people at Quilting Central was less stressful, but to work on a memory quilt that would commemorate Gigi's life? Sadie wanted to make a run for it back to the quilting dorm.

True to her word, Deydie stood right beside her as they went through Gigi's fabric and decided which pieces should go into the quilt, and then Sadie found herself sitting behind the sewing machine. She picked up the first pieces of the block—and a rush of emotion hit her. Gigi had always insisted a Jacob's Ladder block should go into every Sampler, saying it anchored the quilt. Sadie wiped a tear from her cheek and sewed the first seam.

Bethia glanced over at her worriedly. "Are ye okay? Can I get ye something?"

"Nay. Leave her be," Deydie said. "She'll have to shed a few tears, but by the end, she'll be fine. Quilting has healing powers."

Funny, but it seemed like something Gigi might say. Sadie knew there'd be more tears, but she was starting to feel as if she might be all right—not today, or even tomorrow, but somewhere in the future. She picked up two more pieces and stitched them together.

After two hours, Deydie stood and declared it was time to shut down for the night.

"I'll need to wrestle those women out of the pub, I'm afraid." She shook her head and the bun at the back of her neck came down. As she put the pins back in it, she spoke to Sadie. "Ye did good work today. I do believe the quilting has taken root in ye again. That's good."

Sadie looked at the two blocks she'd completed for the Sampler. "You might be right."

"Of course I'm right. I always am about such things." Deydie patted her and walked away.

The others told Sadie good night and she walked back to the quilting dorm alone. Once again, Ross crossed her mind, leaving her to wonder if he was thinking of her, too. But she knew the answer. He didn't have feelings for her like she did for him. Maybe when she got her shot on Wednesday from Doc, she should ask if he had anything for lovesickness. Or pills to make her forget what it was like to be in Ross's arms and be well kissed.

She let herself into the empty dorm; the famous quilters were staying in the quilt dorm next door, Duncan's Den. Oliver had moved to the room over the pub. Sadie went to her room and dressed for bed.

Today was Monday. She was heading home on Friday. Back to her life in North Carolina. She wanted to be over Ross by then; she had to be.

For the next two days, she woke up and did it all again. She said good-bye to the retreat ladies on Wednesday evening and on Thursday morning sewed with the Gandiegow quilters. In the afternoon, with a heavy heart, she went in search of Oliver, to make sure all was set for them to go home the next day.

Oliver didn't want to go anywhere. He looked down at Kirsty as she cuddled into him on the sofa. Her little studio apartment, set at the back of the school, was the perfect space. She said it had once been a storage room, but the town had turned it into a flat before she'd taken the job as their new teacher.

There was a light tap at the door.

Kirsty jumped and he stilled her.

"It's okay. We're not doing anything." Now, if Deydie or one of the other quilting ladies had stopped by two hours ago . . . that would've been a different story. "Do you want me to answer it?"

Kirsty pulled away. "Nay. I've got it." She took the few steps across the room and opened the door.

Sadie stood on the other side. "Hi."

"Come on in." Kirsty stood back and let her pass through.

"Can I speak with you a moment, Oliver?" His sister looked miserable. Even more so than when they'd arrived. Coming to Scotland hadn't helped her a bit. It had only made her worse.

Kirsty grabbed her jacket from the hook by the door. "I was just going to run over to the restaurant and pick up some food. Sadie, will ye join us?" Oliver had installed a second hook for his jacket yesterday.

"Thank you, but no." Sadie looked as if she'd lost weight. "I need to get packed for our trip home."

Kirsty's face fell and Oliver felt as if he'd been punched in the gut. He was going home. He and Kirsty both kept forgetting that he was really leaving tomorrow. It felt like a bad dream. He'd only just found her, and he wanted to build a future with her. It was going to be hard to maintain a long distance relationship, but he had no choice. He had to get Sadie home and see her through her illness.

As soon as Kirsty was out the door, he turned back to his sister. "What's going on?"

"I just want to make sure everything is set for tomorrow. You said you were going to get us checked in." She frowned at him. "Or did Deydie volunteer me to teach another quilt class?"

"No." He wished she would. Then he could stay a while longer with Kirsty.

Sadie cleared her throat, but it wasn't to get his attention. Was she getting sick?

"Are you feeling all right?" he asked. Maybe he should ask Doc MacGregor to take a look at her.

"My throat's a little scratchy. I might be getting a little summer cold."

Oliver pulled out his phone. "I'll call the doc and tell him you're on your way over."

Sadie rolled her eyes. "Don't be ridiculous, Oliver." She shivered.

"Come here and sit down." Oliver held out the quilt that Kirsty had given to him this morning. She called it Four Crowns.

Sadie looked around, embarrassed.

"Just get warmed up a bit. We're not in North Carolina. Scotland is chillier than home."

She sat down and pulled the quilt over her shoulders. "I know." For a moment, she sat silently.

"It's going to be hard, going home, with Gigi not there."

"I know. Nothing feels like it's ever going to be the same again." That was a huge confession so he backpedaled. "But we're going to be okay. Do you hear me?"

She wrapped the quilt around her more tightly. "I need to tell you something. And you're not going to like it."

Hadn't they all had enough bad news? He sighed heavily. It better not be about that *Ross Armstrong*. Oliver was glad he was gone, and good riddance. He was certain that Ross had taken advantage of Sadie, and Oliver hated him for it. His sister didn't deserve to be used.

"Go ahead and tell me," he said.

"It's about Gigi."

"What about Gigi?"

She sat there so quietly, it reminded him of when their parents had died. She hadn't cried. She just sat there looking blank. And the only thing he could do for her then was to read to her. Like their parents had done for them every night. It took a long time, but finally she started to laugh again. Live again. He wanted that for her now . . . but he didn't think that reading to her this time would work.

They weren't a huggy-type family, but he wanted to reach out to her now. "Go on. What is it?"

"I wasn't sure how to tell you before, but you have a right to know. I may be somewhat responsible for Gigi's death." She told him about her application to grad school.

"We knew about that," Oliver said.

"What?"

"Sadie, *good grief*, the way you leave things lying around . . . Gigi and I both knew you wanted to apply for the library science program. We were just waiting for you to tell us."

"So you two were discussing it behind my back?"

Sadie had accused him and Gigi many times of having their own little club because of their early morning chats. "You know Gigi just needed someone to talk to, so she used me as a sounding board. She loved you very much. You know that."

Sadie hung her head. "I know she loved me. But what you don't know is that we argued. The day she died. She wanted me to pick up the fabric from the quilt shop, but my application was due." She wiped at the tears that began leaking from her eyes.

"Oh." He grabbed a tissue off the side table and handed it over. He'd promised Gigi to never tell Sadie, but that was a moot point now. "It's not your fault."

"That's what Emma said."

"Emma? You talked to her?" Why hadn't she come and talked to him? He was her brother.

"It just kind of came tumbling out. She has a way with people," Sadie said.

"I guess I can see that. She got me talking the other day, and I was telling her all sorts of things before I even knew it."

They sat there not speaking for a long moment. Sadie was probably still beating herself up, and he needed to find the right words to tell her the truth about Gigi.

Finally he did reach out and touch her shoulder. "Sadie, when I say it's not your fault, I mean, it's really not your fault."

"What the heck does that mean?"

"You're probably right about Gigi telling me things when maybe she should've been talking to both of us." He shook his head. It had been so difficult carrying this around. "Gigi made me promise never to tell you."

Sadie got that look in her eye . . . that she was on the verge of becoming irate. "Tell me *what*?"

"It was right after your diagnosis and Gigi didn't want to worry you."

Sadie stood, the quilt slipping from her shoulders to the floor. "I swear, Oliver, if you don't spit it out . . ."

"Sit down." He picked up the quilt and held it.

Sadie towered over him, glaring, waiting.

He stood, too. "Gigi got some bad news, too, right after you did. Her heart was bad. It was only a matter of time."

"What?"

"She didn't think you could handle it, with everything going on. As I said, she didn't want to worry you."

"She should have told me. *You* should have told me."

"She made me promise that I wouldn't. I can see now that was a huge mistake." Gigi also made him promise that he would take care of Sadie no matter what. He thought about Kirsty. He would honor his grandmother's request, even if it meant he might lose his true love.

Kirsty opened the door and the smell of Italian meatballs came in with her. She seemed to be taking the temperature of the room, then carefully made her way to the table and set down the sack. "I'm going to step into the schoolhouse for a moment to check on a few things."

"It's okay," Sadie said. "I'm leaving." She didn't say good-bye. Oliver couldn't blame her. Once again, Sadie had been dealt a load of crap.

Kirsty came and rested beside by him, rubbing his back. "Is she going to be all right?"

"God, I hope so. I don't know what to do. She's so young and has had to deal with so much grief."

Kirsty wrapped an arm around his waist and squeezed. "Don't forget, Oliver, that you're grieving, too." She leaned up and kissed him on the cheek. "And Sadie isn't a little girl. She's a woman, and I can see a strength in her that perhaps you can't. She'll cope. And rise above."

He sighed and gazed into Kirsty's face. "You have a way about you. Whenever I look into your eyes, I start to believe that everything is going to be okay."

"Trust in that." She wrapped her arms around his neck and kissed him until the rest of the world fell away and it was just him and Kirsty, and tomorrow wouldn't come.

All the men on board the *Betsy Lane* were celebrating as the sun went down, making her the loudest fishing vessel in the fleet. They'd fished through a bad storm, caught their quota, and were heading home sooner than expected. As the vessel rounded the bend, Gandiegow came into sight, and Ross checked the time—Friday, eleven p.m. Good thing they didn't finish any earlier or he may have run into Sadie.

When they pulled up to the pier, Ross grabbed his duffel and stepped off the boat. He'd much rather be fishing on the *Indwaller* with his brother, but the *Betsy Lane* had served her purpose.

He made his way home knowing his grand plan had failed miserably. He'd done everything he could to keep Sadie off his mind, even taking extra shifts on the boat, but the lass still haunted him. No matter where he went on the boat, or what he did, the thought of Sadie was right there with him. He just felt fortunate now that he was back in Gandiegow that she was gone.

As he passed the schoolhouse, Oliver came out the side door. Ross stopped and stared. *Did Sadie go back to the States without him?*

Oliver stalled and glared. "I thought you were gone."

"I thought ye were gone, too."

"There was a storm. Our flight was canceled."

What? Ross looked about nervously.

"Yes, my sister's still in town. But you better stay away from her."

Ross planned to, but he sure as hell didn't like getting ordered around. For an answer he only stared back.

"I mean it," Oliver said. "She's been jerked around enough."

"What do you mean?" Had someone put the moves on Sadie while Ross was out of town?

"I mean, she doesn't need you sniffing around." Oliver went on.

Ross rarely had the urge to punch someone besides Ramsay, and that was usually in good fun, but he had the urge to punch Oliver now. Maybe instead, he'd give him a verbal jab, threaten to sic Deydie on him for being at Kirsty's at this late hour. "If I were you, laddie, I'd be careful. Ye're on our turf. Our rules." He nodded toward the school building. "I'm sure the folks in town wouldn't like ye *sniffing* around our schoolteacher, either."

"Just watch yourself." Oliver glared at him another second, and then huffed off.

Ross was tempted to go by the quilting dorms, to see for himself if Sadie was really there. Just to know for sure.

But, showing great restraint, he headed home instead. When he got there, no one was awake. He went into the kitchen for a glass of water and gulped it down. But his thirst still wasn't quenched. He set his duffel in his room, intent on going to the pub.

Ross was kicking himself. He should've asked Oliver when their flight was rescheduled for. Would they be leaving in the morning? Afternoon? Later? And if it was later, what was Ross going to do then? He'd probably see Sadie. Then what?

As he approached the path that led to the quilting dorms, he came to a decision. He needed to see the lass, and settle this once and for all. He'd had his fill of cozy moments with her. She needed to understand that it was over. There was no future for them. Friends, or otherwise. She was leaving, and he was going to embrace his freedom.

His step quickened. When Thistle Glen Lodge came into view, he saw that all the lights were on. Why the heck wasn't she in bed, getting her rest? He marched up to the door and knocked.

In the next second, he changed his mind. He should just walk away. He turned to leave as the door opened. She stood there in a cotton robe, pulling the belt into a bow.

She looks angelic. And desirable! The sight of her was like a boom swinging and hitting him in the chest. He wanted to both protect her and devour her at the same time.

She stopped short. "What . . . ? Why . . . ?"

"Can I come in?" His voice sounded hoarse as if his throat had been lined with sand.

"No!" She perched her hands on her hips. "I'm glad you're okay," she said—and moved to shut the door in his face.

He put his hand up to stop it. "Why wouldn't I be okay?"

"The storm! The town was worried sick," she said, glowering at him.

"I doubt that. It was only a wee thing," he said.

"Well, it didn't look *wee* or feel *wee*. But it's good you're alive. Now go away." She pushed harder at the door.

He understood why she was angry. "Give me a minute to explain." What could he say? He'd been a coward to leave as he had? That while he was gone his plan had backfired and he still hadn't been able to get her out of his mind? He definitely couldn't say he wanted to peel her out of that robe and make love to her.

She glared at him. "You left without saying a word." Her voice cracked.

He reached out to touch her, but she backed away.

She shook her finger at him as if Deydie had given her lessons in how it was done. "You've told everyone in the country that we're such great friends, yet I was left looking stupid when you snuck off in the middle of the night."

"Nay. I worked on the shelves through the night and left early in the morn."

She glared at him harder. "You know what I mean."

He didn't like that he'd upset her. A flush had crept up her neck into her face.

And he got it. He hadn't just upset her; he'd hurt her. Didn't he promise that he would never do that? "Come here." He pulled her into his arms quickly and spoke before she could pull away from him. "I'm sorry, lass. I didn't think it through."

"No. You didn't." She stood as rigid as a plank on the deck of the *Betsy Lane*.

He rubbed her back, hoping to soothe, but really hoping she would forgive him. "Ye want the truth?"

She nodded into his chest.

"I respect you too much to use ye."

She pulled back and nailed him with a sneer. "Yet you didn't respect me enough to say *good-bye*."

She wasn't listening. Or he wasn't being clear. "Do I really have to spell it out for you, lass?"

She stood there, waiting, staring him down.

He stepped away, laying a hand on the banister, not meeting her gaze. "I came here just now to tell ye that we can't see each other again. I can't be near you." There. He'd gotten it out.

But still she said nothing.

"Don't ye get it? I'm a strong man, Sadie." He tilted his head back and gazed up at the simple chandelier in the foyer of the quilting dorm. "But I'm not strong enough to be around you and not want to take ye to bed."

Chapter Fourteen

Sadie breathed in sharply. Had she heard him right? He wanted to take her to bed? *Her? Plain Sadie?*

Ross faced her, and she found herself staring into his eyes. Kind eyes. Genuine. "I'm sorry," he said. "I shouldn't have been so blunt."

She grabbed his shirtfront and pulled him down. Before she kissed him, she sent a message with her eyes . . . *I may be plain but I'm not meek, and I want you, too.* When she was pretty sure he got the message, she went for the gold . . . she kissed him long and hard.

At first, he seemed shocked, but then he kissed her back, hungrily. After a moment, he grabbed her arms and set her away, panting.

"No! I'm not going to use you. I told you that I care too much about ye to do that."

Yeah, yeah, I get it—we're just friends.

But so much had been taken away from her. But she could have this one thing, couldn't she? She mustered up every brave cell in her body and said what was on her mind. "Well, I'm not quite as noble as you. I plan to get a proper good-bye this time. And if in the process, I happen to use *you*, then you'll just have to deal with it."

She held her breath, waiting. She'd never said anything so bold in her whole life.

It took a couple of seconds for him to react. Maybe he was warring with himself. Or maybe her being so direct and straightforward was hard on his system. Finally, he growled and wrapped her in his arms. She grabbed him by the shirt, kissing him back. She was so desperate for him that she would've done anything to be with him.

He scooped her up and carried her to the sofa in the living room. When he set her down, he knelt beside her. "What's that?" he said, gesturing toward the blazing hearth. "A fire? At this time of year?"

"I was cold," she said. "And I wasn't waiting around for some man to keep me warm."

He laughed. "Ye're full of yereself right now. Bringing this big man to his knees has ye feeling pretty cheeky, doesn't it?"

He stopped laughing and stared into her face, as sober as the fire was warm. He touched a finger to the birthmark above her mouth, and traced it. "I'm quite fond of this heart of yeres."

He closed his eyes and leaned in, kissing her birthmark tenderly. It was intimate. Exquisite.

"Take me to the bedroom," she murmured. "Anyone could walk in. Like Deydie. Or my brother."

He pulled back, giving her a slow smile. "Good point."

He stood and helped her to her feet. But he didn't take her to the bedroom. Instead he pulled her to him, kissing her again. At this rate, they'd never make it down the hall. To move things along, she ran her hands under his shirt, up and over his chest. He ducked his head and she pulled off his shirt, dropping it to the floor. For a second, she soaked him in, but she couldn't do that for long without touching him. She ran her hand down his chest and abdomen as if she was counting the muscles. But it only made her antsy and she was done messing around. She wrapped her arms around his neck and hopped into his arms, wrapping her legs around his waist, the whole time kissing the heck out of him. That got him moving to the bedroom.

Once inside, he flipped on the light switch and closed the door.

"Lock it." She unwrapped her legs and slid down.

He did as she asked and came back to her. "I want to see you."

She gave a half smile. "Are you sure? There's not much to see."

"Oh, luv, I bet there is." He reached out and with two fingers carefully lifted the tie of her robe. "May I?"

"Don't say I didn't warn you."

As if he was dragging out the anticipation of opening a present, he slowly untied the bow.

He was killing her, but she remained still.

"Can't you hurry up?" she teased.

"Don't spoil this for me, lass. I've wanted to peek under yere clothing from nearly the first moment I met ye."

"Ha, ha. Very funny," she said.

He pulled away, cocking an eyebrow.

"Why'd you stop?" Her disappointment was real.

"Because I don't like ye putting yereself down."

"I'm not. I'm just reporting how it is. I own a mirror."

"Then ye're not seeing what I see." He took another step away from her.

She took a step forward. "That's it? You're going to hold out on me?"

"Aye."

"That's not very friendly." And from the big lug who loved to tell everyone that they were great friends.

But he was a man, after all, and men like seeing women naked. She would just have to oblige.

Sighing heavily, she toyed with her belt that he'd been undoing a moment ago. "I feel bad for you." She undid it and let her robe part. Granted, there wasn't a lot there to look at. She had on a spaghetti-strapped cotton night-gown that came to just above her knees.

But the poor guy was looking at her, as if she was built like Jennifer Lopez.

She pushed the robe from her shoulders, taking one of the straps down with it. "Well, I guess you'd better leave then. I'm going to bed." The robe slid to the floor.

Ross watched silently.

Hmm, now came the tricky part. Did she really have the gumption to strip completely naked with him look-ing on? She pulled back the covers, trying to decide if she did.

Ross moved closer, standing right behind her. He ran his finger under the other spaghetti strap. "Just once, say ye're beautiful out loud. That's all I'm asking." His voice rumbled deep, his burr rich with emotion. No, she thought. Not emotion . . . desire.

She tilted her head to the side, willing him to pull down the other strap, but Ross only drove her crazy with his finger stroking back and forth.

"I can't," she whispered.

"Ye will." He leaned down and kissed the strap, then ran his tongue along her neck. "For me."

People lied in the bedroom all the time, so maybe this once, she would lie, too. "I'm beautiful."

The waiting was over. He spun her around and kissed her as if he'd ached his whole life to put his mouth on hers.

She moaned, glad things were moving quickly now. She undid the buttons of his jeans as he kissed her face, her eyes, her neck. In the process her other strap fell and with it went her nightgown. She was left with nothing but her panties.

"Aw, lass, ye *are* beautiful." While gazing at her, Ross stepped out of his jeans, as natural and effortless as water.

She knew that her breasts were no bigger than lemons, and her underwear was nothing special either—plain, white Hanes. But he looked as if he might drop to the floor and worship at her feet.

Pointedly, she gazed at his boxers. "Is that for me?"

He didn't even glance down. "Still feeling cocky, heh?"

"No." She gestured to the obvious. "Looks like you've cornered the market, though."

"Come here." He reached out and tugged her, pulling her to his chest for a kiss.

But a sobering thought hit her. She tore her mouth from his. "Do you have any protection?" She had never even considered bringing condoms to Scotland. And she was pretty sure Oliver hadn't packed any for her either.

Ross glanced at his jeans lying on the floor. "In my wallet."

"Good." She wondered how many he had at the ready.

He cupped her face. "Can I get back to kissing ye now?"

Only if you do it in such a way that I don't fall desperately in love with you.

She kissed him, but upped the ante by cupping his backside and pressing herself into him.

He groaned. "Aw, lass, don't ye want it to last?"

She did. Forever and ever. "It's your fault that I'm impatient." She rubbed intimately against him.

"Ye're killing me," he mumbled indistinctly, because he was nipping at the pulse in her neck.

"I can't help myself." He was her fantasy lover and she would take advantage of this moment, the opportunity of a lifetime. She was never going to see him again, after tomorrow.

Oh, God!

Tears sprang to her eyes . . . *I'm never going to see him again!*

Instead of becoming a blubbering mess, she kissed him harder. And Ross responded. He eased her back on the bed and returned her fervor. He kissed every inch, starting at the top and working his way down. When he got to her panties, he peeled them away slowly, gently scraping her skin with his nails, then laid kisses everywhere his hands had been. Before he even got around to removing his boxers, she was frazzled, writhing on the bed, pleading with him.

"Ross. Now. Please."

He nipped at her hip bone. "Patience, lass."

But she'd had enough of his blasted calm. Turnabout was fair play. Or was it *all's fair in love and sex?* She didn't know. She wanted to make him feel as desperate for her as she was for him. She scooted out from underneath him.

She pushed him onto his back and crawled on top, though he had to have a hundred pounds on her. "My turn." Her voice had become a husky rasp. She started at the top and began kissing her way down, but didn't get too far when she realized that suckling at his ear drove him absolutely mad.

One second she was in charge, and in the next, he was back on top.

He reached over the side of the bed for his jeans. He cursed as he fumbled with the wallet and then the package. She didn't even know how he'd gotten his boxers off. He wasn't even suited up for a second, or gave her a cursory *brace yourself*, before he drove into her.

It was pure bliss, the most thrilling sensation of her life. To make him that crazy for her—*the power of it*—and then for him to fill her, wholly, completely . . . she was breathless for him.

"Sorry," he gasped. "I couldn't . . . stop. I had. To have. You." He drove into her again and again.

And she was with him. To the edge too quickly. She wanted it to last. She felt beautiful in his arms, *absolutely beautiful*. Sex, at this moment, was everything it was supposed to be. *She* was everything she was supposed to be! She spilled over into the abyss, crying out his name. Over and over.

And then it really was over. He rolled off, both of them panting hard.

She didn't know what she expected next, but she certainly didn't expect him to sit up, rake his hand through his hair, and reach for his boxers.

By the pull of his brow, he looked conflicted. She didn't know what to do. Seconds ticked by, but that only seemed to frustrate him more.

He glared at the floor while pulling on his boxers. "Dammit, Sadie. I shouldn't have done it. And didn't I tell you this would happen? Now, what am I supposed to do? We made a right mess of it, and I'm sorry for it!"

She wanted to punch him. Sorry? She wasn't sorry. She was spent, and at the same time, she wanted more. He sounded angry. At her? At himself? She didn't know.

He turned on her. "I told you this wasn't in the plan." He looked into her eyes, and as he did, the anger slipped away and was replaced by self-loathing. "And bluidy hell, not only that, I should've been gentler."

"No." Her voice hitched. He should just be quiet. He'd been perfect. Too perfect. And now she was afraid she was going to cry.

Ross ran a hand through his hair, more confused than ever. What was wrong with him? He came here to the dorm intending to do one thing, but had done the opposite. *Now* wasn't the time to be tangled up with some damned Yank who was leaving.

Now was his time to start living. For himself!

And *gawd*, if he was going to make love to her, he should've done it right, not been a horny bastard with zero self-control. He should've been a gentleman. But he'd taken her hard and fast. As if she didn't matter. But she did. He was supposed to be her friend.

He had to apologize. She had to forgive him. "I'm—"

Sadie cut him off. "I don't want to hear it." Her voice was wobbly.

He had to know. "Did I hurt ye, lass?"

Her bark of laughter was derisive. "That was nothing, stud."

She may have thought she sounded tough, but she was too genuine to pull it off. Sadie was the sweetest person he'd ever met, and now she was upset.

He looked at the door. "I screwed everything up." They couldn't be together.

Even though being together was so . . . right.

"I think you'd better go."

Ross pulled on his jeans. He made it as far as the door, but couldn't leave—*again*—without saying the right thing. He spun back around, ignoring her eyes. He had to. Her eyes held all the power.

"Good-bye, lass." He couldn't get out of there fast enough.

As he closed the bedroom door, he heard an *erghh!* from the other side, along with a pillow slamming against the frame.

Deydie knocked louder on the front door of the Armstrong cottage. Maggie had told her that Ross was home, but he wasn't coming to the door. She turned the knob and went inside. She had to speak to him right away.

When yesterday's storm blew in out of nowhere, canceling flights, keeping Oliver and Sadie here, Deydie knew it was a message from the Almighty—*Keep the two of them in Gandiegow*. At first, she hadn't seen the lass's worth, but she was starting to see it now. The town quilters were thrilled with her library, and surely the out-of-town quilters would be, too. And Sadie had done a hell of a job teaching the master quilters. Kilts and Quilts could always use an extra teacher. And her talent for reading to others. Well . . .

"Ross," Deydie hollered. "Where are ye?" Surely, he wasn't still in bed. It was eight o'clock, late by fishing standards.

Deydie pounded on Ross's bedroom door anyway. "Are ye here?"

He opened the door, shirtless, his hair a mess, and a mean scowl on his face. "I'm here."

"Good. I heard ye were back. We need to talk. First, I need some tea." She went to the sofa and sat.

He sighed heavily, following her. "What is it that ye want?"

"Less attitude. And tea," Deydie said. "Earl Grey or oolong. Then ye and I are going to talk."

When he didn't move from his spot, Deydie got angry. "I don't have all day. The wedding is almost here and there's still a damned lot of work that has to get done."

Ross went into the kitchen, put the kettle on, and then took the wing chair beside the sofa. "Tell me what's on yere mind."

These were desperate times, desperate times, indeed. "I need ye to keep Sadie in town."

"What? She's leaving today. And ye're the one who told me to stay away from her."

"It's really Oliver. We need the lad here in Gandiegow."

"Her brother told me to stay away from her, too."

Deydie leaned forward. "I don't care what he said; this is for his own good. And Gandiegow's. He loves

Kirsty, and he needs the right kind of push to marry her. The whole town needs him. If we're to keep the Kilts and Quilts retreat top-notch, then he has to stay and do our *computering*."

Ross looked away, muttering to himself.

"Speak up," Deydie said. "Me ears aren't what they used to be."

"And Sadie? How do ye propose I make her stay? Handcuffs?"

"I don't care. If handcuffs is what ye have to use, then I'll look the other way. But I'd prefer that ye keep out of her bed."

"Oh, good grief." Ross's cheeks turned red.

Deydie smacked the coffee table. "Ye have a way with the lass. We've all seen it." And, well, it seemed as if the Almighty was on Ross's side—He'd sent a storm to keep Sadie here long enough to see the lad again. That was a strong sign in Deydie's book.

"I don't want to do this," he said.

"But ye will," Deydie countered.

Ross looked away and ran a hand through his hair. "When are they scheduled to leave?"

"At five this evening. That's why ye have no time to waste."

The kettle whistled. Ross unfolded himself from the chair and went to the kitchen.

Deydie rose, too, and spotted a plate on the counter. "I'm going to skip the tea. But I'll take one or two of Maggie's oatcakes on my way out."

Sadie lay awake all night, replaying every second of what had happened in this bed. If she went over it enough times, then maybe she could change the outcome. *Complete insanity.* She might've dozed, but her brain had never turned off. She just couldn't believe Ross had left like that. Yes, she'd told him to go, but not before he was nearly dressed and halfway out the door. He'd taken off as if a rocket had been strapped to his backside and lit. Bam—he was out of here!

Just another abandonment. Her parents' deaths. Gigi's heart attack. CKD robbing her of a normal future. And then to not have five minutes of joy after experiencing the most wonderful encounter. She would never forgive Ross.

But that wouldn't be fair.

He was right. It was her fault. He'd said he didn't want to be near her, or that he couldn't be, or some such statement . . . she couldn't remember which. But she'd just had to have her way and seduce him. To act so tough, saying he'd have to deal with it if she used him. But he hadn't dealt with it. She buried her face in her hands, trying to hold back the tears. She'd ruined everything. He was her friend and she'd run him off. She owed him an apology for putting him in such an awkward situation and forcing him to make love to her.

Well . . . had she really *forced* him? "Argh! I don't know!" She was going nuts.

Someone was knocking at the front door. Surely they would go away, if she ignored them. Instead, she heard them come in. *Them* was really one person, if she heard the footsteps right. And she knew those footsteps. Sadie pulled her quilt over her head. She couldn't deal with him now.

He tapped at her bedroom door. "Sadie? It's me, Oliver. Can I come in?"

"I'm still mad at you," she said.

Oliver opened the door. "I know. But one day, you'll understand why I couldn't tell you."

"I'm not a child! I understand now. But I'm still angry." And if she was willing to admit it, maybe she was angrier at Gigi than at him. But that made her feel guilty in ways she couldn't explore right now.

"I need to talk to you." He sat on the end of the bed.

"You're acting weird. What's wrong?"

He examined the pattern on the quilt. "This looks familiar. Did you and Gigi make a quilt like this?"

She sat up and propped herself against the wall. Being sleep deprived made her impatient. "Out with it, Ollie. What has you being so nice?" *And had her being direct.*

"I have a favor to ask."

Well, that was a switch. He wasn't one to ask so much as issue marching orders.

"Go on," she said, kind of intrigued.

"I want to see if we can stay a while longer. I'm not done setting up the computers for the school. I also have a list of repairs I've agreed to make for various folks around town."

Sadie knew what he was really looking for . . . more time with Kirsty. "You can stay. I'll go home."

He shook his head. "I know that. But I would feel better if you were here with me."

Some things never changed. He wanted to keep an eye on her.

"I'm a grown woman, Oliver."

He looked at her with earnestness. "I know. I'm working on seeing you that way. Be patient with me. Kirsty said to tell you that I'm a work in progress, especially when it comes to you."

Sadie knew she liked that girl for some reason. "Kirsty has a good head on her shoulders."

Oliver gazed out the window across the room. "I *really* like her, Sade."

"I know you do." And Sadie could feel herself caving. The most vulnerable look she'd ever seen came over his face. "Can you do this one thing for me? Please?"

"You need to see where this leads," she said for him. "To see if it's real?"

"Yes."

"For how long?" she asked. Would she be stuck here forever while Oliver made up his mind?

"Another week? Until after the wedding?" He almost seemed like the little boy she remembered before their parents had died. Excited. As though he was sure he was getting a new bike for his birthday or something.

She nodded. "All right. I'll do it. For you." She would be miserable, but at least one of them would be happy.

Chapter Fifteen

Ross watched with disgust as Deydie lumbered out the door. He didn't have much time, not nearly enough to come up with a real plan. Five o'clock was only nine short hours away. Hurriedly, he showered, dressed, and skipped breakfast in lieu of finding Sadie and saying something to make her stay.

He was doing this for Deydie . . . *not himself. He* wanted Sadie gone. He was exhausted from thinking about her all the time. And he was tired of losing sleep. Last night, after he'd ruined their lovemaking—no, sex—he hadn't slept well at all.

He just hoped to God that he was given the right words before he got across town to Thistle Glen Lodge. And that she didn't find something more lethal than a pillow to lob at his worthless head. He was halfway there and he still had nothing.

"Ross? Hey, Ross, can ye come here for a moment?" Doc was coming out of the General Store with a package of disposable diapers under his arm.

"I'm in a hurry."

"I only need a minute," Doc said. "I need an extra set of hands to move Angus's crib."

"Okay. But only if it's quick." Ross followed him to the doctor's quarters, now not only worried about what he was going to say to Sadie but about time running out.

Deydie would be upset with him if he didn't complete his mission.

Doc glanced over. "Maybe ye should tell me what's troubling you while you have a chance." He opened the door to the doctor's quarters and motioned for Ross to head upstairs. "Emma isn't home."

Maybe he *should* talk to Gabe. Ross remembered how it had been with Gabe and Emma: at war with each other one minute and married the next. Maybe Gabe could help him sort out his feelings for Sadie—or at least give him an idea of how to get Sadie to stay. But how to explain?

"What's going on?" Gabe asked.

"It's Deydie," Ross said.

Doc followed him up, shaking his head in complete understanding. "It usually is. What is she up to now?" He opened the door and motioned to Ross. "The crib's in our bedroom."

"So?" Ross looked confused.

"Ye'll understand when you have yere own bairns. I'm taking a stand. I'm kicking Angus out of our room. I want my wife back."

"How is Emma going to feel about it?" Ross figured Doc would probably have to sleep with Dominic's pig, Porco, in the lean-to behind the restaurant.

"In exchange, I'll take care of the lad at night. She'll

agree to it. I have my ways, plus she's sleep deprived. Now, back to Deydie. What has she done?"

Ross understood about being sleep deprived. If he wasn't, he probably wouldn't tell Doc what was going on. "Deydie wants me to find a way to keep Sadie in town."

"Ye don't sound happy about it." Gabe grabbed one side of the crib. "Why don't you just ask her to stay?"

"I may have done something to complicate things," Ross admitted.

"I see," Gabe said, as though he knew perfectly well what had happened. He pulled the crib away from the wall. "Get the other end there."

"If there was a way to keep her here without me actually asking her to stay, I wish I knew what it was. What would make you stay, if you were in her position?"

Doc seemed to be thinking about it as the two of them tilted the crib on its side and angled it through the door.

"Well, maybe if you had a terrible accident. But you might not want to maim yereself for *Deydie's* sake." Doc paused for a second. "Or . . ."

Ross was really feeling desperate. Maybe getting his arm caught in the conveyor at the North Sea Valve Company like Ramsay had done wasn't a bad idea. But would it be dire enough for Sadie to agree to stay on? "Or what?"

"My wife wouldn't approve of what I'm about to say. And I don't condone this either."

"Condone what?"

"I'll tell you exactly what to say, and I'll back you up. But if you ever tell anyone that this was my idea, I'll call ye a liar in front of the whole damn town and then kick yere arse afterward for blabbing."

"Just tell me," Ross said as they pushed the crib up against the wall in its new room, the nursery.

"If I were you . . ." Then Doc told him the plan.

Sadie lay in bed for a long time before dragging herself out and taking a shower. There were plenty of things for her to do today now that she wasn't going home. She could work more on Quilting Central's library, sew on Gigi's memory quilt, or pretend that Ross had sailed off to Mars.

But that wouldn't fix the ache in her heart.

As she was drying off, she heard a knock at the front door. She slipped on her robe, tied the knot, and went to answer it.

Ross stood there with his duffel bag in hand.

Which made no sense. Hadn't she banished him to Mars? And she couldn't see him now. She hadn't figured anything out yet.

The man didn't wait for her to speak, but came in. "Sorry about this, lass. Doc said I should stay here. Medical emergency."

Sadie scanned him from top to bottom, seeing only gorgeousness. "Bullsh—"

He put a finger across her lips, stopping her. "Listen. Will ye? While I was away, ye know, on the *Betsy Lane*—"

She cut him off. "So that was her name. How was she? Better than me?" Sadie had a lot of anger built up—at herself, at him—and she hadn't gotten any rest.

"The lobster boat, Sadie. Her name is *Betsy Lane*," he said patiently as if she was dim-witted. He set his duffel down.

"I know what you meant." She walked down the hallway into the living room, trying to put some distance between them. She couldn't think clearly with him so close.

Ross followed. "I just got word that one of the crew members has come down with the measles. My bunk-mate, Rabbie. The problem is that I've been exposed. And I don't want to give it to anyone else."

She turned around to see if Ross was lying, but he wasn't meeting her eyes. She had to hand it to him though. It took guts to walk back in here after he'd hightailed it out so fast only, what, nine hours before?

"Any chance I could get some breakfast?" he asked. "I rushed right over to Doc's . . ."

Ross had trailed off and was staring at her robe as if remembering how she'd peeled out of it earlier.

Finally he pulled his eyes away. Hopefully, he didn't realize that she was naked under there this time. Unfortunately, she was well aware, and she heated up at the mere reminder of how wonderful it had been being underneath him while he made love to her.

Concentrate. She took a deep breath. "Why did you need to rush to Doc's?"

"I needed to find out what to do. Ye know, because of baby Irene." Ross's expression was sincere, but there was a small glint in his eyes that said he was enjoying himself.

"Hasn't she been vaccinated against the measles?"

He shook his head. "Nay. She won't get her vaccination until she's a year old. Doc says it's very dangerous for her to be exposed, too. Good thing I haven't seen any of the family yet."

"Really? Where did you sleep after you left here last night?"

He didn't miss a beat. "On the family boat."

She could tell that was clearly a lie. "And where did you shower this morning? Off the pier?"

"Doc's," he said as if rehearsed.

"And why exactly are you staying here instead of next door at Duncan's Den?"

His expression fell. "Too many memories." The pain that creased his brow was absolutely genuine.

"Sorry."

"Doc says it's best if I'm here, in case I do come down with the measles. There's no one in town who'd have time to nurse me, except you. Of course, ye won't be able to leave today. Ye'll have to wait until I'm out of the woods."

She shook her head and asked sardonically, "How long will that be?"

"The incubation period is seven to twenty-one days. If I don't get sick in the next three weeks, then ye're free to leave."

"I'll give you a week. It's the best I can do." And it would give her a chance to apologize for forcing him into her bed . . . after she figured out some way to say it.

"You—?" He seemed shocked that she'd agreed, and so quickly. Of course, he didn't know about Oliver's visit earlier, and she had no intention of telling him.

"I'll take it," he finally said. "But if I get sick after ye leave, it'll be on yere head."

"Wait a minute," Sadie said, her brain finally catching up. Sleep deprivation and his damned good looks were muddying the waters for her. "Haven't *you* been vaccinated against the measles?"

"Yes and no. I missed my booster. I should've had it five years ago. Doc checked the date."

"And what about me?" Sadie said, but she already knew the answer. "Aren't you worried about infecting me?"

"My question exactly, but Doc says you had a booster before you came to Scotland."

Which she had. And Doc MacGregor knew that because Oliver had given him her medical file.

"I'm having a hard time believing that you're going to stay quarantined in this quilting dorm for the next three weeks."

He looked stumped for a second, but recovered. "Doc said I can go fishing. John and Ramsay got their boosters on time."

She had to hand it to Ross. He'd done well on his answers. The problem was she was out of questions.

Ross had to congratulate himself for not getting thrown out in the first three seconds. By the look she was giving him, she wasn't buying the whole measles-exposure-thing, but she wasn't calling him on it either. He pushed his luck further. "Now," he said, "can I have some breakfast?"

"Help yourself. I'm getting dressed." She was still mad at him, clipping her words, as if throwing stones.

He blocked her path and laid his hands on her shoulders. She stiffened, but didn't blow past him.

He bent down a little so she could see his face, and to know that he spoke the truth. "I'm sorry for how I acted last night. I was a cad. A complete and utter fool."

Her eyes said she agreed with him.

He went on before she could voice it. "For all my talk about what good men do and don't do, well, I was terrible. I hope you can forgive me. I never should've left like I did, or blamed you for that matter."

She hung her head, sighing. "No. You were right. I am to blame. At least for part of it." She paused, a blush creeping into her cheeks as if she was remembering how she'd kissed the hell out of him. "I never should've forced you into having sex with me."

"That's not exactly what happened."

Her eyes met his. "But I hope you'll forgive me just the same."

He grinned at her. "On one condition." He shouldn't do it, but he couldn't help himself as his eyes drifted down to her robe. "I promise to forgive you for forcing me to take ye to bed, if ye tell me what you have on underneath there." The way she chewed her bottom lip for a brief second, he knew she liked how much she turned him on.

In the next moment, she shot him a stern look that said he'd lost all rights to seeing her cute little body. "You can ask all you want, but I'm not saying."

He touched a strand of her wet hair. "Well, I'm yere man, if ye need assistance with a zipper. Or anythin'."

She raised her eyebrows and stared at him pointedly to let him know that he still wasn't off the hook.

He let go of her hair and stepped aside.

She walked away, but paused. "You can have one of the bedrooms upstairs. We don't even have to see each other while you're here."

"I was hoping to share with ye. I'll be lonely upstairs all by myself," he said, forlornly.

"I'm sure you'll survive." As if to escape, she hurried toward her room.

But his stride was longer than hers, and he came up from behind, touching her arm. It was as if he could feel her soft skin underneath, the memory still powerful of how they'd been together. He'd been playing with her since he'd gotten to the dorm this morning—except when he'd apologized—but playtime was over. A wave of seriousness washed over him. "But lass . . ."

She looked into his eyes.

"Ye can banish me from yere room, and spout that ye won't be seeing me. But ye can't keep me from *seeing you*. The real you."

He wasn't looking at her robe this time. Ross was gazing into her eyes, and it was unnerving. Sadie had never felt more flustered, more vulnerable, and more exposed.

And yet more safe.

Without responding, she slipped away. What could she have said anyway? He was the most confusing and irritating man. As she dressed, her irrational thinking returned with a vengeance. She'd been able to talk to him like she had because she was still angry about how abysmally last night had turned out. But now, alone in her room, with nothing but her crazy thoughts, she had to ask herself: Why did Ross want to stay here with her?

On its heels came another thought: What would Oliver do when he found out that she and Ross were cohabitating? He'd probably make her get a doctor's note from Gabriel. But Sadie felt pretty certain Ross had cooked up this plan all on his own. But the question still remained . . . *Why?*

Her heart turned sappy. *Hopeful.* But she pulled out her mallet of reason and squashed those little flutters of promise.

When she came out, Ross was gone. For a moment,

she wondered if she'd made up the whole encounter. But as she walked to the foyer, she tripped over his duffel bag. It was almost as if he'd left it there to remind her that he was coming back.

The second she entered Quilting Central, Deydie rushed toward her. "How are ye this morning, lass?"

Thrown off balance by such unprecedented friendliness, Sadie answered cautiously. "I'm fine." She looked around for Oliver, but he wasn't there. She guessed it was up to her to talk to Deydie about extending their visit. "I was wondering how you would feel if we stayed in Gandiegow a while longer. My brother and myself." Sadie decided it was best to make it sound as if it was her idea; Oliver might not want the whole world to know that he was trying to figure out what was going on between him and Kirsty. "Would it be okay if I stayed at the quilting dorm for another week?"

Deydie clapped her hands excitedly, then latched on to her arm, looking relieved. "Of course, 'tis fine. I'm so happy ye're going to stay." She turned to the room. "Sadie and Oliver are going to be with us a mite longer." Everyone there smiled at Sadie.

Sadie was baffled at how Deydie's attitude toward her had changed. Even more puzzling: She had warmed to the old woman as well.

Deydie pulled her over to her sewing machine. "Now, come sit and work on yere quilt while I get some of the wedding things done."

I could get used to this feeling of belonging, Sadie thought. Everyone but Deydie had made her feel so welcome in Gandiegow, and now Deydie had joined in as well. It was wonderful to be wanted.

Sadie settled in behind the machine. As she worked on the next quilt block, the Old Maid's Puzzle, her mind wandered back to Ross and her heart beat double time. She didn't buy his measles story; he was definitely up to something. But she was willing to drop her questions and let it play out.

When the quilt block was done, she held it up. "Damn." She'd stitched one of the pieces wrong. She dug in her sewing bag and found a seam ripper. The mistake was with an interior piece, too, so nearly the whole block would have to be taken apart and redone.

If only she could undo the mess she'd made of her life as easily, undo what she'd done with Ross. The Old Maid's Puzzle block suddenly seemed fitting.

As she attacked the first seam, Bethia wandered over and took the chair beside her. She pulled out a white handkerchief and blue embroidery floss.

"It's for Father Andrew, for the wedding. I'm putting his initials on it."

Sadie nodded, but her mind was on ripping out the seam. "Ugh, this seam isn't cooperating." There was a knot that didn't want to get undone. The more Sadie dug into it, the more she feared she might make a hole.

Bethia began hand-stitching. "You might be able to put things to rights by ripping out a seam, but I say, sometimes it's best to leave a block as it is. Part of a magnificent patchwork, and a way to look back on the messes we've made and think how in the end, it all turned out fine. Lovely, in fact."

Sadie stopped what she was doing and looked at Bethia, pretty sure she wasn't talking about quilting.

Bethia laid a fragile hand on Sadie's. "Don't ye think it's best to let things lie as they may and move on?"

Sadie nodded in agreement and put the seam ripper down.

Kirsty clapped her hands at the front of the room, getting their attention. "It's time to put our sewing away and turn Quilting Central into wedding shower central. Moira will be here within the hour."

For the first time, Sadie noticed a table was already dressed in white tulle and piled with gift boxes wrapped in white paper. She would've had a present for Moira, but she never imagined she would still be here.

Deydie nudged her. "Don't worry, lass. We saved something special for you to give to Moira—the last bit of sewing on her wedding dress. Tradition says the dress shouldn't be finished until the last moment. We left two small tasks for the end. It's extra special to be the one who sews in the strand of hair."

"Hair? Really?" Sadie asked.

"For luck, of course. As yere present for Moira, ye can sew the hair into an inner seam and finish the last few inches of the hem."

Working on the dress had been a community effort, and Sadie felt honored to be included. She also liked the idea of doing something for her new friend, Moira.

"Would ye like to help with the tablecloths or setting out the food?" It seemed strange that Deydie asked instead of ordering her; maybe the old woman was really starting to like Sadie.

The next hour rushed by with a flurry of activity, making everything perfect for Moira's arrival.

She showed up in a white dress, cut the same way as the plum-colored dress that had to be her favorite. Her brown hair was pulled back in a clip, and she seemed embarrassed to be the center of attention.

"Sit here, lass," Bethia said, guiding her to a small table. "We're going to begin this celebration with the Passing of the Recipes."

Deydie, who had taken the seat next to Sadie, dug in her dress pocket and produced two index cards. "I printed up one for ye to give Moira when I found out ye were staying. Later, it would be grand if ye wrote out yere own favorite recipe."

"Thank you," Sadie whispered.

"I figured ye wouldn't have time. Now, shhh."

"Let's start at this side of the room, and one at a time, bring yere recipe up to Moira for her box." Bethia pulled out a beautiful dark wood box adorned with a Celtic knot on the front face and a tartan bow on the top. She set it on the table beside Moira.

"It's the MacBride tartan. Father Andrew's clan," Deydie explained.

One at a time, each Gandiegow woman rose solemnly, announced what recipe she was gifting the bride and why it was a favorite, and then presented it to Moira. As if it was a dance, Moira nodded each time, said *thank you*, and stowed the recipe in the gorgeous box.

"What a lovely custom," Sadie whispered to Deydie.

"Aye," Deydie whispered back. "We're blessing Moira's table with our favorite recipes to nourish their marriage."

Deydie's recipe was for her mini cherry cheesecakes. Sadie followed with her index card, titled Deydie's Chicken Stew.

Next it was time to play a game: *What's in Moira's Sewing Basket?* Each attendee wrote down what she imagined was hidden away there. Maggie helped Glenna write down her answers, and in the end, the child won a stack of fabric fat quarters.

When Bethia moved to the table with the presents, Deydie tapped Sadie on the shoulder. "Get a needle and thread. I'll get the wedding dress so you can finish it and gift it to Moira."

Sadie went to her sewing bag, keeping her eye on the front so as not to miss a thing.

Bethia pulled the first wrapped box from the top of the pile and handed it to Moira. As she opened it, Bethia explained, "I made ye an herbal first aid kit."

Moira beamed up at her and then took out a couple of the vials, reading the contents. "Thank ye."

Maggie's gift was next. "It's a centerpiece for yere table," she said of the pretty vase filled with pebbles at the bottom, some shells in the middle, and a candle on the top. "To light yere way."

Deydie returned, laying the white gown across Sadie's lap, and then handed her a small Ziploc bag. "A strand of hair from Moira's mama, Pixie."

Sadie was confused. "I thought her mother was gone."

Deydie frowned at her as if she was daft. "She put it away in Moira's hope chest for this very day. Now stitch it into the seam to bring Moira good luck in her marriage."

Amy presented Moira with a quilted travel tote bag stocked with essentials. "For yere honeymoon," she said gaily.

Moira looked at her quizzically. "But we're not having one."

Cait got up and held out a folder to Moira. "Graham and I gift you with one."

Moira gave a little gasp before slowly reaching out to take it.

"Tell us where ye're off to!" Rowena called out.

Moira opened the packet and gazed at the itinerary inside. "Five days in Italy . . . Oh, my!" She looked up again, worried this time, her eyes darting to Glenna for a second.

Amy laughed, placing a hand on Glenna's shoulder. "Glenna is going to stay with us and help me with baby Wills. Aren't ye, Glenna?"

"Aye," the young girl said, beaming up at Amy.

Soon all the wrapped presents had been opened, from sundresses for their trip to practical items for their new home. Sadie had finished the last few inches of the seam and was waiting for Deydie to tell her when to present her gift to Moira.

But Deydie went over to her desk, where she sometimes sat with her notebook, and pulled a box out from under it. She lumbered over to Moira and put it in her lap. "Open it."

Moira took off the lid, pushed back the tissue paper and pulled out a quilt. This was a Sampler quilt, too, but made entirely of different kinds of Celtic knots. "Oh."

"We thought ye and Andrew would like it. We all had a hand in it over the last few months, even Glenna," Amy said. "Show Moira which block we did together."

Glenna hopped up and pointed it out as the room smiled, and Moira gave her a big hug. "'Tis the most beautiful quilt I've ever seen. Truly."

"All right." Deydie took the quilt from Moira; Bethia grabbed the other end. "Ye won't see this again until the ceremony."

Sadie wondered if that was another Gandiegow tradition. She'd have to remember to ask Deydie later.

Deydie stowed the quilt back in the box and said, "Now listen closely, Moira. I have some last minute instructions for ye. Tomorrow, when ye leave yere house for the last time as a single woman, don't forget to step out with yere right foot. Do ye ken?" As Moira nodded, Deydie dug in her pocket for a coin, which she held out to Moira. "Put this sixpence in yere bridal shoe."

Moira didn't take the proffered coin. "Thank ye, but I have Mama's sixpence from her own wedding day, along with her handkerchief."

"Aww, that's lovely," Bethia said.

"Aye. Rightly so. It should be passed from mother to daughter. That'll be yere *something old* then," Deydie said nodding her head.

Amy piped in. "I gave her a new pair of earrings to wear for the wedding. Her *something new*."

Cait came forward, unclasping the necklace from her neck. "I would be honored if you'd wear this tomorrow. The wise women say the *something borrowed* should come from a happily married couple, and I'm exceedingly happy with my Graham."

Sadie chuckled to herself, *What woman wouldn't be?*

When Moira nodded solemnly Cait clasped the necklace around her neck.

"And now for something blue . . ." Deydie said.

Claire sauntered forward with a flat square box in the

palm of her hand. "I might've picked up something for ye and Andrew while I was shopping at the Slip of the Tongue."

The women tittered. Was Claire giving Moira lingerie? Surely not, especially in public.

Cautiously, Moira took it and gingerly lifted the lid. Then she tilted the box for them all to see. Inside was a perfectly respectable garter, but the bride blushed anyway.

Claire hugged her. "Blue symbolizes the steadfast love that ye and Andrew feel for each other."

Deydie came forward again and cleared her throat. Sadie thought she might even be a little choked up. "'Tis a shame your parents aren't here to see you married," Deydie began, "but all of us here love you, Moira. And how nice that your uncle George will be there in your da's place."

Moira smiled bravely. "Aye."

Amy came to stand next to her. "And I'll be beside ye as yere matron of honor."

Moira glanced up, looking grateful to have her best friend by her side.

Glenna ran over and leaned against Moira. "And you have me as the flower girl."

Moira wrapped an arm around her waist. "Ye'll walk with me up the aisle?"

The girl hugged her. "Aye."

Deydie smiled at them all. "Before we wind this up, there's just one more thing. Claire, tell Dominic to keep that pig of his penned up tomorrow. It's bad luck for a pig to cross the path of the bride."

Claire laughed. "I will. But Porco was hoping to catch

a glimpse of Moira in that beautiful wedding dress that Sadie's just finished."

Sadie had completely forgotten that she was holding it across her lap, so enthralled was she with Gandiegow's traditions. She stood and held it up. "It *is* gorgeous." She walked it over to Moira.

"Thank you for finishing it for me." Moira glanced around the room. "Thank you all."

The women converged on Moira with chatter, laughter, and hugs. Sadie was nearly overwhelmed by the love in the room. Her whole life, she'd believed that big weddings were a waste of money, stressed everyone out, and only complicated things. But here in Gandiegow, it seemed like pure joy. What a beautiful gift they'd given Moira today. And for Sadie to witness it, and be part of it, was a gift to her as well.

The room was cleaned up in a whirl of activity, during which three more people hit Sadie up to add their loved ones to her *read-to* list. She jotted down the information, and when the crowd had left, sat down in her little library area to make notes on what books they might like.

Tonight, she would make up a schedule for the week: when she would read to others, when she would quilt— and when she'd have a chance to read a book for herself. But thinking about the evening ahead made her shiver. Ross would be at the quilting dorm. Big, handsome Ross, who seemed to take up all the space in the bungalow . . . and all the air. A severe case of the butterflies attacked her stomach and spread out to the far reaches of her nervous system.

Deydie lumbered over and plopped down on the library's sofa. "I'm beat. It's a good thing we don't have a wedding every month here in Gandiegow. I'm not sure me old bones could take it." The old woman glanced up. "What are ye doing for tea this evening? Would ye like to come back and eat with me at my cottage? I've leftover stew."

Sadie sat down next to Deydie and looked at her fondly. "I would love to, but I'm beat, too. I'm going to have the soup Freda left in the refrigerator and go to bed early."

The old woman patted her hand and scooted to the edge to rise. "Are ye ready to head home then?"

"I just want to pick out some novels to take with me."

Deydie gave her a nod. "'Night, lass."

Sadie smiled at how much Deydie had grown on her. "Good night."

At the door, the old woman spun around. "Tomorrow's a big day. Make sure ye get plenty of rest. Do ye hear?"

Sadie smiled. "I will."

"I don't want to come after ye with my broom." Deydie left without a backward glance.

Sadie picked out two books, stowed them in her Mondo bag, and headed for Thistle Glen Lodge. When she opened the door, the smell of fresh bread and garlic hit her nose.

"What in the world?" Somebody from Quilting Central must've snuck over here and left her dinner.

She dropped her Mondo bag on the couch and went to the kitchen. And stopped short when she saw the back of the big Scot in a black apron, stirring white sauce. Then he leaned over the pan and took a taste from the spoon.

As if Ross had used his superpowers to know she was there, he spoke over his shoulder. "Can ye nip off some fresh parsley for me?" He tilted his head to the potted plant on the windowsill.

She didn't move. "How . . . Why . . ."

"The parsley first. Then you may ask yere questions."

She pinched off a few leaves, rinsed them, and put them in the pot. "You surprised me, is all." She glanced at the homemade bread, cooling on the rack, and squashed the feelings that rose up; he'd said that he *saw the real her.* "You made bread? All by yourself?"

He laughed. "I'm not admitting to anythin', but I might've nabbed a pan of Maggie's dough while it was rising on the counter, and baked it here."

"What are you doing going back home if you're supposed to be contagious?" She had him now.

But he answered immediately. "I had to go back for my vitamins." He flexed his spoon-holding arm and a bicep bulged.

Sadie's middle squeezed deliciously, remembering the feel of those muscles as his strong arms held her last night. "You risked giving your niece the measles to get your vitamins?"

"'Twas no risk. Little bug wasn't home. I wore a mask and used antibacterial hand sanitizer before entering."

"Right. And I'm Miss Universe."

He turned and studied her from head to foot. She couldn't tell if he was imagining her in a bathing suit contest or taking her clothes off with his eyes.

She went to the cabinet and pulled down two plates, busying herself. And changing the subject. "So you know how to cook?"

"Dominic taught me how to make his Alfredo sauce. And Kit gave me her breakfast casserole recipe when she moved out, the same recipe she gave my mum, so I figure I have breakfast and dinner covered. Now I only need someone who can make lunch for me." He raised his eyebrows as if Sadie should offer.

"You're on your own, buddy," she laughed. He had a way of lightening her mood.

He made an aggrieved face. "Since the new baby came, I've been making my own." He flexed his muscle again, peering at the huge muscle sadly. "I'm wasting away."

She patted his back as she walked by. "I think you'll live."

"I guess." He dropped his arm.

She smiled. "That sauce smells amazing. When will dinner be ready?"

Sadie was pleasantly surprised that things weren't the least bit awkward between them, and they had a lovely dinner together. They really were great friends. She just needed to keep her head from entertaining pipe dreams. She was both saddened that she wouldn't experience being in his arms again, and grateful that they could still be friends.

Afterward, while they cleaned up the kitchen together, she wondered if he was going to figure out a way to go to the pub while maintaining his ruse.

Ross hung his kitchen towel over the oven handle. "Do you have any plans for the rest of the night?" The words sounded promising, but he wasn't acting as though he wanted to get her naked.

She told him the truth. "I picked up a few books at Quilting Central. Would you like me to read to you? You might like them." She tried not to think about how nice it'd been at his aunt's house in Glasgow, sitting beside him in her bed.

"A Dean Koontz novel?" he asked hopefully.

"No, Janet Chapman. I want to reread her books about the time-traveling Scottish warriors."

He grimaced. "Is it like Jane Austen?"

"Not exactly."

"Judging by your grin, I think I better stay away from her books, too." He looked about the room as if the book might jump up and attack him.

"I can't believe you're frightened of a little romance."

"Who said I was afraid?" His eyes flashed and Mr. Swagger himself sauntered toward her. He took her hand, admired it as if it was a cherished map before turning it over. His eyes came up to meet hers as he brought her palm to his lips.

Her pulse escalated and at the same time her breath hitched. He'd turned into a character from a Jane Austen novel and she—well, she was a sappy mess when it came to a charming Regency romance hero. A marshmallow melting over a flame.

"More?" he asked.

Her wobbly legs couldn't take much more, but she nodded.

He tipped her chin with his finger and kissed her tenderly, all restraint and propriety. But those qualities slipped away two seconds later as Mr. Romance turned back into the hot Scot. The kiss morphed from sweet nothings to let's-go-mess-up-the-sheets.

He pulled away, sounding out of breath. "Cards?"

She crumpled into a chair. "What?"

"Let's play cards." He didn't wait for her answer, but walked out of the kitchen.

Cards? She wanted him to come back and do that all over again! She followed him to the living room. "What are you talking about? Gin rummy?" *Or strip poker?*

"Nay. Haggis."

She wrinkled up her nose. "The stuff made from a sheep's stomach?"

"It's a card game. I believe Cait left a deck in each of the dorms." Ross opened the cupboard and moved around the board games. "Here it is."

They sat on the floor on either side of the coffee table. After he explained the rules, he dealt the cards. Just as they were getting started, there was a knock at the door and people entered.

Sadie had gotten used to the townsfolk popping in to the quilting dorm, but when it was her brother, she would've liked to be on a more even footing and not sitting on the floor. She was so grateful Ross had cooled things between them earlier. Oliver looked angry enough as it was without finding her in a compromising position.

Her brother towered over her and jabbed a finger at Ross. "What is he doing here?"

Kirsty laid a hand on Oliver's arm as if to calm him.

"Playing cards with yere sister," Ross offered.

"I thought I told you to stay away from her," Oliver said.

Ross got to his feet, maybe a power play as he was a few inches taller than her brother. "And I made it clear I take orders from no one."

"Enough." Sadie stood as well and put herself between

them. "As you can see, *Ollie,* everything is on the up-and-up here. Ross has made it *perfectly clear* that we're only *friends.* So why did you stop by?"

Kirsty let go of Oliver's arm and stepped forward. "It's me. I wondered if you'd like to join our yoga class tonight."

Gandiegow has yoga? Sadie glanced at the Haggis cards on the coffee table. "I don't know anything about yoga."

Kirsty looped her arm in hers. "Not to worry. It's just a restorative class. Very beginner, very basic. I figured with the wedding coming up that some of the town could use a class to unwind."

Sadie looked at her brother. "Are *you* going to do yoga?"

"Not tonight. I'm headed up to Cait's house. She's having trouble with her Wi-Fi. I'm just walking with Kirsty as far as Quilting Central."

"That's where we're going to hold our class," Kirsty said.

"Go on, lass," Ross said. "I'll clear away the cards. We can play another time."

"If you're sure," Sadie said. Ross was a clever one. He had found a way to stay behind without saying he would be sleeping there.

Sadie let Kirsty pull her to the door. She grabbed her sweater off the hook as she passed by.

Once they were outside, Kirsty looped her other arm through Oliver's, and they wound their way along the walk three abreast. "Ye've nothing to fear about Ross, Oliver. He's a good man. Verra polite. Last spring, we went on a couple of dates."

"What?" Oliver stopped and clenched his fists, but Kirsty pulled him forward again.

"Listen," she said. "Ross never laid a hand on me. Not so much as a good night kiss. There was no chemistry between us."

Oliver exhaled. "Then the man must be blind or gay."

Neither of them looked in Sadie's direction, or they would have seen the shock that she felt. Kirsty was gorgeous. *Gorgeous!* Curvy, with a face beautiful enough to be on a fashion magazine.

Ross never made a move? Sadie couldn't wrap her brain around it. She had the urge to go back to Thistle Glen Lodge and demand an explanation.

What the hell had he been thinking? If he'd dated Kirsty, then why didn't he take advantage of her perfectly pouty lips? Why didn't he have his rebound fling with *her?*

And then it hit Sadie. There could be only one answer and it hurt, really hurt. Ross kept telling her over and over what a good friend he was. When he'd kissed Sadie the first time, he'd made it clear that he wanted to give her some experience, because he'd been sure that she didn't have any. All the other kisses . . . more practice before she hit the road. Risk free, because she was leaving soon, no chance of her trying to hook him into a long-term relationship.

And them making love? Sadie wanted to sob at the truth of it. *Damn him.* Had he felt sorry for her, certain she couldn't get anyone into her bed? Once again, he'd only been trying to be a good friend. She didn't need him as a friend! She needed something more. The thought made her ill. Because *something more* wasn't possible for someone like her.

Chapter Sixteen

Sadie stepped into a different Quilting Central than she'd left an hour ago. The muted lighting, the soft guitar music, did nothing to dissuade her from not wanting to be there. In fact, she didn't want to be in Scotland at all. She wanted to be anywhere except in the same village as Ross Armstrong. She'd had enough of his pity, everyone's pity.

As she followed Kirsty to the far corner of the room, where the tables had been cleared and mats were laid out and battery-run candles were glowing, an anger, not remotely associated with yoga, grew inside Sadie.

"The others will be here shortly." Kirsty sat on the floor and slipped off her shoes and socks. She stopped and studied her. "Are you all right?"

Sadie copied Kirsty and slipped off her shoes and socks, too. "Oh, I'm grand."

Kirsty seemed to weigh her words but went with I'm-going-to-pretend-you're-okay. "One of the first things I do at the beginning of a session is to ask everyone if they have any injuries or medical conditions that I should know about before we start."

Sadie tensed even more. Was she was expected to talk about her CKD?

"Have you been hiking up the bluff? Or does your back hurt from quilting?"

"No." Sadie couldn't tell Kirsty about her aching heart.

The door opened and more women arrived—Cait, Emma, Claire, Moira, Amy, and Kit.

"That looks to be everyone," Kirsty said. "Usually the older crowd doesn't join us for the evening classes."

But the door opened again and a very pregnant Pippa came in. "Can I join ye?"

They all looked around nervously. "Ye can stay," Amy said, "but only if ye promise not to have the twins during downward facing dog!"

Pippa laughed. "I promise." She sat in a chair, but Kirsty jumped in and helped her slip off her shoes.

"She'll be fine," Kirsty said. "We're just going to do restorative yoga. I'll get you set up with a bolster."

"That would be great. I've been feeling so uncomfortable lately."

Amy set a bolster on Pippa's mat, the one next to Sadie's. "Ye should rest as much as ye can. After the babes arrive . . . well, there won't be much time for it then."

Both Emma and Claire agreed. Cait seemed quiet on the subject. Sadie had overheard Deydie speaking of the miscarriages that her granddaughter Cait had endured. All this baby talk must be hard on her.

"So what is restorative yoga?" Sadie asked, hoping to change the subject for Cait's sake.

Kirsty explained, and the others joined in to tell her

what they liked about it. Kirsty queried them if they had any injuries, too, then they got busy setting up their mats.

Cait said to Sadie, "I have to thank you for what ye've been doing for Mattie. He's really enjoying reading with you. A couple of times, he's even spoken about it."

Emma looked over and beamed. "I knew you would be great with him."

"And Dand," Kit chimed in. "Maggie hasn't stopped praising you. You've really made a difference here, between working with the children and the elderly."

"Yesterday," Pippa said, "when I stopped to see Mr. Menzies, he said he didn't know what he was going to do once ye left."

Sadie was blushing, not used to attention, let alone praise. And the thought of leaving made her sad.

Moira touched her arm. "I know ye're busy, but Glenna wanted to be put on yere list, too. I read to her, but the way Dand talks about ye, she thinks she's missing the fun. Do ye mind?"

"I'd love to read to Glenna." Sadie would definitely have to get that schedule together. And make sure to drop by Mr. Menzies's more often. Maybe she should get audiobooks for the library, too. Yes, the quilters would like that—something to listen to while they worked.

"What about a story time at the school?" Kirsty interjected. "That way you could take care of a lot of children at once. It would be good for them to be reading over the summer months."

Emma leaned over. "And you could have the children read out loud. Mattie might be ready for a bigger audience. The other children are supportive and I think Mattie would feel safe. I could be there to make sure it went smoothly."

Cait looked over at Emma gratefully.

Even though Sadie was supposed to go home soon, she got a picture in her head of dressing up as a princess and reading to the children. Or as a wizard. Or as a zombie . . . but only to the older kids who liked that sort of thing. For such a small town, things to do seemed endless.

"Okay, everyone," Kirsty said in a soothing tone, taking charge, "let's all lie back on our bolsters and open up our chests. Pippa, let me help ye get to the floor."

Sadie and Cait both jumped up, too.

Pippa laughed. "Ye might be able to get me to the floor, but I'm afraid ye'll have to get the crane from the factory to get me back up. Or find Max. He's the one who got me in this predicament."

"Aye," Claire said. "And ye had nothing to do with it."

They all laughed.

Kirsty had them start with some deep breathing. Sadie was self-conscious at first, but gradually she let herself relax. She couldn't imagine a nicer group of women to hang out with. And the most surprising thing happened— when she put her shoes on and headed back to the quilting dorm, she felt restored.

Ross snuck out as soon as Sadie was gone. He wanted to be a good chap and put in an appearance at Andrew's stag party at the pub. He rushed to The Fisherman and joined the crowd.

Brodie stood at the doorway and lifted an eyebrow. "Ye get hung up?"

"Something like that."

The door opened behind them, and Gabe walked in. Behind him was another. Gabe clasped Ross on the shoulder. "Ross, Brodie, this is my father, Casper Mac-Gregor. Be on yere best behavior tonight. He's the minister marrying Andrew and Moira tomorrow."

Ross and Brodie greeted him and Gabe went on to introduce his da to the rest of the men.

From halfway across the room, Coll nodded to Ross and hollered above the crowd, "What can I get ye?"

"Cola."

Brodie raised his eyebrow again. "Are ye driving somewhere later?"

"Nay." But Ross needed a clear head as he was trying to figure out what was going on with himself.

Why in the world had he been honest with Sadie and told her that he saw the *real* her? He shouldn't have said anything at all. He'd gone all sappy on the lass. Which was ridiculous. And although he'd never visualized a future with someone who had a serious illness like Sadie, he had moments of picturing what that might look like now. Caring for her. The whole deal. But the truth of it was he didn't see her as sick or fragile. He just saw her as Sadie.

His friend.

But then he'd made his friend his lover.

Max whistled to get the floor, but Ross didn't catch all of the toast. He had his own worries.

Surprisingly, even though he and Sadie had some issues after they'd had sex, they seemed to be okay now. And that's what he liked best about her. She wasn't a drama queen. She was steady. And she seemed to have forgiven him for—he hated himself for it—*nailing her.* He was going to make it up to her. He would. The next time they made love, he would be as attentive as a painter crafting a masterpiece. That is, if she'd let him.

Several others made toasts before Ross realized his drink was gone. He glanced at the door.

"Are you expecting someone?" Brodie asked. "Ye're as fidgety as Andrew was earlier. That is, until his brother called and said he wouldn't make it to the wedding."

Ross shoved his empty glass at Brodie. "I have someplace to be. I'll see you later."

When Ross arrived at the quilting dorm, he was relieved to find the place was empty; Sadie was still gone. He stretched out on the sofa and waited for the lass to come home. Maybe he'd get the opportunity to make up for what he'd done last night.

The door to Thistle Glen Lodge opened and closed. He shut his eyes, pretending to be her manly Sleeping Beauty. *Maybe she'll kiss me awake.*

"What in damnation are ye doing?" came a grumpy old voice.

His eyes popped open. "What the . . ." The fairy tale had turned into a nightmare in the form of Deydie's glare.

She kicked the leg of the sofa. "Get yere arse up from there. When I told ye to keep Sadie in town, I didn't mean for ye to shack up with her."

"How did—"

"Maggie. When she stopped by for the vases for the centerpieces, she said that ye'd announced ye were going to be gone for a few days. I figured it out. What the hell were ye thinking? How did ye come up with such an asinine scheme?"

Ross wanted to send her to Gabe for the answer. He opened his mouth, but Deydie apparently wasn't finished.

"Ye better not have set yereself up in the lass's bedroom." She looked as if she was going to head down the hall for proof of a love nest. "Didn't I tell ye I wouldn't have it?"

"As I recall, you said ye'd *prefer* I didn't."

Deydie's color turned angry. "I—"

Ross held a hand up, cutting *her* off this time. "Sadie told me to sleep upstairs." He didn't mention he was hoping she'd reconsider.

"Git that look off yere face." Deydie slammed her hands on her hips. "And git yere things and move back home."

"Nay. Ye have to admit that if it wasn't for me, Sadie would've been long gone from Gandiegow."

Deydie, like a stubborn ole mule, didn't budge from her position.

"Ye need me here at the quilting dorm. I'll be yere insurance policy. Let me be Sadie's friend while Kirsty finishes reeling in Oliver."

Deydie's arms dropped and she looked as if she might be considering his proposition. "Aye. But only because having Oliver here is that important to Gandiegow."

The front door opened.

"I'll head out the back," Deydie said, and was gone.

As Sadie walked into the room, his chest warmed. "Hallo, lass." The wake of Deydie was history, replaced by what Ross had planned for this evening—plans of finessing Sadie back into bed. He'd even let her read one of her romances to him if it was what she wanted.

What she wanted, he wanted.

"How was yoga?"

"Lovely." She looked all relaxed and dreamy-eyed.

"Are ye ready for bed?" He tried not to sound anxious, *but gawd*, he couldn't wait to hold her again.

She smiled at him. "Yes. I believe I am."

This is good. This is verra good.

He stood, rounded the couch, waiting as she walked toward him. He felt a little choked up at how much she affected him, and was so glad that he was here.

Feeling confident, he reached out to Sadie, anxious to have her lips on his. "If ye're off to bed, then I hope ye don't mind if I join ye." He couldn't wait to worship every inch of her, from her perfect breasts to that place behind her ear that he was sure would drive her wild.

She smiled at him sweetly and patted his chest. "Ross, you forget that I'm only your friend." Then her eyes met his. Her gaze now held steel and determination. "Do I look like I've had a lobotomy?" She patted once more, then walked past him, down the hall, slamming her bedroom door behind her.

Grace arrived late that night; the friend who would be caring for Glynnis while Grace was gone had been delayed. But in the end, she left her sister in good hands, the two friends excited for time together to catch up.

There were advantages to coming into town this late. Grace could take it all in and get some of her feelings under control as she headed to the cottage. The cottage she'd entered as a young bride and raised her three boys in. The cottage where she'd dressed in black and then bade farewell to the love of her life. She missed Alistair terribly, every day. Glynnis needing her, moving to Glasgow, had saved Grace. Taking care of her sister gave her life meaning and purpose. But sometimes it was lonely, too.

As the cottage came into view, she felt unsettled. She hadn't lived here in two years and she'd accepted that Maggie was the woman of the house, while she was just visiting. But that was the thing—she was just visiting everywhere, with no real home of her own anymore.

She let herself into the cottage and went to Ross's room, the bedroom closest to the front door. Maggie had told her that Ross would either take the couch or use a bedroll in the nursery. He was a good lad.

She stowed her things and went to the kitchen to get a drink of water. She was quiet so as not to wake Ross if he was on the couch. She peeked into the living area, but he wasn't there. After turning on the light over the stove, she walked to what was once Ramsay's room, but was now the nursery, and didn't find Ross or her granddaughter either. She wasn't worried about Irene—John had complained that the babe was still in their room. For a moment, she wondered where Ross was.

She smiled as a thought hit her—the lad must be out with Sadie.

Sadie needed to go back to yoga. Ross had ruined her buzz. She shouldn't have slammed the door, but it had felt good, and it nicely conveyed what she thought of his proposition.

She could share the same address with him and not succumb to his charms. She could sleep alone in this room. She could do this. She was strong. Strong enough to withstand a diagnosis that would've brought most people to a screeching halt. Strong enough to withstand her grandmother's death. Strong enough not to get her heart more broken than she already had.

She yanked open the dresser drawer and pulled out her nightgown, remembering how he'd slipped it from her shoulders. She ached to go find him and tell him that she didn't mean it; she'd take him no matter the circumstances. But after Scotland was over, she'd have to live with herself. There was a line, and she had to remember to keep it firmly fixed in her mind. It had been one thing to willingly offer herself up to him as his rebound fling. It was quite another for him to bury himself deep inside of her out of pity.

There was a slight rapping at the door. "Lass?"

She ignored him.

He tapped again. "Sadie? Let me in. Let me talk to ye."

She wiped away the few stupid tears that had leaked out. "Go away." Her voice broke a little, but she was certain he hadn't heard.

"Sadie, lass, I need for ye to forgive me."

For a *good friend*, he didn't listen very well.

She didn't say anything back. She wanted to yell at him that pitying her wasn't what she wanted. She wanted what he couldn't give. She wanted . . . she wanted . . .

"I'm right here, if ye change yere mind. I'm not going anywhere. I can't until you accept my apology." His voice reverberated through the door, as if he was sitting on the floor with his back against the wood. "I tried to apologize last night. And I'm sorry if ye took offense at me wanting to go to bed with ye again."

Enough was enough. She yanked open the door and he fell backward, but caught himself before his head hit the floor.

"You're apologizing for the wrong thing!" she growled, surprising herself further by standing up to him.

He rose from the floor. "Then tell me what I did. I can be pretty thickheaded when I've got other things"—he gave her the once over—"on my mind."

"You had sex with me because you felt sorry for me!" Sadie blurted.

"What?" He looked as though he didn't understand plain English.

"Pity, Ross! I hate to be pitied." She wiped away another tear, not caused by sadness, but by anger. "I was fine with being your rebound fling." That wasn't completely true. "But I never wanted you to go to bed with me because you pitied me . . ." She faltered. Thoughts bounced around in her head, but she couldn't voice them out loud.

Ross had the audacity to break into a grin. Then he chuckled. "Oh, *gawd*, lass"—he burst into full-out laughter—"ye've got it all wrong. Weren't ye listening last night?" He collapsed on the bed, shaking his head, laughing even harder.

"Stop it. It's not funny." She may even have stomped her foot.

Like lightning, he grabbed her arm and pulled her down beside him. Her backside hit the bed and made him bounce a little. He held her there, trying to get control of himself.

"Ye're so far off, that when ye hear the truth of it, ye're going to laugh, too." He shook his head some more.

She wished he would just get to the point. With his hand wrapped around her arm, her stomach was warm, and her anger melted. She needed to stay mad at him. It was the only way to keep her heart from falling in love.

Finally, he turned to her. "Ye're a goofy lass if ye think that I took you to bed because I pitied ye. The truth is, Sadie, I took ye to bed because I had no choice in the matter. I can't resist ye, woman." As he said the words, all mirth slipped away, replaced by seriousness.

"Oh." She stared at the armoire, thinking she'd rather have him laughing at her because it was easier to handle.

He brushed his index finger under her chin so she'd turn back to him. "I'm sorry that I rushed it. That I made it more about me than you."

She had no rebuttal to that.

He tipped her chin up and planted the sweetest kiss *in the history of kisses* on her lips. Warm, soft, gentle. She wanted to weep for the tenderness his kiss conveyed.

He ended the kiss and gazed into her eyes. "Do ye believe me? Will ye forgive me, lass?"

She nodded, not breaking eye contact with him. It occurred to her that they'd gotten this kiss backward. Weren't they supposed to maintain eye contact before the kiss and not afterward?

"Good." He hooked her hair behind her ear. "Now, if there's one of us that has to be pitied, it's me. I've figured out my perfect punishment for treating ye poorly."

"You have?" she whispered. She'd liked how they'd made love. She'd liked it very much.

"Aye. Ye're going to make me sit and listen while ye read"—he grimaced—"one of yere romance novels. Apparently, I need to learn how to properly woo a woman." He patted her knee. "Read more Jane Austen. That would serve me right. And maybe, just maybe, ye'll make a gentleman out of me yet."

But Ross was the gentlest man that she knew. Gentle with his words. Gentle with his feelings. Gentle with his touch.

"All right then."

He stood and pulled her to her feet. "But we're not going to do it in here."

She glanced up at him. "Why not?"

He raised an eyebrow as if she should know the answer, but then he told her. "Too much temptation. I'll go start the teakettle while ye get settled on the sofa."

After about fifteen minutes of reading *Sense and Sensibility*, Sadie started to yawn.

"Off to bed with ye." He took her hand and pulled her from the sofa. "We have a full day tomorrow and ye don't want circles under yere eyes. It's going to be grand having so many folks in town for the wedding."

"Like who?"

"Like my cousin Sophie, and her new husband, Hugh. She moved away, but of course she wouldn't want to miss Moira's wedding. Oh, and lots of friends who live in other villages around here."

"Is the church big enough to hold everyone?"

"We'll squeeze in." As if demonstrating, his hand engulfed her arm and he squeezed gently.

That little contact jolted her hormones—and the rest of her—awake. She wanted him to squeeze a few other places on her body. She liked being with him. He was great company. But she yawned again.

He kissed her on the cheek, and as if she needed guidance, he turned her toward the hallway and patted her on the bottom to get her walking.

"I'm going," she complained. It wasn't much of a *good night*. She wanted more. "Aren't you going to bed?"

"I'm going to stay up a while longer and read more about that hottie Elinor Dashwood."

She laughed. "Elinor is the opposite of *hot*."

"Maybe to you. But to me . . ." He whistled and then smiled. His gaze turned caring. "Ye rest now."

"Okay." She did as he said, but as she got into bed, she wondered at the game she was in: plain-as-walnuts Sadie playing house with the gorgeous Scot. She had to muster up some serious willpower not to return to the living room, just to be near him longer. She yawned again and her eyes watered. He was right—she needed her rest.

She fell asleep instantly, and was so tired that it barely registered when he quietly pulled the other twin bed next to hers and climbed in. He wrapped her in his arms and kissed her head. She was so relaxed and so warmed by his presence that she went right back to sleep and slept more soundly than before.

Chapter Seventeen

The first thing Sadie did when she woke up was to realize that she was alone. Ross was gone. She figured as much . . . *fishermen*. Today was the big day—*the wedding*—but that wasn't going to stop the fishermen of Gandiegow from doing what they had to do.

She took a long shower, then wrapped herself in her robe, and went to her bedroom, closing the door. As she was pulling on her underwear, she heard the front door open and footsteps approach down the hall.

"Sadie, I'm home," Ross said through the door. "Are ye all done in the bathroom?"

"I just finished."

"I'm going to shower. I hope ye left me plenty of hot water," he added.

Oops. He'd find out soon enough.

She went to the closet and peered at the dresses she'd bought with Ross. If Deydie hadn't warned her against it, Sadie would've chosen the green dress to wear to the wedding. But she didn't want to get in trouble with the superstitious woman for welcoming the fairies to Moira and Andrew's big day. She pulled the flowing purple dress from its hook and put it on.

From the bathroom across the hall came the outraged, "What? No! Sadie! How long did ye run the water?"

She smiled and ignored him. A little cold water would perhaps be good for the hot Scot.

Sadie pulled out her cosmetics case and peered inside, thinking it was bare enough to belong to the Amish. But she did have the basics—mascara, blush, eye shadow, and lip gloss. And because the occasion was a wedding, Sadie primped longer than usual—blow-dried her hair, used the curling iron, and applied makeup to her plain face. In the end, she wasn't unhappy with the results.

She left the bedroom in search of breakfast, but found more than she bargained for. When she reached the kitchen, her need for oxygen outweighed her need for food. She stopped and stared at the man before her.

Ross's cold shower hadn't taken away one drop of his hotness. In fact, he looked twice as handsome in a navy plaid kilt, thick knee-high socks, boots that laced at his shins, a dress shirt, tie, and jacket.

"Wow," she whispered.

He turned and smiled. Then he took her in. "Ye look lovely, lass."

"Not as lovely as you do!" she exclaimed.

He shook his head. "Sit down and I'll dish ye up some porridge. We'll want to be ready when the wedding party starts the wedding walk."

"What's that?"

He smiled. "Ye'll see."

They had their tea and oatmeal in companionable

silence. Afterward, they left their dishes to soak and argued over who would brush their teeth first. In the end, they shared the bathroom and brushed them together. It wasn't weird at all, except how comfortable she felt with him.

As he helped her into her light sweater, she stopped suddenly. "Wait a minute. You can't go to the wedding. What about the measles? What about being contagious?"

"Oh. Aye." He seemed to be working this one out. "Didn't I tell ye? I received a text this morning from Rabbie, my bunkmate on the *Betsy Lane*. False alarm. It wasn't measles after all."

"No?"

"Aye. Only prickly heat."

"So you're in the clear?"

"Well . . . aye." He didn't look happy about it. Was that because he had no excuse to stay here with her anymore? No, her eyes and her imagination must be muddling her good sense yet again.

With great formality, he offered her his arm. "Are ye ready to see a real Scottish wedding?"

She latched on to him, promising herself to let go the moment she saw anyone around. She didn't want to start any more rumors than were already bobbing around the village.

As they made their way along the path from the bluffs, Ross explained, "We have to go down to the boardwalk to see the wedding party, but most of the townspeople only have to wait at their doors for them to pass."

On the wind, a bagpipe skirl rang out and rose above the village.

"It's starting." He picked up his step, hurrying her along. When they arrived at the edge of the walkway, Ross pointed. "There they are."

Sadie unlatched herself from him and gazed at the far end of town. A bagpiper was leading the way, a small entourage following.

"Who is that playing the bagpipes?" she asked.

"Graham. Graham Buchanan." Ross grinned down at her. "He loves doing stuff like this."

The group came nearer and Sadie could see it really was the famous movie star.

He was dressed like Ross, but in a kilt that was yellow, red, and green, and he wore a hat on his head. Behind him was Andrew decked out in his kilt, a green-and-black plaid with a small stripe of purple in it, a black full-cut Argyll jacket with high-buttoned waistcoat, and his clerical collar. He looked handsome and proud as he walked beside Amy MacTavish in her midlength red plaid dress.

Behind them walked the best man, Max McKinley, in his kilt and suit jacket, and at the end came Moira holding Glenna's hand. Across her wedding dress, from right shoulder to left hip, she wore a sash of vibrant green and blue; Glenna's dress was made of the same tartan. Moira wasn't looking down at her feet today. She had her eye on the prize near the head of the pack—her man, Andrew. Every few steps, she would turn to Glenna and smile, as if this walk was but the first steps to the wonderful life that they had ahead.

As the wedding party walked past each house, the residents left their doorways and fell in behind the group. The music, the spectacle, the ocean as their backdrop—it was pure magic to Sadie.

"Oh, Ross, isn't it wonderful?"

He beamed down at her as if her excitement was contagious. "Back there, behind Ailsa and Aileen, is my cousin Sophie and her husband, Hugh." He sent up a wave to her.

The bagpipes became louder as the group got closer. When it was their turn, they joined in at the back.

But as the couple neared the church, a lone kilted figure stepped out between the houses, leading a gray horse by the reins. Sadie saw Moira's look of happy surprise, and was as overwhelmed by Andrew's thoughtfulness as the bride was. The horse's owner circled the path in front of them, as if displaying the horse, and then led the horse back between the houses so the wedding march could continue on to the church.

Graham stood beside the door and played on as everyone processed into the building except Moira and Glenna. As Sadie took her seat next to Ross, she thought the wedding couldn't get any lovelier, but then the service started.

The robed pastor, Andrew, Amy, and Max took their places at the altar, and Graham and his bagpipe led Glenna and finally Moira down the aisle. As his bride made her way to him, Andrew's face held such love that Sadie's eyes filled with tears.

Ross dug in his coat pocket and handed her a handkerchief. He leaned over and spoke quietly. "I've another one, if ye need it."

Sadie took the square from him and dabbed under her eyes. "Is that Doc's father?" The pastor looked so like Gabriel that if he were twenty years younger she wouldn't have been able to tell them apart.

"Aye. Casper MacGregor."

The ceremony included readings, like any other service, and Andrew and Moira exchanged rings and said their vows, but then there was something she'd never seen at a wedding. The couple knelt and the minister used one end of his stole to wrap Andrew and Moira's hands together.

In a deep, clear voice, Reverend MacGregor said, "We have witnessed the promises of Andrew and Moira. Together we now handsel them."

Sadie leaned against Ross and sighed, it was so lovely.

"As they are pledged to each other in love, so we promise, in hope, to be a living sign of love in the world. I declare that you are joined in marriage." The reverend unwound the stole and the couple stood. Next he took the Celtic Sampler quilt that Amy and Max had presented to him, which he proceeded to wrap around Andrew and Moira's shoulders.

"May the peace of the Lord be with you," Casper said, smiling.

At that, Andrew and Moira kissed each other joyfully.

"I present to you the new husband and wife," Reverend MacGregor announced, as everyone applauded.

Amy retrieved the quilt and laid it over a chair. Andrew undid the pin at Moira's shoulder and removed her tartan. Max retrieved another tartan from the front pew and gave it to the groom.

Ross leaned over. "The MacBride tartan. To welcome the bride into his clan."

Andrew held the tartan to Moira's shoulder and she helped him secure it in place with a brooch. Then to Sadie's surprise, Max reached into his pocket and gave a smaller brooch to Andrew, who knelt and pinned it to Glenna's sash.

"The MacBride crest," Ross whispered into Sadie's hair.

She was enjoying this play-by-play from her Scottish escort.

When Andrew was done, Glenna threw her arms around her new father and hugged him, kissing his cheek.

More tears leaked from Sadie's eyes. Glenna had lost her parents, but she was given a new family today. Ross handed her the other handkerchief.

While Sadie dabbed at her eyes, the wedding party walked to the table under the crucifix and took turns signing papers and the church registry.

Afterward, Reverend MacGregor motioned for everyone to stand for the final prayer. After *Amen,* the bagpipe sounded from the back of the church and Graham marched down the aisle to the front, turned and led the wedding party out again, first Max and Amy, then Andrew and Moira with Glenna holding their hands between them. The church bells began to ring.

Sadie's heart swelled. And because all eyes were on Andrew and Moira, when Ross took her hand and squeezed, Sadie didn't immediately let go. What a blessing to witness this wedding. She had rarely felt such happiness.

No wonder so many hookups happened after weddings. All that love had a tendency to spill over onto the guests, until everyone was oozing wonderful endorphins. And that's why Sadie was going to ask Ross to come back to her bed tonight.

Chapter Eighteen

Sadie's face throughout the wedding had all the excitement and wonder of Dand's on Christmas morn, Ross thought. He had never enjoyed a wedding more. As the crowd filed out of the kirk, he followed behind Sadie, guiding her with his hand on her lower back.

As the village and guests processed down the walkway to the restaurant, Ross lingered behind on purpose. When Sadie began to fall in line behind them, he pulled her between the buildings.

"Not so fast." He cupped her face. "I've been wanting to do this all morning." And he kissed her sweet lips.

She grabbed his biceps and mewed.

Gawd, she was enticing.

He let her go and stepped back. "That was because I didn't say *good morn* to ye properly."

She stepped closer and laid a hand on his chest. "I like *how* you said it."

"We'd better get to the reception," he said huskily.

"Yes. Before we are missed." She was probably thinking about her brother and the ruckus he would cause if he knew Ross had her alone again.

Together, they rushed to the reception, but when they arrived, people were still funneling in. When they finally made it upstairs to the grand dining room on the second floor of Pastas & Pastries, Max was standing beside Andrew with a dome-shaped mantel clock in his hands.

"I understand," Max was saying, "it's Scottish tradition for the best man to give the groom a clock." As he passed the clock to Andrew, the room applauded.

Andrew set the clock on the table behind them.

Max held up his hand. "But because I'm from the States, it's only fitting to give our man of the hour the traditional American gift, too." From beneath the table he pulled a bottle of whisky and held it up high for everyone to see.

The room broke into laughter, and Max and Andrew ceded the floor to Amy and Moira.

From the table, Amy retrieved a tray with a tea set. "If you are cold, tea will warm you," she recited. "If you are too heated, it will cool you; if you are depressed, it will cheer you; if you are excited it will calm you. William Ewart Gladstone." She passed the set to Moira.

Once again, everyone clapped.

Deydie hurried up to the front. "And now the cutting of the cake. Graham?"

"One of the piper's duties is to present his dirk for the couple to cut the cake," Ross explained to Sadie.

The famous movie star came forward and pulled a long decorative knife from the scabbard hanging from his kilt belt.

"Wait a minute, Graham. That won't do a'tall." Ramsay strode to the front, and produced his grandfather's sword from behind his back. "You agree, don't ye, that mine is bigger than yeres?"

Graham laughed and stepped back, allowing Ramsay to hand off the sword to Moira. Andrew laid his hand atop hers and together they sliced the first two pieces of wedding cake. One they gave to Glenna, and the other they fed to each other, while Ailsa and Aileen began cutting the cake for the rest of the attendees.

Ross leaned into Sadie. "I'll run up and get ye a piece, on one condition."

"What's that?"

"Ye save me a dance."

Sadie snorted. "Like anyone else wants to dance with me."

"Stay here," Ross said. "I'll be right back."

As he wound his way through the crowd, the cake line grew longer and longer.

Deydie stepped in front of the table and hollered to the room. "Don't fill up too much on sweets. Dominic has luncheon ready." She motioned to a long table where a pot-holdered Bethia was arranging steaming pans.

Ross glanced over at Sadie and almost abandoned the cake line; Abraham Clacher was introducing his grandson Brodie Wallace to her.

The band began to play, and Andrew led Moira out on the floor for their first dance. A few moments later, Amy, Max, and Glenna joined them. A few beats later everyone changed partners and Coll took Amy into his arms, while Max gently led the pregnant Pippa onto the floor. He wouldn't let her do more than lean against him as he swayed back and forth.

Ross finally reached the head of the cake line and

grabbed two plates. But when he turned around to find Sadie, he saw she was on the dance floor, too . . . with Brodie! Ross set the plates back on the table, ready to tell Brodie to buzz off. *This is my dance!*

But Bonnie tapped him on the shoulder. "How about we get this party started?" She took his hand and pulled him onto the floor.

Bonnie, who worked at the pub, was always on the hunt for a man. Being promised to Pippa all those years had provided *some* protection against her advancements, but since Max and Pippa got married, she'd tried to reel Ross in on more than one occasion. She was pretty and buxom, but always overdone, constantly changing the style and color of her hair and painting her face. Ross glanced over at Sadie. Today was the first time he'd seen her wearing makeup. She looked nice, but he decided he liked her better without it.

Bonnie brought him out of his musing. "Do ye have plans for later?"

"Aye," Ross said automatically.

"What kind of plans?" Bonnie was a persistent one.

"Fixing holes in the fishing nets," Ross said flatly.

Bonnie looked around, searching for her next prospect, and her eyes landed on poor, unsuspecting Brodie. "I wonder what he's up to tonight."

The song came to an end, and Bonnie shot off in Brodie's direction.

Ross wasn't much better; he wanted to snag Sadie before anyone else did.

Into his path stepped Maggie, with her sisters in tow. "Which one are ye going to dance with first?"

Ross was getting the terrible feeling that the rest of

the afternoon would be like this. He should've seen it coming. Between Kit and the rest of Gandiegow, if he'd had an actual dance card, he was sure they would have filled it for him.

He didn't get to answer before Rowena laid a hand on his shoulder and stepped forward. The next song started, a reel, and she dragged him onto the floor. He was thankful that the reel was fast so he wouldn't have to listen to a bunch of small talk. Rowena was a little too loud for him, a little too pushy—a lot like Maggie, in fact. Maggie was a good sister-in-law, but he certainly didn't want to be married to a lass like her.

Out of the corner of his eye, he caught Sadie being whirled around in Graham's arms and felt a pang of jealousy. Ross looked around. *Where the hell is Cait?*

When the song ended, he was able to take only one step in Sadie's direction to claim her for the next dance when Deydie insisted on dancing with him, and Sadie was nabbed by his own brother Ramsay. *It's beginning to feel like a conspiracy.* But hadn't they all been against him being alone with Sadie from the beginning?

When he saw Sadie make a plate of food, he got in line, too, hoping to sit beside her during the meal. But by the time he arrived at her table, Deydie and Bethia had taken up camp on both sides of her, and Ailsa and Aileen were sitting across. He decided to plant himself next to Sophie and Hugh instead, taking the opportunity to catch up on the news from their wool community, located an hour away.

After he cleared his dishes, he was, once again, passed from one woman to the next on the dance floor. And

Sadie . . . she was passed around, too, but looked to be having a fine time. Well, he was happy the lass was enjoying herself.

To no one's surprise, Brodie walked up to the band and took the microphone; they'd all been waiting for him to sing.

"Moira and Andrew," Brodie said, "Deydie says it's time for yere love song to send you on yere way. As for the rest of Gandiegow, the party will keep going."

A love song. Ross swung around and located Sadie at the punch bowl. He hurried in her direction, but out of nowhere, Maggie thrust her little sister Sinnie in his path.

"Fair's fair," Maggie said. "Ye can't do for one and not the other. I promised them both that ye'd take them around the floor."

He worked very hard at not losing it with his sister-in-law. Did she not understand that he wanted to dance with only Sadie? But instead, he held out his hand to the blushing Sinnie. "May I have the honor?"

Sinnie took it as the slow dance began.

Sinnie was Rowena and Maggie's opposite, her quietness music to a man's ear. Before Kit came along, Maggie had tried to marry one of her sisters to Ramsay. Now she was hoping for Ross to take one of them off her hands. Neither would do. Rowena was too bossy, and Sinnie was too young. Although, wasn't she the same age as Sadie?

His eyes sought out the American lass at the punch bowl, but she was gone . . . and found her dancing in Colin Spalding's arms!

She was smiling up at the bloke as if he was some romantic hero for bringing the gray horse to town for

Moira and all to see. Nonsense. The young gentleman farmer from up the road wasn't a good match for her. He just wasn't.

"Are ye all right?" Sinnie asked. "Are you angry about something? Didn't the wedding set well with ye?"

He looked down at her. "Ye're full of questions."

She stared at her hand on his shoulder. "Once ye do as Maggie wants—*dance with me and Rowena*—then ye're free to ask the American lass to dance."

He was a little shocked. He never knew Sinnie to be so observant. Only quiet.

"Sorry," he said. Sinnie deserved a more attentive dance partner. He twirled her out and then back. "What about you? Whatever happened to Davy the rich whisky maker?"

She laughed. "He was fun for a bit, but too full of his own comings and goings for my taste."

"Is there someone here ye might fancy?" Her eyes darted away and Ross followed her glance. "Colin, eh?"

She looked over Ross's opposite shoulder as if to ignore him, but her blush deepened.

"I'll see what I can do to help." Ross moved them in Colin's direction. When they were close enough, he tapped on the other man's shoulder. "Do ye mind if we switch?"

Colin smiled at Sinnie and Ross spun her into the man's arms.

On the next beat, he took Sadie's hand and tucked her in close, breathed her in, and relaxed. "Finally."

She cuddled into him, and he felt at home.

"How are ye doing, lass?" he said into her hair. "Are ye having a good time?"

"The best," she said.

"Are ye getting tired? Ready to go back to the quilting dorm?"

She nodded her head *yes* into his chest.

He danced them toward the entrance. As the song ended, he pushed them through the swinging door, and held her hand as they started down the stairs.

"Shouldn't we tell Moira and Andrew good-bye?" she asked.

Ross kept walking. "I bet they have more important things on their mind than missing us." He opened the next door and pulled them out into the night.

He took the path leading alongside the restaurant back toward the bluffs and the quilting dorm. When they were out of sight of the boardwalk, he pulled her into his arms and kissed her.

She was compliant, sweet, and intoxicating, but kissing her only made him hungry for more. *Much more.*

He pulled away and looked down. "The answer to yere question is *yes*."

"And what was the question?" she said with a knowing smile.

"Ye wanted to ask me back to yere bed."

She stroked his arms. "You're feeling pretty sure of yourself, aren't you?"

"Aye." He ran his hands through her silky hair. "I can feel the *want* in yere kiss. See it in yere eyes. Feel it in the way ye press up against me."

"Really?" she said, cocking an eyebrow. "Are you sure that's what I'm feeling?"

"Don't deny it, lass. I recognize it. Yere *want* matches my own."

Sadie laughed and wrapped her arm around his waist. "I guess we better get to the dorm then."

"And?" He held his breath. He needed to know for sure.

She tipped her head up and gazed into his eyes. "So you can join me in my bed."

Sadie opened the door to Thistle Glen Lodge. Without a word, she wrapped her arms around Ross's neck, and stared into his eyes, knowing this time would be different. This time she knew what *was* and what *wasn't*. This wasn't the beginning of Sadie's happily-ever-after, just a beautiful moment in time. And this intense emotion passing between them was a product of Moira and Andrew's wedding, a miasma of romance that would gently fade away. But she was going to enjoy every single moment until it did.

Without breaking eye contact, he picked her up, stepped inside, and shut the door with his foot—straight out of an old movie. Only then did he lean in for a gentle kiss. Yes, this time would be different.

He took her straight to the bedroom, but by the time they got there, the gentle kiss had worked itself into full-blown passion. He laid her on the bed and stepped back, running his hand through his hair and breathing hard. "Lass, we're going to have to slow down."

She kicked off her shoes. "Says who?"

"Last time I got carried away and went too fast."

"Last time, you were perfect." She crawled off the bed, feeling like a sex kitten, because this beautiful man looked absolutely miserable with desire.

"Ye're killing me. Ye know that?"

She shot him a seductive smile right before she pulled her dress over her head. She stood before him in bra and panties. "I like you looking at me."

"Ah, lass, that's good, because I so verra much like to be doing the looking." He kept his eyes on her while he began unbuttoning his dress shirt.

"No," she said. "Let me." She moved forward and continued what he'd started.

He ran his hands down her arms to her back, his gentle touch costing him. She read him like a book. With every caress, another clue would pop up that he was on a slippery slope to losing control. His eyes dilated, his nostrils flared, and his gaze warned her that he had to have her . . . now.

She kissed his chest as she quickly undid his kilt belt. He took care of her bra.

"Next time," he said, his breath short. He unfastened his kilt and let it fall to the ground. "I promise, next time—"

"Shhh," she said. "It's what I want, too. Now kiss me."

He did. As he laid her on the bed, he reached for his sporran and retrieved what they needed. But instead of putting it on, he kissed her neck, then moved downward to her breasts, and lower still. He pulled her panties off and kissed her *there*. Again and again. She squirmed under his loving assault, and when she was sure she couldn't take it anymore, she pulled on his shoulders.

"Please, Ross. I need you now."

He smiled up at her. "I like it when ye say *please*."

"This is no teasing matter," she complained.

"I know, luv. I know." He put the condom on and positioned himself above her.

Impatient, she pulled him down to her, joining them.

"*Gawd*," he groaned as he moved. "Sadie, ye feel so good."

If she could've spoken, she would've said he felt good, too. But he'd primed her too much. He pulled out, and when he slid in the next time, she came. *Stars! Blinding lights! Fireworks!* She felt every cliché. She was so overcome she was afraid she might cry.

"Aww, lass," he murmured into her hair. "Ye're so very beautiful." He kissed her forehead and then her cheek. He pulled out. "Are you crying?"

"I'm okay." She gripped his backside and pulled him close. "You made it happen too quickly."

He chuckled as he withdrew a little ways. "I did?"

"Oh. Yes." She liked her handhold, and met him halfway, lifting herself up as he came down to her. It felt so good. She began nibbling his neck. "Again."

He obeyed, figuring out a rhythm they both enjoyed. Pretty soon, it was impossible for either one to talk.

And then he lost it. Once again, his out-of-control orgasm sent her over the top.

"Oh, Ross, I—I . . ." She bit her lip to keep from telling him everything that was in her heart. She loved him with all that she had. Telling herself not to fall for him had been fruitless. But she wouldn't have missed this moment for anything. To be with the man she loved, in his arms like this . . . she had so much love that it didn't matter that he didn't love her back.

When the quake subsided, he laid his forehead on hers. "That was amazing, lass."

Then he moved to get up.

Instantly, she thought about how he'd vaulted from

her bed the last time and left her alone; surely he wouldn't do it again.

"I'll be right back," he assured her. "Don't go anywhere."

"Okay," she said, smiling.

He left the room for only a minute, and then he was back, crawling into bed and handing her a small towel. He lay on his side and faced her. "So that was good for you then?"

She laughed. "You know it was. You're just fishing for compliments."

His eyes twinkled. "And what am I, after all?"

"A fisherman."

He stilled suddenly, becoming thoughtful, serious as if he was crossing a major roadblock. In the next second, a spark of happiness came over him. And then elation. He kissed her quickly. "*Gawd*, Sadie, that's it."

"What's it?" She was still fuzzy-brained from their lovemaking.

"What I'm going to do for the rest of my life." He rolled onto his back and stacked his hands behind his head.

She rolled into his side. "And what is that?"

He shot her a quick smile. "Ye know how I've been trying to figure out what I love?"

Her brain latched on to the word *love*. Her heart, too. But he wasn't talking about her.

"Don't ye see? I love to fish. I love my job. To the outside world, it may look as if I've settled, that I haven't moved from the same spot. But it doesn't matter. Being on the water and fishing for a living is the only life for me. Do you know how freeing it is to know that I don't have to keep searching for a different career? I've had my dream job all along."

She leaned up farther and kissed his lips. "I'm happy for you." She'd found what she loved, too. She loved reading to people. Maybe she could start a reading service when she got back home.

She dropped her head on his chest. She didn't want to go home. She wanted this time with Ross to last forever.

He wrapped his arm around her. "Will ye go fishing with me in the morn?"

"With John and Robert and Samuel?"

"No. Just you and me. I want to share it with you. We'll take Ramsay's boat. I'm certain he doesn't have anything lined up."

"All right. It sounds like fun." But the sadness of her imminent departure still lingered. She cuddled into him even more closely.

He leaned down and gazed into her eyes. "Do ye know what else sounds like fun?"

"No. What?"

He rolled her on her back. "I guess I'll just have to show ye." And he did.

They talked, laughed, and made love again . . . and again. Every extra second she spent with Ross, she fell deeper in love with him.

After dozing very little and before the sun rose, Ross helped her dress in a T-shirt and capris for a short fishing excursion.

"I know ye're tired, and *gawd* knows I'm exhausted from ye putting me through my paces all night." He shook his head in wonder at her. "We'll only go out for an hour or so, and then we'll come back and rest. Or find something more interesting to do."

Thirty minutes later, out on the water and anchored in Pirate's Cove, Sadie learned that she loved fishing, too. Ross set her a chair next to his, and while he cast his line and waited, she basked in the sunshine and read one of her books, stopping every few pages to chat. Being together like that reminded her of her rock, where she'd relaxed, where she'd first begun to heal. She'd found such peace in Scotland, and all the while, Ross had been by her side.

On their fishing excursion, Ross didn't catch any fish big enough to keep, but he seemed content to have been out on the water with her.

When she started to yawn, he pulled anchor, rounded the bend, and docked the boat in Gandiegow. On the way to Thistle Glen Lodge, they kept up a conversation that seemed to have no beginning and no end.

Once inside, Ross took her hand, spun her to him, and kissed her like they'd been doing it forever. "Thank you for going with me, lass. I really enjoyed it."

"Me, too."

"I'm going to take a shower. Do ye want to join me?"

"Tempting. But I have to finish this chapter first."

"Yere loss," he said, laughing.

"I know. But save me some hot water." She thought about the cold shower that he'd taken. "Please. I want to soak in the tub for a while."

He smiled at her. "Sure."

Sadie stretched out on the sofa and opened her book. Before she knew it, Ross was done.

He appeared in front of her in only his towel. "The tub's all yeres."

She reached out and ran her hand along his calf. This playing house thing had its advantages. "Thanks."

There was a knock at the door. Before Ross could head for the bedroom, or before it registered that Sadie should've moved her hand, the Inquisition marched in . . . Deydie, Oliver, and then Grace.

Chapter Nineteen

Ross held onto his towel as Sadie dropped her hand from his calf and scrambled to sit up. His mother seemed more curious than scandalized, while Deydie clenched her fists, probably wishing she had her broom.

But it was Oliver who stormed forward and jabbed a finger at Ross's naked chest. "What are you doing here?"

Ross was at a disadvantage. A man needed his skivvies to argue effectively. "Excuse me while I find my clothes." He glanced down at his shirt at his feet. His mum seemed to have seen it before him.

"Stay right there." Oliver moved forward and yanked on Sadie's arm. "Go to your room."

Ross tucked the towel in extra tight. "Ye'll unhand the lass. Now."

Sadie unlatched herself, shooting a quick glance at Ross before lighting into her brother. "What gives you the right to come in here and tell me what to do?"

"Just tell me why he's here," Oliver ground out.

Ross had had enough. "The only reason I'm here is to help *you* out."

Instantly, Sadie spun on Ross. "What?"

Her hurt look made Ross wish he'd put it another way. He grimaced down at his towel, blaming his slipup on his lack of clothing.

It was easier to focus on Oliver than on Sadie's confusion—confusion that was fast turning to anger—so Ross glared at Oliver.

Oliver's attention was fully on him. "What do you mean, *help me out*?"

Ross looked to Deydie, but the old woman had gone mute. He wouldn't out her, but *dammit*, he didn't want to take the fall by himself either.

Oliver rounded on Deydie; "Do *you* know what's going on?"

Deydie's humped shoulders fell, but she wasn't one to look sorry for the things that she did; not for too long, anyway. "It could be that I talked Ross into keeping Sadie around. But I never told him to bring his toothbrush!" She glared at Ross for a long second and then turned a kinder face to Oliver. "I figured if *she stayed, you'd stay*."

"Why would you want *me* to stay?" Oliver asked.

"Everyone likes ye, lad. You'll make a fine match for our Kirsty, and we need folks like ye in the community. Someone with skills. Like the computering." Deydie seemed to genuinely care about Oliver. Ross had never heard her use such a gentle tone.

But he didn't have to see Sadie's face to know that, once again, Deydie's words had hurt the lass.

"Well . . . that's very kind," Oliver said. "But what's that have to do with *him* taking advantage of my sister? I talked to Sadie myself about staying for another week, and she said she would. You see, there was no reason for *him* to be involved at all."

It was Ross's turn to be a little peeved for being put in this situation. "The lass never said a word." Why hadn't she? He cocked a brow at Sadie, but she avoided eye contact.

"Son," his mum said, "go get dressed."

But nothing has been resolved yet. She was right, though. He needed to cool off, because he had no idea what he was going to do next.

Sadie watched Ross stalk from the living room. It felt more like he was exiting her life for good. *Playtime was over. Back to reality.*

Shoulders sagging, she turned to her brother. "Why did you come here, Oliver?"

He was still frowning after Ross, but took a deep breath and said, "I stopped by earlier today to tell you the good news. When you weren't here, I went to Quilting Central to see if Deydie might know where to find you."

Grace came forward and gave Sadie a quick hug. "I tagged along."

"What *good news*?"

"Last night, I asked Kirsty to marry me. She said *yes*. We're engaged."

Sadie didn't expect it to be so soon, but she should've. Everything always worked out perfectly for Oliver. She mustered up her good wishes, though it required digging deep. She stepped forward and hugged him. "Congratulations. I know you're going to have a great life together."

"When you know, you know," he said.

Ha, Sadie thought.

"We're going to marry here in Scotland," Oliver continued, "if that's all right with you."

As if Sadie had any say in it. "Sounds fine."

Ross returned, fully dressed, with his duffel bag in hand. Grace reached out and touched his arm as he passed. Then he was out the front door and gone.

Sadie felt as if her heart had gone with him. She was approaching numb. She was exhausted. She needed a shower. She needed the rest of them to leave.

Grace laid a hand on Deydie's shoulder to get her attention, but spoke to Sadie. "Ye look a little tired, lass. Do ye need to lie down for a bit?" She gave Oliver a motherly glance. "How about we let your sister rest?"

"Yes. I do need to lie down," Sadie agreed. She also needed a vacation away from Gandiegow.

Oliver didn't budge; instead he bombarded her with concerned eyes.

"I'm okay, Ollie. Promise."

"If you're sure." He hesitated another second, but Grace laid a hand on his shoulder, too, guiding him away. "We'll talk later, sis. Okay?"

"Oliver," Sadie called to him, before he got completely away. "I really am happy for you. And for Kirsty. She's a lucky woman."

After they left, Sadie didn't sit down and have a good cry over Ross; life was too short for such indulgences, and she had too much to do. She went to the bedroom and stripped the sheets, intending to remove any evidence that Ross was ever here.

From the beginning, she'd known the measles thing was crap, but she'd played along with the charade. A part of her really thought Ross had come up with a crazy excuse to be near her, that he had feelings for her. But he'd only been doing what he'd been told to do . . . like he'd been told to marry Pippa back in the day. Once again, he'd blindly gone along with what the town wanted of him.

Some things would never change. Ross would never change. And she was stupid for wanting to hang around to see if he would.

And in the next second, she knew she was responsible, too. If she'd told Ross the truth—that she'd already consented to stay for Oliver's sake—she could've saved herself a whole lot of heartache. Wanting Ross was self-destructive. She had enough damaging things going on in her life. She couldn't get rid of her bad kidneys just yet, but she could fix *this* problem.

She grabbed her phone and booked a flight, then ordered a taxi to pick her up. It would take a while to get out of Gandiegow. She would have plenty of time to shower and pack. She wouldn't stop by Quilting Central for Gigi's quilt; she could get it later, when she came back for Oliver's wedding. By then she would be stronger, have her head screwed on straight.

Sadie got everything in order and when it was time to meet the taxi, she rolled her suitcase to the parking lot. As the car pulled away from Gandiegow, she texted Oliver.

I've gone home. I'll be back for the wedding.

Then she shut off her phone.

Alone. Exactly what she wanted. She needed solitude to grieve her most recent loss . . . Ross. She laid her head back on the seat and let the tears flow, hoping they would begin to wash away the pain.

*   *   *

Grace left Deydie at Quilting Central, feeling equal parts giddy and guilty. She couldn't tell anyone that she'd stayed up half of the night, talking with Gabriel's father, Casper MacGregor! She couldn't believe herself, carrying on like a young lass—laughing and enjoying his company . . . and a bit of whisky. She would probably see Casper again today. What would she say to him? Would their easy conversation of last night be easy in the light of day?

Grace worried over the upset she'd witnessed between Ross and Sadie at Thistle Glen Lodge, but those two would surely be okay.

She'd watched them at the wedding. They were so in love, so in tune with each other . . . as she and Alistair had been. She glanced down at the wedding band she was still wearing three years after her husband's death, and guilt, like the tide coming in, washed over her again. Alistair was the love of her life. So why did she feel a connection to Casper?

She shouldn't have spent all that time with him. She shouldn't have let him kiss her good night on the cheek either. *Nay, not night, morning.* She blushed, remembering. She was too old to have a little crush on Reverend Casper MacGregor.

Grace put her mind back on Ross and Sadie, regretting how disheartened the lass had looked when Ross left. Grace had stayed out of Ross's affairs, mostly, but maybe it was time to get involved again. She hurried to Ramsay and Kit's cottage, hoping to catch her daughter-in-law at home.

Kit answered the door before she had to knock twice.

"Are ye busy?" Grace asked.

Kit stepped aside. "Come on in."

Their cottage was a small two bedroom, but it seemed to fit the sophisticated American lass just fine.

"I wanted to talk to ye about Ross and Sadie."

Kit smiled brightly. "After seeing those two together yesterday, I was wondering what I could do for them, too." She tilted her head to the side. "I fear I've been too pushy with Ross. I really should apologize."

"I'm glad ye see what I see between him and Sadie. But they had a wee upset this morn. Maybe later today we could fix it so they both show up at the restaurant at the same time. They can have a private dinner to work things out. If one of them would say how they are feeling, then the other one would surely follow."

Kit sat back. "You know Deydie's against Ross being with Sadie."

"Deydie doesn't have to know what we're doing," Grace said. "But if she becomes a problem, I'll talk to her. She can be reasonable."

Kit guffawed with a grin. "Sometimes. But not very often."

"So how do we get the two of them to play along?" Grace asked.

There was a knock at the door.

Kit walked across the room to get it.

Ross stood there with his hands in his pockets. "Can I speak with you?"

Kit laughed, stood back, and opened the door wider. "I'm popular today."

Ross ducked his head and entered. When he looked up, he seemed shocked. "Mum?"

Grace rose and hugged her boy. "How are ye, Ross?"

He looked a bit haggard. The frown lines between his brows didn't belong there. She and Alistair had raised three wonderful sons, but this one was such a kind man. No wonder he would pick a woman whose soul matched his own.

He looked so uncomfortable. "I came to see . . . if I could hire Kit." He wasn't just kind. He was smart, too. Smart enough to know when he needed help.

"I'll put some tea on, shall I?" Grace offered. "Ye two can sit at the table and talk."

Kit took a chair at the dinette set that was perfect for two, maybe three, when she and Ramsay decided to start a family.

"First, Ross," Kit started, "let me apologize. I didn't mean to harass you and browbeat you with that stream of bachelorettes. I was just worried. We all were. We were afraid you wouldn't get out there and look for your Mrs. Right."

Ross paced, impatient. "All is forgiven. As long as ye help me."

"Tell me exactly what it is you want. I don't want to assume anything this time," Kit said.

The kettle whistled. Grace set mugs in front of them both, and put one on the counter for herself.

"I need help with Sadie." He seemed both embarrassed and perplexed. "What is it ye call it? An introduction?"

Kit nodded.

"I need ye to set up an introduction for me and Sadie. That way, she'll know I'm serious." He looked in his empty mug. "She puts herself down. Saying she isn't pretty. But I think she's perfect." He glanced up at the both of them. "Don't you?"

Grace laid a hand on his shoulder. "Aye. Verra much so."

"Will ye help me, Kit?" He seemed a little desperate.

Before Kit could answer, another knock came; this one sounded angry.

Ross opened the door.

Oliver and Kirsty were on the other side, the lad's face as red as Kit's curtains.

"What the hell did you do to my sister?" Oliver's fist, like an avenging angel, shot out and connected with Ross's jaw.

"Oliver. Stop." Kirsty pulled him back.

Ross didn't retaliate, which was best for the Yank, since he'd been fighting two brothers since he was the size of a midge. He rubbed his chin. Maybe on some level he deserved it. He should've told Sadie how he was feeling, though he couldn't put into words just yet what exactly that was. The only thing for certain was that he couldn't stop thinking of her. But he had to deal with Oliver first.

"I didn't do anything to yere sister." But she'd certainly done a number on him.

"She's fragile," Oliver said.

"Bullshit. She's tougher than you and me put together." Ross sat in a chair and spoke to Oliver man-to-man. And he didn't care if the women in the room heard him or not. "She's certainly the only woman who's brought me to my knees."

His mum came and stood by him.

"What do you mean?" Oliver said. Some of the fire was gone from his voice and his face, too. Kirsty was rubbing his arm, which seemed to calm him.

Ross pointed in the direction of the quilting dorm. "I didn't mean for this to happen."

Tension filled Oliver's face again.

"I didn't want to meet someone special." Ross glanced at Kit. "Which is one of the reasons I was less than thrilled about you setting me up with every woman within a fifty-kilometer radius. I wanted to play the field. But Sadie ruined it for me." Ross was in agony. He couldn't have it both ways—his freedom and the lass. "I guess I'll just have to be with her."

Oliver folded himself into the other kitchen chair. "Not going to happen."

"I think ye've pushed yere sister around enough. Let her decide," Ross said.

"You don't understand. Sadie has decided. She left for home."

Ross hadn't heard right. "What do ye mean?"

"She texted. She left two hours ago."

But . . . Ross hadn't gotten to tell her—*she won*. He would give up his freedom. *For her*.

Suddenly, it seemed ridiculous that he'd dragged his feet. Sadie was *the one* from the start. He couldn't breathe.

He dropped his head in his hands. "Oh, *gawd*. What did I do?"

Mum laid her hand on his shoulder. "It's not yere fault. Ye didn't know."

"What's not his fault?" Oliver growled. "What did he do?"

"Go on and tell him," Mum said.

Ross looked up into Oliver's harsh gaze. "Ye've got to tell me how to find her. Ye said she went home. Give me the address."

"Why would I?" Oliver said. "You're the reason she ran off."

"I'm begging ye." Ross stood. "I—I love her."

Oliver tilted his head to the side. Ross had seen him do this while considering a problem with the computers at Quilting Central.

Standing next to Oliver's chair, Kirsty put her arm around him. "Tell Ross what ye told me . . . about Sadie."

Oliver looked into her face as if he was warring with himself. He didn't turn to Ross, but kept staring at Kirsty. After a long moment, he finally spoke. "I've never seen Sadie so alive as when she's around him." He turned to Ross and spoke to him this time. "She was never the same after our parents died. I thought a part of her had died with them. And then her diagnosis took another piece of her. And I thought I was going to lose her for good when Gigi died." His voice cracked. He looked away, pulling himself together. "As a little girl, she had spirit. Joy. Around you, the old Sadie came back."

That was the woman Ross knew. The woman Ross loved. Sadie was always running away. And he didn't mind, especially if she was running away *with him*. But he didn't like her running away from him. Not one damn bit.

Ross held out his hand. "The address, Oliver. I promise, I'll do anything and everything to make this right."

Chapter Twenty

The taxi driver set Sadie's luggage at her front door while she dug around in her Mondo bag for her wallet. She paid him, feeling more tired than she had in her whole life. Between getting little rest the night before she left Gandiegow and the eight-hour delay at Heathrow because of mechanical problems, she was completely spent. Sleep would help fix her physically, but it would have little effect on the ache in her chest.

She found her key and unlocked the door to their house. *No.* She would have to start thinking of it as *her* house. Only hers. Oliver was gone. Gigi was gone, too, but she was starting to accept it. Oliver's words were helping Sadie to heal. It really hadn't been her fault that Gigi died, only bad timing.

Sadie stepped inside and dropped her bag by the entry, expecting mail to be piled up on the other side of the door where the slot was. But there was none. Oliver must've placed a hold. She'd have to go to the post office tomorrow and take care of it. Everything was on her now. Paying the bills. Mowing the lawn. Upkeep on the house. *Everything.* She would adjust. It wasn't only the house.

She'd have to get used to dealing with her illness on her own, too.

It didn't matter. Not anymore.

Sadie dragged herself into the kitchen and took down a glass. She was going to miss Gandiegow—not just Ross, but Mr. Menzies, Moira, Emma, even the gray-haired ladies of Quilting Central. Maybe most of all, she was going to miss the kids. She would talk to her local library, or when school started in the fall, she'd see if she could read to the kids at the elementary school two blocks over. But those children wouldn't be Dand, Mattie, Glenna, or the other little ones from Gandiegow.

That's all right. Sadie was home now. She would start over, reinvent her life, something she'd been doing every day since finding out she had CKD.

As she filled her glass with water, she noticed the answering machine was blinking. Hope jolted through her. Had Ross called? No. That was the crazy type of thinking she was going to have to eradicate. And now that she was home, it should be easier because she wouldn't see him, day in and day out. Of course, she would see Ross again when she went back to Gandiegow for the wedding. She would have to be over him by then. At the very least, Ross could never know that she loved him. She prayed Oliver and Kirsty would have a long engagement to give her plenty of time to heal her broken heart.

She hit the button on the answering machine.

"Oliver?" It wasn't Ross. "This is Dr. Templeton." Sadie's nephrologist? Why was she asking for her brother? "I called as soon as the results came in. It's good news. The crossmatch came back. You're cleared as Sadie's donor."

She stared at the answering machine. "What?"

"Call me when you get this message." The recording ended.

Sadie hit REWIND and listened again. She couldn't believe it. She didn't even know that he'd been tested. Dr. Templeton had talked to her about looking in the family for a donor, but she'd never found the right moment to broach it with Oliver. She figured she had time.

Sadie's mouth was dry and she gulped her glass of water. "Oliver did this for me?" She loved her brother, even when he was bossing her to death. But now, her heart swelled that he would be willing to make this kind of sacrifice for her.

The doorbell chimed. She stayed rooted to her spot, not in the mood to deal with a solicitor right now. Or anyone else, for that matter. The doorbell rang out again. And again.

"Oh, good grief." She went to the door and slung it open, primed to tell whoever it was to go away.

But she couldn't. She was too shocked. Ross stood there with his duffel bag, the same one he'd brought to Thistle Glen Lodge when he'd lied about the measles.

"Will ye let me in, lass?"

She opened her mouth, but her words came out in a whisper. "What are you doing here?"

"Ye forgot something in Gandiegow."

"What?" She could barely breathe.

"Me. Ye forgot me." He walked in, but before he passed, he kissed her on the cheek.

She almost missed his next words, because she was still inhaling his pheromones. He smelled of home, security, and community. And she better get some rest, because clearly this was all a dream.

He held up his duffel bag. "Which bedroom is mine? Upstairs or down?"

Before shutting the door, she looked outside. Nothing seemed amiss. The sky wasn't falling or filled with flying pigs.

When she turned around, Ross had set down the damned duffel and was looking as gorgeous as ever.

"There are things I should've said to ye, lass."

"I'm still trying to understand why you're here."

He moved closer, but he seemed careful, trying not to scare her off. "Can I fix us a cup of tea? I'd like to sit with ye. Talk." He glanced at her lips as if he had something more in mind, but he shook his head as if to clear the thought.

She pointed. "The kitchen's that way."

She followed him in and pulled the kettle from the cabinet. He took it from her and filled it with water, while she got out the tea and cups. When the kettle was on the stove, heating up, they both sat at the table.

"So?" she said.

"I'd never been lonely until I met you," he said without preamble.

He wasn't making any sense.

"Ross, I haven't been gone but, what, twenty-four hours?"

He shook his head as if she didn't understand. "That's not it. I've never experienced loneliness, even when I've been off by myself. But now, I can be surrounded by the whole town, and I feel alone without ye there. When I went to work on the *Betsy Lane* for all those days, it was pure hell to be without you." He reached out and took her hand.

She stared at how his large hand covered hers. How warm it was. How safe she felt when he was near.

She pulled her hand away. "It's an illusion."

He scooted his chair closer. "My love for you isn't an illusion." He tipped her chin up so her eyes met his. "I love ye, Sadie. I've never said that to another woman."

"Not even Pippa?" Sadie was a little lost in his gaze . . . and in the earnestness in his eyes. The sincerity. The truth?

"I love Pippa as a sister. Nothing else." He took Sadie's hand again and squeezed. "You came along at the wrong time, is all."

She tried to pull away, but he held on.

"Ye've heard the saying, *When man plans, God laughs.* I had a grand plan. I wanted to be free and un-attached. But when the Almighty dropped ye in my lap, He laughed his arse off, wondering if I was going to be smart enough to recognize the gift He'd given me."

"So God's plan is for you to have me, huh? What about what *I* want?" Oh, she was being a tough one, but her heart was at stake.

"I understand. I'm a determined man, and patient. I'll just have to win ye over."

"How are you going to do that? I live here. You live in Scotland."

"Luv, don't ye get it? Wherever you are is where my home is now. I can fish here, you know. I can support us."

The kettle whistled. Ross squeezed her hand one more time, rose, and poured the water over their tea bags.

"But we can't be together. My CKD."

"The truth is," he said, "it doesn't matter to me. Even if your illness was something more dire, I'd still want to marry ye."

Her breath caught.

But he went on as if she wasn't near to passing out. "I've done my research. Having CKD isn't a death sentence. Hell, fishing is one of the deadliest jobs in the world. If ye can stand being a fisherman's wife, then I think I can handle yere crappy kidneys."

"You may have done your research, but there are certain decisions that I'm going to make for myself that would impact you—or whoever else I decide to marry."

He smiled at her slipup.

She dropped the hammer. "What if I decide *not* to have children because I don't want to risk it? You have *family man* written all over you."

He reached for her and pulled her onto his lap. "You're not listening. *You* are my family. I believe I fell in love with you that first night you crawled into bed to comfort me. Marry me, Sadie."

"But my life is here. My doctors. Everything." Except for this wonderful man.

"I know. Ye said that. I'm not going anywhere. Marry me." He pushed her hair behind her ear.

"The rejection drugs," she argued. "I'll be on them for the rest of my life after the transplant. Do you know how expensive that's going to be?"

"I'll take extra jobs. Marry me."

She was running out of arguments, and steam. Could this really be happening? "But you said you don't like desperate women." She was grasping at straws at this point, but she needed to cover everything. "And I love you desperately."

She couldn't believe she'd admitted to it.

He laughed and a relieved smile spread over his face. "Och, lass, I was an uneducated prig back when I said that. I had a laddie's point of view."

"It wasn't that long ago."

"But I've grown since then. There's nothing sexier, or more satisfying, than to have yere woman desperate for ye." He gazed into her eyes. "Ye are my woman, aren't you?"

She nodded.

He stroked her cheek. "I love ye desperately, too." He reached into his pocket and pulled out a brooch. "Will ye wear this? To show everyone that ye're mine?"

"A luckenbooth?" It looked nothing like Moira's, but Sadie recognized the design. This one looked old. It had two entwined hearts set atop flowering thistles.

"It was my mother's," he said. "My da gave it to her when he claimed her as his own."

She ran her fingers over the brooch. "Is that what you're doing? Claiming me?"

"Aye. But only if ye'll have me. Otherwise, I'll just hang around here like a devoted dog. Or yere servant. Just to be near ye." He leaned in and kissed her.

It was sweet and tender, and it melted all her objections into nothingness. At last, her head believed in her heart.

He pulled away suddenly, reaching into his pocket. "I almost forgot. I brought ye another gift." He handed over a folded piece of paper.

Curious, she opened it up and read.

My dearest Sadie,

I wanted to write you a letter to make you fall madly and completely in love with me as I have with you. I wanted to be as eloquent as a hero in a Jane Austen novel. But the best I could do was to steal a line from Wentworth: You pierce my soul.

I love you, always and forever. I will devote my life to being worthy of your love, if you will only give me a chance and love me back.

Yours,
Ross

Sadie felt intoxicated. All her life, she'd lived vicariously through her novels. She never imagined that she could truly have a love that compared with what was written within the pages of a book. Yet Ross's letter had surpassed every hope and dream she'd ever had for herself.

"Oh, Ross." She threw her arms around his neck and kissed him.

When the kiss ended, Ross held her close. "I'm anxious to wed ye. How quickly can we get married here?"

Sadie took his hand, kissed it, and then gazed into his eyes. "Do you mind much if we wait? I want to get moved home to Scotland first. Then I want a Gandiegow wedding."

"Home?" he said hoarsely.

"Aye." She tried on a Scottish burr.

"But I thought ye said yere life was—"

"My heart is in Gandiegow. I'm already missing everyone. Doc MacGregor can arrange the medical care I need. Scotland is where I want to be. With you."

"Aw, lass." Ross smiled brightly and then held her close

again. "We'll go home. But ye told me ye didn't want a wedding with all the fuss. Ye saw what Andrew and Moira had to endure."

"Yes, I did—their community surrounding them, promising to love, honor, and support them, through thick and thin."

"All right." He stroked her cheek. "But Deydie was right about you."

"About what?"

"Ye're nothing but *trouble*." He kissed her nose. "But ye're my kind of trouble."

Sadie and Ross stayed in North Carolina for five weeks, taking care of the things that needed to be done in the US. She found a real estate agent, packed up everything she wanted to ship to Gandiegow, and generally played house with her hot Scot—especially in the bedroom—until it was time to go back. There were many phone calls and congratulations between the two countries. Oliver seemed the happiest of all, promising not to be controlling when she arrived home in Scotland. She doubted he could change overnight, but the first step in correcting a problem was admitting it.

It was early evening when the shuttle service dropped her and Ross off at the parking lot with her two suitcases and his duffel bag.

Sadie looked around. "It's irrational, but I kind of hoped everyone would be waiting here to welcome us home."

"It's okay, lass. The important thing is that we *are* home."

They walked contentedly through the village. How

strange that all the lights were out at the pub—and when they came near the restaurant, they saw the CLOSED sign attached to the door. But they proceeded on to Thistle Glen Lodge where it had been decided Sadie should stay until they got married next month.

"I honestly don't think I can wait that long," Ross said once again.

"Are you still complaining about how much time a wedding takes to organize? Seriously, Ross, I'm standing my ground. I want it all." She paused, went up on tiptoes, and kissed his lips. "I've got the perfect man, and now I want the perfect Gandiegow wedding—from the bridal shower to the vows at the altar to the reception afterward. And Deydie said over the phone that it would take a month to plan. *And that was rushing it.*"

They dropped their bags off, deciding they would look for everyone before Ross took his duffel home to his cottage, where she would move in after the wedding.

Ross wrapped an arm around her shoulder as they left; he seemed to want to keep her close at all times. "Are ye sure ye don't mind moving into my bedroom until we can figure out a place of our own to live?"

Sadie hugged him close with an arm around his waist. "I'm sure. My home is wherever you are." She was pleased to use those words back on him. Besides, they were true.

They neared Quilting Central, the only building in town with lights on.

"I think we found everyone," Sadie said.

"I wonder what's going on." Mischief danced in Ross's eyes.

He held the door open for her as she walked through—and the crowded room broke out into cheers and applause. Her heart was full of love as she took in the faces of these wonderful people, and the room decorated as it had been for Moira's shower, with the addition of a huge banner hung over the gift table: WELCOME HOME, SADIE AND ROSS.

Ross came up behind her, pulling her back against his chest. "It was Deydie's idea."

"Not completely." Deydie stood near and jabbed a finger at Ross. "He threatened to move into Thistle Glen Lodge and take up with ye there if we didn't pull off the wedding by tomorrow."

Sadie turned and looked at him over her shoulder. *"Tomorrow?"*

"I'm a patient man, lass, but I do have my limits." He squeezed her shoulders.

"Take yere hands off of her and go say hello to yere mother and brothers." Deydie took her hand. "Come with me. I've something to say." She dragged her to the kitchen. On the way there, Oliver made a move toward them, but Deydie waved him off. "In a minute, lad."

Sadie wondered what was going on. Everyone else in Gandiegow seemed to wonder, too, as they were all listening in.

Deydie plugged in the electric kettle. "Before we go any further and start the festivities, I need to tell ye that I was wrong." She put her hand up as if Sadie was going to stop her. "I'm not wrong very often, but I was wrong to tell Ross that he shouldn't court ye. I'm sorry. I said some things that might've been hurtful. Ye've got to know . . ." The old woman looked away as if collecting herself. "I lost my daughter to illness. Duncan. Others, too. Sometimes I think it's best not to get attached at all, especially if ye know right off that ye're going to like someone."

Sadie touched her arm. "I understand." It was the reason it was so hard in the beginning to be around the quilters of Gandiegow who reminded her of Gigi.

Deydie gazed at her. "I think that's why I said what I did. I ask that ye forgive me."

Sadie felt herself tear up. "Of course. No harm was done." Not permanently anyway.

"Ye need to know that we care for ye as much as we do Oliver. It just took me longer to see the error of my ways." The old woman glanced at Oliver, then leaned over and whispered conspiratorially, "Perhaps ye belong here more than yere brother. Ye're a hell of quilter, Sadie Middleton. A hell of a quilter."

Sadie smiled, feeling welcomed and loved.

Deydie straightened and grabbed the tea ball. She dumped out the old tea and filled the tea shell with new leaves. "We'll start fresh."

"That sounds wonderful," Sadie said.

To her shock, Deydie suddenly set the tea ball down and pulled her in for a bear hug. The crowd hushed completely with all eyes on them.

Recovering, Sadie returned the hug. "Thank you for everything." She'd never have Gigi back, but she could have Deydie and the other quilting ladies as part of her new life here in Gandiegow.

Deydie dropped her arms and gave a little wave at the room, looking embarrassed at the display of affection. Sadie loved her all the more for doing it, and couldn't help but lay a hand on her shoulder possessively.

Deydie smiled for one brief moment, then barked at

her. "Go mingle until the tea is ready. Then we'll start the party."

Sadie looked around for Ross, but he was in deep conversation with Andrew and Moira. Emma approached, holding Angus. He automatically put his arms out for Sadie to take him.

"Come here, chunker." She hefted him to her shoulder, happy to be cuddling with him again. Only time would tell if she would take that step to become a mother. But it wasn't a decision she had to make today.

Out of the corner of her eye, she saw Oliver make his way to her. When he got within arm's length, she surprised both of them when she pulled him in for a one-armed hug, the best she could do with Angus clinging to her.

"Thank you," she said. She'd already thanked him on the phone, but it hadn't been enough. "You didn't have to be tested."

He pulled away. "Of course, I did. I'm your brother."

Emma relieved her of Angus. "Oliver told us the good news, that he's a match. Ross was devastated when he found out that he wasn't."

"What?" Sadie and Oliver said at the same time.

Emma looked stricken. "Oh, I assumed you knew. He made no secret of it with us." She looked around the room. "He was tested while the two of you were in Glasgow."

"Well, I'll be damned." Oliver gazed upon his future brother-in-law with what looked like newfound respect.

"But we barely knew each other then," Sadie said.

But that wasn't true. They seemed to have recognized each other from the beginning. Ross had said himself that he'd fallen in love with her on the first night that she'd crawled in bed with him.

Oliver squeezed Sadie's arm and left.

Emma gently bounced Angus. "Gabriel said he knew it was love between you and Ross from the start. 'A man will act on it before he can even name it,' is what he said."

"I guess that's right." Sadie laughed. "But wouldn't it be nice if they got a clue a little bit sooner?"

Kirsty stood on the stage and clapped her hands. "Okay, everyone. Deydie said we need to get started. Fellows, go ahead and take Ross away for his stag night."

Grace stood up, pointing a finger at her sons. "And ye better keep things moderate. I want Ross to be up for his wedding in the morning, and not stinking drunk somewhere out to sea on one of yere boats."

The room laughed.

Instead of heading for the door, Ross came for Sadie. He pulled her into his arms and kissed her long and hard.

The whole town hooted and hollered, but she didn't care.

He set her back and beamed at her. "We've got a place to live. Our own place!"

"Where?"

"We're going to rent Moira's cottage. She and Glenna have moved into the parsonage with Andrew. *Gawd*, Sadie, our own place." His eyes twinkled. He whispered the next words. "Unless ye want to live under the same roof as John and Maggie and mind how loud ye yell out my name in bed." He picked her up again and gazed into her eyes.

"Come on, Ross," Ramsay hollered. "Stop accosting her. Can't ye wait one night to start the honeymoon?"

Ross smiled at her. "I love ye, lass. We're going to have the most wonderful life together."

"I know." She kissed him soundly. "Now, let me have the wedding I never knew I wanted." She patted his rump. "Go on now." Because behind Ross, she saw that Bethia was holding a beautiful box. "It's time for the Passing of the Recipes."

Yes, she would have a Gandiegow wedding, and that was just the beginning.

Dear Reader,

Oftentimes I'm asked where the stories come from, and the answer is that they are based on snippets of real life. This story, *The Trouble with Scotland,* is no different.

Last fall one of my closest friends—sister of my heart and matron of honor at my wedding—received some life-changing news about her young adult daughter. Prior to this, her daughter was a vision of health, so you can image the shock when Amber was diagnosed with stage four Chronic Kidney Disease (CKD).

Doctors told my friend that her daughter would need a kidney transplant in the future. I was moved deeply by the news. I remember watching Amber skip down the aisle as the three-year-old flower girl at my wedding. When she was in middle school, I was thrilled when she wanted me to see the quilt that she'd made. Amber is a lovely person, and I'm impressed with the wonderful young woman that she's become. *The Trouble with Scotland* isn't Amber's story, but writing it has been a way for me to process how Chronic Kidney Disease can have a lasting effect on families, friends, and communities.

The National Kidney Foundation® has been a great support to Amber and her family. If you would like to find out more about Chronic Kidney Disease and donate to further research and assist those struggling with CKD, please visit my website at www.PatienceGriffin.com and click on the National Kidney Foundation button.

As of the writing of this letter, we have once again received news. Amber and her doctors had hoped to put off her kidney transplant for five years, but recent bloodwork shows her transplant will be needed within the next two weeks. Please keep her and her family in your thoughts and prayers.

From the heart,
Patience

To contact me, visit:

Facebook: www.facebook.com/PatienceGriffinAuthor
e-mail: patience@patiencegriffin.com

Or through the US postal system:

Patience Griffin
5100 Eldorado Pkwy, Ste 102
PMB518
McKinney, TX 75070

Continue reading for a preview
of the next book in
Patience Griffin's Kilts and Quilts series,

It Happened in Scotland

Coming in December 2016.

Holding her daughter's hand, Rachel stood at the baggage claim alongside the woman with whom they'd sat on the flight from Chicago to Glasgow. Rachel's new friend, Cait Buchanan, was flying home, whereas Rachel was bringing her daughter to Scotland for the first time.

Rachel had been to Gandiegow, the small town on the northeast coast of Scotland, twice before. Once to marry her husband. And again to bury him. She glanced down at five-year-old Hannah, who looked so much like her father, Joe. Rachel had been drowning in a hazy fog of grief and guilt for the last three years, hardly noticing how her spunky daughter had been growing and changing by the day. She was finally pulling herself out of it for Hannah. She had to. This year she was going to give her daughter a Christmas. A Christmas with a real tree, gingerbread cookies, and family.

Cait stepped to the luggage carousel. "There's mine."

"It's huge. Let me help." Rachel turned to her daughter. "Can you stay here and watch my things?"

"Sure, Mommy."

She didn't have to worry; Hannah would guard Rachel's tote along with her own *Frozen* backpack like a belligerent soldier if anyone got near.

As the large suitcase approached, Cait laughed. "I always pack too much." She reached for the handle, Rachel for the wheels. Together they tugged it to the floor with a *whoompf.*

"I'm glad ye're taking me up on my offer," Cait said. "What are the odds of sitting next to someone going to Gandiegow too?" A green tinge came over her face and she grimaced. "Do you mind, um, watching . . . ?"

"Go," Rachel urged. "We've got your bags."

Cait raced for the toilet sign while Rachel rolled the humongous bag over to Hannah.

"Mommy?" Hannah took her hand. "Is she going to be okay?"

Rachel nodded. "Yes. She'll be fine." Nothing seven or so months wouldn't cure.

The way Cait had been downing saltines all through the flight, especially during the turbulence, made her pregnancy obvious. Rachel had experienced the same joy and perhaps fear that stretched across Cait's face at every turn.

Right when Rachel was beginning to worry, because Cait had been gone so long, she appeared—white, wrung out, but with a small smile on her face.

"Sorry about that," she said when she'd rejoined them. She studied Rachel. "So ye've guessed."

"That depends on whether you want anyone to know or not."

"The morning sickness is much worse this time. The

doctor says it's a good thing. But I haven't told anyone. Not even my husband."

Automatically, Rachel's eyebrows shot up, but she got her reaction under control quickly. Cait's relationship with her husband was her own business.

Her new friend bit her lip. "I don't want to get his hopes up. I've miscarried twice. It's been hard on him. He travels a lot and he worries about me so." She glanced at Rachel, hopeful. "So ye'll keep my secret?"

"Mum's the word." She gave her a reassuring smile. Rachel knew a lot about secrets and keeping them hidden.

Her luggage came around the conveyor, much smaller than Cait's, as they were only going to be here a short while. Just long enough for Hannah to spend some time with her grandfather, Abraham Clacher, sing a few Christmas carols, and go back to the States at the beginning of the New Year. In and out without a worry or a fuss.

Rachel pulled off their bags as Cait's cell phone chimed.

"Our ride is here," she said. "I'll wait for you on the other side of customs."

The line for customs was surprisingly fast, and it didn't take long to meet back up with Cait. As their little group wheeled their things through the doors, three people rushed toward Cait, and she tugged Rachel closer to meet her friends.

"This is Ross, his wife, Sadie, and Ross's mother, Grace." Cait smiled at them fondly. Ross and his mother were tall, but Sadie was a brown-haired pixie who looked up at her husband lovingly.

"Thank you for letting us hitch a ride." Rachel hadn't reserved a rental car, not completely certain whether she would chicken out or not. Well, she was locked into going now.

"I'm glad it worked out," Ross said.

"We were closing down the house here in Glasgow," Grace explained. "My sister passed last month, and I'm moving back to Gandiegow."

Rachel already knew the particulars through Cait. Grace's sister had died from complications of pneumonia but had been dealing with MS for years. "I'm so sorry for your loss," Rachel said but cringed a little as it came out. She'd been the recipient of that phrase too often.

Grace smiled at her kindly as one who accepted things easily. "Thank you. Glynnis is in a better place. My hope is that the house will sell quickly."

Sadie took Grace's arm lovingly. "I'm sure it will." They seemed closer than most mothers- and daughters-in-law.

"Let's get on the road. I'm anxious to get home," Ross said.

"And back to fishing?" Sadie interjected with a grin.

"Aye. Fishing."

As they drove to Gandiegow, Ross and Sadie filled Cait in on the gossip from the last two weeks.

When there was a break in the conversation, Rachel inquired after Abraham. "How is he doing?" She knew of his illness only because when she'd called, he'd had a coughing fit. She had no idea how long he'd been sick and how bad it was.

Ross glanced at her in the rearview mirror. "He's the same ole Abraham. But if ye're speaking of his health, he's not well. He quit fishing about six months ago, which told the rest of us how serious it really is."

"Oh." More guilt. Rachel should've brought her daughter sooner to get to know the only great-grandparent she had.

An awkward silence came over the van for a few moments, but then Grace turned to Rachel. "Where will you and Hannah be staying? Thistle Glen Lodge?"

"The quilting dorm," Cait clarified to Rachel.

Cait had explained all about her venture in the village of Gandiegow, the Kilts and Quilts Retreat, turning the sleepy fishing village into a go-to quilting destination.

"I'm not sure," Rachel answered sheepishly. Though she'd talked to Abraham last month, and he'd asked her to come and bring Hannah, she'd made no promises. She'd booked the flight and a hotel room in Glasgow to get her bearings. Over the years, she'd learned to have a contingency plan. If she'd had second thoughts about going to Gandiegow at the last minute, she and Hannah would simply have had a special Christmas vacation at the Jurys Inn in the big city.

But Providence had stepped in when Rachel had taken her seat next to Cait. Rachel had innocently told her of Gandiegow, having no idea that Cait hailed from the village of only sixty-three houses.

"You can stay with me and my son, Mattie, in the big house," Cait offered.

"That's so kind." But Rachel wouldn't impose. "I think Hannah and I would like to stay at Thistle Glen Lodge. The way you described it, it sounds perfect." She kissed her daughter's head. "That is, if it's okay. Do you have a quilt retreat going on right now?"

"One's starting tomorrow, which is why I couldn't stay longer in the U.S., but there's plenty of room. Deydie, my gran, said we had to keep the group small, as we're so close to Christmas."

"Sounds fantastic."

"When is Graham done shooting?" Ross asked.

For Rachel, all the pieces clicked together. From the first moment, Cait had looked familiar. *That's where I saw her.* On the cover of *People* magazine, along with her famous movie star husband.

"Graham?" Rachel said, more in disbelief than a question. She had been so self-absorbed that it hadn't quite registered when the story came out that Graham had grown up in Gandiegow. So he still lived there?

"Yeah. Graham," Sadie said, kind of dreamily. "My reaction exactly."

"Hey, now, lass," Ross said with mock hurt. "Yere husband's in the vehicle with ye."

Sadie patted him. "You've nothing to worry about. Graham only has eyes for Cait."

Cait reached over and laid a hand on Rachel's arm. "Sorry I didn't say anything sooner."

"I get it."

Cait nodded and spoke to Ross. "Graham'll be home next week. The production shuts down until after the New Year. It'll be nice for Mattie and me to have him back."

Rachel wondered if Cait would tell him then about the pregnancy. Surely, she wouldn't keep it hidden from him too long. She wondered if Cait's chest was always so expanded. Graham would certainly notice a change there, wouldn't he?

The conversation switched to Christmas, and Rachel turned inward, thinking more about her own turmoil than about the joyous occasion they were describing. Hannah leaned against her and fell asleep. Rachel dozed, too.

She came awake as the van pulled down the hill toward the parking lot. Ross was talking on the phone.

"Good. We can use the help getting my mum's stuff to the cottage." He hung up.

Rachel gently woke Hannah. "We're here, sweetie." She glanced around at the familiar sight of the bluffs looming out of the earth at the back of the village and how the small houses seemed to sit precariously on the edge of the ocean—a quaint row of dwellings daring the sea to engulf them.

Ross parked the van and jumped out to help his mother.

Rachel felt stiff from the flight and then the long drive to Gandiegow. She climbed out and then helped Hannah.

As she reached in to grab her tote, something caught her eye on the walkway. *No.*

Someone caught her eye. Strolling toward the parking lot, he looked so much like Joe. Tall, broad, with dark hair. But where Joe's hair had been kept short—the better to peddle pharmaceuticals—his cousin's long hair blew in the wind off the ocean. Six years had changed him. His features were chiseled, and where an easy smile for her had once existed, a stony frown remained.

But he was as beautiful as ever.

Rachel stopped breathing, but the voice in her head shouted loud and clear, *What is he doing here?*

"Mommy, are you all right?"

For the life of her, Rachel couldn't stop staring at the

man she never thought she'd see again. They all turned to look at her.

When he got close enough, he nodded in her direction. "Ye're back."

How could he have no emotion on his face? She was dying here.

"Hey, Brodie," Ross said. "Grab a bag from the boot. It's going to take us a couple of trips."

What in the blazes is she doing here? Brodie Wallace couldn't believe his eyes. It felt as if Ross had sucker-punched him in the stomach. And yet here Rachel was, standing in Gandiegow's parking lot. The only woman who had ripped his heart out. The only woman he'd ever loved.

And he'd never forgive her.

Never.

Six years ago, he wasn't the only one toppled by the instant attraction. He knew she had felt it, too.

His cousin Joe had brought her home to Gandiegow two weeks before their scheduled wedding. Brodie was taken with Rachel from the start, which was no surprise. He and Joe had always gone for the same type of lass. Funny, smart. Even as lads, they'd competed, and Joe had won. Whenever Brodie found a girl, Joe would swoop in and steal her away. Brodie understood. Joe was a charmer with the gift of gab, and women couldn't help but fall under his spell.

Day in and day out, Brodie tried to keep his distance from Joe's bride, but they had been constantly thrown together at Abraham's house. They danced around and avoided their feelings. But on the day of the wedding, he'd climbed up the bluff to clear his head and hide out in the ruins of Monadail Castle. When he arrived, Rachel was there, as if it was meant to be. She turned at his approach but didn't budge from the stone ledge. He had noted her puffy red eyes. She'd been crying.

He'd lifted her chin so she would look at him. "What's wrong?" The question was fatal.

"Why didn't I meet you first?" she cried, and threw herself into his arms, kissing him and knocking him from his moorings. His heart had slammed in his chest like a tidal wave.

"What are you going to do about it?" he'd asked, and she'd only shaken her head.

But that kiss and the way she'd looked at him, they had meant something—*they had meant everything.* For an hour they held on to each other, Brodie confessing to her that he'd never felt like this before. He knew it was love, but he couldn't tell her that until she called off the wedding. Which he was certain she would. More certain of it than the snow on the ground, the tide in the ocean, and the blood in his veins. Rachel loved him as he loved her. But then Grandda always said, *Women can't be trusted.* Just an hour later, Rachel walked down the aisle and repeated her vows, tossing Brodie away as if he was nothing more than spoiled bait.

Ross nudged him, pulling him back to reality.

"What?" Brodie said, the voice sounding harsh.

Cait eyed him curiously as if he'd cast his line into an opposing wind. "You two know each other?"

"Aye." Brodie's gaze dropped down to the little girl holding Rachel's hand. The child gaped up at him. *God, the girl has Joe's eyes. Brown. Rich as the soil on Here Again Farm.* Where he'd hidden out after Rachel betrayed him. He snapped his gaze away from hers.

"Brodie was best man at my wedding," Rachel provided to Cait. "To Joe." As if clarifying which wedding.

Has she married again? Brodie's gaze slid to her hand, and he hated himself for looking because he sure as hell didn't care. He didn't care if she was married. He didn't care if she was in town. He didn't care if she disappeared altogether.

She was frowning back at him now.

Good. Let her frown. He didn't give a damn. She was nothing to him. Nothing. Just another heartless female.

He stalked to the rear of the van, yanked out a couple of bags, and stomped away with them, not certain where he was supposed to drop them off.

As if Ross had read his mind, he hollered after Brodie, "Thistle Glen Lodge."

Thoughts, like fists, pummeled Brodie.

A little warning would've been nice. Why hadn't Abraham—his own grandda—told him that she was coming? Brodie didn't need this right now. He had his hands full with taking over Abraham's fishing business and trying to nurse the old man back to health.

Brodie wondered if he dropped the bags in the sea whether Rachel would leave. *And take the kid with her.* Maybe he should call Ewan and head back to Here Again Farm. Or maybe Ewan's cousin Hugh could use help at the wool factory. Anything to get out of town and away from *her.*

He took the bags to the quilting dorm, but didn't return to the vehicle for a second load. Instead, he headed home to have it out with Grandda.

As he opened the door to the cottage, he heard Abraham coughing, and Brodie's fury disintegrated. He couldn't roar at the old man. He owed his grandda nothing but gratitude for first taking him and his mother in when Da had died, and then for letting Brodie stay on when his mother remarried shortly afterward.

He found his granda nearly hacking up a lung in the kitchen while trying to pull down a mug.

"Here," Brodie said. "Let me get the tea. You sit."

Abraham nodded and coughed in response.

Having Rachel back was ripping open all the closed wounds. Grandda never questioned why Brodie hadn't come back for Joe's funeral. But just having Rachel over at Thistle Glen Lodge made Brodie want to give his grandfather that explanation now: Though he'd wanted to pay his respects to Joe, he hadn't been able to bear seeing her again.

The kettle whistled and stopped him. Brodie poured water into the teapot and put the lid on.

He turned to Abraham. "She's here."

His grandfather spun around, searching the kitchen with rheumy eyes. "Who's here? Deydie?"

Brodie looked around, too, in case the old head quilter had miraculously appeared. But it was just the two of them. He settled in next to Abraham. "Joe's widow has arrived."

"What?" His grandfather looked truly confused. Then a smile stretched across his face, one that Brodie hadn't seen in quite a while. "So she came. Did she bring the babe?"

The girl was hardly a baby. "Aye." He stared hard at his grandda. "So ye really didn't know she was coming?"

The old man rose, ignoring him. "If Rachel's in the village, why isn't she here right now?"

"She's settling into Thistle Glen Lodge."

Abraham had that confused expression again. "Nay. Ye know she has to stay here."

No!

"She wants to stay at the quilting dorm." *I can't have her here.*

"Git over there now and tell her she's staying with us." Abraham might have been sick, but he could bark out a command as if still captaining his boat.

Brodie stared back at him for a long moment but finally caved. If his grandfather hadn't done so much for him his whole life, he would've argued.

"Fine. I'll fetch them after you have your tea." Brodie poured the steaming liquid into their cups.

"Go now. I want to see the lassie." Abraham started coughing, and for a moment, Brodie wondered if he did it to get his way.

To stall, Brodie pulled down the to-go mug he took out with him on the ocean and filled it for himself. "I'll bring her back," Brodie said out of duty. Aye, that was all it was . . . duty.

Once outside, he sipped his tea while making his way to the back of the bluffs where the quilting dorms were— Thistle Glen Lodge and Duncan's Den.

He paused at the doorway, steeling himself to set Rachel straight. There would be no repeat of the crazy attraction that he'd felt before. He was over her.

Automatically, his hand covered his heart, the place

where a tattoo artist had inked the bluidy partridge into Brodie's chest. While the man worked on him, Brodie had drunkenly told him about Rachel, the love of his life. How they'd kissed. How they'd clung to each other. How time had stood still while a partridge had lingered nearby in the snow at the ruins of Monadail Castle. One minute the partridge was there, and in the next it had flown away. *Like Rachel.* From that moment on, Brodie had no intention of ever seeing Rachel again, but the souvenir of foolishly loving her remained embedded on his chest. *Forever.*

He dropped his hand and knocked on the door to Thistle Glen Lodge. Running could be heard on the other side. The door flew open, and the little girl stood there.

She cranked her head around toward the hallway. "Mommy, the man that looks like Daddy is at the door."

Brodie nearly dropped his cup. He stabilized his hand, then shoved his free one in his pocket.

She gazed up at him, studying every inch of his face. "I have a picture of my daddy. Do you want to see?"

He didn't get to answer. She grabbed his hand and tugged. He was too surprised to stop her from pulling him over the threshold. She towed him down the hallway to the living room. When Rachel saw him, she looked as stunned as if the little girl had dragged in a ghost.

"He wants to see Daddy's picture," the girl said.

"I never said—" Brodie started.

"Don't worry about it." Rachel gazed down at her daughter with a mixture of exasperation and love. "I never know what she's going to do or say next."

"What's her name?" Brodie asked for lack of anything else to say.

"Hannah," the two females said together.

Hannah dropped his hand and leaned over her roller bag, unzipping it. "I wrapped my guzzy around it."

"Guzzy?" he said.

"The quilt I made for her," Rachel answered.

"She made it from Daddy's soft shirts." The kid pulled out the guzzy, which was a patchwork of different plaid flannels. She unwrapped the small frame and held it up to Brodie. "See?"

It was Joe. Not in jeans and a T-shirt, as he had worn here in Gandiegow, but in a suit, standing next to a Volvo.

"Mommy says Daddy was handsome."

The cold finger of betrayal stabbed through the tattoo on Brodie's chest.

Hannah turned to Rachel but thrust a thumb at him. "That makes him handsome, too. Right, Mommy?"

"Abraham wants you over at the house," Brodie said abruptly.

At another time and in another place, he might've found the kid cute or funny. But it was Rachel and Joe's kid, and there was nothing cute or funny about what was going on here. He was holding the picture of his dead cousin, and he was standing in the same room with the woman who had obliterated Brodie's chances of ever having a family of his own. Gandiegow was filled with dozens of happy families; the village seemed to sprout them as easily as the vegetables in the kitchen garden on Here Again Farm.

Rachel took the picture from Brodie, not glancing at it. "I want to see your grandfather. Hannah does, too. We're just going to settle in first. Maybe take a nap. It was a long flight."

"Nay." God, he didn't want to do this. "Ye've got it all wrong. My grandfather wants ye to stay at the cottage. With him."

Not me. Brodie wanted her and her kid to return to Glasgow, Chicago, or Timbuktu. It didn't matter. Everything about her made his blood pump faster, ruining the semblance of peace that he'd had since returning to Gandiegow.

She stared from one of his shoulders to the other, as if he was too broad to fit in the cottage with them. "We'll be much more comfortable here."

As would I. "Old Abraham insists. He's not well."

Rachel chewed on the inside of her cheek. He'd forgotten that she did that when she was worried. Six years ago, he'd caught her looking at him many times, gazing at him with yearning and worrying the inside of her cheek. Because she wanted him, too. He knew it.

"I can't stay there," she admitted.

"Why?" he asked as if the question wasn't filleting him, too.

"It would be too . . . hard." She looked away. "Too difficult."

Tough shite. She didn't know the half of it. She couldn't possibly know the fresh hell she was putting him through.

He wouldn't tell her either or give her the satisfaction of knowing the pain of her forsaking him as she'd walked down the aisle and pledged herself to Joe.

"Ye'll do as Abraham bids." He took the picture from her and handed it back to the little girl. "Put that away. Ye're going to go see yere great-grandda."